THE LINDISFARNE LITURGY

JOHN REGAN

ISBN-13:9781686769368

DEDICATION

To Vicky with love. My biggest fan and harshest critic. Without which, I would never have finished this book.

ACKNOWLEDGEMENTS

It goes without saying that to produce anything worthwhile, requires help from others. The process of writing a book such as this is aided and abetted by numerous people. Some of who only subtly assist, and others, who profoundly do so. Some of the content in this book was suggested by friends and acquaintances, you know who you are. My thanks go to anyone who however small, contributed to this novel. My principal appreciation, however, is to the people who purchased and read my first five books: The Hanging Tree, Persistence of Vision, The Romanov Relic, The Space Between Our Tears and The Fallen leaves. Your support is greatly appreciated. Many thanks go to my writing friends for their invaluable support and help in making this book possible. Finally, to anyone who is reading this book. I hope you find it enjoyable, and any feedback is always appreciated.

January 2020.

DISCLAIMER

Many of the places mentioned in this book exist. However, the author has used poetic license throughout, to maintain an engaging narrative. Therefore, no guarantee of accuracy in some respects should be expected. The characters depicted, however, are wholly fictional. Any similarity to persons living or dead is accidental.

CHAPTER ONE

Sam flopped onto the settee next to Emily, who held their daughter in her arms.

'Can I feed her?' he said.

Emily handed him the baby and bottle. 'Sam?' she said, and placed a hand on his leg. 'When are we going to name her?'

Sam cradled the baby in his arms and popped the end of the bottle into her mouth. 'We can't agree. I don't like the names you've come up with, and you don't like my suggestions.'

'But she's almost six weeks old. We can't keep calling her *baby*.'

'I know that.' Sam said. 'It'll be awkward when she starts nursery.'

'You're not taking this seriously. We haven't even registered her birth, and that has to be done in the next few days.'

'What are they going to do? Throw us in prison?'

Emily huffed. 'Sam! What are we going to do when we christen her?'

Sam raised his eyebrows. 'Vivian.'

'Vivian? Where the hell did you get that from?'

'Gone with the wind was on last night.'

Emily sighed. 'It's too old-fashioned.'

'See. Any suggestion I make, you don't like.'

'That's because most of the names you suggest are the names of women you've slept with. I'm not having my daughter named after one of your bedroom conquests.'

Sam kissed his daughter on the cheek. 'Who's a beautiful girl?' He glanced at Emily. 'I've slept with a lot of women, Em. So that rules out a lot of names.'

Emily stroked the baby's head. 'I overheard a name I liked yesterday. Daisy.'

Sam furrowed his brow. 'Never slept with a Daisy.'

'Good. Can we call her Daisy, then?'

'I knew a Rose and a Violet. They're flowers, too.'

'Sam!'

He tapped a finger on his chin. 'Daisy Davison. Not sure if I like the alliteration.'

Emily threw her hands up. 'Sam. You're impossible.'

'I do like Daisy, though.' He smiled at his daughter. 'What do you think, Daisy?'

Emily beamed. 'So, it's settled. We can call her Daisy?'

'On one condition.'

She frowned. 'What?'

'I get to choose her middle name.'

Emily narrowed her eyes. 'What were you thinking of?'

'After my mam.'

Emily pouted. 'Agnes? We can't call her Daisy Agnes.'

'There's nothing wrong with Agnes,' Sam said.

'I never said there was.'

Sam lowered his brow comically, staring at Emily. 'However, you're wrong. Agnes was my mother's middle name. She preferred Agnes for some reason.'

Emily smiled. 'Ok. Let me have it.'

'Donna.'

Emily's mouth dropped open. 'I thought you said you didn't like the alliteration. That would be, *Daisy Donna Davison*.'

Sam shrugged. 'It's growing on me. In for a penny ...'

'Daisy Donna it is then.' She leant forward and kissed Sam on his cheek. 'One more thing ...'

Sam's eye's narrowed. 'Yeah?'

'I was looking through your wardrobe, and I couldn't see a suit in there.'

Sam scoffed. 'A suit?'

'Yeah. For the christening. Now we have a name we can get Daisy christened. So you'll need a suit.'

'I haven't got a suit.'

Emily stared at him. 'Oh. But you are getting one?'

Sam laughed. 'You're kidding. There are only two ways you'll get me in a suit. Pay me forty-grand a year or die.'

'Sam,' Emily said. 'It's your daughter's baptism.'

He stood. 'No, I'm adamant about this. Jeans and a t-shirt will do fine.' He kissed Daisy and handed her to Emily. 'I have to go to work.'

Emily stood. 'Sam ...'

He held up a hand. 'End of discussion.' Sam made his way into the hall, smiled to himself, and left.

'Phillip,' Kim shouted. 'There's someone knocking. Can you get it?'

'Yeah,' he said, and opened the door. Their neighbour stood outside, holding a box. 'Mrs Winthorpe,' he said. 'Can I help you?'

'You can do something about these,' she said, and thrust the box towards him.

'What is it?'

'I believe they belong to you.'

Phillip peeked inside the box. 'Puppies? I think you've made a—'

'There's no mistake, Mr Davison. They belong to you. Or should I say they belong to that mongrel of yours.'

'Baggage? Are you sure?'

She rolled her eyes. 'Of course I'm sure. They've all got that pathetic lopsided head of his. Look at them.'

Phillip glanced inside the box again. 'I suppose they could be.'

'Take it from me, they are. I caught him in my garden months ago. My poor, *Shimmering Light of the Golden Orient*, has been defiled,' she shrieked.

Phillip frowned. 'Shimmering light ...?'

'It's her pedigree name. We call her Shimmer for short.'

'Right. Is it possible—?'

'There's no doubt. I did think I'd caught them in time but obviously the Don Juan of the canine world, there ...' She pointed a finger at Baggage who had popped his head around the corner. '... is more tenacious than I thought.'

'What do you want me to do with them?' Phillip said.

Kim appeared at the top of the stairs, wrapped in a bath towel. 'Who was it?'

'Mrs Winthorpe,' Phillip said.

'What did that daft cow want?' she said.

Mrs Winthorpe glared at Kim as she made her way down. 'Oh,' Kim said, as she spotted her. 'Mrs Winthorpe. What appears to be the problem?'

'As I'm explaining to your ...' She looked Phillip up and down. 'Your boyfriend's bloody hound has defiled my Shimmer.'

Kim joined Phillip at the threshold. 'What are you on about, you silly woman?'

'Look, look,' she said, and furiously tapped the box in Phillip's hand. 'In there.'

Kim lifted the lid. 'Aw,' she said. 'Puppies. How lovely.'

'They're not lovely.' She lifted her eyes skywards. 'These are offspring of that fecund mutt of yours.'

'Are you sure?' Kim said. She folded her arms. 'Is there a canine paternity test we can do?'

'Very amusing, young lady.'

'As I was saying,' Phillip said. 'What do you want us—?'

'What I'd like you to do, Mr Davison, is whatever you want. I did think of taking them to my vets to be destroyed—'

'Destroyed?' Kim said, elbowing her way in front of Phillip. 'You bloody heartless—'

'Kim,' Phillip said. 'Let me handle this.' He focused his attention back on Mrs Winthorpe. 'I don't think we have to resort to that. We'll deal with them.'

Baggage padded over to Phillip and poked his nose into the box, he sniffed, pulled it back out and tilted his head at an angle. Mrs Winthorpe glared at the dog. 'Look at the stupid cant?'

Kim glowered. 'What did you call him?'

Phillip placed a hand on Kim's arm. 'Calm down, Kim.'

'Didn't you hear her? She called Baggage a—'

'Cant,' Phillip said. And tilted his head to one side. 'As in head-cant.'

'Oh,' Kim said.

'One more thing, Mr Davison. Keep that bloody flop-eared, flea-bitten hound off my property.' With that, she stomped off.

'Yeah, piss-off,' Kim quietly mouthed after her.

Phillip locked eyes with Baggage. Lowering the box towards the dog, he opened the lid. 'Know anything about these, boy?'

Baggage poked his head back inside and sniffed again. He glanced at Phillip, turned swiftly, and trotted off.

'You need run,' Phillip said.

Kim slammed the door. 'I hate that haughty cow.' She peeped inside the box again. 'Aw, puppies. They're gorgeous.'

'The canine Casanova ...' He nodded towards the living room. '... has left us with a huge headache. It appears boyo, in there, has been sneaking into her garden somehow and having a right old time with her poodle.'

'I told you months ago there's a hole in the fence.'

Phillip rolled his eyes. 'Little did I know that we're living with Sam Davison of the dog world. We could have a host of owners knocking on our door.'

'Stop exaggerating.' Kim lifted one of the puppies from the box. 'Can we keep them?'

'Don't be daft, Kim. How the hell can we have five dogs.'

'Can we keep one of them, then. Please? A girl.' Holding one of the pups aloft, she kissed Phillip. 'I'll be really grateful.'

Phillip blew out, holding up an index finger. 'One. No more.' He paused. 'I have one condition, though.'

Kim kissed him on the cheek. 'Thanks, gorgeous.' Kim raised her eyebrows. 'Condition?'

'I name her.'

'You won't give her a daft name, will you?'

'I'll give it some thought,' he said. 'What are we going to do with the others?' He followed Kim through into the living room. Baggage lay on his bed, his head between his front paws. His eyes lowered.

'You need look sheepish,' Phillip said.

Kim nudged him. 'Can dogs look sheepish?'

Phillip rolled his eyes again. 'I'm going to make breakfast,' he said, and headed out of the room.

Kim knelt next to Baggage. 'Who's a clever boy?' And then planted a kiss on his head.

Albert stared into the cupboard at the multiple packets of biscuits, neatly stacked in rows. There was definitely no Kit-Kats. He sighed loudly and glanced at the printed piece of paper sellotaped to the inside of the door, neatly typed from one to eight, with the names of different makes of biscuits on it. He'd eaten a Trio - number four on his list – the previous evening with his cocoa and it had been the last one. He picked up the empty packet to confirm this. Next on his biscuit rota was a Kit-Kat. But he had no Kit-Kats. He'd forgotten to buy some. He balled his fists and placed them either side of his face, resting his elbows on the worktop. How could he allow this catastrophe to happen? He so wanted something sweet to go with his early-morning Darjeeling, but how could he if he had no Kit-Kats?

'Now, Albert Jackson,' he said quietly. 'This is stupid. Just have a Penguin. It's next on the list after Kit-Kats. You can always return to the rota when you have Kit-Kats.'

He reached for the packet, but as he did so his hand began to shake. Beads of sweat pushed through the skin and appeared on his forehead. He stopped and took hold of the worktop as the room started to spin. Albert closed his eyes as dizziness swamped him. He blew out hard and slowly counted to twenty, allowing the feeling to subside. Albert closed the cupboard door with a thud and brought his hands to his face.

'Bloody Kit-Kats, I hate you,' he said, and slapped his hand on the worktop. He would just have to have his tea without a biscuit. He picked up a piece of chalk from the countertop and wrote, *buy Kit-Kats, lots of them,* on the blackboard hanging from the wall.

The front-door bell sounded. Albert, shaken from his musings, trudged into the hall and opened the door. A tall, grey-haired, bespectacled man stood outside.

He smiled warmly. 'Albert Jackson?' he said.

Albert nodded. The man offered his hand. 'George Knight. I'm Stanley Knight's brother.'

Albert grinned. 'Mr Knight, the history teacher?'

'That's right. I saw the piece in The Evening Gazette ...The Romanov Eagle.'

Albert beckoned him inside. 'Yes, The Romanov Eagle. But how did—?'

'You mentioned my brother in the interview,' he said, following Albert though into the living room.

'That's right, I did. Mr Knight was my favourite teacher at school. How is he by the way?' Albert pointed to the settee, indicating for Knight to sit.

'Stanley's dead, I'm afraid.'

Albert eased himself onto a chair. 'I'm sorry to hear that.'

'I'll come straight to the point, Mr Jackson.'

'Albert. Call me Albert.'

'Albert. My brother had a great passion.'

'Lindisfarne?' Albert said.

'That's right. Stanley had this.' He paused. 'Ridiculous idea that a cross was saved from the marauding Vikings and brought across to Middlesbrough.'

Albert's eyes widened. 'Really?'

'Stanley was obsessed with it. When I visited his house, he had mountains of stuff about Holy Island.'

'You don't believe there is a cross, then?'

Knight rubbed his chin. 'I don't know what to believe. My brother was up at Alnwick when he died. According to his diary, he was meeting someone ...' Knight took out a small notebook. 'Professor Haldine. A good friend of his.'

'How did he die?' Albert said.

Knight lowered his eyes. 'He fell from a hill next to the castle.'

Albert brought a hand to his mouth. 'Oh, that's terrible.'

'The police said it was an accident.'

'And you don't believe it was?'

'Let's just say, I have some doubts.'

Albert glanced at the clock on the wall and stood. 'How rude of me, George. I haven't offered you a drink. Would you like one?'

Knight smiled. 'Yes, please. Tea would be super.'

'We'll have a cuppa, and then you can tell me all about it. Any particular type? I'm a bit of a tea fanatic.'

Knight tapped his chin with his index finger. 'Well, I'm not sure—'

'Darjeeling ok?'

'That's fine,' Knight said.

Albert walked towards the kitchen and stopped at the door. 'I would offer you a biscuit.' He glanced into the kitchen. 'But I'm right out at the moment.'

'That's all right. I'm watching my waistline.' Knight patted his stomach.

Albert nodded and went to make the tea.

Tommo took a slurp of tea from the mug and surveyed the almost finished cocktail bar. ‘Ewen,’ he shouted.

Ewen popped his head up from behind the bar. ‘Yeah?’

‘I’ve made you some tea.’

‘Great,’ Ewen said.

‘It’s looking fantastic. Have you much more to do?’

Ewen took a sip of his drink. ‘No. I should be finished in an hour or so.’

‘Brilliant. I’m hoping to open it on Friday.’

‘Tommo,’ Sam shouted from the pub next door.

‘In here,’ Tommo shouted back.

Sam wandered through. ‘This is where you are.’

Ewen raised his mug at Sam. ‘Sammy-boy.’

Sam scowled. ‘Ewen.’ He looked back towards Tommo. ‘I see you called it, *Black Mamba*?’

‘Yep,’ Tommo said.

‘I don’t know what your obsession with snakes is.’

‘I love snakes. I wanted a snake when I was a kid. Our mam wouldn’t let me have one.’

Sam rolled his eyes. ‘I remember. She had sense, your mam. So, you didn’t like my suggestion?’

Tommo rolled his eyes. ‘No, I didn’t.’

‘What’s that, then?’ Ewen said.

‘The Hairy Bush Viper,’ Sam said.

Ewen chuckled. ‘Has a certain ring.’

‘Like I said,’ Tommo said. ‘It’s too long.’

‘Is it a real snake?’ Ewen said.

‘Of course it is,’ Sam said. ‘That’s why I suggested it. I don’t go around making up random snake names.’

‘Anyway,’ Tommo said. ‘Black Mamba it is.’

‘You could have shortened it,’ Sam said. ‘And called it Hairy Bush.’ Ewen chuckled again.

‘Is there a reason you came around here?’ Tommo said. ‘Or are you just here to annoy me?’

‘Oh,’ Sam said. He reached into his back pocket and took out an envelope. ‘Your invitation.’

‘Invitation?’ Tommo said.

‘To my daughter's christening.’

‘Have you decided—?’

‘Daisy,’ Sam said. ‘Daisy Donna Davison.’

Tommo smiled. ‘Lovely. When is it?’

‘Next month. Don’t forget, you and Deb are godparents.’

Ewen took a loud slurp of tea. ‘Don’t I get an invitation?’

Sam glanced towards him. ‘Sorry, family and friends only.’

Phillip entered the office carrying a box in his hands. Sam, his feet on his desk, glanced up from the magazine in front of him. 'Morning,' Sam said.

Phillip placed the box on his desk. 'Morning. You look busy.'

'Not much on, mate. I've got to meet someone later today. A friend of a friend. Apparently, someone's been nicking hardy perennials from his garden.'

Phillip hung up his coat. 'Riveting.'

'Wants me to set up some cameras.' Sam jumped from his seat. 'What's in the box?'

'Baggage,' Phillip shouted. The dog came padding in and stopped beside his owner, he looked up, cocking his head. 'Would you like to explain to Sam?'

Baggage glanced across at Sam and then back at Phillip, turned and headed out. 'Coward,' he shouted after him. Phillip opened the box and took out one of the puppies, holding it aloft for Sam to see. 'Casanova of the canine world, in there, has been sneaking out and, well, you can see the result.'

Sam grinned. 'Has he really. The rascal.'

Phillip rolled his eyes. 'I've got three pups to find homes for.'

'We'll have one.'

'You will?'

'Yeah. Emily was only saying the other day that she thinks we should get a puppy for Dee Dee.'

'Dee Dee?'

'Oh, yeah. We finally thought of a name for the baby. Daisy Donna Davison.'

'Has a certain ring,' Phillip said.

Sam stood and walked over to Phillip. He took the pup from him, lifted it up, and checked its sex. 'Have you a bitch? This one's a dog.'

'Yeah. Why?'

'Bitches are better,' Sam said. 'More faithful. And they don't clamp onto someone's leg when you have people around.'

'Help yourself,' Phillip said. 'Only two more to home.'

'Were there only three pups?'

'Four. Kim persuaded me to keep one.'

Sam pulled out another pup. 'She'll do. Holding the dog to his face, he kissed it.'

'Will Baggage be ok with another dog in the house?'

'He'll have to be, it's his fault. We're going to have to get Luggage spayed, though. We don't want any other accidents.'

Sam smiled. 'Luggage?'

'Yep. Luggage.'

'Kim all right with that name?'

Phillip sat and grinned at Sam. 'Loves it.'

Albert entered, swiftly removed and hung up his coat. He faced Phillip and Sam. 'I may have a big job for us.'

Sam lifted his eyes from his desk. 'It doesn't involve biscuits, does it?'

Albert shuffled his feet. 'No.'

Sam leant back on his chair. 'Only last week you nearly went into meltdown when I opened your packet of Hobnobs without following the Albert Jackson biscuit protocol.'

Albert rolled his eyes. 'I wasn't at my best last week. I'm getting my biscuit issues under control.'

'What about your new therapist?' Phillip said.

'I'm seeing him on Friday.'

Sam allowed his chair to drop back onto four legs. 'Can you make sure you don't tell him all our secrets this time?'

'I've said I'm sorry—'

'Ignore him, Albert.' Phillip said.

Sam exhaled. 'Ok. I promise I won't mention it again. Tell us about this job.'

Albert settled behind his desk. 'It's for the brother of my old history teacher, Mr Knight. Apparently, he was looking for a cross from Lindisfarne.'

'Holy island?' Phillip said.

Albert took out a small notebook from his top pocket. 'Mr Knight was really interested in the history of the place. There is a legend that a very valuable cross was smuggled off the island when the Vikings invaded.'

'Don't suppose we have a map with an X on it, do we?' Sam said. He placed his hands behind his head and grinned. 'The Lindisfarne Liturgy.'

Albert furrowed his brow. 'How do you—?'

'It was mentioned in the chronicles,' Sam said. 'It's almost certainly lost.'

Phillip followed Albert's stare. 'You seem to know a bit about it?'

Sam pushed his chair back onto two legs and placed his feet on the desk. 'The Vikings sacked Lindisfarne in 793 AD. And after the collapse of the Northumbrian Kingdom, the monks fled taking St Cuthbert's body with them in 875 AD. They didn't name it Holy island until the priory was re-established in Norman times as a Benedictine house. This continued until its suppression in 1536.'

Albert glanced at Phillip and then back at Sam. 'How?'

'I did a history degree,' Sam said. Albert's jaw dropped open. 'It was years ago.'

'You've got a degree?' Phillip said.

'Yeah. I only did it because of Katherine Mosely.'

'You've got a degree?' Albert said.

Sam closed his eyes and sighed loudly. 'Yeah, Katherine Mosely. She was gorgeous and had the most perfect pair of breasts I have ever seen.'

'This degree?' Phillip said.

Sam waved his hand dismissively. 'Katherine was uber-intelligent. I was smitten. She wanted to be an archaeologist. In an attempt to woo her, I joined her class.'

Albert rubbed his face. 'You must have gained A levels, then?'

'Yeah,' Sam gritted his teeth. 'Five.'

Albert's jaw dropped open again. 'Five,' he whispered.

'Yeah, five. Why the bloody interest in my education? I'm trying to tell you about Katherine Mosely here. Her breasts ...' Sam shaped his hands together.

'Sam,' Phillip said. 'I think the fact you have all these qualifications is—'

Sam jumped to his feet. 'If you're not interested in hearing about Katherine Mosely, I won't tell you. I'm going to make a cup of tea.' He wandered towards the exit and stopped. 'They were fabulous, though.' He disappeared through the door and popped his head back around the corner. 'I have a photo of them if you're interested?'

Albert gaped at Phillip. 'Five A-levels and a degree,' Albert said. 'How ...?'

Phillip narrowed his eyes. 'Now that's a mystery we need to get to the bottom of.'

Sam returned with a steaming cup of tea, slid into his seat and pushed it back on two legs. 'This ex-teacher of yours,' he said. 'What's the mystery?'

'His brother, George,' Albert said. 'Thinks there's something suspicious about his death.'

Sam flopped his chair forward. 'Suspicious?'

Albert studied his notebook, again. 'He was meeting a friend of his called Professor Haldine in Alnwick. He fell from a hill. Mr Knight, not Professor Haldine.'

'Accident?' Sam said.

'The police think so,' Albert said.

'This Knight?' Phillip said. 'What does he want us to do?'

Albert glanced between Sam and Phillip. 'Mr Knight has loads of paperwork relating to Lindisfarne. He wants us to see if there's any truth about the cross, and find out if his brother was murdered.'

Sam raised his eyebrows. 'Does he know what we charge?'

'Yeah,' Albert said. 'Seems quite happy with the cost.'

Phillip held up a hand as Sam was about to speak. 'Why us?'

Albert smiled. 'He read about The Romanov Eagle in the paper.'

Sam stood. 'Sounds good to me. We could do with a big job. I'm going to make a sandwich. Who wants one?'

'I'll have one,' Phillip said.

'Sam?' Albert said.

Sam paused, and Albert continued. 'There aren't any Kit-Kats, are there?'

Sam rolled his eyes. 'There he goes with the biscuits again.' He threw his hands in the air and marched out.

'Albert,' Phillip said. 'I don't suppose you fancy owning a dog?'

CHAPTER TWO

SIX MONTHS EARLIER - Stanley Knight sat at his desk scribbling notes. His mobile rang and still writing, he answered it.

'Stanley Knight,' he said.

'Stanley,' a voice said. 'It's Bob Haldine.'

'Hi, Bob. How are you?'

'I'm well. The cross ...?'

Knight stopped writing. 'Yeah?'

'I may have a lead.'

'To its whereabouts?'

'Let's not get too excited, Stanley. But it's a possibility.'

'Well, you have my undivided ... Go on.'

'Bit of a coincidence really. I was at a party the other night, and I got talking to this gentleman. He's a bit of a history buff. Anyway,' Haldine continued. 'He particularly specialises in historical court cases. When I mentioned that you, Randy and I, were looking for the Lindisfarne Liturgy, he was interested.'

'Has he heard of the cross?'

'No. But he remembers a case dating back to the eighteenth century concerning the theft of a cross.'

Knight groaned. 'It could be any cross.'

'There was a detailed description of it. On the back was an inscription.'

'Go on,' Knight said.

'He couldn't remember exactly. But it mentioned Lindisfarne and Cuthbcrt.'

'Can we meet him?'

Haldine chuckled. 'Already way ahead of you. I've booked us lunch today.'

'I'll phone Randy,' Knight said.

Haldine and Knight were joined by another gentlemen. He shook hands with the pair and sat.

'This is Austin Fagerson,' Haldine said to Knight.

'Nice to meet you,' Knight said.

Fagerson placed a thick file onto the table. 'I had a bit of trouble locating the exact bit of information.' He opened the file and began flicking through the pages.

Haldine placed a hand on Fagerson's arm. 'We have another gentleman joining us,' Haldine said. 'Maybe we should wait until he arrives?'

'If you like,' Fagerson said.

Knight caught the attention of the waiter. 'Perhaps a drink while we wait?'

Fagerson smiled. 'Yes. A glass of merlot would be lovely.'

'Another glass of merlot,' Knight said. The waiter nodded at the three men and left. 'Maybe you could tell us a little about your research.' He fixed his gaze on Haldine. 'Bob was telling me you're writing a book?'

'Yes,' Fagerson said. 'I've been collating crime and punishment cases from the late nineteenth century. Around the Teesside area.'

The waiter and Randolph Edwards arrived together.

'Apologies for my tardiness, gentlemen. My meeting took a little longer than I anticipated.'

Knight raised his eyebrows at Randy, who smiled back at him. Randy signalled to the waiter. 'A brandy, my good man. I feel I've earned it.'

Knight smiled. 'This is Austin Fagerson,' Knight said.

Edwards held out his hand. 'Delighted to meet you, Austin.'

'Austin was just telling us about a book he's writing,' Haldine said.

The waiter returned with the brandy and placed it down. 'Are you gentlemen ready to order?' he said.

'Yes,' Edwards said, looking at the men in turn for confirmation. 'I think we are.'

PRESENT DAY – Sam sat, propped on the back legs of his seat, staring outside of the office window as Phillip entered with Kim.

'Morning,' Phillip said. 'You look busy.'

Sam allowed his chair to rest on four legs. 'I thought we might have a trip across to Guisborough.'

'Guisborough?' Phillip said.

Sam sighed. 'Emily is giving me grief about the christening. She wants me to wear a suit.'

'You should wear one,' Kim said. 'It is your daughter's special day.'

Sam scoffed. 'What's wrong with jeans and a t-shirt?'

Kim glanced at Phillip and raised her eyebrows. 'I'll leave you to it. I've got someone coming to have a look at the flat.'

Phillip kissed her on the cheek. 'See you later.' He slid into his seat and looked at Sam. 'So, what's so special about Guisborough?'

'The case Albert's working on ... The murdered history teacher?'

'We're not sure it's murder,' Phillip said.

'Well.' Sam stood. 'One of the guys who knew him ...' He glanced at his notebook. '... called Randolph Edwards, has a shop. Men's clothes, suits etc.'

'Ah,' Phillip said. 'And you thought ...?'

'Kill two birds. Ask him about Stanley Knight and get kitted out at the same time. It'll put a smile on Emily's face.'

'Where is Albert?'

Sam rolled his eyes. 'Biscuit therapy.'

'Who was the other bloke Albert mentioned?'

Sam glanced at his notebook again. 'Professor Haldine. He's abroad at the moment, though.'

'You've been busy. Anything else I should know?'

'Not really. I think this is a wild goose chase. Like I said, there is a cross mentioned in the chronicles, but—'

'Didn't you say something similar about the Romanov Eagle, and that turned out to be real.'

'True enough,' Sam said. 'No one's infallible.'

Sam and Phillip parked on Guisborough High Street and got out. Sam stretched and yawned.

'Tired?' Phillip said.

'Daisy had us up half the night. It's exhausting work this parenting thing. When are you and Kim going to join that particular club?'

Phillip smiled as Sam followed him along the pavement. 'We haven't discussed it. I'm not even sure she wants kids.'

Sam caught him up. 'What about you?'

Phillip stopped. 'Never given it much thought.' He carried on a little more then stopped again. He stared at the brightly coloured sign above a doorway. '*Randy Ted's*.'

Sam raised his eyebrows. 'Great name,' Sam said.

'Shall we?' Phillip said, theatrically pointing the way.

The pair entered and climbed the stairs to the floor above. It opened into a large room with rows of jackets, shirts, trousers and waistcoats. Sam ambled across to a rack and began perusing the suits. The pair turned as a tall, portly, black gentlemen emerged from a room at the back of the shop, accompanied by two other men.

'I'll have them ready for you next week,' he said to his customers. His voice a deep, honey-coated baritone. 'I'll call and let you know when they're ready to collect.' The men thanked him and disappeared downstairs.

The man switched his attention to Sam and Phillip. 'Good morning, gentlemen. Can I be of assistance?'

Sam glanced at Phillip, then fixed his view back to the man. 'Randolph Edwards?' Sam said.

'Yes,' he said. 'And you two are ...?'

Phillip stepped forward and offered his hand. 'Phillip Davison. This is my associate, Sam Davison.'

Sam screwed up his face and moved past Phillip, glancing at him. 'Associate?'

Phillip smiled. 'Sam and I are cousins. We work at the Erimus Detective Agency.'

'Yes, Yes,' Edwards said. 'Of course. The Romanov Eagle. I read about it in the papers.' He let out a huge belly-laugh. 'What a tremendous caper.'

'What it is, Mr Edwards,' Sam said. 'We are ...'

'Randy,' Edwards said. 'Call me Randy. Everyone does. Mr Edwards is so impersonal.'

'Randy.' Sam smiled. 'I like that name.'

Edwards winked. 'Randy by name, randy by ...' He let out another belly-laugh. 'The fairer sex love it.'

Phillip glanced at Sam and then back at Edwards. 'We would like to have a chat with you.'

'My suit,' Sam said. 'Don't forget my suit.'

Phillip rolled his eyes. 'My friend here.' He nodded in Sam's direction. 'Needs a suit.'

'Ah,' Edwards said. 'You've come to the right place. This chat ...?'

'It's about a case we're working on,' Phillip said.

Edwards consulted his watch. Pulling the timepiece from the pocket of his waistcoat, he flicked open the cover. 'Perhaps we should sort your friend out with his suit first. I close for lunch, and can perhaps spare you ten minutes or so for our chat.' He raised an index finger high. 'Not a minute longer, mind. I have another meeting. A liaison.' The last word stretched in a long and suggestive manner. 'I'm sure you two men of the world understand.'

Sam smiled. 'Perfectly, Randy. Now ...' Sam performed a 360. 'Point me towards the threads.'

SIX MONTHS EARLIER - Edwards sipped on his second brandy and studied Fagerson. 'So ...' He leant back in his chair '... You have a lead?'

Fagerson put down his glass. 'As I was telling your two friends here, I'm putting together a book about nineteenth-century crime and punishment.' He opened his file. 'While researching, I came across an interesting case. Well, interesting to you, gentlemen.'

Knight and Haldine leant in closer. 'Jeremiah Fagerson,' he continued. The three men glanced between themselves. Fagerson smiled. 'No relation. However, it is why my interest in the case was piqued. Normally, I'm only interested in ...' He sipped at his wine. '... the more scandalous cases. Murders and suchlike. One has to keep the reader's attention.'

'This Jeremiah Fagerson?' Knight said. 'How is—?'

'He lived on the outskirts of Stainton Village. He owned a small piece of land. Unusual in those days. By all accounts, his father had been gifted it by the Pennyman family.'

'Of Ormesby Hall fame?' Edwards said.

'Yes. Unfortunately, it appears Jeremiah was a wastrel. By the time of his death, the house and land had fallen into a bit of a state. It appears he liked a drink or two.'

'Was he murdered?' Knight said.

'No. Two men tried to burgle his house. One of them, James Smith, was shot and killed by Jeremiah. His accomplice, Thomas Barwick, managed to escape.'

'With the cross?' Knight said.

'Apparently so. Sadly, Jeremiah suffered a heart attack and died soon after. No one, but Jeremiah, saw the cross.'

Edwards emptied his brandy glass. 'How do they know he had the cross? And what makes you think it was The Liturgy?'

Fagerson held up his finger. 'Yes, The Liturgy. The professor told me a little about it the other night. He said you were looking for an ancient cross.'

'Yes,' Knight said. 'There was a cross that came from Lindisfarne. A precious and revered cross. Dating back to the ninth century.'

Fagerson scoffed. 'Surely you don't think it's the same one?'

Haldine smiled and glanced at Knight. 'Stanley knows more about the cross than anyone else.'

'But how did it get to ...?' Fagerson said. 'I mean if it did get to ...?'

'Have you heard of the Monk's Trod?' Knight said. Fagerson shook his head, and Knight continued. 'The Monk's Trod, as the name implies, was a path travelled by monks from Durham to Whitby Abbey. As well as passing through Hartlepool and Middlesbrough, called Middleburgh in those days, Stainsby—'

'A medieval village,' Haldine said. 'It was located near to where the A19 now runs.'

'It also passed through ...' Knight took a sip of his drink and raised his eyebrows.

Fagerson grinned. 'Stainton?'

'Indeed,' Knight said. 'There are still remnants of the Monk's Trod in the village.'

'But this cross,' Fagerson said. 'How do you know it left the island?'

'There is a book in Dorman's Museum from the tenth century. It was held at a small monastic cell in Middlesbrough. A monk arrived from Lindisfarne and died soon after. He had a Celtic cross which he was taking to Whitby Abbey. One of the small order of monks set off with it in his possession. It's in one of the entries. Unfortunately, he never arrived, and the cross has never been heard of since.'

'I see,' Fagerson said. 'And you think it may have ended up in Stainton?'

'It's possible,' Knight said.

'What happened to the cross in your case?' Haldine said.

'It was never found,' Fagerson said. 'Thomas Barwick was soon apprehended by the authorities. He and James Smith were well-known villains. He confessed to taking the cross but claimed he hid it at the edge of the village. When a search was done, it wasn't found.'

Knight looked at Haldine. 'It could still be out there, somewhere,' Knight said.

Edwards grunted. 'It's unlikely to have remained undiscovered, Stanley.'

'It's possible,' Haldine said.

Edwards waved the waiter over. 'Can we have some more drinks?' he said.

'The same as before?' the waiter asked. The other three nodded their approval and the waiter left.

'If this is indeed the same cross,' Edwards said. 'What proof have we got that Jeremiah Fagerson had it?'

'Ah,' Fagerson said. 'Before his death, the old man did a sketch of it. It was mentioned at the trial of Barwick. A description of the cross and the inscription on the back ...' He consulted his notes again. '*Ad honorem Cuthberti.*'

Knight smiled and clasped his hands together. 'To honour Cuthbert. It is The Liturgy, gentlemen. It matches the description in the chronicles exactly.'

'What happened to Barwick?' Haldine said.

'Clearly, the judge didn't believe Barwick when he showed them where he'd hidden the cross and, because Jeremiah died in the burglary, Barwick was hanged a week later.'

'Without the cross being found?' Knight said.

'I've checked,' Fagerson said. 'There is no mention in the newspapers of its discovery.'

The waiter placed the drinks down, and Knight picked up his glass. 'A toast,' he said. 'Sit primo quaerere. Let the search begin.'

'I take it,' Fagerson said, 'that this cross is valuable?'

'Priceless,' Knight said. 'Bloody priceless.'

PRESENT DAY - Sam strutted out of the changing room, stylishly dressed in a suit. He winked at Phillip and held out his arms. 'What do you think?'

Phillip stopped perusing the rows of jackets on a rail and turned to view Sam. He nodded slowly. 'Very dapper. Emily will be pleased.'

Edwards finished serving a customer, handed them an embossed paper bag, and joined Sam and Phillip in the rear of the shop. 'My word,' Edwards said. 'What a transformation.' He wandered across to Sam and pulled at various parts of the garment. 'It just needs a nip and tuck in places. My seamstress will make it a perfect fit.'

'Will that take long?' Sam said. 'I have a mal-function to go to.'

Edwards raised his eyebrows. 'Mal-function?'

'Yeah. They never go to plan.'

Edwards belly-laughed. 'We'll have this done by the middle of next week. Would that be acceptable?'

Sam nodded. 'Brilliant.'

Edwards rechecked his watch. 'If you would like to come into the back, I'll mark up the adjustments. Time is of the essence.' Edwards glanced at Phillip. 'Give me a shout if anyone comes in, young man.' Phillip nodded and resumed his rack search as Sam followed Edwards.

'Is this liaison of yours ...' Sam comically raised his eyebrows. 'A lady?'

Edwards smiled. 'Amour dans l'apres-midi.'

Sam smiled and tapped the side of his nose. 'Love in the afternoon.'

'The ladies love a bit of the Gallic.'

'I had to give up all that malarkey when I got together with Emily.'

'But you're so young to settle down.'

'She's the one ... You know ...' Sam smiled. '*The One.*'

'Ah,' Edwards said. 'Love. The enemy to a successful lothario.'

'Have you ...' Sam coughed. 'Slept with many women?'

Edwards guffawed. 'Samuel my dear, if they're sleeping, you're doing something wrong.' Sam joined in with Edwards' laugher. 'My midday clandestine ...' He licked his lips. 'Is a rather charming brunette. She's married, you see, but she can't resist a little bit of Randy.'

Sam and Phillip followed Edwards into a coffee shop. Phillip ordered the coffees as Edwards and Sam found a seat.

'So,' Edwards said. 'You said you had something else that demands my attention?'

'Yes,' Sam said. 'Stanley Knight.'

'Stanley?' The smile fell from Edwards' face. 'He was a good friend of mine.'

Phillip joined the other two and placed the coffees down. 'Has Sam told you—?'

'I was just telling him now,' Sam said.

Phillip sat. 'His brother has asked us to look into his death.'

'The police think it's an accident,' Edwards said. 'I've no reason to believe it was anything else.'

Phillip took a sip of coffee. 'It was in Alnwick?'

Edwards nodded. 'Up near the castle.'

'What about the cross?' Sam said. 'The Liturgy?'

Edwards smiled. 'Stanley had this hobby, almost verging on obsession. The Lindisfarne Liturgy has been missing for over a thousand years. It was probably taken by—'

'The Vikings?' Sam said.

'Most likely.' Edwards said.

'He must have had some reason for searching for it,' Phillip said. 'A clue, a lead?'

Edwards huffed. 'A wild-goose chase, boys. Stanley was a lovely man, and a dear friend, but he was prone to flights of fancy.'

Phillip sideway glanced at Sam and leant in closer to Edwards. 'Why was he in Alnwick?'

Edwards pulled out his pocket watch, glanced at it, and pushed it back into his waistcoat. 'I've no idea. Our time, gentlemen, is at an end. There's a comely wench requiring Randy's amour.' He stood and downed his coffee in one. 'I'll ring you when your suit is ready to collect, Samuel.' With that, he left.

'What do you think, Sam?' Phillip said.

'Randy by name, randy by nature.'

'Not about that. About his reaction when we asked about Stanley Knight?'

Sam shrugged. 'Maybe he's telling the truth. Like I said before, The Liturgy was probably plundered by the Vikings. And even if it wasn't, it'll have been melted down years ago.'

Phillip fixed his stare on the door which Edwards had left by. 'I think a little digging into Randy's past is in order.'

'So,' Sam said. 'What do you think of my suit?' Phillip rolled his eyes.

CHAPTER THREE

Tommo moved to the far end of the room. He raised his glass high and tapped on the side to attract the attention of everyone. The hubbub of noise receded, and he smiled at the gathered guests.

'Thank you all for coming tonight.' Deb joined him. 'Deb and I are grateful that you managed to fit us into your busy schedule.'

Sam lifted his glass. 'Free drink and food. We'd be mad to miss it.'

'Thanks, Sam,' Tommo said. 'So, without further ado, I'd like the lovely Deb to cut the ribbon and officially open our new cocktail bar ... Black Mamba.'

Deb accepted the scissors from Tommo. 'I was hoping you'd have one of those giant pairs,' she said.

'Size isn't everything,' Tommo said, and winked.

Tommo pulled himself a pint of beer and slumped onto a stool. Deb framed his face between her hands and kissed him. 'You look absolutely knackered,' she said.

'I am. I won't take much rocking tonight.'

'Nearly over, gorgeous.' She kissed him again. 'I'm just going to have a chat with Emily and Kim. Save a little bit of energy for later.' She winked and sashayed off. Tommo watched as she headed across the room and sighed a loud, contented sigh.

'Tommo,' Albert said.

Tommo spun around. 'Hi, Albert,' he said. 'On the cocktails, are we?' He nodded at the giant fishbowl in Albert's hand.

Albert glanced at the concoction. 'Gene insisted. If I'm honest ...'

Tommo took the glass from him and put it behind the bar. 'How about a proper drink? This ...' He tapped the pump. 'Is a cracking pale ale.'

Albert beamed. 'Yes, please.' Albert rubbed his chin and fidgeted. 'Tommo,' he said.

'Yeah.'

'You've known Sam quite a while, haven't you?'

Tommo glanced over at Sam, who was attempting to balance a large number of beer mats on the tip of his nose. Tommo puffed out his cheeks. 'Yeah, since we were at primary school.'

Albert followed Tommo's stare towards Sam, who now had Emily on his lap with her arms wrapped around him. The pair kissed passionately.

'Get a room, you two,' Tommo shouted. 'My bar is not the place for creating a little brother or sister for Daisy.' Emily blew Tommo a kiss.

'Sam.' Albert said.

Tommo gave Albert his full attention. 'What about him?'

'He did rather well at school?'

Tommo looked skywards. 'Yeah.'

'But how?' Albert said.

Tommo chuckled. 'I know.' He glanced towards Sam and Emily, who were now performing a Salsa. 'Sam is a bit of an enigma.'

'He said he got five A levels.'

'Yeah.' Tommo shook his head. 'Sam plays the fool, but he's intelligent. Don't ask me why, but he could have been, could be, anything he wanted to be.' Tommo stared directly at Albert. 'I struggled and fought for every GCSE I got. Sam would breeze through the exams.'

'What A levels did he get?'

Tommo raised his eyebrows. 'English, maths, history, physics and modern and classical languages.' Albert's jaw dropped open. Tommo leant in closer. 'He got four A stars, and an A in physics.' Albert slowly shook his head as Tommo continued. 'Claimed he would have had all A stars, but he didn't get on with the physics teacher. He told me he deliberately did badly in the exam.'

Phillip joined the pair. 'What are you two talking about?'

Albert turned to face him. 'Sam got four A stars in his A levels.'

Phillip raised his eyebrows. 'Wow!' He followed the gaze of the other two as they watched Sam piggy-backing Emily outside. 'He has a degree, too?' Phillip said.

Tommo took a large swig of his beer. He let out a riotous laugh. 'It's hilarious, isn't it? Sam Davison, who goes through life as if he's fifteen, has a degree.'

Albert and Phillip shook their heads in unison. Tommo beckoned them closer. 'Not just any degree … A first.'

'No!' Albert said.

Tommo nodded and then let out a great belly-laugh. 'A bloody first. At one point he gained the highest mark nationally.'

'It's so bizarre,' Phillip said, and slumped onto a stool next to Albert. 'He …' Phillip threw his hands in the air. 'It's … bizarre.'

Tommo reached into his back pocket and pulled out his wallet. 'Wait until you see this.' Tommo carefully removed a piece of paper and unfolded it. The pair stared at the photo of Sam, under the heading - Durham University – ***'Aim high like Samuel Davison. Our shining star.'*** Tommo chuckled. 'I used to call him "The Campus King."'

Albert picked up his pint and took a large gulp. 'Bizarre.'

Kim opened the door to the flat, allowing Emily with her pushchair inside. 'Phew,' Emily said. 'Those stairs are challenging with a pushchair.'

'You should have phoned. I'd have come down.'

Emily waved a hand. 'All good exercise.' She followed Kim through into the lounge. 'Where are the boys? I popped into the office, and it's empty.'

'I've no idea where they are,' Kim said. 'Probably chasing a lead on a case. Although Phillip did mention something about Sam going to get himself a suit.'

Emily slumped onto the chair. 'Really ... He's a bugger. He likes to wind me up. He told me he was wearing jeans and a t-shirt.'

'Well, I think he intends pushing the boat out.'

Emily grinned. 'Bloody good.'

'Phillip was telling me about Sam's qualifications ... I didn't know if he was winding me up or not.'

Emily rolled her eyes. 'Yeah. GCSE's, A-Levels and a degree. Sam has qualifications coming out of his backside.'

'How come we're only learning about this now?' Kim said.

'Because he hates the fact that he is bright. He thinks it's uncool to have all these certificates.'

'Why?'

Emily held her hands up. 'I don't know. It's just ... Sam. Sam is Sam. I stopped trying to fathom him out years ago.'

Kim slowly shook her head. She checked her watch. 'She's late. She should've been here by now.'

'The woman who wants the flat?' Emily said.

'Yeah. She sounded quite mature on the phone.' Kim picked a piece of paper from the coffee table. 'Mary Huff. Spelt H-o-u-g-h.'

'What does she do?' Emily said.

Kim raised her eyebrows. 'Spiritualist, tarot-reader and Indian mystic practitioner.'

'Oooh,' Emily said. 'That sounds interesting.'

'That's what I thought.' The doorbell sounded. The women pulled a face at each other. 'That'll be her,' Kim said. She grinned at Emily, stood, and went to answer the door. Emily waited, straining to hear the conversation.

Kim re-entered, closely followed by a large woman with long wavy hair, dyed the colours of the rainbow. Her flowing dress cascading behind her in a cavalcade of satin and taffeta. Despite her size, she glided gracefully in her vivid pink sandshoes, the sound of the abundant necklaces and bangles around her neck and wrists jangled musically as she moved. Emily stared wide-eyed at her.

'Emily,' Kim said. 'This is Mary Hough.'

Emily smiled and held out her hand. Mary walked forward and took hold of it within both her hands, closed her eyes and lowered her head. Emily glanced at Kim, who pulled a face and shrugged.

Mary's eyes blinked open. 'Sorry about that,' she said in upper-class, clipped tones. 'I do like to know whom I'm dealing with.'

'… I'm Emily,'

Mary let out a guffaw. 'You misunderstand me, my dear. I meant your aura.' She grasped at thin-air with her fist.

Emily smiled. 'My aura … Is it … Ok?'

Mary tapped the top of Emily's hand while holding onto it with her other. 'It's more than ok, my dear. It's positively radiant.' She closed her eyes again. 'Mm,' she said. 'You're a new mum.'

Emily's jaw dropped open. 'Yes, I am. I have a little girl. But …?'

Mary's eyes blinked open again. 'Your maternal glow. It coruscates.'

'Does it?' Emily said. 'Does it really?'

Mary lifted a hand and gently placed it on Emily's cheek. 'Positively coruscates.' She twirled and performed a pirouette. 'And this is the flat, Kimberly?'

Kim nodded. 'Yes. What do you think?'

Mary clasped her hands together. 'I love it,' she purred. 'Its ambience is magnificent. It's been a happy home, I feel.' She studied the two women, looking for affirmation. Emily nodded, but Kim frowned. Mary closed her eyes. 'And yet …' Her eyes snapped open. 'I sense loss.'

'Bill,' Kim said.

'Your partner?' Mary said.

Kim shook her head as tears pooled in her eyes. 'No. He was …' Kim brought a hand to her mouth.

Emily hugged her friend. 'He was murdered,' Emily said.

'Oh, my,' Mary said. 'But not here?'

Emily shook her head. 'No.'

'I feel his presence,' she said. Mary closed her eyes once more, hands clasped together. 'He was happy here. I feel a deep love and affection for you, Kimberly.'

Kim sniffed and wiped her hand across her face. 'He was like my dad.'

Mary walked over to her and took hold of her hand. 'He was,' she said softly.

The three women sat at the kitchen table. Mary sipped at her tea. 'I'm sorry if I upset you, my dear. It wasn't my intention.'

Kim smiled. 'Don't worry, you didn't.'

'Kim was telling me,' Emily said. 'That you read Tarot cards.'

Mary nodded. 'I do, and a lot more. I'd be happy to do a reading for you two.'

'We'd pay of course,' Kim said.

Mary waved a dismissive hand. 'Wouldn't hear of it. I don't abuse my gifts by charging people money for it. I come from a long line of mystics. My mother and grandmother were both blessed with the gift. We'll arrange something.'

'Thanks, Mary,' Kim said.

Mary stood and wandered about. 'You don't mind if I change the décor a little?'

'No,' Kim said. 'Feel free.'

'I must have colour.' She bounced around the room, then stopped and closed her eyes. 'I can see it in my mind's eye.'

Kim and Emily glanced at each other. 'Blues, reds, greens and yellows,' Mary said. Her eyes blinked open. 'There must be yellows.'

'When would you like to move in?' Kim said.

'Immediately,' Mary said. 'One has to grasp the nettle in life.'

'Well,' Kim said. 'I can give you the key today.'

Mary clasped her hands together. 'Wonderful.' She opened her bag and pulled out an envelope. 'I have the bond and two months of rent here.' She handed it to Kim and clasped her hands together again. 'Yes, there must be yellows.'

Mary bounded outside and into a car. She took out her mobile and phoned.

'How did the flat hunting go?' a male voice said.

'Very well. The flat needs a bit of my touch, but it's ideal.'

'And the people from the agency?'

'I only met Kimberly, the secretary, and her friend. I haven't met any of the men. However, I don't think winning their trust will prove difficult.'

'Good. I'm back in England shortly, we'll meet and discuss our plan of attack.'

CHAPTER FOUR

LINDISFARNE - The day broke softly on 8th June 793. A shimmering light reflected on an almost still sea. After early morning prayer, Eadred went about his daily tasks in one of the gardens, tilling the soil and collecting food for the evening meal. He leant on his shovel and looked skywards. A bright, blue unbroken blanket stretched in every direction. As he walked back towards the monastery with his basket of foodstuffs, the bell in the tower began to chime and Eadred stopped as Leofric came running from the building.

'Eadred,' he said. 'Come quickly.'

'What is it?'

Leofric pointed to the sea. 'Heathens.'

Eadred dropped his basket and stared. 'What can we do?' He followed the retreating Leofric inside as the pair raced along the passageways and into a hall. Leofric bent and opened a large wooden trunk. From it, he pulled out something covered in cloth and held it out to Eadred.

'... but,' Eadred said.

'It must not be taken by the Heathens. You must save it.'

Eadred stared at the object in his hands. 'Why me?'

'You are the youngest and also the swiftest.'

'Where?'

'Take a donkey and travel to Whitby. Deliver it into the hands of the Abbot. No one else.'

'I'm—'

Leofric took hold of his shoulders. 'It is vital that the cross is saved,' he said, as the bells continued their peel outside.

'Yes,' Eadred said. 'I understand.'

Leofric placed a hand into his robe and pulled out a piece of folded paper with a wax seal over the join. 'This will give you passage. Travel via Middleburg. There are people who will help you.' Leofric took hold of the young monk's arm and pulled him towards the door. 'Quickly, my friend.'

'But what of our brethren?'

'We will do what we can. Godspeed, Eadred.'

Eadred trudged across the causeway and onto the mainland, his feet wet from the crossing. He paused and gazed back across to Lindisfarne. Black smoke billowed upwards from the monastery in an almost vertical plume. He slowly shook his head and climbed on the donkey. Eadred glanced at the package fastened to the side of the animal, encouraged the beast onwards with his heels, and set off.

Eadred clung onto the animal's neck as he made his way into the small hamlet of Middleburg. The exhausted donkey stopped and Eadred, unable to hang on any longer, fell from its back. A woman came rushing from one of the ramshackle buildings and was quickly joined by another.

'He's a monk,' the first said. 'Go and fetch someone.'

The second woman hurried off and quickly returned with two robed men.

'Who is he?' the second woman said.

One of the men searched through Eadred's belongings and pulled out the letter. 'He's from Lindisfarne,' he said to his companion. 'He has a letter.'

The second man knelt and placed a hand on Eadred's head. 'He has a fever. We need to attend to him.'

The young man stood next to his elder. 'Who is he, Cedric?'

The older man, his hands clasped together, sighed. 'His name is Eadred. He's from Lindisfarne.'

The young man sucked in air. 'He has travelled a long distance.'

'Yes. His condition is worsening. I fear he has drunk unclean water.'

'What does he want?'

'Something must have happened on the island. He would not make such an arduous journey otherwise.' Cedric turned to his companion. 'He was carrying that.' He pointed to a table in the corner. The young man moved across to it and gazed at a large, gold Celtic cross which gleamed in the candlelight.

'There is a letter,' the young man said, and picked up the piece of paper next to the cross.

'Indeed,' Cedric said. 'It was intended for the Abbot of Whitby. The cross is sacred.'

'What shall we do?'

The old man faced his younger companion. 'We pray that he recovers, Osgar.'

The men pushed the soil into the hole until the body could not be seen. They rested from their toil and drank greedily from their flasks before resuming again. The sun lowered in the sky, lengthening their shadows as the pair gathered their breath.

Cedric made his way over to them and placing the crude wooden cross in the ground, hammered it in. The other two stood and lowered their heads as words were said over the grave.

Osgar followed after Cedric. 'What about the cross?' Osgar said.

The old man stopped. 'It must be delivered to Whitby.' He stared at the younger man. 'I am too old to attempt such a journey,' he said. 'You must complete …' He glanced back at the grave. '… Our dear brother's task.'

Osgar brought his hands together. 'If you see fit.'

'Come,' Cedric said. 'We must ready you for the task ahead.'

Half a day's ride from Middleburg, Osgar stopped for a rest allowing the donkey to graze and drink from a nearby stream. He slumped onto a small grassy hillock and pulled some bread from his satchel.

Unsure how long he had dozed for, he woke as he heard a twig snap nearby. Instinctively, Osgar reached for his sword as two men came running from the trees, brandishing weapons and screaming madly. He jumped to his feet in readiness as the donkey, spooked by the noise the men were making, bolted into the undergrowth. It careered on, bounding past trees and shrubs as the cross, still strapped to the animal's flank, loosened with every hoof-fall. The donkey halted abruptly near the edge of a pond, the cross fell, bounced a couple of times, before sliding down the bank and dropping into the inky-black water with a loud plop.

STAINTON 1865 - The old man peered through the filthy glass of his dilapidated cottage. His dog barked wildly at something nearby. He strained his eyes, trying to decipher what it was. He mumbled some words. Then, pulling the old musket from above the fireplace, he headed outside.

'Toby,' he shouted. The dog momentarily stopped barking and briefly observed his owner before resuming its yapping. He wandered closer. His weapon levelled should anything make for him, slowly he edged forward. He reached the dog and looked over the edge of the riverbank. A small fawn bleated helplessly, its mother standing resolute on the opposite side.

'Ah,' the man said. 'You're stuck, are you?'

He lay the gun on the grass and gingerly edged his way down the bank and into the water. The fawn bleated louder as he approached. The doe stared on. He moved closer and grasped the youngster, pulling it into his arms. Gathering his breath, he waded through the shallow water and deposited it onto the other bank. The doe slowly walked forward and licked the fawn. She turned, and the youngster unsteadily followed in her wake. The man grunted and plodded his way back across the beck. He reached for a large branch on the other side to aid his exit but stopped as a glint in the water caught his eye. He peered closer, trying to decipher where the sparkle had come from. Slowly he edged nearer, his eyes scanning the surface of the water. Trying not to disturb the liquid, he squatted and gently probed with his fingers. His hands fell onto something and grabbing hold of it, he pulled it free. The man held the object in his hands, the weight surprising him. He sluiced it in the river while rubbing with a hand until slowly the object revealed itself. The old man held it aloft and gazed in awe at its beauty. The Celtic cross, the bright yellow gold, glinted as the sunlight glistened from it. He quickly clambered up the bank and carried the object into his cottage, laying it carefully on the table. He chuckled to himself as he realised its worth. The dog slowly padded over to him and raised its head.

'Manna from Heaven, Toby,' he said. 'Manna from Heaven.'

The old man whistled his way along the road, his dog faithfully by his side. He stopped at the tavern and entered. The large red-faced man behind the counter smiled broadly as he wandered in.

'Jeremiah,' he said. 'I haven't seen you in here for many months.'

The old man rubbed his fingers and thumb together. 'It was a choice between bread and ale. Without the coins, I had to forsake your splendid brew.'

'And now?'

Jeremiah chuckled. 'And now I have the wherewithal.' He tossed a couple of coins onto the counter and eased himself onto a bench. 'Some of your wife's fine bread and butter too.'

The landlord swept the coins into his hand and deposited them into a pocket in his apron. 'Right away, Jeremiah. Wife! Wife!'

An equally rotund woman pushed her portly figure through the door. 'What's all this noise, Jacob?' she said, glaring at her husband.

'We have a customer, Meg. He wants some of your bread and butter. Now be quick with it, before I take a broom to you.'

She huffed. 'You'll never be man enough.'

Jeremiah lifted his feet onto a stool and reclined with his hands behind his head as the landlord placed a flagon of ale in front of him. 'So,' the landlord said, and put his hands on his ample belly. '... What's this good fortune you've had?'

Jeremiah tapped the side of his nose. 'I'm not at liberty to say. But by sunset tomorrow I'll be a wealthy man.' He pulled a piece of paper from his jacket and held it aloft. A crude drawing of a cross sketched on it. 'Here is a clue, though.' The Innkeeper studied the picture before Jeremiah refolded it and deposited it back inside his pocket.

Meg returned and placed a dish in front of him. 'Come on, old man,' she said. 'You can't keep a secret.'

Jeremiah shook his head. 'Toby and me.' He patted the dog next to him. 'Will be quite comfortable.' He pulled a piece of bread from the dish and tossed it to the dog. 'Quite comfortable indeed.'

Jeremiah wobbled and held onto the bar. He slammed down his empty tankard and turned to face the occupants of the Alehouse. 'I'm off to my bed,' he slurred. 'Take a good look ...' He hiccupped. 'Tomorrow you'll be doffing your cap to me. Come, Toby,' he said, and patted the hound. 'We need our sleep. We have much to do in the morning.' He staggered towards the door and turned again. 'Good health,' he said, and tottered out.

The two men crept from the tavern and followed Jeremiah at a distance. They watched as he reached his cottage and staggered inside, closing the door with a resounding bang. Silently they made their way around the back of the property and squatting close to the rear door, they waited.

Jeremiah was soon fast asleep, his loud, drunken snores reverberating around the room. Through the open window, something was dropped to the floor. Toby, awoken from his own slumber, barked a little, before making his way over to the small pieces of meat lying on the flagstone below the window. He sniffed them before wolfing down the offering. The two men outside waited for the poison to take effect. Toby, oblivious to what the meat contained wandered back to his bed and slumping down, was soon snoring as loudly as his owner.

The man crept silently past the sleeping Jeremiah and stopping at the front door, carefully pulled the bolts back.

His friend joined him. 'Where's the old man, Thomas?' he said.

'He's sleeping.'

'And the dog?'

'I don't think he will give us any trouble. We're doing the animal a favour. The old mangy thing was on its last legs anyway.'

He nodded at his friend and moved towards the small front room. The floorboards creaked as he reached the threshold.

His friend reached for him and grabbed his arm. 'We must be quiet, James,' he whispered. 'We don't want the old fool waking.'

'What is it we're looking for?' James said.

'I'm not sure. But it must be gold or silver. He was bragging in the tavern tonight.'

James smiled. 'We'll be rich.'

'Come,' Thomas said. 'We'll search together.'

Jeremiah was roused from his slumber by a noise. He sat upright in bed, glanced around and listened. Hearing movement in the room next door he grasped hold of his musket and crept forwards. He strained to see in the dim light but spotting a figure crouching in the corner, he levelled his weapon as the man stood.

'Don't move,' Jeremiah said.

Thomas spun around to face the old man, the cross dangling from his right hand.

'You thieving bugger,' Jeremiah said. 'I should shoot you where you stand.' Jeremiah looked to his right as a figure moved towards him. He fired, the force of the blast hitting James in the chest, flinging him back as he fell to the floor dead. Thomas seized his opportunity and pushed past Jeremiah, causing the old man to stumble over.

Thomas was out of the door in a flash, closely followed by Jeremiah. 'Thief,' Jeremiah shouted. The younger man quickened away from the cottage and out of the village.

'Thief,' the old man shouted again. He slowed and dropped the weapon. Occupants from nearby properties flooded into the lane. A burly man reached Jeremiah, who had slumped to his knees.

'Jeremiah,' he said. 'What's wrong?'

Jeremiah raised his head. 'They've stolen the cross ...' He brought a hand to his chest as an excruciating pain gripped him. The old man let out a low moan and then slumped to the floor.

Hearing the sound of the voices pursuing him, Thomas ran as fast as his legs could carry him until he reached the outskirts of the village and stopped. With the cross held tightly in his hands, he searched around for some place to secrete it. Spotting a hole in a hedge, Thomas made his way through. He glanced around, his heart hammering at his chest. Dropping to his knees, he dug a small hole in the soft earth and deposited the cross into it. Quickly replacing the soil, he lifted a large stone nearby and placed it over his excavation. He stood, glanced in all directions, and headed off.

A figure standing nearby, stepped from the shadows as Thomas disappeared into the distance. Walter Littleby, the church gravedigger, made his way across to where Thomas had dug and dropped onto his knees.

CHAPTER FIVE

Inspector Comby picked unenthusiastically at his salad. Sitting in the front of his car parked in Middlesbrough police station, he watched as his junior, Detective Sergeant Mick Hardman, made his way over. Hardman reached the car and struggled to open the door with the large paper bag, drink cup and several chocolate bars in his hands. Comby leant across and opened the door for him. Hardman lumbered inside, the car dropping 3-4 inches with the additional bulk it now had to carry.

Hardman tossed the sweets on the dashboard, pushed the drink into the holder next to him and smacked his lips. 'Bloody packed at the café.' He glanced towards Comby's meal. 'What the hell is that you're eating?'

Comby appraised his food and then at pointed his fork at Hardman. 'Salad.'

Hardman snorted. 'Salad? What the hell?'

'It's healthy,' Comby said. 'And tasty.'

Hardman slipped his hand inside the paper bag and pulled out an enormous breakfast bun. 'Not as tasty as this bad-boy.'

Comby sniffed. The smell of the sandwich filling his nostrils with a delightful aroma. 'Heart attack in a bun, that.'

Hardman squeezed his butty and took a huge bite. 'It's never bothered you before, guv,' he spluttered through his half-full mouth.

'Well I've decided,' he said, looking at the cherry tomato on the end of his fork. 'That I'm going to look after myself from now on and lose a bit of weight.'

'You're not that fat, guv.'

'Not compared to you,' Comby said. 'Jesus, Mick, the suspension on this car is just about shot with you. You must have put on a stone since last month.'

Hardman frowned. 'Me and the missus are going through a rough patch. I'm comfort eating.'

'You need to try some of this stuff.' He shook the salad container under Hardman's nose.

Hardman took another bite of his bun. 'Never much liked veg and that. Too bland.'

'Have you tried going to the gym?'

Hardman scoffed. 'Gym?'

'Yeah, gym. Where you exercise. I've started going three times a week.'

Hardman gave a puzzled look. 'Wait a minute. Healthy food, gym ... What's going on here? You haven't got a woman on the go, have you?' Hardman let out a roar of laughter, splattering the dashboard and window with bits of sausage, egg and bacon.

'What the hell are you laughing at? What's so funny about me having a woman?'

Hardman fixed him with a stare. 'Are you serious?'

Comby tossed the remainder of his salad down. 'Yes. And I don't need you—'

Hardman held a hand up. 'Sorry, guv. I thought you were joking. Of course there's nothing wrong with you having a lady friend.'

'Too right,' Comby said.

Hardman shifted in his seat. 'Where did you meet her?'

'I'm not discussing my love-life with my junior officer.'

Hardman pursed his lips. 'I thought we were mates, too.'

Comby sighed. 'Yeah, well.'

'I could give you some pointers. It's been a while. It must be ten years since your missus left.'

'What do you mean, give me pointers? You've just told me you and your lass aren't getting on.'

Hardman scoffed. 'Oh, that. It's just a little tiff. It won't be long before we're bumping hips again.'

'Jesus, Mick, way too much info.'

'I'm just saying.' He patted his substantial stomach. 'I might be on the large size but I can still put it about a bit in the bedroom.'

Comby rolled his eyes. 'I hope you have understanding neighbours?'

Hardman stared blankly. 'Why?'

'Come on, Mick. Your Natalie's no light-weight either.'

'That's why we're so compatible. Anyway, why should the skinny people have all the fun? Us biggies ...' He began to slowly thrust his hips forward and backwards. 'Have all this to bang it in with.' He guffawed. 'I'm built for comfort, me.'

Comby rolled his eyes again. 'Thanks for that image, Mick.'

'When I get Nat on our memory foam mattress ...' He smiled at Comby and raised his eyebrows.

'I hope it's got amnesia.'

'What does this woman look like, then?' Hardman said.
'As I said, I don't wish to discuss my—'
'Is she a dog?' Hardman said.
'No, she bloody isn't. She looks very attractive in her profile picture.'
'Profile picture. You mean you haven't met her yet?'
Comby growled. 'Hardman!'
'Sorry, guv. It's a bit of banter, that's all.'
Comby sighed loudly. 'Guisborough.'
'Guisborough, guv?'
He tutted and stared at Hardman. 'Yes, Guisborough.'

Phillip pulled the car into a parking spot outside *"Randy Ted's"* and switched off the engine. 'We'll get your suit and then have some lunch.'
'Great,' Sam said. 'I'm bloody starving.'
'I'd like to ask Randy some more questions,' Phillip said. 'He knows more than he's letting on.'
'Well, let me get my suit first before you start upsetting him.'
'Yeah.' Phillip glanced at the shop. 'Definitely knows more than he's told us.'
The pair made their way inside, ascended the stairs, and entered the main shop. Sam wandered across to the suits in the corner. 'I not sure I should have got the blue one, now. I like this check.'
'Randy,' Phillip shouted. He looked over at Sam. 'I wonder where he is?'
Sam wrapped his arms around himself and pouted. 'Probably giving some chick a bit of Randy luuurve.'
Phillip wandered into the back of the shop. 'Randy?' he said. Phillip stopped and stared, open-mouthed, at the prone form of Edwards on the floor. He moved across to him and bent down, placing two fingers onto the shop owner's neck. He slowly shook his head and hurried back into the shop.
Sam viewed himself in the large, ornate mirror and held up a piece of material. 'Do you think I'd suit a cravat, Phillip?'
Phillip slumped onto a chair. 'He's out the back.'
'Good. Tell him to hurry up, I'm starving. My stomach thinks my throat's been cut.' Sam picked up a flat-cap and pushed it onto his head. 'Look … I'm a Peaky Blinder.'
'He's dead, Sam.'
Sam furrowed his brow. 'Who is?'
'Randy.'
'What are you on about?'
Phillip inhaled. 'He's in the back. He's been murdered.'
Sam raced towards the other room, stopped at the threshold, and gawped at the proprietor. 'Bloody hell, he has and all.'

Phillip nodded to an item on the floor. 'Looks like he was hit over the head with that antique shoehorn, and then strangled with a tie.'

Sam sucked in air. 'A Dolce and Gabbana silk tie!' He raised his eyebrows. 'Classy killing.'

'Sam,' Phillip said. 'This is no time for levity.'

'Probably some woman's husband. It was a risky game Randy was playing.'

'What are we going to do?' Phillip said.

'I don't know. What do you think?'

'We should phone the police, really.'

Sam grimaced. 'I'd rather someone else found him. We haven't got a great relationship with Cleveland Constabulary.'

'Only because you wrote all those awful things about Comby.'

'That was the journalist,' Sam said. 'He embellished.'

'Well, I think we should go. Let someone else find him.'

Sam glanced back at the body. 'Yeah. Better all-round if we did.'

Phillip moved towards the door. 'Come on. Let's see if there's a back way out.'

'Hold on,' Sam said. He disappeared into the storeroom.

'Sam,' Phillip whispered. 'What are you doing?'

'Eureka!' Sam said, and emerged carrying a suit-holder.

'What's that?'

Sam held it up. 'My suit.'

'You're robbing a dead man?'

'It's not robbery, I've paid for it. If I come home without this, Emily will—'

'I don't believe you. Come on.' Phillip exited and made his way downstairs. He froze as the door to the street opened and Comby, accompanied by Hardman, entered.

Comby glowered at Phillip, who had stopped halfway down. 'Well, well, well,' Comby said. 'If it isn't Mr Davison.' Sam came out of the shop and started his descent, but stopped as his eyes locked with Comby. 'And look here,' Comby continued. 'We have the other member of the comedy duo.'

'Inspector,' Phillip said. 'Fancy meeting you.'

'What are you two doing here?' Comby said.

'Erm ... well,' Phillip said.

Comby tapped the package Sam was carrying. 'A new suit? Is that for your next court appearance?'

'Good one,' Sam said. 'Actually, it's for my daughter's baptism.'

Comby scoffed. 'The poor child. Having you as a parent.' Comby waved them down. 'Come on, out of my way. I have Mr Edwards to see.'

Phillip and Sam moved to one side, as Comby and Hardman, who glared at the pair, pushed past them.

'There's a problem,' Phillip said.

The two officers stopped. 'Problem?' Comby said.

Phillip trudged back up, followed by Sam. They made their way into the shop and waited as Comby and Hardman joined them. Phillip nodded towards the back room.

'This had better be good,' Comby said, and motioned for Hardman to take a look.

Hardman plodded through into the other room, as Phillip and Sam hung on to a collective breath.

'Guv,' Hardman shouted. 'He's dead.'

Comby pointed at the cousins. 'Don't move an inch, you two.'

Phillip closed his eyes and winced as Sam wandered across to the suit-rack again. 'I definitely should have got the check one,' Sam said. Phillip spun and glared at him.

'You two,' Comby said. 'Come in here.'

Phillip lowered his eyes as he and Sam trudged through and stopped next to the two officers.

'Would you like to tell me what happened here?' Comby said.

'He was like that when we arrived,' Phillip said.

'Of course he was,' Hardman said. 'What did you do it for, the takings?'

'We didn't do anything,' Sam said. 'We only came here to collect my suit.'

Comby chuckled. 'And of course, you have your suit. At what point did you feel it was the appropriate thing to do, find a body and steal a suit?'

'I resent that,' Sam said. 'I've paid for it.'

'Oh, well that's all right then,' Comby said. 'Were you just going to allow this gentleman to decompose here.'

'No,' Phillip said. 'We were on our way to summon help.'

'What's wrong with the phone,' Hardman said.

'We didn't want to contaminate the murder scene,' Sam said. Phillip grinned at him.

'Mobiles, gentlemen,' Comby said. 'Your mobiles.'

'In the car,' Phillip said. Sam surreptitiously pulled his from a pocket and slipped it into the suit holder.

'You wouldn't mind being searched, then?' Hardman said.

'Not at all, Sergeant,' Sam said. Comby waved his junior away as he moved towards the cousins.

Comby pointed at the corpse. 'I take it this is Randolph Edwards?'

'Randy to his mates,' Sam said. He moved closer. 'A bit of a ladies' man. It was probably some irate husband who did this.'

'We'll see,' Comby said. 'You two are not off the hook yet.' He glared at Sam. 'I still haven't forgotten that interview with the Gazette you did.'

'Oh, that,' Sam said. 'That reporter stitched me up. I never said any of that. He embellished.'

'Mmm,' Comby said. 'Or the tyres on my car.'

'We've told you,' Phillip said. 'That was probably kids.'

Comby glanced at Hardman. 'Get on the phone to forensics.'

'Yes, guv.'

'You two,' Comby said. 'Can tell me everything you know.'

CHAPTER SIX

Tommo lay in bed with Deb's arm draped across him. He sighed a deep and contented sigh. 'I could get used to this,' he said. 'Making love in the afternoon.'

Deb purred. 'So could I. It's a shame you have to get up and go to the pub.'

'The vagaries of being a publican.'

'Can't Gene look after it? We could have a second round.'

Tommo eased himself into a sitting position and checked the bedside clock. 'I suppose I could be a little late.'

'You're the boss,' Deb said.

Tommo and Deb entered the sidewinder two hours later. Gene flicked a bar-towel over his shoulder and glanced at his watch. 'What time do you call this?' he said.

'Sorry about that,' Tommo said. 'We were held up with something.'

Gene leant forward on the bar and smiled at Deb. 'I bet you were.'

Deb winked at him. 'Emily not in?'

'No. It's been dead in here,' Gene said. 'I need a favour Tommo.' Tommo tossed his coat behind the bar and raised his eyes as Gene continued 'We need a barrel changing.' He tapped the middle pump. 'The IPA's gone off.'

'Yeah, I'll do it. Anything else your Majesty?'

'No, I think that's it.' Gene winked at Deb as Tommo disappeared into the cellar. He waved Deb closer. 'What were you and Tommo doing that made you an hour and a half late?'

Deb took out her lip balm and applied a little. 'What can I say … The big fella can't get enough of me.'

Gene tapped her on the arm. 'He's a one, isn't he? I wish I had a big strapping bloke like him.'

'You've got Ricardo.'

Gene lowered his eyes and shook his head. 'He went back to his old boyfriend.'

'Oh, no,' Deb said. 'I thought you two were getting on so well.'

'I bent over backwards for that man, and forwards.' He let out a laugh.

Deb studied the names on the pumps. 'You're slipping. I've been in here five minutes, and you haven't asked me if I want a drink yet.'

Gene glanced at the clock. 'Isn't it a bit early ... Even for you?'

Deb screwed up her face. 'It's seven o'clock at night somewhere in the world.'

Gene smiled. 'I suppose it is. What's your poison, gorgeous?'

Deb tapped a pump. 'I'll give that one a try.'

'It's quite strong.'

'Good,' Deb said. 'More bang for your buck.'

Tommo emerged from the cellar and placed an empty bucket on the bar. 'Pull that through when you finished helping Deb drink my profits.'

Deb pouted. 'You've been paid in kind.'

'True enough,' Tommo said, and patted her backside as he passed. 'I'm going through into the cocktail bar to stock-up the mixers.'

'What about food?' Deb said. 'I'm starving.'

'Give the lady a bag of nuts, Gene.' He smiled at Deb, winked, and disappeared next door.

Gene held out a packet, and Deb plucked them from him. She raised her pint to her mouth and took a large gulp. 'Cheers,' she said.

Deb swivelled on her stool as Emily and Kim entered. 'I was wondering when you'd turn up,' Deb said.

The pair made their way across to her. 'How many have you had?' Emily said.

'Two,' Deb said.

'Three,' Gene shouted.

Deb stuck her tongue out at Gene. 'Bloody grass,' she said. 'I couldn't sit here waiting for you two without a drink, could I?'

'Aren't the boys in?' Kim said.

'No. It's been like a morgue in here. I'm waiting for my cuddly-bear next door to finish stocking-up so we can go for something to eat.'

'I think you need something to soak up that alcohol,' Emily said.

Deb giggled. 'It wasn't that last week when you and Sam were re-enacting last year's Grand National.' Deb slurred. 'Where have you been, anyway?'

'We've been to a tarot reading with Mary Hough,' Emily said.

Deb spluttered and laughed. 'Mary Hough!'

Kim and Emily stared blankly at each other. 'Sam always laughs when I mention her name,' Emily said.

'Get the two soft-lasses a drink, Gene,' Deb said. 'And then they can tell me all the rubbish Mary Hough ...' She laughed again. '... told them.' Kim looked at Emily, who shrugged at her.

Sam and Phillip strode into The Sidewinder. 'That's a couple of hours of my life I'll never get back,' Phillip said, as he stopped at the table where Kim, Emily and Deb sat.

'What's up?' Kim said.

Phillip lifted his head upwards and blew out. 'We've had the pleasure of DI Comby for the last two hours.'

'Why? What's happened?' Emily said.

Sam held high the suit holder. 'We went to pick this up.'

'Is that your new suit, Sam?' Emily said.

'Yeah. Although I'm not sure I got the right one. The check one might have been better.'

Emily took hold of the garment. 'Let's have a look.'

Phillip held out his hands. 'Never mind the bloody suit, Sam. It's not the most important thing here.'

Sam paused. 'Randy's dead,' he said.

The jaws on Kim and Emily dropped open. 'Dead?' Emily said.

'Yeah,' Phillip said. 'Murdered in his own shop.'

'And Comby thinks you two had something to do with it?' Kim said.

Sam rolled his eyes. 'The fat detectives are still pissed off with us—'

'You, Sam,' Phillip said. 'They're pissed off with you.'

'All right, with me. He hasn't forgiven me for that article in the Gazette.' Sam held out his hands. 'They embellished.'

Phillip groaned. 'You don't help. You're constantly winding him up.'

'Boys ...' Deb slurred. 'Who's Randy?'

Sam smiled about to speak, but Phillip raised his hand. 'Don't even think about cracking a funny.'

Sam pulled an imaginary zip across his mouth. 'Randolph Edwards,' Phillip said. 'He is, he was, the owner of Randy Ted's, men's tailors.'

'Oh,' Deb said.

'Someone hit him over the head with a shoehorn, and strangled him with a tie,' Phillip said.

Sam's eyes widened. 'Not just any tie. A Dolce and Gabbana Paisley, silk tie. They're about £150.'

'Oh,' Emily said. 'Classy killing.' Sam held out his fist to her, and Emily tapped it with her own.

Phillip threw his hands up. 'I'm going to the bar.'

'Do the police think you had something to do with it?' Kim said.

'Nah,' Sam said. 'Comby was just being a dick. We found Randy, so he made us give a statement. It took ages. He did it on purpose. He's a vindictive—'

Emily unzipped the suit holder. 'How did you get this if he'd been murdered?'

'I just took it.'

Kim's eyes widened, Emily's jaw dropped open, and Deb giggled. 'You stole it?' Emily said.

Sam grabbed it back from her. 'No, I didn't steal it. I'd paid Randy for it. It's not theft if you've already paid for something.'

Emily looked at Kim, who shrugged. 'I suppose,' Emily said.

Phillip returned with a pint for him and Sam and slumped onto the stool next to Kim. 'What have you three been up to?' he said. 'Apart from getting drunk.'

'Where are our drinks?' Kim said.

Phillip stared at the three of them and checked his watch. 'I think you three have had enough. It's only five o'clock.' Phillip gestured at Deb, who now had her head on the table. 'How many has *she* had?'

'She's been on the IPA,' Emily said. 'But I don't think she realised it was 6.2%.'

Sam slurped his pint. 'Where's the big fella?'

'Next door,' Kim said. 'One of the staff phoned in sick. He has to work until Maria comes in.'

'Guess what, Sam?' Emily said. 'Kim and I had a tarot reading today.'

Sam scoffed. 'Tarot reading ... It's mumbo jumbo.'

'How do you know?' Kim said.

Sam sniggered. 'How can you tell the future with cards. I mean, the universe is just waiting for you to pick a card. The pair of you are so gullible. What are you planning on doing tomorrow? Going into town to buy a couple of bottles of snake oil?'

'Just ignore him,' Emily said. 'What do you think, Phillip?'

'I'm with Sam.'

'Well,' Kim said. 'She told us some interesting things.'

'Like what?' Sam said.

'She said I was going to have six children,' Emily said.

Sam tutted. 'Not while a vasectomy is still legal, you won't.'

Emily punched him playfully on the arm. 'Who said you'd be the father of them all?'

'How much did this rubbish cost?' Sam said.

'Mary did it for nothing,' Emily said.

Sam laughed. 'Mary Hough?' Deb, her head still on the table, giggled.

Kim and Emily glanced at each other. 'Yeah,' Emily said.

Sam shook his head. 'Are we going for something to eat? I'm starving.'

'We'll have to pick Daisy and the dog up first.'

Sam held out his hands. 'Well ok, then. Shake a leg.'

Emily stood. 'See you lot later. Are you ok, Deb?' she said, and put a hand on her friend's head. Deb grunted.

Sam took hold of Emily's hand. 'Do you think I would suit a cravat?' he said to her, as they made their way towards the door.

STAINTON 1865 – Walter Littleby paused in his digging and lit his pipe. He glanced into the half-dug grave and grunted. 'A little breather, Walter,' he said to himself.

A lady appeared from inside the church and steadily made her way over to him. 'Ah,' she said, looking at the hole as she reached him. 'You've already started to dig the grave.'

'You know me, Alice. I like to get things done.'

'I'm afraid it's a bit of a waste of time.'

Walter leant on his spade. 'Why?'

'Mrs Jesmond has been to see the vicar. She doesn't want young Harry burying here.'

'But this is the Jesmond's family plot.'

Rose thrust her hands into her apron pocket and pulled out a handkerchief. She blew her nose. 'Poor little mite. She's adamant, though. Told the vicar she wants him buried near her family home.'

'What do I do with this, then?' Walter pointed at the half-dug hole.

'Fill it in, I suppose,' Rose said. 'Don't worry, you'll still get your money.'

Walter gripped the handle of his spade. 'How come?'

'Because you'll have another to dig anyway.'

'Who's?' Walter said.

'Did you not hear about the commotion last night?'

'Commotion? No,' Walter said. 'I travelled over from our Mabel's. I only got back first thing this morning. You're the first soul I've laid eyes on this day.'

'Jeremiah Fagerson.'

Walter's eyes widened. 'How?'

'Two men from another village burgled his house. Old Jeremiah killed one of them stone dead with that gun he keeps above the fire, and the other got away.'

'What were they after?'

'A cross.'

The blood drained from Walter's face. 'A cross?'

'Yes. No one's sure how Jeremiah came by it.' Rose crossed herself. 'People in the village are saying it's cursed.'

'Surely not.'

'Well …' Rose folded her arms. 'Poor Jeremiah's dead. One of the burglars too, and even Jeremiah's dog.'

'What about the other burglar?'

'Thomas Barwick is his name. A right wrong 'un. They caught him early this morning. It'll be the rope for him. That'll be three.'

'And the cross?'

Rose glanced about. 'They haven't found it. Mark my words, Walter. It'll be a good thing if no one does. Nothing good will come of it.' She shook her head and hurried off.

Walter stared at the empty grave. 'Cursed,' he mumbled to himself.

Walter patted the ground with the back of his shovel. He peered down at the filled grave. 'If you are cursed,' he whispered. 'That's the best place for you. He crossed himself, tossed his shovel onto his shoulder and made his way out of the graveyard and towards his home.

CHAPTER SEVEN

Albert stared vacantly out of the window as a slim, grey-haired man, with an immaculately coiffured beard, entered the room.

He smiled at Albert and positioned himself opposite. 'Hello, Albert. I'm your therapist, Charles. How are you?'

Albert looked towards the floor. 'Not bad, I suppose.'

'When we spoke on the phone…' He opened his file and glanced at the notes. '… you mentioned something about biscuits.'

Albert nodded. 'I'm a little fixated with them.'

Charles clasped his hands together and scrutinised Albert. 'In what way?'

'I like biscuits,' Albert said. 'Especially with my morning cup of tea.' Albert shifted in his seat. 'I have a rota … I have to eat biscuits in order.' The therapist jotted something on his notepad, and Albert continued. 'For example, … Monday may be a Penguin. Tuesday a Blue Ribband and so on.'

'And this is causing disruption in your life?'

'The other morning the biscuit was supposed to be a Kit Kat, and—'

Charles gazed into the distance. 'I do love Penguins. They're not my favourite though …' Albert shifted in his seat again. 'I'm sorry,' Charles said. You were saying?'

'Yes,' Albert said. 'I …'

'Kit Kats?'

'Oh, yes. I had none, you see.'

'Kit Kats?' Charles said.

Albert threw his arms in the air. 'Penguins, Blue Ribband, Trio's—'

'Oh, Trio's,' Charles said. 'Now there's a biscuit.'

'Yes,' Albert said. 'They are rather nice, aren't they?'

Charles lowered his head and reached inside his jacket pocket for a tissue. '2003,' he said.

'2003?'

'My annus horribilis.' Albert slowly shook his head, and Charles continued. 'They stopped making Trio's.'

'Really? But they—'

'They brought them back out in 2015. But I had to endure a twelve-year hiatus.'

'Ah,' Albert said.

'It was a terrible time for me back in 2003. My wife left me, you see. What with that and the demise of Trios ... Well, let's just say I was pretty low.'

'Your wife?' Albert said. 'That must have been hard?'

'Oh, good God no! Couldn't abide the woman.'

Albert's brow knitted. 'But I thought ...?'

'She left with my best friend, Kevin.'

'Oh, I see.'

'We were so close, Kevin and I. We would spend our weekends fishing. Oh, Albert ...' A smile spread across Charles' face. 'The happy hours we spent together.'

'But your wife?'

He sneered. 'She was a cold woman. I'm sure she only left with Kevin to spite me.'

'I'm sure she didn't,' Albert said.

'I have a picture.' Charles dug inside his pocket and pulled out a photo. 'It's a little tattered now. I was going to have it repaired.' He plucked another tissue from the table and blew his nose.

Albert stared at the picture of a man holding a massive fish. 'This is?'

'Kevin,' Charles said. 'How handsome he looks.'

'Yes, I suppose he does.'

'Why he left with that bloody woman, I'll never know.'

'Have you heard from them since?' Albert said.

'I get an occasional postcard from Kevin. Usually with him holding some impressive fish, in a sunnier clime, with the emerald-green sea lapping at his shapely ankles.'

'Have you tried to find another companion to go fishing with?'

Charles scoffed. 'Good God no. No one could replace what I had with Kevin. Those cerulean eyes, his manly chin.' Charles blew his nose again. He fixed Albert with a stare. 'No man cast a line like Kevin. He was ...' Charles stood and threw out his hands. 'Magnificent.'

Albert shifted on his seat. 'I've often thought of going fishing.'

'Have you, Albert?' Charles said. 'Have you?'

'Yes. I think it would be the solitude that would attract me.'

Charles glanced at the clock. 'My, my, hasn't time flown. I think perhaps we need to schedule an hour-long session, next time, Albert. We're making excellent progress.'

Albert frowned. 'Are we?'

'Oh, yes. I have so much more ...' Charles chuckled. 'We have so much more to discuss.'

Albert stood. 'Thanks,' he said. With that, he turned and left. Pausing outside the door, he slowly shook his head and headed off.

Sam carried his bacon and egg sandwich into the dining room and placed it on the table. He returned to the kitchen and picked up a bottle of beer.

He smiled across at the pup asleep in the dog basket. 'You know, Southgate ...' he said. 'Life doesn't get much better than this. A bacon and egg butty, and a bottle of beer.' The sleeping dog didn't stir.

'Sam,' Emily shouted from the utility room. 'Can you come in here, please?'

Sam rolled his eyes. 'And yet, Southgate, something always comes along to spoil it.' He stood and trudged to where Emily was. 'What's up?'

Emily nodded towards the floor at a massive dog turd. 'Jesus,' Sam said. 'Has she done another one?'

'Well I didn't do it, and Daisy wears a nappy. So, unless there's something you need to confess?'

'How can something so little produce so much?'

Emily folded her arms. 'I've no idea, but it can't go on. You said you would house train her.'

'I've tried. I take her outside and she has a wee, but seems to want to save her poos for inside.'

'Well ...' Emily said. Her arms now on her hips. 'You'll both have to do better. Daisy will be crawling soon. I don't want her getting dog mess all over her. And it's dangerous.'

Sam scoffed. 'Dangerous?'

'Yeah. I stood on one the other day, and I nearly slid the length of the room.' Sam stifled a laugh. 'It's not funny, Sam.' she continued. 'I could have injured myself. I had to put my Converse trainers through the wash. You know what happens to shoes when you wash them ...?' Sam shrugged and Emily held her arms out. '... They're never as good.'

'Can't we put one of Daisy's nappies on her?'

Emily sucked in air. 'No, we bloody can't. People would think we're mental. Putting a baby's nappy on a dog.'

'Surely you can get canine ones?'

'Sam!' Emily threw a look towards the ceiling. 'We'll do what my dad always did.' Sam shrugged again, and Emily continued. 'We'll cover the floor with newspaper. The dog associates going to the toilet with the paper. Then over time, you gradually reduce it. Until you have one piece near the door. Then you move it outside, and voila! Southgate is crapping in the garden. Where she should.'

'Any particular newspaper? The Times or Telegraph, perhaps.'

Emily snatched a carrier bag from the top of the washing machine. 'I'll leave that up to you.'

'Can I finish my sandwich first?'

'Yes. But I want it cleaned straight after.'

Sam sighed and trudged back to the dining room. He picked up his sandwich and took a bite. Emily followed him and slumped onto a seat next to Sam.

'You all right, Em? You seem a little fraught.'

She rubbed the back of her neck. 'Sorry, Sam. It's the christening. I'm really stressed about it.'

Sam scoffed. 'What's to worry about. We hand Daisy to a man in black wearing a dog-collar, he pours water on her head, Daisy cries, he says a few words and Bob's your uncle.'

'Is that all?' she said. 'He is my uncle, actually.'

'Who is?'

'Bob. He's my uncle. My mam's brother. He's travelling from Kent for the christening.'

'You've never mentioned him before?'

Emily raised her eyebrows. 'He's a bit of a black sheep.'

'Why?'

'We don't talk about it. Anyway, he's coming. He phoned me yesterday.'

Sam nodded towards the carrier Emily was holding and took a bite of his sandwich. 'What's in the bag?'

Emily closed her eyes and giggled. She opened the bag to allow Sam to see inside.

'Dildoes,' he said.

'Yeah.'

Sam put his hand inside and pulled one out. 'Christ,' he said. 'Look at the size of this one? I hope you take a couple of painkillers before using it.'

Emily scowled. 'It's not mine, you cheeky get.'

Sam slowly swung it. 'You could play cricket with it.'

'It's Stella's.'

Sam dropped the sex-toy. 'Bloody hell, Emily.' He snatched at a piece of kitchen roll and rubbed his hands.

Emily rolled her eyes. 'I've washed them.'

'Why the hell have you still got mad Stella's dildoes here?'

Emily crossed her arms. 'They were at the flat ... And when we moved ... Well, I just brought them along.'

'Why on earth—?'

'I was going to throw them out. But ... Do you know how much these things cost?' Emily stared at the offending article.

Sam took a swig of beer. 'No! Why would I? I've got my own. It comes readily attached and free with the rest of me.'

'I suppose I could throw them in the bin.'

Sam took another bite of his bun. 'Have you seen the way our binmen work. There's litter all over the road when they've been. It'll look good when that ...' He nodded towards the floor. '...ends up in the street.'

'I should ring her, really.'

Sam folded his arms. 'I don't want that soft cow coming around here. I can't stand her.'

'Only because she broke your nose.'

'Exactly. She's mental. I mean it, Emily. I don't want her stepping foot over the threshold.' He nodded at the carrier. 'Donate them to a charity shop. The old dears will have the time of their life. It'll give them something to talk about at the knitting club.'

'Sam,' Emily said. 'Don't be disgusting. You're so inappropriate at times.' Emily stooped and picked up the sex-toy and deposited it inside the carrier. 'I need a favour.'

Sam pushed the last bit of sandwich into his mouth. 'Yeah?'

'Can you go across to Tommo's Aunty Anne's?'

'What for?'

'I need Daisy's Christening cake collecting.'

Sam exhaled loudly. 'Why can't you? I was going to paint the fence.'

'I'm meeting Deb in town. She's going to help me choose a christening gown for Daisy.'

Sam puffed out his cheeks. 'I suppose so.'

Emily leant forward and kissed him. 'Good lad.' She stood and pushed the bag into the under stairs cupboard. 'I'll decide what to do with those later.'

Sam sucked on his beer and glanced across at the sleeping puppy. 'You make plans, Southgate, and Emily intervenes.'

Sam peered at the puppy who stared at him, wagging its tail. 'Right, Southgate. Don't blame me. The newspaper was Emily's idea. Apparently, you have to get used to it.' He picked the puppy up and gave it a kiss. Depositing the dog in its bed, he placed a stuffed toy next to it. 'This is your friend, so you shouldn't get lonely. I'll see you later.' He stooped, rubbed the top of the dog's head and left, closing the door behind him. Sam collected his house keys, pulled on his coat, and headed for the door. He opened it to find Lydia, his middle-aged, next-door neighbour, stood outside.

'Lydia,' he said.

'Hi, Sam,' she purred. 'I need a favour.'

Sam glanced at his watch. 'I was just on my way out.'

'It won't take long. Seconds in fact.'

'Yeah, ok,' Sam said.

'I need a screwdriver. I have something that needs ...' She giggled like a young girl. '... Screwing.'

'Phillips or flat-blade?' Sam said, unfazed. He headed into the garage with Lydia following closely behind. As she passed the bannister, she pulled off her coat and tossed it over, revealing a low-cut blouse beneath.

Lydia leant back against the worktop and pouted. 'Is there a difference?'

'Yeah,' Sam said, and rolled his eyes while rummaging through a cupboard 'What did the top of the screw look like?'

'I'm not sure,' she said. Sam turned and looked at Lydia.

'Jesus,' he said as he caught sight of her breasts, spilling over the top of her blouse. 'Are those real?'

'They cost me £5000,' she said. 'Paid for them from my divorce settlement.' She edged closer. 'You can see them unfettered if you wish.'

Sam gulped. 'No. I think they should remain inside that inadequate bra of yours.'

Lydia tittered. 'You don't know what you're missing.'

Sam ignored her, moved across to a cupboard, and pulled out a small toolbox. 'There's a selection in here. One of them should fit.'

'I don't suppose you'd fancy screwing it for me, would you. I'm useless around tools. Well, some of them.'

'As I said, Lydia. I have to go somewhere.'

Lydia moved closer, pushing Sam against the garage wall. 'You're just a big tease,' she said.

Sam's libido, which was snoozing with its feet up, stirred. 'I'm not going to have sex with you, Lydia. I've stopped all that stuff. I'm faithful to Emily.'

'But don't you find me attractive, Sam,' she said, fluttering her eyelashes. 'Haven't I got a nice figure for my age. I've taken care of myself.'

'I can see that,' Sam said. 'Those leather trousers you're wearing look sprayed on.'

'Do you like them?' She moved closer, pressing her breasts against him.

Sam's libido jumped to attention, pulled up its shirtsleeves, and rubbed its hands together. 'Now, Lydia,' Sam said, acutely aware of his resolve steadily slipping away. 'Emily could come back at—'

'She'll be hours. I was talking to her earlier. She's gone shopping.'

'But ...' Sam turned away and extricated himself from Lydia. '... I can't.' Sam headed out of the garage and back into the hall, pursued by Lydia.

She positioned herself between the front door and Sam. 'I know you want me, Sam,' she said. 'Why fight it?'

'... But Emily might come back. I ...' Sam closed his eyes and exhaled loudly. 'Listen,' he said, as Lydia pushed him against the wall and began grappling with his trousers. 'I can't ...' Sam grabbed hold of her arms and held on fast. He gawped at her. 'That was a car.'

Emily pulled the car to a halt outside her house. She got out, opened the boot and took out a carrier bag.

'Hello, Em,' a female voice said.

Emily spun on her heels and stared at Stella. Her hair cropped short and dyed blonde. 'Stella?' Emily said.

Stella stepped forward and held out her arms. 'Don't I get a hug?'

Emily slammed the boot shut and placed the bag on the pavement. 'Of course.' The pair of them embraced.

Stella edged towards the house. 'This is where you're living now?'

'Yeah ... with—'

'Sam,' Stella said. 'I heard.'

'Ah. I wondered if you had.'

Stella scoffed. 'I couldn't believe it when that cow, Amber, told me. Where's the baby then?'

'Daisy's at my mam's.'

'Daisy? Lovely name. My niece is called Daisy.' She gazed at the house again. 'You and Sam ... How did that happen, then?'

Emily lowered her head. 'It just did. Turns out we were both attracted to each other.'

Stella walked towards the property and peered into the garden. 'Never thought you'd be the type to change horse mid-stream.'

Emily collected the carrier and moved forward. 'Neither did I.'

'Are you sure this is what you want? Even if you have switched sides, Sam was never the most reliable of men.'

'I love Sam. He's a fantastic Dad,'

'Do you remember when we discussed having a kid?'

Emily lowered her eyes. 'A lifetime ago, Stella.'

Stella shook her head. 'I'm happy for you.' Emily looked up. 'I really am Em. Of all the woman I've had relationships with, you're the one that meant the most.' Emily forced an unconvincing smile. 'So,' Stella said. 'Doesn't your old friend get a cup of tea, then?'

'Oh ...' Emily glanced towards the house and then at her watch. '... Yes, of course.' She strode past Stella and fumbled for her key, desperately hoping Sam was still out.

Sam pushed Lydia into the garage. 'Jesus, Lydia. If Emily finds you here ...'

'But, Sam,' she purred. 'You were just about to crack.'

'No I wasn't,' Sam snapped. 'Now stay quiet until I get Emily out the back. Then you can slip out.'

Lydia pouted. 'So close, Sam. I was so close.'

Sam opened the door to the garage and checked both ways.

Lydia scoffed. 'It could be anybody's car.'

Sam pushed her away and peeked through the glass in the door. 'Shit! It is Emily. If she finds you in here, I'm dead.' He glared at Lydia. 'And so are you. You haven't seen her angry.'

Lydia's face dropped. 'What … I mean … Can't we …?'

Sam grabbed her by the arm and bundled her along the passage and into the kitchen. 'Get inside the utility,' he said. 'I'll …' He threw his hands up. 'I'll think of something.' Lydia disappeared inside, closing the door behind her.

Sam raced into the hallway and stopped, spotting Lydia's coat across the bannister, he shrieked. 'Jesus,' he said. Grabbing the coat, he mounted the stairs two at a time and raced through into the spare bedroom. He paused, looking for somewhere to secrete it.

Emily entered with Stella. She peeked sheepishly around. 'Sam,' she shouted.

Sam stood still. The coat still hanging loosely in his hand. He took a deep breath and held onto it.

Emily bit her bottom lip. 'I think he's out.'

'I don't know what you're so worried about,' Stella said. 'It's as much your house as his.'

Emily led Stella into the dining room. 'He still hasn't forgiven you for breaking his nose.'

Stella scoffed. 'Oh, that. It was his fault for calling me a big, fat dyke. Not very politically correct.'

Emily huffed. 'He only called you that because you poured a pint over his head. That's bound to annoy anyone.'

'Yeah, well, I wouldn't have done that if …'

Emily held up her hands. 'I know, Stella. I was there. Anyway, long story, short. Sam doesn't want you in here. I don't want to fall out with him, especially with Daisy's christening coming up.'

Stella sat. 'Ok, I get it.'

'Tea did you say?'

'Yeah. You know how I take it?'

Emily smiled. 'Yeah, I remember.'

Sam hadn't moved a muscle. Straining to hear the sounds from below, he crept slowly towards the cupboard and deposited the coat inside. He tiptoed forward and stopped at the door, listening intently.

Emily, opposite Stella, placed a cup in front of her guest. 'Anyway,' Emily said. 'How have you been?'

Stella shrugged. 'Ok, I suppose.'

'No one new on the horizon?'

'There's been a couple, but none that compare to you.'

Emily lowered her gaze. 'Stella—'

'I know,' she said. 'You love soft-lad.'

Emily smiled. 'I do. There's no one else I would have …'

'No.' Stella sipped her tea.

Southgate, who had been sleeping, stretched and jumped from her bed. She ambled her way across to Stella and stared up, cocking her head to one side.

Stella scooped her up. 'Who's this little beauty?'

'Southgate,' Emily said.

'After the England manager?'

'After the Middlesbrough defender,' Emily said. 'It's important to know that.' Emily rolled her eyes. 'Sam is very clear on that point.'

Stella lifted the pup and examined its undercarriage. 'I hate to tell you this, Em, but Southgate's a girl.'

'I said that to Sam, but he doesn't care. So, Southgate it is. I wasn't about to argue, though, after the problem we had choosing Daisy's name.'

Stella cuddled the dog. 'We had some good times, Em.'

Emily blinked slowly. 'Yeah, we did.'

'Do you remember that Christmas Eve?'

Emily giggled. 'When we ordered all those sex-toys and had them delivered to Jade's?'

Stella threw her head back and cackled. 'God yeah. She still doesn't speak to me. It's been three years for Christ's sake.'

'She did nearly get divorced over them,' Emily said. The pair burst out laughing. 'Talking of …' Emily moved to the under-stairs cupboard and pulled out the carrier. She shook the bag and held it up. 'I found these. They're yours.'

Stella put Southgate down, wandered over, took the bag from Emily and peeped inside. She grinned. 'I wondered where these had got to.'

The pair locked eyes. 'Well now you know,' Emily said.

'You're beautiful,' Stella said. She tucked a stray piece of Emily's hair behind her ear. 'Those eyes.' She lifted her free hand and placed it on Emily's cheek.

Emily placed her hand on top of Stella's. 'I can't,' Emily said. 'Even for old-time's sake.'

Stella moved closer, took Emily's face in her hands, and gently allowed their lips to meet.

Emily groaned. 'Please,' she said. 'Don't.'

Sam couldn't quite decipher what was being said. It was Emily's voice, but he couldn't make out who the other person was. He stepped closer to the landing, and a floorboard creaked.

Emily and Stella looked upwards. Still in each other's arms, they stared at each other.

'Sam,' Emily said, and pointed towards the ceiling. 'He must be home.'

Stella mouthed. 'Oh, shit!'

'Quick,' Emily said. 'Hide.'

'Where?'

Emily snatched up the carrier containing the sex toys, thrust it into Stella's hand, and shoved her towards the utility. As she did, a massive dildo fell from the bag and onto the floor. 'Hide in here. I'll let you know when the coast's clear.' Stella nodded and entered the utility, softly closing the door behind her.

Emily raced to the foot of the stairs. 'Sam, is that you?'

Sam appeared at the top. 'Hi, Em. I didn't hear you come in.' He made his way down and joined her. 'I thought you'd still be out shopping.'

She glanced towards the kitchen. 'We got a gorgeous christening gown in the first shop we went in.'

Sam peered towards the kitchen. 'Let me have a look then.'

Emily darted into the living-room as Sam, raced into the kitchen. He stared towards the utility door and gulped.

Emily joined him. 'Here it is,' she said, and held out the carrier. 'Go and have a look in the front room, and I'll make us a cup of tea,' she said. Her eyes were drawn to the two mugs on the dining-room table. Sam opened the bag and peeped inside. 'It looks lovely,' he said.

Emily positioned herself between the table and Sam, concealing the mugs from his view. 'I'll tell you what, Sam,' she said, moving closer. 'Daisy's at Mam's until teatime, why don't we go upstairs for a bit of ...' She raised her eyebrows.

Sam glanced past Emily towards the utility-room door. 'Upstairs?' he said.

'Yeah.' Emily took hold of his hand. 'We get little time on our own these days.'

Sam smiled. 'Yeah, upstairs. Why don't you go and get yourself ready? I'll only be a minute.'

Emily tugged his hand. 'Sam,' she said, reaching to nibble his ear as she surreptitiously viewed the utility door. 'What happened to spontaneity?'

'Spontaneity,' Sam said. 'Yes, of course.' Emily pulled him towards the door and through into the hall. The pair stopped and locked eyes with each other. Emily nodded upstairs. 'Shall we?'

'I need a drink of water,' Sam said, and moved towards the kitchen again.

'I'll get it,' Emily said, grabbing hold of his arm.

'No, I'm fine. I can get a glass of—'

The doorbell sounded. Both Emily and Sam looked skywards.

'If you go and get that,' Sam said. 'I'll get the water.'

'I'll get the water, and you can answer the door. It's probably for you, anyway.' She started to move.

Sam tugged Emily back. 'Why don't we both get the door?'

Stella listened intently in the darkness. She had heard voices, Emily's and Sam's, and groaned loudly. 'Where's the friggin' light?' she said, as she fumbled along the wall.

Lydia sucked in air, and Stella stopped. 'Who's that?' she whispered.

'Lydia Colman. From over the road. Who are you?'

'Stella Jones, a friend of Emily.'

'We're both thinking this ...' Lydia said. '... so one of us should just come out and say it ... What are you doing in here?'

'I'm an old girlfriend of Emily's. I popped round to see her. Sam doesn't like me, and Emily bungled me in here when she found out Sam was home.'

Lydia chuckled. 'I came around here to seduce Sam. I thought Emily would be out all day.'

Stella scoffed. 'Is he up to his old tricks again?'

Lydia pulled aside a curtain that covered a window, allowing the two women to view each other. 'Sadly, no. Sam was proving a hard-nut to crack.'

'Wow,' Stella said, eyeing Lydia up and down. 'He's obviously changed.'

'I reckon another ten minutes and I would have worn him down, though.'

'Yeah. I almost had Emily going, too.'

'You're gay?' Lydia said.

'You don't have a problem with that, do you?'

Lydia smiled. 'Not at all.'

Stella nodded towards Lydia's cleavage. 'Are those your own?'

Lydia smiled again. 'No. I paid for them out of my divorce settlement.'

'They're spectacular. They look real. What do they feel like?'

Lydia pushed her breasts further forward. 'Have a fondle.'

Stella ran her hands over them. 'God,' she said. 'They just like the real thing.' She gazed into Lydia's eyes. 'Have you ever thought of ...?'

Lydia shook her head. 'No. But I'm ...'

'Where do you live?'

Lydia ran her tongue across her lips. 'Over the road. Why?'

Stella moved her mouth to within an inch of Lydia's. 'Fancy giving me a tour of your bedroom?'

Lydia allowed their lips to meet. The pair kissed passionately and slowly parted. Stella stooped and picked up the carrier. 'I have these.' She opened the bag and showed the contents to Lydia.

Lydia's eyes widened, and she beamed. 'What are we waiting for?' she said.

Emily turned back. 'Yes, I think we both should.' The pair wandered through into the hall and stopped at the door. Sam pulled it open. Phillip, holding baggage, and Kim, cradling Luggage, stood outside.

'Hi, you two,' Emily said.

'What a surprise,' Sam said.

Kim and Phillip glanced at each other. 'Hi,' Phillip said. 'Kim was saying you two might fancy taking the dogs for a walk.'

'Yes, we would,' Sam said. 'Come on through.' The four-headed into the lounge and stopped. 'How about a cup of tea, first,' Sam said.

Kim glanced at Phillip, who nodded. 'Yeah,' Kim said. 'A cuppa would be nice.'

'I'll make it,' Emily said.

'No, I will,' Sam said, as the couple disappeared into the kitchen.

Phillip looked at Kim. 'What's up with those two?' he said, as the pair sat.

Kim pulled a face and bent closer to him. 'I think they've had an argument,' she said quietly. 'I can tell.'

Phillip rolled his eyes. 'Great. I don't fancy spending the afternoon with those two moody buggers.' He unclipped Baggage from his lead, and the dog wandered off.

'Shh,' Kim said. 'They'll hear you.'

Sam and Emily came back in, each carrying two mugs. 'Sorry we're right out of biscuits,' Emily said.

Sam laughed nervously. 'It's a good job Albert isn't here. He'd be on his knees blubbing like a ten-year-old.'

Phillip glanced at Kim. 'Yeah, he would.'

Kim stared at Emily and raised her eyebrows. Emily rolled her eyes and mouthed, 'Later.'

Kim nodded. 'Did you get the dress?' she said.

Emily blinked slowly. '... Oh, the dress ... yes ... it's lovely.'

'Can I see the cake?' Kim said.

Sam playfully banged his forehead with the palm of his hand. 'The cake. I knew—'

'Oh, Sam,' Emily said. 'You haven't forgotten the cake, have you?'

'No ... I was going to phone Tommo for a lift, but got distracted.' Sam glanced towards the kitchen.

'Maybe you should go now,' Emily said.

Sam scoffed. 'I can't go now. We have guests. Anyway, we're going for a walk. I'll pick the cake up tomorrow.'

Emily frowned. 'How are you two, anyway?' she said, fixing her attention back on Phillip and Kim.

Phillip glanced at Kim. 'We're good.'

'We're looking forward to the Christ …' Kim said. Her eyes followed Baggage as he wandered into the middle of the room with a massive dildo in his mouth and allowed it to fall to the floor in front of him. He looked up and viewed the four people one by one, wagging his tail furiously.

Sam glanced at Emily, who glanced back at him. Phillip glanced at Kim, who glanced back at her. The four humans remained motionless in a silent Mexican standoff.

Emily leant forward and snatched the item from the floor as Baggage sat and stared at her. He cocked his head to one side and wagged his tail faster.

'It's mine,' Emily said. Phillip's jaw dropped open, and Kim winced. 'I was having a clear-out,' she continued. 'Spring cleaning and all.'

Sam nodded towards the dog. 'I think Baggage wants you to throw it for him.' Phillip and Kim stifled a laugh.

Phillip raised his eyebrows at Kim. 'You don't normally get those at Pets at Home,' he said. Kim covered her mouth with her hand.

Emily glared at Sam. 'I'll just put this away.' She stood and moved towards the kitchen. Sam sprung to his feet. 'Where are you going?'

'The kitchen,' she said.

'I'll help you.'

'I'm fine.'

'I can help you carry it.' Sam grabbed hold of the dildo, but Emily wrestled it back from him.

'It's not that big, Sam. I can …' Sam's eyes followed Emily's as the pair glimpsed movement outside. Stella and Lydia raced across the road and into Lydia's house. The couple looked at each other, forced an unconvincing smile, and turned to face their guests again.

'Another cuppa?' Sam said.

'Oh, yes,' Emily said, taking hold of Sam's hand. 'You must have another.'

Phillip held his still-full cup up. 'When I've finished this one, maybe.'

'So,' Kim said, glancing back at Sam and Phillip who were some distance behind. 'What the hell was going on back there?'

Emily rolled her eyes and began.

Sam pulled at Phillip's arm. 'Don't get too close,' Sam said. 'I don't want Emily to hear.'

'So, this next-door neighbour ...?'

'Lydia,' Sam said.

'She was trying to seduce you when Emily came home?'

'Yeah. Jesus, Phillip, I almost cracked.'

Phillip huffed. 'It would have taken some explaining.'

'She must have got out of the utility room somehow. I saw her making her way over to her house with some other woman.'

'Bloody hell. Do you think Emily suspects?'

Sam shook his head. 'No. I think I got away with it.' Phillip and Sam stopped as the girls, ahead, raucously laughed.

Phillip nudged at Sam. 'I shouldn't really say anything about the—'

'Dildo?' Sam said.

'Yeah. It was huge.'

Sam smiled. 'God knows how Baggage got it in his mouth.'

Phillip laughed. 'I know.'

'It isn't Emily's.' Phillip raised his eyebrows and Sam continued. 'It was an ex-girlfriend of hers. Mad Stella.'

'Mad Stella?' Phillip said. 'That explains the size.'

'Exactly,' Sam said, as the girls erupted into laughter once more.

CHAPTER EIGHT

Albert waited in his therapist's office and stared out of the window as an intransigent dog pulled its owner along the street. Albert shook his head. 'You need to train a dog,' he said to himself.

The door opened, and Charles strode in carrying a tray with tea and biscuits on it. 'I wasn't sure what the biscuit of the day was,' Charles said. 'So, I've brought a good selection.'

Albert pulled out a small notebook and flicked through the pages. 'Twix,' he said.

'Well.' Charles grinned and held a biscuit aloft. 'You're in luck.' Albert plucked it from the therapist's hand and smiled.

'Of course, you do know that the Bar Six was the king of all biscuits?' Charles said.

'I don't think—?'

'You're much too young, Albert. They were discontinued some time ago. Cadbury deserved to go bust for that decision. Bloody Philistines.'

Albert leant forward. 'Were they nice?'

'Nice!' Charles stared at Albert. 'They were absolutely gorgeous.'

'What were they like?'

Charles clasped his hands together and closed his eyes. 'A creamy chocolate bar with a wafer centre.'

'Like a Kit-Kat?'

Charles scoffed. 'A bloody Kit-Kat was no match for a Bar Six. The Bar Six was covered in Cadbury's chocolate for one. It also had this velvety hazelnut cream.' Charles licked his lips. 'Six pieces of heaven-sent scrumptiousness.'

'It does sound rather good,' Albert said.

'It was,' Charles moved forward in his seat and fixed Albert with a steely stare. 'I'm not one for hyperbole, Albert, but if the Bar Six was still around you wouldn't be vacillating with these inferior types.' He waved a dismissive hand across the plate of biscuits and selected a chunky Kit-Kat. 'The Bar Six was a diamond among biscuits. This ...' He tossed the confectionary to the opposite side of the room. 'is cubic zirconia.'

'I see,' Albert said. He sat back in his chair and stared at the chocolate bar on the floor.

Charles pulled a tissue from the box in front of him and blew his nose. 'Bastards,' he said.

'Maybe they'll bring it back.'

Charles threw back his head and snorted. 'Of course they won't. They've all gone now. Rowntree, Terry's of York. Taken over by the Swiss! What do they know about the art of chocolate making?' He stared at Albert.

'Well, I'm not—'

'Triangular monstrosities.' Charles made a triangle shape with his fingers. 'Toblerone. Hah! What sort of sweet is that?'

Albert looked about nervously and shrunk further into his seat.

'While the rest of Europe was fighting a war to end all wars, what were the Swiss doing, eh? Answer me that. I'll tell you what they were doing, Albert. Making crap confectionery, and plotting to take over our chocolate factories.'

Albert shakily lifted his cup to his lips and took a sip. 'The rain's stopped.'

'Has it?' Charles said. 'Has it really?' He covered his face with his hands and sobbed.

Albert leant forward and patted his arm. 'They might make a comeback. We should never lose hope, Charles.'

Charles lowered his hands. 'A chocolate renaissance, you mean?'

'Yes.' Albert nodded enthusiastically. 'A chocolate renaissance.'

Charles smiled. 'You're so perceptive.' He stood, wandered across to the door and pulled a carrier from the hook on the back. 'I have a present for you.'

Albert grinned. 'For me?'

'Yes.' He walked back over and pulled a picture frame from the bag. 'Here,' he said.

Albert inspected the photo and then stared back at Charles.

'It's a picture of Kevin,' Charles said.

Charles pulled his chair next to Albert. 'That's a Carp. It was a monster.' He chuckled. 'Even Kevin with those rippling biceps of his, and those rock-hard glutes couldn't land it. I had to help him haul the beast ashore.'

'What did you do with it?'

'We put it back. It's a battle between man and fish, Albert. Once victorious, we carefully place him back in the water and look forward to meeting on another day.'

'I see.'

'I thought you might like to put it on your mantlepiece.'

Albert looked at the photo again and then back to Charles. 'Yes. I'd love to.'

'You have got a mantlepiece then?'

Albert nodded. 'A huge one.'

Charles stood. 'Fantastic,' he said, and punched the air with his fist. 'The photo will take centre stage. It will be a great talking point.' Charles scrutinised it again. 'It doesn't do Kevin justice, though. It doesn't capture his ...'

Albert's eyes widened. 'No?'

'No. You see Kevin's hands?' Albert nodded slowly. 'They're huge. My God, the power in those hands, was, is ... incredible. And yet ...'

'And yet?' Albert said.

'They were capable of such delicate dexterity too. I've never seen anyone make a fly like Kevin. Those massive sausage-like fingers were a joy to behold.'

'Did I tell you I have a dog?' Albert said.

'A dog?'

'Yes. He's just a pup, but—'

'Kevin had a dog once. Oh, how he loved it.'

Albert rolled his eyes and flopped back in his seat.

Albert gazed at the photo of Kevin and frowned before placing it on his desk.

Sam walked into the office and stopped near to Albert. He picked up the photo and studied it. 'Who's this then?'

Albert shuffled on his seat. 'Kevin.'

'Kevin who?'

'He's a friend of Charles'.'

Sam lowered his eyes. 'Charles, your therapist?'

'Er ... yes.'

Sam placed the picture back on the desk and smiled. 'I'll let Phillip ask you about this one.'

Phillip looked up from his paperwork. 'Albert,' he said. 'Why have you got a photo of your therapist's friend on your desk?'

Albert lowered his eyes. 'Charles gave it to me.'

Sam wandered back to his desk, slumped onto his chair and leaning back, placed his feet up. 'Well, that answers that,' he said. 'I'm sure I've got a photo of the surgeon who took out my appendix and his mother, somewhere.'

'How's your biscuit therapy going?' Phillip said.

Albert coughed. 'Very well. We had an interesting discussion about a biscuit called the Bar Six today.'

'Really.' Sam yawned. 'That sounds riveting.'

Phillip glanced at Sam and winked. 'Where do you stand on the Jaffa Cake, Albert?' Phillip said.

'Jaffa Cake?'

'Yeah,' Sam said. 'It's got a personality disorder. Is it a biscuit, or is it a cake?'

'I'm going to ignore you two,' Albert said.

'It can't be a biscuit,' Phillip said. 'There's no crunch. Biscuits should crunch.'

'True,' Sam said. 'But is it really a cake? I'm not too sure.'

Albert huffed and stood. 'I'm going to take Zeus for a walk.' He snatched his coat and hurried out.

Sam and Phillip both laughed. 'We shouldn't tease him,' Phillip said. 'It's a bit wicked.'

'He'll get over it. Anyway,' Sam said. 'I have something to show you.'

'Oh, yeah?' Phillip said.

Sam stood and pulled a photo from his back pocket. He held it out to Phillip. 'Katherine Mosely,' Sam said.

Phillip studied the photo. 'Wow,' he said. 'You were right. They are impressive.'

'I was going to burn the photo now I'm with Emily. But …'

'But you couldn't bring yourself to?'

'No. They were a work of art.'

'I wonder if they're still as impressive?'

Sam sneered. 'No. I saw a picture of her in an archaeology magazine a few years back. She's a big, fat knacker now.'

Sam reclined on his chair cradling a steaming-hot cup of tea while Albert polished his desk and Phillip scanned the local newspaper.

Emily walked in, carrying Daisy. 'Sam,' she said, easing the baby bag off her shoulder and onto a chair. 'I need you to look after your daughter.'

Sam planted his chair down. 'But I'm at work.'

Emily surveyed the room. 'Oh, yeah. I can see, you're bloody rushed off your feet.'

Sam stood, walked across and took Daisy in his arms. 'Where's my little princess?'

'Your little princess has been in a right mood this morning.'

'Can't your mam watch her? A big job might come in.'

'I'll only be an hour,' she said. 'Besides, Mam and Dad have gone away for a few days.'

'Where are you off to?' Phillip said.

'Pilates.' Emily pulled a piece of paper from her back pocket. 'Pilates, pas de vetements. Mary said it's all the rage, apparently.'

'I once thought of doing Pilates,' Albert said. 'But all that lying down on the floor put me off.' Sam rolled his eyes, and Albert frowned at him and continued. 'The floor houses an enormous amount of—'

'Yes, yes, Albert.' Sam sighed. 'I'm sure it does.' Sam eased himself onto a chair with the baby on his knee. 'Are you going alone?'

'Kim's coming too.'

'Is she?' Phillip said.

'Mary says it will help with our wellbeing.'

Sam laughed. 'Not Mary *Hough?*' Emphasising her surname for effect.

Emily narrowed her eyes. 'Yeah. She runs it at the community centre.'

'Well,' Sam said. 'You had better run along. Enjoy!'

Emily frowned. 'I will.' She turned and flounced out.

Sam bounced Daisy on his knee. 'Who's a silly mammy.' He laughed again.

'What's so funny?' Phillip said.

'Neither of you two speaks French, do you?'

Phillip and Albert glanced at each other, and Sam let out another roar of laughter. 'Pas de vetements. Wait until your mummy has to strip off. Completement nu.'

'What are you on about?' Phillip said.

'Pas de vetements,' Sam repeated. 'No clothes.'

'You mean …' Albert gulped and waved his hands down his body. 'In the n—'

'Completement nu,' Sam said. 'Stark naked.'

'Maybe Emily knows,' Phillip said.

Sam stood and moved over to the baby-bag. 'Of course she doesn't know. Emily hates anyone seeing her naked. I've only just persuaded her to have sex with the light on.' Albert blushed, turned away, and picked his duster back up. 'It's like having a relationship with a vampire.'

'Shouldn't you have told her?' Phillip said.

'No way. I would love to be a fly on that wall.' Sam sat back down with Daisy. 'What about Kim …? Is she ok with nudity?'

'Yeah,' Phillip said. 'She walks around the house and cleans with her kit off.'

Albert polished faster and then stopped. 'I'm making some tea,' he said. 'Does anyone want one?'

Sam held up his still half-full mug. 'I'm good.'

'Me too,' Phillip said, as Albert raced off.

Phillip looked across at Sam. 'It doesn't take much to embarrass Albert,' Phillip said.

'I know,' Sam said. 'I don't know why he just doesn't become a monk.' Sam chuckled again. 'Mary Hough,' he said. 'I bet she has.'

'Has what?' Phillip said.

Sam threw his head backwards and roared. 'Mary Hough!'

Phillip shook his head and resumed reading his paper.

Emily and Kim reached the community centre and climbed the stairs. 'Are you sure these leggings are ok?' Emily said.

'I told you,' Kim said. 'You look great. You look as if you've never given birth.'

'I'm nearly back to the weight I was before I had Daisy. It's just ...' She pulled at the waistband of her outfit. 'They feel a little tight.'

'They're fine.'

'What about when I bend over?' Emily bent and touched her toes. 'You can't see the outline—'

Kim huffed. 'No.'

'What about the crotch?' She stood straight again. 'They're not a little tight down there, are they? I haven't got a ... you know. Because I wouldn't want my lady-bits on show. I'd be mortified.'

Kim blew out loudly. 'Em,' she said. 'You look fine. Your lady-bits are well covered.'

'Good.'

'Is this the Emily who used to bed a different woman every week?' Kim said.

'Not every week, you cheeky cow. Besides ... I'd normally had a drink. It emboldens one, does alcohol.'

'True enough. Ready?' Kim said, and took hold of the door handle.

'Ready.' Emily said.

The pair edged their way inside. 'Hi,' Kim said to Mary, who had her back to them. She twirled to face the couple, the gown she wore floating in the air as she moved towards a wide-eyed Kim and Emily.

'Hello, my dears. So nice to see you.'

Emily and Kim stood, drop-jawed, as they peered into Mary's open gown. She was naked beneath it. Her huge pendulous breasts hanging loosely.

'You're ... naked,' Emily spluttered.

'Of course, my dear. Did I not say? Au naturel?'

'No,' Emily said. 'I think you neglected to ...'

Mary roared. 'Come, come. You'll love it once you give it a try. It's so liberating.'

'But ...' Emily said.

'Don't worry about privacy. We lock the door and close the blinds. It's all females in here. We're all girls together.' She clapped her hands. 'Now, off you go and get changed. We start in five minutes promptly. My other ladies are getting ready now.' With that, she twirled and bounced off.

Kim nudged Emily. 'It's not really changing if you're just getting your kit off.'

Emily stared at Kim. 'Are you all right with this?'

Kim snorted. 'Yeah. I clean in the nude. It doesn't bother me.'

'But I'll be naked with a bunch of strangers.'

'Did you see Mary's bush?' Kim said. 'I've never seen so much hair since I went to the zoo.' Kim walked towards the changing room, pursued by Emily. 'It was like she was wearing a sporran.'

'But, Kim …'

'I bet it's never seen a waxing strip.'

Kim and Emily exited the community centre and stepped into the sunshine. 'Fancy a coffee?' Kim said.

'I've never been so uncomfortable in all my life,' Emily said. 'It's just not natural bending and stretching while you have no clothes on.'

'You have a beautiful body. You've nothing to be embarrassed about.'

Emily covered her face with her hands. 'I'll never live this down.'

'Come on, Em. You used to be gay.' Kim raised her eyebrows. 'Didn't you see anything … anyone you fancied?'

'You're having a laugh. There was only you and me under 65.'

'True.'

'I'll need counselling after this.'

Kim giggled. 'Haven't you ever played nude Twister?'

'No, I bloody haven't.' Emily banged her forehead with her palm. 'That's why Deb couldn't keep a straight face when I asked her to come.' Kim looked blankly, and Emily continued. 'She has an A-level in French.'

'Ah, I see,' Kim said.

'And wait until I see that Sam. He knew too.'

'I'm sure he—'

Emily grimaced. 'Of course he did. He speaks the bloody language.'

'Sam speaks French?'

'And German, Spanish and a smattering of Italian too.'

Kim slowly shook her head. 'Well, fancy that.'

Emily raised her eyes skywards and huffed. 'I'll swing for him.'

'That's what he'll expect,' Kim said. 'Tell him you loved doing it. That way …' She tapped the side of her nose with her index finger. 'You'll have the upper hand.'

'Yeah,' Emily said. 'I suppose …'

'It was a laugh, Em.' Kim nudged her playfully. 'Wasn't it?'

Emily smiled. 'I suppose it was an experience. Did you see that ginger woman?'

'Oh, God, yeah. I couldn't look away. It was like a pubic car-crash.'

Emily hooted. 'It looked as if she was hiding Ed Sheeran down there.'

Kim burst into laughter. 'It did.'

Emily slowly shook her head. 'I didn't know your pubes went grey, either.'

'Yeah. I'd never given it much thought. It's like every other part of the body, I suppose.'

Emily tutted. 'The things you see when you haven't got a gun.'

Kim put an arm around her friend. 'How about that coffee. My treat?'

'And a cake?'

'Obviously' Kim said.

'Tell us that again,' Tommo said.

'Emily and Kim did nude Pilates,' Sam said.

Tommo continued along the street. 'Why?'

'They didn't realise. Margaret Rutherford encouraged them to do it.'

Tommo frowned. 'Who?'

Sam theatrically rolled his eyes. 'Mary Hough.'

'Oh, Mary Hough.'

'Yeah. The thing was …' He chuckled. 'The daft lasses didn't know it was nude until they got there.'

'Ouch,' Tommo said. He drew to a halt outside a café. 'Right, here we are. Cake you said?'

'Yeah. For Daisy's christening.'

Tommo hauled his large frame from the car. 'Everything sorted on that?'

'Yeah, just about. It's costing us an arm and a leg. All this fuss for one day.'

Tommo marched towards the shop and inside, closely followed by Sam. A woman with long, flowing, auburn hair glanced at them and made her way out from behind the counter.

'Hello you two,' she said. 'Just what I need. Two strapping lads to do some heavy lifting.'

Tommo smiled. 'It's as if you knew we were coming, Annie.'

'I had an inkling,' she said. 'Let me have a look at you.' Wandering across to Tommo, she placed a hand either side of his face. 'Look at him, Sam. My Howard's like a great, big Teddy bear.'

Sam smiled. 'Not how I'd describe him.'

She kissed Tommo on his cheeks and stepped back. 'Now that's how a man should look. Like he's going to throw you onto the bed and ravish you.'

'Steady on, Annie,' Sam said. 'He is your nephew.'

'Only by marriage. I was reading yesterday about an aunt and nephew who had a torrid affair. It was in my Take a Break magazine. It caused a rift in the family.'

'Unfortunately, I'm spoken for,' Tommo said.

'I'm only teasing,' she said, and pinched his cheek. She turned her attention to Sam. 'And look at you,' she said. 'Are you as hirsute as Howard under that shirt?'

Sam glanced across at his friend. 'There are creatures living in a cage at Chester Zoo not as hirsute as him.'

Annie giggled. 'I love that sense of humour. If I was twenty years younger, I'd have you. Your Emily would have no chance.'

'If you were twenty years younger, I'd let you.'

She hugged Sam. 'Right, boys.' Moving back behind the counter, she clapped. 'If you two would do me a big favour and bring in those boxes from the back, I'll rustle up a bit of breakfast for you.'

CHAPTER NINE

Albert opened the door to Phillip and Sam. He ushered them inside and through into the living room.

Sam held up a carrier bag. 'I brought biscuits. I didn't want any biscuit related meltdowns.'

Albert lowered his gaze. 'I'm trying to get it under control.'

Phillip patted his arm. 'Ignore Sam. He's just annoyed we're having this meeting here and not the office.'

'Well, I can't see why we didn't have it there. It is our place of business.'

'I told you,' Albert said. 'Mr Knight said he works nearby. It was convenient—'

'Yeah, yeah,' Sam said, and slumped onto a chair. 'Just get the kettle on.'

'The tea's made,' Albert said. He left the room and returned moments later with a tray.

'What does Knight want to see us for?' Phillip said.

Albert began pouring the tea. 'He's interested to find out if we've made any progress on the case yet.'

'Have you told him about Randy?' Sam said.

Albert put down the pot. 'He knows. He saw it in the paper.'

'I thought Randy knew something,' Phillip said.

'What?' Albert said.

'I'm not sure. But I had this impression there was something he was keeping from us.'

Albert leant forward. 'I wonder what?'

Sam picked his tea up and took a sip. 'We don't know. And now he's dead, we never will.'

'You don't think Randy's death had something to do with the case?' Albert said.

'Probably not,' Sam said. 'He was a bit of a lad. I'd put money on a husband or boyfriend.'

'But we can't rule it out,' Phillip said.

Sam hummed. 'I suppose not.'

Albert showed George Knight into the living room where Sam and Phillip sat. 'These are my associates,' Albert said. 'Sam and Phillip Davison.'

'Delighted to meet you both.' He shook hands with Phillip and Sam. 'I particularly liked that piece the gazette did. Especially the incompetence of the Middlesbrough police.'

'They embellished it a little,' Sam said. ''I'm not their favourite person if I'm honest.'

'Would you like a cup of tea?' Albert said.

'I'm good, thanks, Albert. I've only just had one. I'm more interested in how you three are getting on with the case.'

'You heard about Randolph Edwards?' Phillip said.

'Yes, I did. The police don't seem to know who did it.'

'You don't think it had anything to do with the case, do you?' Phillip said.

Knight shook his head. 'I don't think so. Randolph was a bit …'

'Of a lad,' Sam said.

'Yes. I suppose you could say that. Maybe a partner of one of his many women friends did it.'

'That's what I think,' Sam said.

'Did you know him well?' Albert said.

'A little. He's a friend of my brother's. I only met him on a few occasions.'

'Sam and I spoke with him,' Phillip said. 'I got the impression he knew more than he was letting on.'

Knight's eyes widened. 'Really?'

Phillip opened a small notebook. 'Your brother was also friendly with another gentleman. Professor Haldine.'

'Yes, that's right. They go back a long way. Professor Haldine and Stanley worked together for a while.'

Sam took a bite of his biscuit and slurped his tea. 'He's been out of the country, but he should be back next week.'

'He lives in Alnwick. Are you thinking of going there?'

'My daughter gets christened tomorrow,' Sam said. 'We may go there next week.' Sam looked at Phillip, who nodded.

'I'm not sure I can make it,' Albert said. 'I have a meeting with my …' He coughed. 'And of course, there's Zeus.'

'Zeus?' Knight said.

Sam rolled his eyes. 'His dog.'

'Ah, I see.'

'Don't worry, Albert.' Phillip said. 'I think Sam and I can handle it.'

'So,' Albert said to Knight. 'You said you had some information for us?'

Knight held out a carrier bag. 'There is a load of Stanley's paperwork in here. Maybe you three can shed some light on it. A lot of it is to do with Holy Island.'

Phillip nodded at Sam. 'Sam's our resident expert on Lindisfarne.'

Sam stuffed the remainder of a second biscuit into his mouth and took the bag from Knight. 'I'll have a look.'

'Well I'm sure you three know what you're doing,' Knight said.

'Anything else you feel may help?' Phillip said.

Albert closed the front door behind Knight and joined the other two. Zeus ambled into the living room, sat in front of Albert, and began to whimper.

'Ah,' Albert said. 'He needs the toilet. He comes and tells me when he needs a wee.' Albert picked the dog up and carried him out.

'Lucky you,' Sam said. 'Bloody Southgate is still doing it on the newspaper. I've managed to get it down to one sheet, though.'

'You should get a puppy pad,' Phillip said.

'A what?'

'A puppy pad. It's a pad that the puppy goes on. It's absorbent, and after a few days, you throw it out.'

'I didn't know they existed. The paper was Emily's bright idea.'

'Twenty-first century, Sam. That's where we live. The twenty-first century.'

The Black Mamba resounded with a hubbub of noise. Sam cradled his sleeping daughter, dressed in her christening gown, and placed her into her pram.

'That's Daisy exhausted,' Sam said.

'I'm not surprised,' Emily said. 'It's been a long day.'

'Are we going?' he said.

Emily stood. 'Mam and Dad are going to drop me off. You can stay if you want.'

'Are you sure?'

'Yeah. I'm absolutely zonked. You and the boys have a drink. You can discuss whatever case you're working on at the moment. But don't get too drunk.'

Sam stood and hugged Emily. 'The Lindisfarne Liturgy,' he said.

'The missing cross?'

'Yeah,' Sam said. 'It's a wild goose chase.'

'Didn't you say that about the Romanov—'

'Yeah, yeah. I know. But take it from me, that cross will never be found.'

Sam bent and kissed his daughter. 'I won't be too late.'

Emily kissed him, waved at the others, and left with her parents.

Sam joined Tommo and Deb at the bar. Deb glanced towards the door. 'Emily off home?'

'Yeah. She's knackered.'

Deb slowly shook her head. 'Having a baby has really changed you two.'

'In a good way?' Sam said.

Deb smiled. 'I suppose. You couldn't keep on with your wild ways forever.'

Tommo popped a pint in front of Sam. 'On the house,' he said.

Sam pulled his wallet out. 'No. Put it on the tab. Get one for you and Deb. Where are Phillip, Kim and the OCD kid?'

'Next door,' Tommo said.

Sam held out his credit card. 'Let me square up. Don't tell me how much it is, though. I'll wait until my bill for that wonderful surprise.'

Tommo laughed. 'Will do.' Sam paid and headed into the Black Mamba.

Deb leant forward and raised her eyebrows. 'Are we going to get off home while you still have a scintilla of energy?'

'Scintilla,' Tommo said. 'I love it when you use big words. It's a turn-on.'

'Well,' purred Deb. 'Why don't you and I head off home and I'll run through my lexicon for you.'

Sam made his way over to Phillip's table. 'Can I get you and Kim a drink?'

Phillip stood. 'I'll get these. You've bought them all night.' He looked at Kim. 'Another?'

'Oh, yes,' Kim slurred. 'Love this porno star Martini.'

'Porn star.' Phillip chuckled, and made for the bar.

Sam slumped opposite Kim and nodded across the room towards Albert. 'Who's the woman Albert's talking with?' he said.

'New barmaid,' she said.

'Her face seems familiar.'

Kim's eyes widened. 'You haven't slept with her, have you?'

Sam laughed. 'I haven't slept with every woman on Teesside.'

Phillip put down the drinks. 'Just most.'

Sam narrowed his eyes. 'I definitely know her.'

Kim glanced back over at her. 'A friend of Emily's?'

Sam shook his head and furrowed his brow. 'Whoever she is, Albert seems to be getting along fine with her.'

'So,' Kim said. 'Emily's gone home?'

'Yeah. She's given me a pass for the rest of the evening. I won't stay out too long, though.'

Albert stood and tottered across to their table. 'Sam,' he slurred, as he swayed from side to side. 'I wanted to thank you and Emily for asking me to be Godfather to Daisy.'

'No problem,' Sam said.

Albert put his drink down. 'No, I'm really ...' He gulped and reached in his pocket for a handkerchief. 'I'm really ...'

Sam stood and put his arm around him. 'Come on, mate. Don't go all girly on me.' Albert composed himself and nodded.

Phillip picked up Albert's drink and held it high. 'What's this? I thought you hated cocktails?'

'Billie made it for me,' Albert said.

Sam squinted at her and furrowed his brow. 'Billie,' he said to himself.

'What's in it?' Kim said.

'I'm not sure,' Albert said. 'But it's really nice. She made it especially for me. It's called an Albert.'

Billie stood and made her way over to the table. 'Anyone want a drink?' she said.

Sam studied her. 'I know your face ...'

'Sam Davison,' she said. 'You used to go out with my sister, Lisa.'

Sam's mouth dropped open. 'Of course. Little Billie.'

'Lisa's coming in shortly,' she said.

Sam lowered his eyes as Phillip studied him. 'I have to go,' Sam said. 'I told Emily I wouldn't be too long.'

'Never mind,' Billie said. 'I'll tell her I saw you.'

'Yeah.' Sam stood. 'I'll see you lot later.'

Phillip got to his feet and followed Sam towards the door. 'You all right, Sam?' he said.

'Yeah, fine.'

As Sam turned again, Phillip took hold of his arm. 'Are you sure?'

Sam patted Phillip on the arm. 'Yeah, mate. Just a bit tired, that's all. Long day and all that.'

Phillip nodded. 'Ok. See you Monday.'

Sam left and headed along the street. He stopped as he heard footsteps behind him.

'Sam,' Lisa said. 'I thought it was you.'

He spun around as she reached him. 'Hi.'

'Going this early. I thought we could have a catch-up.'

Sam's shoulders slumped. 'It was my daughter's christening. I'm a bit tired.'

'I heard. You and Emily eh?'

'Yeah. You remember her?'

Lisa smiled. 'I remember she's gay.'

'Was.'

'Dad as well. That's a turn-up.'

'I'm in my thirties, Lisa. I couldn't play the field forever.'

Lisa smiled. 'True enough. Listen. How about coming back for a drink. My treat.'

'Another time, maybe.'

'Yeah, sure.' Lisa hugged him tight and gave him a peck on the cheek. 'Another time.' She smiled and headed for the Black Mamba. Sam watched as she entered the pub, sighed, and raced off.

Ewen, who was perched on the stool at the bar of the Boys' End pub, looked over as Sam walked in. Sam headed for the bar and stopped.

'Sam,' Ewen said. 'I thought it was the christening today?'

'It was. Just fancied another.'

'I'll get this,' Ewen said.

'No, it's fine.' Sam reached into his pocket and pulled out his wallet.

Ewen put a hand on Sam's arm. 'It's just a drink, Sam.'

Sam pondered for a moment then shrugged. 'Yeah ok. Double Jim Beam. What are you doing here, anyway?'

'Steph and I had a bit of a barney. I thought I'd come here and get pissed.'

'What was that over?'

'Family, or should I say her family. Her brother is a waster. She wanted me to give him some work.'

Sam raised his eyebrows. 'I take it you didn't fancy that?'

Ewen closed his eyes and shook his head. 'There's not a day's work in him, and he's a bit of a tea leaf. I have to watch him like a hawk as well.' Ewen took a swig of his drink. 'Steph and I started shouting at each other. You know how arguments tend to escalate.' Sam nodded, and Ewen continued. 'The cups and plates started heading my way. I don't know what we're going to eat off.'

Sam huffed. 'I've had that with Emily. She can be really fiery at times.'

'Then Steph came at me with a knife.'

'A knife?' Sam said.

'She wasn't serious.'

'How'd you know?'

Ewen laughed. 'It still had butter on it.' Sam burst out laughing too. Ewen rolled his eyes. 'I might have been worried if I was a croissant.'

Sam shook his head. 'Will she have cooled down when you get home?'

Ewen rubbed the back of his neck. 'Maybe. No doubt I'll be sleeping in the spare bedroom tonight, though.'

'Will that last long?'

Ewen waved across to the barman and ordered some drinks. 'No. She'll soon get over it. You and Emily ok?'

'Yeah. She went home early with Daisy.'

Ewen was served and pushed the glass towards Sam. 'Did you hear?' Ewen said.

Sam took a sip. 'Hear what?'

'Lisa's back.'

Sam took another sip. 'I know. I ran into her at Tommo's.'

'Ah,' Ewen said. 'Our lass saw her in town. Apparently …' Ewen took a drink of his pint. 'She's thinking of moving back for good.'

Sam stared at his drink. 'It's a free world, I suppose.'

Ewen stared at Sam. 'She caused havoc last time.'

Sam slowly nodded. 'I know, but we're a lot older.' He faced Ewen. 'It put a wedge between us, though.'

'Yeah. It seems such a long time ago now.'

Sam drained his glass. 'Another?'

Ewen downed his pint. 'I'll have the same as you. This beer isn't doing it for me.'

Sam groaned as light flooded the room. He quickly pulled the duvet over his head and curled into a ball.

'Are you getting up?' Emily said.

'What time is it?' Sam said. His voice muffled by the cover.

'Nearly one o'clock in the afternoon.'

Sam groaned again. 'Another hour.'

Emily stopped at the edge of the bed. 'What time did you get in last night?'

'I dunno.'

'Two o'clock,' Emily said.

'Well, why did you ask if you knew?'

'I hope you behaved yourself?'

Sam heaved himself into a sitting position and squinted bleary-eyed at Emily. 'Of course I did.'

'Good. I've checked your clothing for lipstick and … random bodily fluids.'

'What do you mean by that?'

'Mmm,' she said, and moved towards the door. 'Just one more thing, Sam …'

Sam raised his eyebrows. 'What?'

'Is there a reason why Ewen is asleep on our sofa?'

'Ewen?'

'Yeah, Ewen. Tommo's cousin.'

'Sort of. He had a run-in with Steph, and I said he could crash here.'

'But I thought—?'

'I met him in town. We got chatting and buried the hatchet over a few drinks. Is that ok?'

'Fine by me, I've always liked Ewen. It was you—'

Sam groaned and pulled the duvet back over his head. 'Are there any paracetamols?'

'Yeah, if you get off your arse and get them. I've cooked you two some breakfast. So, if the pair of you meet me in the kitchen, we can attempt to pull you out of this hangover.'

'I'm not sure I'm hungry.'

'The sooner you get something into you, the sooner you'll be ready to take on the world again.'

Sam trudged into the kitchen and slumped onto a seat opposite Ewen. He peered at him and forced a smile. Emily put a plate in front of Sam with a full-English on it and placed a bacon butty in front of Ewen.

Emily glanced between the pair. 'Tea?'

'Yes, please,' Ewen said.

'How come I've got a big breakfast, and Ewen only has a roll?'

'That's all he wanted.'

Sam unenthusiastically cut through a sausage. 'How's your head?' he said to Ewen.

'I've got a marching band playing in it.'

'Me too. Have you had painkillers?'

'Yeah, Emily gave me a couple.'

Sam nodded, and the pair began eating.

Ewen pushed the empty plate away from him and stood. 'Thanks for the sandwich, Em. And the use of your sofa.'

'Do you want dropping anywhere?' she said.

'No. I think the walk might help clear my head.'

'See you two later.' He nodded at Sam, who waved a hand and then Ewen left.

Emily picked her cup up and sat opposite Sam. 'You and Ewen mates now?'

'I wouldn't say that.'

'It's been a long time since you two fell out. You fell out over—'

'Lisa,' Sam said.

Emily took a sip of her tea. 'Yeah, Lisa.' Emily smiled and tapped his hand. 'Wasn't she the love of your life or something?'

Sam stood. 'I'm struggling with this breakfast.'

Emily pulled the half-eaten meal across from him. 'Waste not …'

Sam rubbed his eyes and downed the rest of his tea. 'I'm going for a shower.'

'What are your plans for the rest of the day?'

He stood. 'I don't know. What did you have in mind?'

'Mam and Dad have got Daisy, so we could go out for tea later.'

'Yeah,' Sam said. 'That would be nice. I might feel better by then.'

'We can try that new Italian in town. I've heard they do the most amazing pizza.'

'Yeah, ok,' Sam said, and gulped. 'But can we not talk about food for the moment.'

Emily laughed and pushed a large piece of bacon into her mouth.

CHAPTER TEN

Sam tramped into the office with a steaming cup of tea and flopped onto his chair with a loud thud.

Phillip looked over from his desk. 'Morning,' he said.

Sam grunted. 'Morning.'

'What's up with you, grumpy?'

'Nowt. I was thinking.'

Phillip raised his eyebrows. 'Oh, yeah?'

'Alnwick.'

'What about it?'

Sam rubbed his chin. 'I think it would be a good time to travel there and see what we can find out about Stanley Knight.'

'What's brought this on? I thought we were going next week?'

Albert walked in. 'Morning,' he said, a huge smile filled his face.

Phillip eyed him. 'You're in a good mood.'

'I slept well, and I feel that I'm getting my anxiety problems under control.'

Sam grunted again. 'No biscuit issues?'

'No.'

'So, you're not still eating them in a strict rota. Monday is Penguins, Tuesday is—'

'I'm not rising to your bait, Samuel.' He stood. 'Anyone want a nice cup of Lapsang?'

Sam held up his full mug. 'I'll stick with my Yorkshire.'

'I'll have one,' Phillip said.

Albert walked towards the door and stopped. 'It's a cake.'

Phillip and Sam exchanged a glance, and Albert continued. 'The Jaffa Cake. Apart from the clue in the name of course. There was a court case.' Sam leant back in his chair and waved for Albert to continue. 'There was a landmark case in 1991.'

'Of course, there was,' Sam said.

'The court found in McVitie's favour,' Albert said. 'For tax purposes, Jaffa Cakes should be treated as a cake.' He viewed the puzzled Sam and Phillip. 'Chocolate-covered cakes are exempt from VAT. Chocolate covered biscuits aren't.'

'Well, there you go,' Phillip said.

'And ...' Sam rolled his eyes, and Albert ploughed on. 'Cakes go stale when left out, but biscuits go soft. As simple as that.'

Sam sighed loudly. 'This is all very exciting, but—'

'However,' Albert said. Sam put his head on the desk and covered his ears. 'In 2012 they were ranked as the best-selling cake or biscuit in the UK.' Albert grinned and then left.

Sam lifted his head. 'Has he gone?'

'Yeah.'

'Thank God. I think I like him better when he's depressed.'

Phillip pulled his chair closer to Sam's desk. 'Come on,' he said. 'Spill the beans. Why do you want to go to Alnwick now?'

Sam rubbed his face and slowly pulled his hands down. 'Do you remember me telling you about Lisa?'

'The girl you were in love with?' Sam nodded. 'The girl you and Tommo's cousin, Ewen, fell out over?'

'Yeah.'

'What about her?'

Sam sighed again. 'She's back in town.'

'Right. How'd—?'

'I ran into her after the christening outside Tommo's. Her sister, Billie, is his new barmaid.'

'Is that why you made a hasty exit?'

'Yeah. I knew she was coming. So, I decided to leave, but ...'

'You ran into her?'

Sam took a gulp of his tea. 'I just think it would be best if I got away for a few nights.'

'Come on, Sam. Lisa was years ago.'

Sam stood and wandered over to the window and Phillip moved over to join him. 'You don't still have feelings for her, do you?'

Sam continued to gaze outside. 'I just think it would be good to get away.'

Phillip nodded. 'Yeah, ok. I'll give Kim a ring to make sure it's all right. What about Emily?'

'I've okayed the trip.' He grabbed Phillip's arm as he turned. 'She doesn't know about Lisa. Please don't say anything to Kim.'

'I won't.'

Albert returned. 'Another fact about Jaffa Cakes ...' he began, as Sam slowly banged his head on the window.

Sam bent forward and kissed Daisy on the head. 'Daddy's going to be away for a couple of days. You be a good for Mammy.'

Emily entered the room and placed a pile of ironed clothes on the kitchen table. 'There you go,' she said.

'Christ, Em,' Sam said. 'I'm only going away for a couple of nights.'

'Well, you want to make sure you have enough clean stuff. Is Phillip picking you up?'

Sam glanced at his watch. 'He should be here any minute.' The doorbell chimed. 'Speak of the devil.'

Sam opened the door, and Phillip stepped inside. 'Bang on time,' Sam said.

'Where's my goddaughter then?'

Sam nodded over his shoulder. 'In there. I'm just going to get my holdall.'

Phillip made his way along the hallway and into the kitchen. 'There she is,' he said.

Phillip leant down and smiled at Daisy. 'Isn't she gorgeous. Oh …' He held out a carrier to Emily. 'Kim sent this.'

'What is it?' she said, looking into the bag.

'An outfit. You know Kim, she can't resist anything cute.'

Emily kissed Phillip on the cheek. 'Thanks, but you two have already bought her loads.'

Phillip shrugged. 'It wasn't expensive.'

'Do you want a cuppa?'

Sam walked in. 'We haven't time. We don't want to hit the Metro Centre traffic.'

'Another time, Em,' Phillip said. 'Kim said to ask if you and Daisy fancy going around for tea.'

'Oh, yeah. Save me cooking.'

Sam pushed his clothes into the holdall and pecked Emily's cheek. 'Well, that's everything.'

'Drive carefully, you two.' She moved forward and kissed Sam. 'I'll see you on Thursday.'

'You will,' Sam said.

Sam jumped into the passenger seat and Phillip moved off. 'Have you got an address for this hotel we're staying at?' Phillip said.

'I'll programme it into the sat-nav when we get a little closer. It's the same hotel Stanley Knight stayed at.'

'Right,' Phillip said. 'I suppose it's as good a place as anywhere to start. What about Professor Haldine?'

'I spoke to his secretary. He's still away. He probably won't be back until next week. She said she would tell him we need to talk.'

'Is it worth going there?' Phillip said.

'We won't know until we get there. Before we hit the A19, can we stop for a coffee and a sandwich? I'm starving.'

'Yeah.' Phillip glanced across at Sam. 'The problem won't go away, Sam. Lisa will still be there when you get home.'

Sam stared out of the window. 'I know, but …'

'But?'

'I just need a couple of days to get my head around it.' Sam studied his phone. 'That's all.'

Phillip stopped outside the bakery. 'All right. Greggs ok?'

'Yeah, Greggs will do nicely.'

Emily opened the rear door to her car and began getting Daisy out of her seat.

'Hi, Emily,' a female voice said.

Emily turned with her daughter in her hands and viewed Lisa.

'I don't know if you remember me?' Lisa said. 'I'm—'

'Lisa,' Emily said.

'Yeah. I was friends with Sam way back.' She smiled at Emily. 'Is this Sam's little girl?'

Emily forced a smile. 'Our little girl.'

'God,' Lisa said. 'You can't half see Sam in her.'

'Visiting family?' Emily said.

'Yeah. My mam lives on this road. Although it may turn into something a little more permanent.'

'Really?'

Lisa smiled again at Emily. 'Yeah. I'm sick of travelling. I always believed I'd end up back here.' Lisa opened her handbag. 'Let me give you a little something for …?'

'Daisy,' Emily said.

'For Daisy. For her piggy bank.' She plucked a £50 from her purse and offered it to Emily.

Emily shook her head. 'That's too much, Lisa.'

'Go on. I'm not badly off.' She pushed the note into Emily's coat pocket. 'I can't believe Sam is a dad. I never thought he was father material.'

'Well, he is.'

'He's still as handsome as ever. I saw him the other night outside The Sidewinder. Did he mention he'd seen me?'

'Of course,' Emily said. 'He tells me everything.'

'Anyway,' Lisa smirked. 'Nice to see you again, and Sam's gorgeous little girl. We'll have to have a coffee some time. You can tell me how you managed to tie him down.'

Emily watched as Lisa made her way along the street, placed Daisy into her pushchair, and kicked the door shut with the sole of her foot.

She opened the boot, took out Daisy's changing bag, and headed along the path to Kim's house.

Kim opened the door to a stern-looking Emily. 'Hi,' Kim said. Emily entered and followed Kim into the lounge. 'You ok?'

Emily slumped onto a chair and huffed. She rubbed at her face and blew out hard. 'Lisa's back.'

Kim cocked her head to one side. 'Lisa?'

Emily threw her hands up. 'Lisa Sandsfield.'

'The Lancashire singer?'

'Sandsfield, not Stansfield.'

Kim slid onto a chair opposite Emily. 'Ok,' Kim said. 'And who is this Lisa—?'

'Sam's ex-girlfriend.'

'I see. And?'

Emily gently rocked Daisy's pushchair as the baby began to stir. 'It's a long story.'

Kim stood. 'Listen,' she said. 'I'll put the kettle on and make us a cup of tea, and you can tell me all about it.'

Phillip parked the car behind The Black Horse Hotel. He switched off the engine and nudged the sleeping Sam. 'We're here,' he said.

Sam stretched and rubbed his eyes. 'That was quick.'

'Of course it was quick when you're asleep, and someone else is driving.'

'You found the hotel on your own then?'

Phillip scoffed. 'I had to. You were sound asleep.'

Sam stretched and yawned. 'What's the plan?'

'We'll book in and have a nap.'

'I'm not tired. I feel refreshed after that sleep.'

'Well, you do what you like. That drive has tired me out.'

Kim took a sip of tea and studied Emily, who was feeding the baby. 'Sam's probably forgotten about this, Lisa,' Kim said.

'She said she ran into him after the christening.'

'So?'

'Sam didn't mention it.'

'He probably forgot.'

Emily lifted Daisy onto her lap and gently rubbed her back. 'You don't understand, Kim.'

'Then explain.'

'Sam loved Lisa. He always used to talk about her. She was the love of his life.'

'But that was years ago. He won't feel the same now. He adores you and Daisy.'

'But what happens if he still has feelings for her? What happens—?'

'Emily,' Kim said. 'You're worrying over nothing. I'll make us another cup of tea, shall I?'

'Yeah, because that will make everything ok.'

Kim sighed at her friend and moved across to the kettle.

Sam slouched on the stool at the end of the bar sipping his drink as Phillip walked in. Phillip slipped onto the seat next to him. 'How many have you had?' Phillip said, nodding at the glass in his friend's hand.

Sam grinned at him. 'Four.'

'Four!' Phillip said. 'It's not even six o'clock.'

'Well, I've been stuck here on my own all afternoon while you were pushing out the zeds. However, ...' Sam took a swig of his drink and waved across at the young barmaid in the corner. 'I haven't been wasting my time.' He tapped the side of his nose.

She moved over to the pair of them. 'Another, handsome?'

'Can I have the same, Sara. And whatever grumpy here wants.'

She looked at Phillip. 'Pint of Timothy Taylors please,' he said.

Sam watched as she moved along the bar and began preparing the drinks. 'She's nice-looking, don't you think?'

Phillip glanced across at her and then back towards Sam. 'Never mind the attractiveness of the staff. What have you found out?'

The barmaid returned and placed the drinks in front of them. 'Anything else, boys?'

Phillip pulled out a £20 and handed it to her. 'No that's everything, thanks.'

'Get yourself one, Sara,' Sam said, winking at her.

Phillip nudged him. 'You've very liberal with other peoples' money. Well? Stanley Knight?'

'He stayed here quite often. The lovely Sara ...' Sam smiled at her as she handed Phillip his change. '... said he was a really nice man.'

'That's it?'

'No.' Sam took a swig of his drink. 'There's a guy called Aaron who works here who knew Knight very well. Apparently, he's doing a degree in history. That's Aaron, not Stanley Knight of course.' Phillip rolled his eyes and Sam continued. 'The pair were always talking about historical stuff.'

'Is he here?'

Sam consulted his watch. 'He should be here soon. He was working on the night Knight fell.' Sam laughed. 'Knight night.'

'Or was murdered,' Phillip said.

'Yeah. Or was murdered. I thought maybe we could have a word with him later. Maybe buy him a drink or two. See if we can wheedle any interesting information from him.'

'Good idea,' Phillip said. 'But I think you should leave the questioning to me. You are a little worse for wear.'

Sam waved at the barmaid, who made her way back over. 'Same again, gorgeous,' he said.

She glanced at Phillip's still full pint. 'Same again for you?' she said.

'I'm ok, thanks.'

Sam leant forward, resting his chin on his hand, and eyed her as she prepared his drink. 'If I wasn't celibate,' he said. 'I'd have a crack at her.'

'Celibate?' Phillip said.

Sam giggled. 'I mean faithful.'

'I think with the problem of Lisa on the horizon, you had better throw yourself into work and forget about the females in your life.'

Sam glared at his friend. 'You had to mention Lisa, didn't you?'

Phillip smiled at himself through the mirror. 'Anyway, this Aaron ...?'

Emily pulled off her coat and slumped onto the chair.

'Did you get Daisy away ok?' Kim said.

'Yeah. Mam's having her overnight. You don't mind me coming back and bending your ear again, do you?'

'Don't be daft, that's what friends are for. You're worrying over nothing. Sam would never ...' She stopped as the doorbell sounded. 'I wonder who this is?'

'Probably Deb,' Emily said.

'Deb?'

'Yeah. She rang when my mam came around to pick Daisy up, and I told her I was coming here.'

Kim disappeared and returned with Deb, who was carrying a bag. 'Evening,' Deb said.

'Evening,' Emily said.

Deb slumped into a seat opposite Emily. 'What's up?' she said to Emily.

'Up?'

'Yeah. I can always tell when somethings up.' Deb folded her arms. 'Come on, spill the beans.'

Kim flicked the kettle on. 'Lisa's back,' Kim said.

'Lisa Sandsfield?' Deb said, and Emily nodded.

'And?' Deb said.

'Sam spoke to her the other night but didn't tell me.'

'How did you find out?' Deb said.

'Her mam still lives up the road, and I ran into her when I came here.'

'Emily thinks Sam still has feelings for her,' Kim said.

'He probably does,' Deb said. 'If he has, there's always more fish in the sea. And you've still got Daisy, so the relationship wasn't a total waste.'

'Deb,' Kim said. 'Don't say things like that.'

'It's true,' Emily said. 'Sam has always been besotted by Lisa.'

Deb threw open her hands. 'He has. It's a shame, I was looking forward to organising your hen night.'

'Who said I'm getting married?' Emily said.

'I just thought it was only a matter of time before Sam popped the question. It's always good to plan.'

'Who said I'd ask you to organise it, anyway. I might ask Helen.'

Deb scoffed. 'Helen. Boring, boring Helen. The most exciting thing she's ever done is to grow her fringe out.'

'You're definitely not getting the job, now,' Emily said. She folded her arms together.

'It doesn't matter anyway. There isn't going to be a wedding, is there. I can always take the hat back.'

Emily scoffed. 'You in a hat. That'll be a sight.'

'Deb,' Kim said. 'You're supposed to be making Emily feel better.'

Emily stood. 'I'm going to the loo.'

Deb popped the bag onto the table and opened it. 'I did bring wine and crisps.' Emily disappeared into the toilet.

'Bloody hell, Deb,' Kim said. 'That was a bit brutal.'

Deb scoffed. 'Kim,' she said. 'I've known Emily a lot longer than you. When she's in a mood like this, she's a pain in the arse. She gets all mardy.'

'Even so.'

'She'll be in the bog having a word with herself and giving her head a shake, and then she'll come out of there in a better humour.' Kim frowned. 'Take it from me. Emily can self-pity like nobody I've ever met. No one, and I mean no one, likes self-pity Emily. She'll be fine.'

Emily returned and slumped back into her seat. She patted Deb on the arm. 'Thanks for that, Deb. I needed telling.' Deb raised her eyebrows at Kim.

'Crisps?' Deb said.

Emily pouted. 'Are they prawn cocktail?'

'Of course.'

Emily smiled. 'Well, what are we waiting for.' She picked up one of the bottles. 'Where's the corkscrew?'

Phillip assisted Sam along the corridor and into his bedroom. Sam slumped on the bed and kicked off his shoes. 'What am I going to do, Phillip?' Sam slurred.

'Maybe now's not the right time to tackle that question. You've had a lot to drink.'

'I love Emily. I really do. And Daisy, my little Daisy.'

'Well, there's your answer.'

Sam threw his arms upwards. 'You don't understand. You don't know what Lisa and I had. I love Emily Simpson, but I love Lisa Sandsfield. You can love two people simul …' Sam burped. 'At the same time.'

'Lisa—?'

'No!' Sam said. 'Not like the singer. Sandsfield, not Stansfield.'

'Anyway,' Phillip said. 'You get some sleep, and I'll go and have a word with Aaron.'

Sam propped himself up in bed. 'Why did she have to come back? All those feelings I'd managed to keep buried for years have come flooding back.'

Phillip rolled his eyes. 'God, you sound like a Barbara Cartland novel.'

Sam rolled onto his side. 'Do I stick or twist?'

'Have you considered that Lisa might not want you back? She may have someone else.'

Sam turned back. 'She does want me. I could see it in her eyes. The look of love.'

'Jesus. This is straight out of Woman's Weekly. I'm going.'

Sam put his head underneath the pillow. 'Yeah, you go and leave your mate when he needs you.'

Phillip smiled and left.

Kim pulled the duvet over the sleeping Emily and headed back into the kitchen. 'That's her out for the count.'

'You shouldn't have let her drink so much,' Deb said.

'Me! You were the one who went for some more booze.'

Deb laughed. 'She'll have a right head on her in the morning.'

Kim slumped down. 'So will I. Do you want to sleep as well? I can put you up on the sofa.'

'Nah. I'm a bit long in the tooth for sofa sleeping. Tommo's picking me up. I phoned him while you were tucking Emily in.'

Kim gulped. 'So, what do you think about her and Sam?'

Deb shrugged. 'I don't know. The Sam of a year ago would have jumped at the chance, but …' Deb pondered for a moment. 'I'm not sure now. The soft lad really does love Emily.'

'And there's Daisy of course.'

'Yeah,' Deb said. 'Maybe I should warn Lisa off.'

Kim's eye's widened. 'What, threaten her like?'

'I never really liked her. She was in the year above me at school. She always had the lads fawning over her.'

'I didn't know you knew her.'

'Not that well,' Deb said. 'She would have all the lads wrapped around her little finger. Sam was just one of many she toyed with. It was down to her that Ewen and Sam fell out.'

'Tommo's cousin?'

Deb leant back in her chair. 'Yeah. Sam and Ewen were good mates. She caused the rift. That's the sort of thing she would do.'

'We can't have her coming between Emily and Sam,' Kim said.

'No.'

The doorbell sounded. 'My cuddly bear's here,' Deb said.

Kim answered the door and returned with Tommo. Deb stood and put her arm around him. 'Thanks, gorgeous,' she said.

'Tommo,' Kim said. 'You know Sam really well.'

'Unfortunately,' he said.

'Do you know Lisa?'

'Lisa Sandsfield?'

'Yeah,' Kim said.

'She was Sam's girlfriend years ago. Her sister works for me. Why?'

'She's back,' Deb said.

Tommo stroked his beard. 'I know. Does Sam know yet?'

'Yeah,' Deb said. 'He ran into her the other night.'

'Right.'

'How does Sam feel about her?' Kim said.

Tommo scratched his beard. 'He was heartbroken when they broke up, and he was gutted about it when she left.'

'I mean now.'

'I don't know. I haven't spoken to him about it.'

Kim closed the door. 'Emily's asleep next door. She bumped into Lisa outside. Apparently, her mam lives on this road.'

'Oh,' Tommo said. 'And?'

'Two and a half bottles of wine later.' She nodded in the direction of the bedroom.

'I thought I could warn her off,' Deb said.

'What's this, a gangster movie?' he said.

'If she tries to come between Sam and Emily,' Kim said.

Tommo shook his head. 'Listen. It's Sam and Emily's problem. You don't even know that Lisa is trying to break them up. Besides, Sam ...' Tommo laughed. 'I never thought I'd ever say this about Sam. He loves Emily. He adores her.'

'That's what we were thinking,' Kim said.

'I'll see if Sam mentions her when he gets back from Alnwick. He normally opens up to me. If he does, I'll remind him what he has to lose.'

'And if that fails,' Deb said. 'I'll duff her up.'

'Yeah, ok, Ma Baker. You'll duff her up.'

Phillip leant against the bar and waited as a young barman served a customer. He finished, then focused his attention on Phillip. 'What can I get you?' he said.

Phillip glanced at the barmen's name tag. 'Aaron?' he said.

'Yeah.'

Phillip pulled a card from his back pocket and handed it to him. Aaron studied it for a moment. 'Erimus Detective Agency?'

'Yeah. I wonder if you could help me?'

'What with?' Aaron said.

'Stanley Knight.'

'Stanley knight?' Phillip nodded. Aaron glanced at the card again. 'He was a customer. He stayed here quite often.'

'One of the other staff, Sara, said you knew him well.'

'I'm doing a history degree, and Stanley would help me out. He was a teacher, you see.'

'Yeah, I know.'

'I'm not sure what else I can tell you,' Aaron said.

'A member of Stanley's family has asked us to look into his death.'

Aaron's eye's widened. 'It was an accident ... That's what the police said. A tragic accident.'

'I know the police said that but—'

'I'm a bit busy,' Aaron said. 'I'll get into bother if the bar manager finds me chatting.'

'But I'm a guest at the hotel. I'm sure he won't mind. There will be a drink in it for you.'

'It's just ...' He began clearing glasses away. 'I'm not sure how I can help.'

'The night he died,' Phillip said. 'Someone left a message for him at reception.'

'I work behind the bar Mr ...' Aaron glanced at the card. 'Davison. I have nothing to do with reception.'

'Is everything all right, Aaron, you seem a little uptight?'

Aaron forced a smile. 'No. I'm fine.'

Phillip took his wallet out and pulled out a £50 note. 'Just ten minutes of your time. That's all I'm asking.'

Aaron examined the note for a few seconds but didn't take it. 'I'm on a break in fifteen minutes. Maybe we could chat then?'

'Yeah. I'll have a pint of IPA and a seat over there.' Phillip nodded into the corner. 'Come and see me when you can.'

Aaron pulled the pint and placed it on the bar. Phillip opened his wallet again, but Aaron waved it away. 'It's ok. On the house.'

Phillip smiled, picked up his pint, and headed across to the other side of the room. He watched as Aaron took out his phone and wandered outside. Phillip sprung to his feet and headed over to the window. Aaron stood in the car park shouting into his phone. Phillip continued to watch until Aaron hung up, pushed the phone into his pocket, and came back inside.

Phillip's phone sounded. 'Hi,' he said.

'How're things going?' Kim said.

'I'm hoping to have a chat with a lad that works behind the bar about Stanley Knight.'

'How's Sam?'

'Sam?'

'Yeah. Emily's here. Her and Deb came around earlier for a few drinks. Unfortunately, Emily had more than a few.'

'Oh. Sam's in bed.'

'On his own, I hope.'

'Of course he's on his own. He hit the booze as soon as we got here. He's pining over a woman called—'

'Lisa.'

'Yeah. How do—?'

'Emily's the same. This Lisa is a past girlfriend of Sam's, and Emily's frightened Sam will go off with her.'

'Sam wouldn't do that.'

'How do you know,' Kim said. 'Has he mentioned anything about her?'

'Not really.'

Kim huffed. 'Phillip, what do you mean by not really?'

'He mentioned her. But he was drunk.'

'Find out what you can. This Lisa sounds as if she's a right trouble-maker.'

'Is it any of our business, though?'

'Phillip. Think of poor Daisy.'

Phillip sighed. 'I'll have a chat with him in the morning.'

'Good lad. Love you.'

'Love you too,' he said.

He pushed the phone back into his jacket and looked across to the bar. Aaron had gone. He stood and ambled over. Another barman moved towards him. 'Yes, sir?'

'Is Aaron there?'

'Aaron's had to go home. He wasn't feeling very well.'

'I see.' Phillip stroked his chin. 'Thanks,' he said to the barman, and headed to bed.

CHAPTER ELEVEN

Phillip pushed his empty breakfast plate away and picked up his cup. Sam wandered in and slumped into a chair opposite.

'Feeling rough?' Phillip said. 'I'm surprised you're here at all, the way you look.'

Sam rubbed his stomach. 'Yeah. I've got a banging headache. You haven't any tablets, have you?'

'Afraid not.'

A waitress stopped at the table. 'Can I get you anything?' she said.

Sam groaned loudly. 'A gun … Or paracetamol will do if you haven't got one.'

She smiled. 'I'm right out of guns, I'm afraid. I can get you some painkillers if you want?'

'Yes, please. And a full English.'

'Tea or coffee?'

'Tea,' Sam said.

She smiled at the pair of them and then left.

'Your hangover hasn't dulled your appetite, I see,' Phillip said.

'You have to attack a hangover with food. Otherwise, it will loiter about all day.'

'I spoke to a barman called Aaron last night.'

Sam poured himself a glass of water. 'Oh, yeah?'

'He seemed a little shifty.'

The waitress returned with a pot of tea and some tablets. 'Thanks, gorgeous,' Sam said. 'Shifty?'

Phillip waited until the waitress was out of earshot. 'He seemed reluctant to talk about Stanley Knight. I offered him £50.'

'£50!' Sam said. 'Jesus, this case will cost us money at this rate.'

'He wouldn't take it.'

'£50? I'd have snapped your hand off.'

'Well, he didn't.' Phillip sipped his tea. 'He said he would chat with me when he had his break, but while I was distracted on the phone, he went home. He told the hotel he was ill.'

'He may have been.'

Phillip scoffed. 'There was nowt wrong with him. He just didn't want to talk to me.'

The waitress arrived with Sam's breakfast. 'Can I get you any sauces?' she said.

'Brown, please.'

The two men remained silent until she returned and popped the sauce down. 'Enjoy,' she said.

Sam waited for the her to leave, then fixed his attention on Phillip. 'Go to his home,' he said, as he buttered his toast. 'Have a word with him there. Maybe ...' Sam took a large bite and chewed as Phillip waited for him to finish his sentence. '... He was frightened to say anything at the hotel.'

'Possible, I suppose. Unfortunately, we don't know where he lives? And I'm pretty sure the hotel won't give out the addresses of their staff to anyone.'

'We'll have to come up with a ruse,' Sam said. 'Let me finish my breakfast, and I'll think of something. I always do better on a full stomach.'

Phillip rested back in his chair. 'About Lisa.'

Sam growled. 'What's all the concern about Lisa? Tommo woke me out of a deep sleep to ask about her.'

'Emily knows you saw Lisa.'

Sam paused with half a sausage mid-air. 'How do you know?'

Phillip nodded. 'That's what Kim told me.'

'So, everyone knows?'

'Listen, mate. If there's anything you want to discuss with me, I'm—'

'I think we've got more important things to think about than my past girlfriends. Like I said. I'll finish my breakfast, and then we'll head around to Aaron's.'

Phillip stood by the reception as Sam, carrying a book, descended the stairs and joined him.

Phillip glanced at the book. 'What's that?'

Sam tapped the side of his nose and wandered over to the desk. 'Morning,' he said to the receptionist.

She looked up from her computer and smiled at him. 'Morning, sir.'

'Is Aaron about?' Sam said.

'No, I'm afraid he went home ill last night.'

Sam held out the book. 'I said I would lend him this. He has an exam or something coming up, and he needs it to help him pass.'

'I'm not sure when he'll be back in.'

Sam leant forward. 'That's a shame.' He turned away as if deep in thought, and then spun back around. 'Does he live far from here?'

'No. Just by the college.'

'I don't suppose you have his address handy. I'll pop it around to him. I'm on my way back to Teesside today, and it'll be a shame if he fails his exam because of it.'

'Well, we're not supposed to give out addresses.'

'In case I'm a nutter or something?' Sam said, waving his arms around for effect.

The receptionist giggled. 'I'm sure you're not.'

Sam smiled broadly and tilted his head slightly to one side. 'Those history exams are tricky little customers. It would be a shame for all that hard work to go to waste.' He held up a finger. 'For want of a nail, the shoe was lost, for want of a blah, blah, blah. I promise I won't harm him, gorgeous.' Sam leant in closer and winked.

The woman paused and scribbled on a piece of paper. 'Don't tell anyone I gave you this.'

Sam gently tapped her hand. 'Of course not. Mum's the word.' He took the paper from her, smiled again and headed off closely followed by Phillip.

'I don't believe she gave it to you,' Phillip said. 'What is that book, anyway?' Sam held it up for Phillip to view. 'I'm not sure the Gideon Bible would help him much with his exams.'

Sam shrugged. 'I was improvising. It got us the address, didn't it?'

'That, and your outrageous flirting.'

'Just a little trick I leant from Baggage.' He paused and tilted his head. 'Now, Let's go and see this Aaron.'

Phillip pulled the car to a halt outside an old Victorian house. 'Is this it?' he said.

'Yeah,' Sam said. 'Flat 1. Probably the ground floor.'

'How are we going to play this?'

Sam stared across at the building and rubbed his chin. 'Leave it to me. You had no luck last night, maybe I can get him to talk?'

The pair made their way over and stopped outside a door with bell pushes for each flat to the side of it. Sam glanced at Phillip before pressing the intercom for flat 1. They waited a few moments, but no one answered.

'Out?' Phillip said.

Sam shrugged. 'Maybe.'

A man deep in conversation on his phone approached the door. Sam and Phillip moved aside allowing him to press the bell for flat 6.

A voice answered. 'Yeah.'

'It's me. Let me in.' The door clicked open, and the man pushed through and headed inside. As the door swung closed, Sam stopped it from shutting entirely with his foot. They waited a moment before following the man inside. The pair stood and watched as he disappeared out of sight up the stairs.

'Well,' Sam said. 'We're inside.'

They wandered across to the door for flat 1 and Sam knocked. Phillip nodded towards the door. 'The door isn't quite shut,' he said.

Sam placed his hand on the handle, pushed, and the door opened slightly.

He pushed again and stepped inside. 'Aaron,' he said.

Phillip followed him into the room and gently closed the door behind him. 'He must be out,' Phillip said.

Sam stepped further into the room and pointed to his left. 'Is that Aaron? he said to Phillip, and nodded towards the prone figure of someone lying face down on the floor.

Phillip moved across and lowered his face towards the man. He placed a couple of fingers on his throat and felt for a pulse. 'It's Aaron. He's dead.'

Sam rolled his eyes. 'Why is it we always find the dead ones. It's as if they know we're coming.'

Phillip lifted Aaron's limp body up a little. 'He's been stabbed.'

'So not an accident then?'

'We'd better phone the police,' Phillip said. He stood. 'We can't do what we did in Guisborough.'

'No,' Sam said. He looked at the dead man again. 'Didn't you say you saw him on the phone after you spoke to him last night?'

'Yeah,' Phillip said.

'Aaron's going nowhere, is he. Maybe we can see who he phoned.'

'Where's his phone, though?'

Sam knelt. 'I'll check his pockets.'

'I'm not sure about this,' Phillip said. 'Even if you do find his phone, it will probably be locked.'

'Eureka!' Sam said, and held the mobile aloft. He lifted Aaron's limp hand and taking hold of his index finger, placed the tip on the back of the phone. Nothing happened.

'He'll be too cold,' Phillip said. 'Mine doesn't work if my fingers are cold.'

'Go and fetch some hot water. We'll dip his finger in.'

'Hot water?'

'Yeah. Boil a kettle or something.'

Phillip shook his head but left the room, returning moments later with a cup half-filled with liquid. Sam placed Aaron's finger inside and waited.

'It's not too hot, is it?' Phillip said.

Sam scoffed. 'I'm sure Aaron won't be complaining. We're dealing with a dead body here, not giving Daisy her bottle.'

'I meant it could leave a mark. What will the police think?'

Sam removed Aaron's finger and wiped it dry. He placed it back on the phone and the device lit up. 'I'm bloody good, me.' Sam held the mobile out to Phillip.

Phillip studied the phone. 'Not that good.'

'Why?'

Phillip showed him the screen. 'It's asking for a passcode.' He tossed it back to Sam.

Sam groaned. 'Bollocks.' He rubbed the phone clean with his t-shirt and slipped it back into Aaron's pocket.

'What do we do now?' Phillip said.

'Call the coppers.'

Emily trudged into the kitchen and slumped on a seat.

'Breakfast?' Kim said.

Emily looked up, bleary-eyed. 'Just some juice and toast, please. And a couple of tablets.'

Kim scooped up two paracetamols from next to her, put there in readiness for Emily's arrival. 'I made you this,' she said, handing Kim the pills and a pint glass full of orange liquid.

'What is it?' Emily said.

'Vitamin drink. It'll put you back in fine fettle.'

Emily groaned and put a hand to her head. 'Sam never phoned last night.'

Kim slipped into a chair opposite her. 'I spoke to Phillip. Sam had one too many drinks yesterday afternoon. He was sleeping it off. It appears you two are very much alike.'

'He could have rung this morning.'

'He will. Phillip said they were chasing a lead.'

Emily's eyes filled, and the tears spilt down her face. 'What if he leaves me, Kim? What will I do?'

Kim moved closer. 'You're just hungover. And you know how alcohol makes people depressed. Sam and you will be fine.' She took hold of Emily's hand. 'I'm sure of it.'

'They're on their way,' Phillip said to Sam. His phoned sounded again. 'Hi.'

'Why hasn't Sam phoned Emily?' Kim said.

'Why are you whispering?'

'Emily's in the bathroom. I don't want her to hear me.'

'Oh. We're a little tied up at the moment.'

'Phillip,' she said. 'This is important.'

'I know, Kim,' he said. 'But at the moment we're looking at a dead body, and the police are on their way here. I think that trumps you.'

'Dead body?'

'Long story. I'll get him to phone when we can. I promise. Listen I'll have to go, Sam's coming back.'

'Love you,' she said.

'Love you.'

'Kim?' Sam said, and handed Phillip a cup of tea.

'Yeah.' Phillip cradled the mug in his hands. 'What's this?'

'Tea. No biscuits though. Albert would be distraught.'

'I meant.' Phillip took a deep breath. 'Why are you making tea? The police are coming and you're tramping all over a crime scene.'

'Well, you had better hurry up and drink it then. I'll wash them before they arrive.'

Phillip huffed. 'You haven't phoned Emily.'

Sam dropped onto the arm of a chair. 'Yeah. I meant to this morning, but when I got up, I felt like shit.'

'You should ring.'

Sam pointed at the body. 'Not the most important thing at the moment.'

Phillip put his hands on his hips. 'I suppose not. I wonder how long they'll be?'

Sam took a gulp of his tea. 'No idea. I've phoned the hotel and booked an extra night.'

'What for? I thought we were going back today?'

'I have a feeling we'll be tied up a little.' Sam thoughtfully took a sip of tea and glanced at his phone.

The uniformed police officer moved away from Sam and Phillip and over to an older man who had just entered the room.

'What have we got?' the older man said as the officer reached him.

'A male. 20-30 years of age, sir. He's been stabbed.'

'Who found him?'

The officer nodded towards Sam and Phillip. 'The two gentlemen over there.'

He briefly eyed the two cousins before walking across to them. 'Inspector Stead,' he said. 'And you two are?'

The uniformed officer joined them. 'Samuel and Phillip Davison, sir.'

'Let them speak for themselves,' Stead said.

I'm Phillip Davison, and this is my cousin, Sam.'

'How do you know the deceased?'

'He works at the hotel we're staying at,' Sam said.

The inspector raised his eyebrows. 'And which hotel would that be?'

'The Black Horse,' Phillip said.

'And you know him well?'

Phillip glanced at Sam. 'Not really.'

Stead pulled out a notepad and began jotting things down. 'Can I ask,' he said, studying them. 'What you're doing in his flat?'

'It's a bit of a long story,' Sam said.

A younger plain-clothed officer arrived and joined them. Stead glanced at his junior. 'Nice of you to join us, Headley.'

'Sorry about that, guv. Flat tyre.'

Stead fixed his glare back on Sam and Phillip. 'This long story.' He smiled. 'I would love to hear it.'

'I was loaning him a book,' Sam said.

'A book?'

'Yeah,' Sam said. 'He's doing a history degree, and I've got a history degree, so I said I would loan him one of my books.'

'Right,' Stead said. 'And you thought you would pop it around to his flat? Why not give it to him at the hotel?'

'He had gone home sick,' Phillip said. 'So, we ...'

'So, you ...?' Stead said.

'Well ...' Phillip said. 'We thought we'd drop it off for him.'

Stead tapped his pad with his pen. 'That's incredibly kind of you.'

'That's us two.' Sam grinned. 'Generous to a fault.'

Stead stared at him. 'I don't believe you.'

'That's because you're a cynical old copper,' Sam said. 'You lot are all the same.'

Phillip nudged him. 'What my friend means, Inspector—'

'Well,' Stead said. 'This cynical old copper thinks we need to have a more formal chat with you two down the station. Find out what you were really up to.'

Sam groaned. 'Why is it you lot always think the worst of people?'

'Because, Mr Davison,' Stead said. 'We have a man found dead in his flat, and two people who hardly know him are here too. Call it my copper's nose.'

'Look,' Phillip said. 'This is getting silly. We'd hardly murder someone, phone the police, and then wait here for you to turn up.'

'Perhaps not,' Stead said. 'But there's something you two are not telling me.'

Another plain-clothed male officer came into the room. 'The forensics are here, sir.'

'Good,' Stead said. 'I want to know when he died.'

'The kettles still warm,' the uniformed officer said.

'Ah,' Phillip said, casting a sideways glance at Sam. 'That was us. We had a cup of tea.'

Stead glared at Phillip, and then at Sam. 'Cup of tea? This is a murder scene, gentlemen. Not *Ye old tea shop*.'

'We knew we'd have a bit of a wait,' Sam said. 'We know how incredibly busy you boys are. So—'

'Headley,' Stead said, continuing to stare at the two cousins. 'Get these jokers down the nick.'

CHAPTER TWELVE

Emily phoned Kim. 'Hi,' Kim said, as she answered. 'How are you feeling?'

'A little better. Have you heard from Phillip?'

'Not this morning. Why?'

Emily sighed. 'Sam hasn't phoned.'

'Oh, hold on. Phillip's trying to ring me now. I'll call you back.' She quickly ended her call with Emily and answered Phillip. 'Hi, gorgeous. How are you?'

'Not great.'

'Why?'

'We're at Alnwick police station.'

'Police station, why? What's happened? They haven't arrested you, have they?'

'We're helping the police with their enquiries, regarding the body we found.'

'Oh, my God,' Kim said. 'They don't think you did it?'

'I don't know.'

'Who is it?' Kim said.

'He works at the hotel we're staying at. It's a long story, but …' Phillip took a deep breath. 'He was a possible lead on the case we're working on but when we went around to his flat, he'd been stabbed to death.'

'Bloody hell. The police must think you two—'

'I hope not. Sam was his usual cocky self with the coppers, and that's one reason why we're here.'

'Talking about Sam, he still hasn't rung Emily. She's getting a little worried.'

'I'll mention it to him, but you know Sam.'

'Yeah. I let her know where he is.'

'Ok, gorgeous. I'll have to go.'

Kim phoned Emily. 'What did he say?' Emily said.

'They're at Alnwick police station. Helping the police with their enquiries.'

'What's happened?'

'They found another body.'

'Another?' Emily said. 'Jesus. It's becoming a habit.'

'I know. Phillip couldn't talk long, but I've asked him to tell Sam to ring.'

'Ok.'

'Don't worry,' Kim said. 'He will.'

Sam and Phillip sat at a table in an interview room as Stead and Headley walked in carrying two cups. The junior officer placed the drinks in front of the cousins.

'We've brought you two some tea.' He stared at Sam and then Phillip. 'I know how much you love your tea.'

Sam picked up his cup, took a sip and grimaced. 'Christ, that's bloody awful.' Phillip nudged him. Sam pulled a face at Phillip. 'Well, it is.'

'I'm sorry our tea doesn't meet your exacting standards,' Stead said.

Phillip tasted it. 'It's fine, Inspector.'

'Now we have the niceties out of the way,' Stead said. 'We can crack on.' He smiled at the pair. 'Why did you really go around to the deceased flat?'

Phillip pushed his tea away from himself. 'We run a detective agency in Redcar.'

Stead glanced at his junior. 'Really? In Redcar, you say.'

'Yeah,' Sam said, and folded his arms. 'We do, ok?'

'And Aaron Morgan ...?'

'He was a lead on a case we're working on,' Phillip said.

Stead leant back in his chair. 'Now we're getting somewhere. What case?'

'Stanley Knight. He was a—' Phillip said

'History Teacher,' Stead said. 'What about him?'

'His brother asked us to look into his death,' Sam said. 'He thinks your colleagues didn't do your job properly.'

Stead leant closer. 'I investigated that case.' Phillip looked at Sam and rolled his eyes. 'And let me tell you—'

'Sam didn't mean to cast aspersions, Inspector.' Phillip said.

Stead continued to stare at Sam for a couple more seconds before fixing his attention on Phillip. 'Stanley Knight fell to his death. It was a tragic accident.'

'Are you sure, though?' Sam said.

'I'm more than sure, Mr Davison. I'm certain. There was a witness who heard him shout, and when they investigated, they found him dead.

There was no one else about. The witness was …' He stared at Sam again. 'Sure.'

Sam re-folded his arms. 'Maybe this witness pushed him?'

'She was a seventy-five-year-old dog-walker, Mr Davison.' Stead said.

'And a churchgoer,' Headley said.

'Yes,' Stead said. 'And a churchgoer.'

'Ok,' Sam said. 'But his brother—'

'Forget about Stanley Knight, gentlemen. I'm more concerned with this murder.'

'Ah,' Sam said. 'So you think it was a murder.'

'Mr Davison,' Stead bellowed. 'Will you shut up about Stanley Knight.'

'They could be connected,' Phillip said.

'Connected?' Stead said.

'I spoke with Aaron last night. He knew Stanley Knight quite well. But when I asked him about the night Stanley Knight was found dead, he became cagey.'

'Cagey?' Headley said

'Yeah. He agreed to talk to me on his break, but then went home. He told the hotel he wasn't feeling well.'

Stead steepled his fingers together. 'I see. But he didn't give you any indication that—'

'Take it from me, Inspector,' Phillip said. 'He knew something.'

'This is pure conjecture,' Stead said.

'Randy,' Sam said.

'Randy?' Stead said.

'Randolph Edwards,' Phillip said. 'He owned a shop in a town near us. He was a good friend of Stanley Knight. He was murdered.'

Stead glanced at his junior. 'I see. I'm waiting on a telephone call from Cleveland Constabulary regarding you two. I'll inquire about this murder of …'

'Randolph Edwards,' Phillip said.

'I have a colleague who's a friend of mine. You might know him. Inspector—'

Sam groaned. 'Comby.'

'Yes. How did you know?'

'Just a guess,' Sam said.

Comby growled at Hardman as his sergeant lumbered into the passenger seat.

'Ready, are we?' Comby said. 'Only we do get paid for this.'

'Yeah. Sorry about that, guv. When you've got to go, you've got to go. I think that sausage and egg bun I had—'

'Spare me the details, Mick.'

Hardman blew out. 'God, I filled that pot.'

'Hardman!'

'Sorry, guv.' Hardman playfully nudged Comby. 'How did your date go by the way?'

Comby smiled. 'Very well, as it happens. We're going on another.'

'Well done, sir. What's she like in the flesh, then?'

'Very nice indeed. And erudite.'

'Erra what?' Hardman said.

'Well read, Mick. She's read all the classics.'

Hardman raised his eyebrows. 'Has she? There's a lot is there?'

'Hundreds. I've started reading Thomas Hardy's back catalogue.'

'And is it a good book, then?'

'What?'

'This back catalogue.'

Comby rolled his eyes. 'I meant his books in general. I'm onto The Mayor of Casterbridge.'

'Is it a thriller?'

'No, Mick. It isn't.'

'Did you …' Hardman winked. 'Manage to … you know?'

'No, Hardman, I didn't. Barbara is a lady. We haven't reached that level yet. I'm taking her to Darlington Hippodrome on Saturday.'

'Oh, yeah. What are you seeing?'

'The Woman in Black.'

Hardman shrugged. 'The woman in black. Who is she?'

'Forget about it, Mick.'

'If you do manage to seduce, Barbara—'

'Hardman, I'm not discussing my sex life with you.'

'Are you sure it still works?'

Comby frowned. 'What?'

'The old fella.'

'Of course it still bloody works, you cheeky bugger.'

'Ah,' Hardman said. 'Just because it works for you, doesn't mean it will work for someone else.'

'What!'

'My cousin Vinnie—'

'Like the movie?' Comby said, and rolled his eyes theatrically.

'His names Vincent, and he's my cousin. What can I say? Anyway, he thought everything was working fine down there. But sitting in an armchair with a box of Kleenex watching Xhamster is not the same as being in bed with a woman.'

'I've never even watched Xhamster,' Comby said.

'He hadn't had a partner for a few years, and you've gone a lot longer than that.'

'What happened?' Comby said.

'Use it or lose it is true, apparently. It took him a while, and my help, to rediscover his mojo.'

Comby raised his eyebrows. 'Your help?'

Hardman put his hand into his jacket pocket and pulled out a little plastic bag. 'Mick's little blue pills.'

'Are those?' Comby said.

'Yeah. They sure are. Super strength.'

'Where did you get those?'

Hardman tapped the side of his nose. 'You don't want to know.'

'Mick.' Comby gripped the steering wheel. 'I'm a copper. I don't want any of your dodgy drugs. Surely I can get it over the counter?'

Hardman laughed. 'Only if you take two of them.'

'Very droll,' Comby said.

'They're here if you want them, guv. Take it from me. One of these little beauties a couple of hours before kick-off and you can hang a hat on it.'

'I'll pass,' Comby said. 'Besides, I don't own a hat.' His phone vibrated in his pocket, and he quickly pulled it out. 'DI Comby.'

'Clive, it's Fred Stead.'

'Hi, Fred. How are you?'

'Very well. Listen, Clive, I need some information.'

'Fire away.'

'Have you come across two cousins who run a detective agency in Redcar, called—'

'Davison.'

'Yeah.'

Comby groaned. 'What have those two clowns been up to?'

'They found someone who'd been murdered.'

Comby sneered. 'Another?'

'Another?'

'Yeah. Those two are making a habit of finding dead people.'

'Who was—?'

'Randolph Edwards.'

'Yes, they told me about him. Although they neglected to mention that they found the body.'

'Yeah. Someone had knocked him out and strangled him in his shop.'

'Are you sure they didn't have anything to do with it?'

Comby groaned. 'Unfortunately not. I'd love to get something on those two. Especially Samuel Davison.'

'Tell me more.'

Stead made his way back into the interview room where Sam and Phillip remained opposite Headley.

'Well, well, well, gentlemen. I've just had a lovely conversation with our mutual friend, Inspector Clive Comby.'

Sam folded his arms again. 'Oh, yeah. How is Clive?'

'He's very well. He told me you two found Randolph Edwards' body. Something you neglected to tell me.'

'We had nothing to do with his murder,' Phillip said.

'Yeah, so I heard. But you do have a habit of being in the wrong place at the wrong time. Most people go through life without finding one body, but you two ...'

'Don't believe anything Comby tells you, Inspector,' Sam said. 'He's still mad about an article in the Gazette.'

'Yes, he did mention that. And something about four tyres?'

'That wasn't us,' Sam said. 'And that reporter embellished.'

'Quite. Ok, gentlemen. This is how it works. I'm letting you two go, and I'll need your addresses. You will have to come back at some time, and we'll get your statements typed up.'

'What about Stanley Knight?' Phillip said.

'You leave it to the professionals,' Stead said. He stood. 'I'll be in touch.'

Phillip and Sam exited the police station. 'They could have given us a lift back to our car,' Sam said.

'They might have if you hadn't kept winding them up.'

'They're just annoyed because we're better detectives than them.'

'Before you do anything, phone Emily.'

'Emily?' Sam said.

'Yeah. She's worried about you.'

'Ok, Dad.'

Sam took out his mobile and wandered away from Phillip.

'Hi,' Emily said.

'Hiya. We've just got out of the police station.'

'Kim said you and Phillip were helping with enquiries.'

Sam grumbled. 'Bloody coppers. Four hours I'll never get back. What a total waste of time.'

'Daisy's missing you ... and so am I.'

'We'll be back tomorrow.'

'Sam,' Emily said. 'We're good, aren't we?'

'Yeah. Why ...?'

Emily sniffed. 'If we weren't, you would tell me?'

'Em. I love you and Daisy. You know that. You mean the world to me.'

'Really?'

'Really. I'll be home tomorrow. We'll have a night out. Like the old days.'

'Not sure I could go on a bender. I'm still a little delicate from last night.'

'Yeah, me too.'

'Will you ring me tonight?'

'Yeah.'

'Promise?' Emily said.

'I promise.'

Phillip watched, and as Sam put his phone away, Phillip made his way over. 'Everything all right?'

'Fine. Emily's a bit teary.' He pulled his phone back out and read the message. '*Nice to see you the other night. Sorry we couldn't chat longer. We'll have to catch up soon. Lisa x*.'

'Everything ok?' Phillip said.

'Phillip,' Sam said. 'I'm fine.' He thrust the phone back into his pocket and marched off, closely followed by his cousin.

CHAPTER THIRTEEN

Albert looked across from his desk as Sam and Phillip entered. 'Morning,' Albert said, smiling at the other two.

'Morning,' Phillip said.

Sam slumped onto his chair and grunted. 'What have you been up to while we've been banged up in a police station?'

'Police station?' Albert said, glancing between Sam and Phillip.

'Long story,' Phillip said. 'Suffice to say ...' He glared at Sam. 'We would have spent a lot less time in there if laughing boy had kept his mouth shut.'

Sam made a face at Phillip and pushed his chair back on two legs. 'We haven't even been home yet.'

'Where's Kim?' Phillip said.

'She went out with Emily and Daisy. Any leads on the case?'

'We had one, but someone killed him,' Sam said.

Albert's eyes widened. 'Murder?'

'Yeah,' Phillip said. He wandered across to Albert's usually pristine desk and stared at the paperwork covering it. 'What's all this then?'

'I've been going through Mr Knight's paperwork,' Albert said. 'I was hoping it might yield some clues.'

'Anything?' Phillip said.

'Well.' Albert scooped a handful of papers and held them up. 'Mr Knight visited Stainton quite a lot. He went on a walk around the village and visited the church several times.'

'Church?' Sam said.

"Yes. He made quite a number of entries in his diary. I asked his brother if he had any friends or family in Stainton, but apparently, he doesn't.'

'I don't suppose he left a location for where the Lindisfarne Liturgy is buried, did he?' Phillip said.

Albert smiled. 'Unfortunately, not.'

'Stainton's an old place,' Sam said. 'It was mentioned in the Domesday book.'

'The Monk's Trod passed through the village as well,' Albert said.

'I didn't know that,' Sam said. 'The Monk's Trod, eh.'

Phillip glanced between the pair of them. 'What's the Monk's Trod?'

'It was a walkway that went from Durham to Whitby,' Sam said. 'It passed through several places on the way. Hartlepool, Middlesbrough etc.'

'Is Middlesbrough that old?' Phillip said.

'It was only a tiny settlement on the banks of the Tees,' Albert said. 'There was a handful of Benedictine Monks there and a few other dwellings.'

'This is all very interesting,' Sam said. 'But how does this help with the case?'

Albert narrowed his eyes and stared at Sam. 'There must be a reason why Mr Knight visited Stainton. I think he found some sort of clue to The Liturgy's location.'

Sam waved a dismissive hand. 'That's a huge leap.'

'There's something in his diary. One of the last entries.' Albert flicked through the pages. 'Meeting Bob Haldine in Alnwick. I have some exciting news to tell him. Our quest may be over.'

Sam sprung to his feet. 'Let me see.' He took the book from Albert and read the words. 'The next page is torn out.'

'I know,' Albert said. 'Someone must have taken it.'

'Why would he write all this stuff down?' Phillip said, and took the book from Sam.

'According to his brother,' Albert said. 'He was going to write a book on his quest and discovery of the cross. There's something else too.' Albert plucked the diary from Phillip. 'A week earlier, he had a break-in at his house.' Albert found the appropriate page. *'Break-in at the house while I was away. Nothing of value taken, but they were looking for something. My papers had been rifled through. Fortunately, I had my notebook with me. I will have to be extra vigilant from now on.'*

'Someone must have known he was close to finding the cross,' Phillip said. He looked at Sam. 'It's beginning to look like the cross does exist.'

Sam pondered. 'Yeah, it is.'

'Anything else, Albert?' Phillip said.

'No. I've scoured this lot twice,' he said, and waved his hands over the paperwork. 'Nothing.'

Sam returned to his desk and sat. 'We could visit Stainton but without a clue of where we are looking, we'd never find it.'

'So you two agree?' Albert said. 'It looks as if Stainton's the place?'

'Well, it looks that way,' Phillip said.

'You said he visited the church quite a few times,' Sam said.

'Yeah, but he also visited the memorial hall on a number of occasions. Plus, Dorman's Museum and Middlesbrough archives.'

Sam stood. 'We'll have to sleep on it. I'm going home.'

The door to the office opened and DI Comby and DS Hardman walked in. Sam groaned and dropped back onto his chair.

'Well, well, well,' Comby said. 'Not content with causing bother on Teesside, you're now giving Northumbria Constabulary a headache as well.'

'We're well,' Sam said. 'And how are you, Inspector?'

'I need a chat with you two. Regarding this case you're working on. You neglected …' Comby picked up a mug. 'I'd love a cuppa if you're making one.'

'I'll do it,' Phillip said.

'No, no,' Comby said. 'Maybe Mr Jackson would like to. I need a word with you and Samuel over there about your little sojourn.'

Albert stood. 'Of course. It's milk and three sugars if I remember right.'

'No sugar for me,' Comby said, as Albert left.

Sam leant back in his chair and put his feet on the desk. 'Trying to lose a little weight, Clive?'

'Bit of a health kick,' Comby said.

'This would have nothing to do with a certain lady.'

'My private life is going to remain private.'

'He's started going to the theatre,' Hardman said.

'Hardman!' Comby said.

'Theatre?' Phillip said. 'I didn't have you down as the theatre-going type.'

'The black woman wasn't it, guv?'

Comby rolled his eyes. 'Woman in black.'

'I've seen the movie,' Phillip said. 'Kim and I enjoyed it. Daniel Radcliffe was in it.'

'Him who played Harry Potter?' Hardman said.

'Yes,' Phillip said.

'Sans broomstick of course,' Sam said.

Hardman frowned. 'What?'

Comby banged his fist on the desk. 'Can we get to the matter in hand, gentlemen.'

'Certainly,' Sam said. 'Don't forget, though. If you need any tips regarding the fairer sex, I'm your man.'

'I've offered him some—'

'Hardman!' Comby said. 'You utter one more word, and I'll have you walking the beat by next week.'

Hardman pulled an imaginary zip across his mouth.

'You're working on a case regarding the death of a gentleman called, Stanley Knight?'

'Yeah,' Sam said.

'The copper in Alnwick is convinced it was an accident,' Phillip said. 'Stanley Knight's brother thinks it was murder.'

'My colleague in Alnwick has reopened the case. With the death of the young man you two found ... I—'

'Which young man?' Albert said, as he re-entered carrying a tray with tea and biscuits on it.

'Have you not told your chum?' Comby said.

'We hadn't got around to that,' Sam said.

Comby picked up the mug and took a sip. 'I must admit, Albert,' he said. 'You do make a wonderful cup of tea.'

'Lapsang,' Albert said.

Hardman took a mug and three biscuits. He glanced around the room as the others regarded him. 'I haven't had any dinner yet.'

Albert dished out the remaining teas and returned to his desk.

'Is Knight's death the only thing you're looking into?' Comby said.

Phillip looked at Sam and gestured for him to continue. 'Tell him,' Phillip said.

'Knight was looking for a cross,' Sam said.

'A cross?' Hardman said, spluttering biscuit fragments from his mouth.

'The Lindisfarne Liturgy,' Albert said.

'Like the island?' Comby said.

'Yeah,' Sam said, and explained in detail about The Liturgy and how the cross was essential to this.

'And where is this cross now?' Comby said.

'We don't know. We think Knight may have been murdered for it.'

'So, Knight had the cross?' Comby said.

'We don't think so,' Phillip said.

'And Aaron Morgan?' Comby said.

'He was friendly with Knight,' Phillip said. 'I had a feeling there was something he knew. That's why we went around to his flat. Unfortunately, someone beat us to it and stabbed him to death.'

'I see,' Comby said.

'Possibly the same person who killed Knight,' Sam said.

'Can I just say, gentlemen, you have been extremely helpful.'

'That's all we know,' Sam said.

'No inkling as to who could have killed Knight?' Comby said.

Phillip took a drink of his tea. 'Knight, along with Randolph Edwards and Professor Haldine were looking for the cross.'

'Randy's dead and Haldine was away at the time of Knights death,' Sam said. 'There was a note left at the hotel in Alnwick where Knight was staying, asking him to meet Haldine. We think Aaron left the note for him to lure Knight out. Aaron was working on the night, so he didn't kill Knight.'

'But he knew who did?' Comby said.

'Exactly,' Phillip said.

Comby drained his cup and stood. 'Right, Hardman. You and I need to begin our enquiries. Thanks again, gentlemen. If you come by any more information ...'

'You'll be the first we ring, Inspector,' Phillip said.

The two policemen headed out and Sam stood again.

'You didn't mention Stainton,' Albert said.

'No,' Phillip said. 'We don't want those two to know everything.'

'That's right,' Sam said. 'If this cross is still out there, it's bloody ours.'

Comby climbed into the car next to Hardman. 'They were helpful for a change,' Hardman said.

'Yeah,' Comby said, staring back towards the office. 'They were. Which means they haven't told us everything. Those three.' He drummed the dashboard. 'Are holding out on us.'

Stainton 1886 – The vicar was ushered inside and along a small corridor by the old woman. 'He's fading fast, vicar,' Mabel said.

'Did he say what he wanted to see me about?'

'No. He's rambling a little. I'm not even sure you'll get any sense from him.'

The vicar placed a hand on Mabel's arm. 'You go and have a rest,' he said. 'You look exhausted.'

'I've made some broth. I'll fetch you a bowl. Maybe I can get Walter to take a little. A man shouldn't go to his grave for want of food.' She took out a handkerchief, dabbed at her eyes and left the vicar to it. He pushed open the door and slid silently onto the chair next to the bed. 'Walter,' he said softly. 'It's the vicar.'

The old man opened his eyes. 'I knew you would come.'

The vicar placed a hand on Walter's arm. 'What is it you wanted?'

'It's my conscience, vicar. I can't leave this life without telling.'

'Telling what?'

'The cross, vicar. Cursed they said. I didn't know what to do.'

'What cross?'

'It was before you came to the village. Poor Jeremiah, and the other two.'

The vicar patted his arm. 'Don't trouble yourself with this now.'

'I buried it. Buried it on holy ground. It kept me safe all these years.'

The vicar furrowed his brow. 'I'm sure it did.'

'She didn't want him buried there, you see?'

'Who?' the vicar said.

'Mrs Jesmond. Wanted the poor little mite buried at her family home.'

'I see. And you dug the grave?'

'Not the one he was interred in, vicar. Not that one. The one here. Had to fill it back in though.'

'I see.'

The old man coughed. 'That's where I put it. It was a wicked thing to do, wasn't it?'

The vicar smiled. 'I'm sure God forgives you, Walter.'

'Best place for it.' Walter's eyes slowly dropped. 'Out of harm's way.'

The vicar turned towards the door as it opened and Mabel came in carrying a tray. 'How is he, Vicar?'

'I think he's going, Mabel.'

The old lady took hold of her brother's hand as the vicar said a prayer over the dying man. He let out a small moan and gave one final cough. The last lungful of air Walter would ever breathe, expelled into the stillness of the room.

CHAPTER FOURTEEN

FIVE MONTHS EARLIER - 'Hi, Bob,' Stanley Knight said, as he answered his phone.

'How are you?' Haldine said.

'Very well. Still searching relentlessly for this dammed cross.'

'No leads?'

Knight sighed. 'Not really. I've been over to Stainton a few times, but it was such a long time ago that the cross was sighted there.'

'To think it could be buried somewhere in that village,' Haldine said.

'I've put a notice on some of the Facebook history pages, asking if anyone has any historical links to Stainton. Nothing back yet.'

'Are you still coming to Alnwick next week?'

'Yes,' Knight said 'We'll meet for dinner.'

'I'll look forward to that. Has Randy come up with anything?'

Knight groaned. 'He isn't convinced the cross is out there. You know Randy, more interested in the fairer sex.'

'Quite,' Haldine said. 'You'd think at his age he'd be hanging up his spurs, but he shows no sign of doing so.'

'Well, keep me informed. I'll have to go. I'm meeting my brother.'

'George?' Haldine said.

'Yeah.'

'I thought things between you two were a bit strained?'

'They are,' Knight said. 'The call came from out of the blue. I thought about declining, but blood and water ...'

'Yes, I suppose.'

'I'll see you next week,' Knight said.

'I'm looking forward to that.'

PRESENT DAY - Sam and Phillip walked into the office together. Albert, writing in his diary, glanced up from his desk.

'Ah,' Albert said. 'I'm so glad you two are here. Professor Haldine is coming to see us this morning.'

'See us here?' Phillip said.

'Yes,' Albert said. 'His secretary phoned and arranged the appointment. Apparently, he's in Teesside for a couple of days.'

'What time?' Sam yawned.

'About half an hour.'

'I need coffee,' Sam said. 'I got about two hours of sleep last night.'

'Daisy?' Albert said.

'Yeah. She's teething. At one point we had Southgate in there too.'

'Oh, dear,' Phillip said.

Sam stopped at the door. 'Wait until you have a baby.'

'Who said we will?'

Sam smiled. 'We all fall for it.'

'I read,' Albert said. 'That it costs on average £230,000 to bring up a child in the UK.'

Sam groaned. 'Thanks, Albert. That really cheers me up.'

Kim showed a man through into the office. Phillip and Albert stood as they entered. Sam, his feet on his desk, slept.

'Sam,' Phillip shouted. 'Sam!'

Sam jumped to his feet. 'What?'

'Professor Haldine is here.'

Sam rubbed at his eyes and yawned. 'Sorry about that. I must have nodded off.'

'Sam has a teething baby, Professor,' Kim said. 'Can I get you a tea or coffee?'

'Tea would be lovely. Milk, no sugar, please.' He perched on the edge of the seat that Phillip indicated. 'A baby?' Haldine said. 'I don't have any children. You're a braver man than me, Sam. I was only reading the other day that it costs £230,000 to raise a child. An enormous undertaking.' Sam groaned.

The three cousins sat as Professor Haldine sipped on his drink. 'Stanley and I had been friends for a long time.'

'Didn't you work together?' Albert said.

'Yes, for a while. But we knew each other before that.'

'Stanley's brother, George, doesn't believe he was murdered,' Phillip said. 'He's asked us to investigate the case.'

Haldine tapped his chin. 'Mmm,' he said. 'George is unusual.'

'Unusual?' Sam said.

'Stanley and George had been estranged for a long time. They only got back together shortly before his death.'

Phillip glanced at Sam and then Albert. 'Really?' Phillip said.

'Yes. He had a meeting with him.'

'And?' Sam said.

Haldine tapped his chin again. 'Stanley was a little cagey. George was his brother, of course, but I got the impression there was something Stanley was unsure about.'

Phillip leant forward. 'Unsure?'

Haldine narrowed his eyes. 'You do know George has been in prison?'

The three cousins glanced between themselves. 'No,' Sam said.

'Yes. Some years ago, before I met Stanley. He was the black sheep of the family. They hadn't spoken for many years to my knowledge.'

'So why would he ask us to investigate his brother's death?' Phillip said.

'It all seems odd to me,' Haldine said.

'So, you've never met George?' Albert said.

'No.'

'Are you saying George could have had something to do with his brother's death?' Phillip said.

Haldine clasped his hands together. 'I wouldn't go that far, gentlemen. The police believe it was an accident.'

'And you?' Sam said.

'Let's just say I'm keeping an open mind.'

'Sam and I travelled to Alnwick last week,' Phillip said. 'Have you heard of someone called Aaron Morgan?'

Haldine shook his head. 'No.'

'Stanley knew Aaron from his visits to Alnwick,' Sam said. 'Aaron worked in the hotel he stayed at. He was murdered last week.'

Haldine raised his eyebrows. 'Murdered?'

'Yeah,' Phillip said.

'How awful.'

'The thing is, Professor,' Sam said. 'Phillip spoke to Aaron the night before he died. He thinks Aaron was holding something back.'

'Such as?'

Phillip shrugged. 'We don't know.'

'And we never will,' Haldine said.

Sam eyed the professor. 'Aaron was the one who gave Stanley a note on the night he died. It was supposedly from you. What do you know about that?'

Haldine blinked. 'Well, we know that wasn't the case. I was out of the country. We were going to meet for dinner the following day when I got back.'

'Would Stanley have known the note wasn't from you?' Albert said.

'I'm not sure. Clearly, he thought it was, otherwise he wouldn't have gone to the castle.'

'We know Aaron never left the hotel,' Phillip said. 'Other members of staff have confirmed this.'

'It seems strange to me,' Sam said. 'That the police didn't find it suspicious that a note was found on his body asking him to meet you urgently at the castle, and then he fell to his death.' Sam leant back in his chair. 'However, having met the copper in charge of the investigation, I understand why.'

'Not your cup of tea?' Haldine said.

'No,' Sam said. 'He seems a bit more interested now, after Aaron's death.'

'Really?' Haldine said.

'What about Randy?' Phillip said.

'Yes,' Haldine said. 'Terrible, really.' Haldine stared into his tea. 'Randy was a bit of a ladies' man—'

'We know,' Sam said. 'We met him.'

'It seems a little odd that he was killed too,' Albert said.

'It does,' Haldine said.

'You and Randy ...' Sam said. 'You were close?'

'Yes, we were. Stanley, Randy and I had known each other for some years. Mine and Randy's interest in the cross was not as fervent as Stanley's. We were.' He paused. 'More interested observers.'

'Can I ask?' Albert said. 'How you became interested in the cross?'

'Ah,' Haldine said. 'The fabled Lindisfarne Liturgy story had been kicking around for years. Stanley was enthusiastic about it. Verging at times on the obsessive. He had a way of drawing you in. Randy and I helped him out over the years.'

'Randy didn't seem the type,' Sam said.

'Randy was a little bit of an enigma. He was a coin collector, so, a story about a fabled cross piqued his interest. As I said, Stanley's enthusiasm was contagious,'

'Is it possible that Stanley found the cross?' Phillip said.

Haldine smiled. 'I think he would have told me if he had.'

'Do you think it ended up on Teesside?' Albert said.

Haldine emptied his cup. 'There is a good chance it did.'

'How—?' Sam said.

'There is documented evidence that a cross resembling The Liturgy reached Middlesbrough. And further evidence that someone living in Stainton had in their possession a cross. This is a fact.'

'What happened to it then?' Phillip said.

'Ah,' Haldine said. 'That's the problem. It has never been seen since.'

'You are sure it was The Liturgy?' Sam said.

Haldine smiled. 'It was inscribed with the words, *Ad honorem Cuthberti*.'

Sam's eyes widened. 'To honour Cuthbert.'

'Indeed. You speak Latin?'

Phillip and Albert rolled their eyes. 'Sam's a polyglot,' Albert said.

'Really,' Haldine said. 'Impressive.'

'He also has a first in History,' Albert said.

'My word, one should never judge a book by its cover.'

Sam waved a dismissive hand. 'Yeah, yeah, old news. It does look as though The Liturgy was there, however. But it doesn't help with finding it.'

'Quite.' Haldine rose. 'I'm afraid we have run out of time, gentlemen. I have another appointment.'

Phillip, Albert and Sam stood and shook hands with Haldine. 'Do you think it's still out there?' Albert said.

Haldine pondered for a moment. 'If The Liturgy had been found, it would have made the news. In academic circles, nothing is secret.'

'In Stainton?' Sam said.

'Perhaps,' Haldine said. 'Or maybe somewhere completely different.' Haldine nodded at the cousins and descended the stairs. He made his way outside and into his car. Pulling out his mobile, he dialled.

'I've just been to the detective agency you employed,' he said.

'And?' Knight said.

'They are not as stupid as you made out. One of them is very intelligent.'

'Well, they did find the Romanov Eagle.'

'Maybe it was a mistake involving them,' Haldine said. 'They asked me about Aaron.'

'You have an alibi. You were out of the country. Aaron was unreliable. Besides, I left something at his flat to muddy the waters.'

'This is getting messy, George.'

'Hold your nerve, Bob. Let them find The Liturgy for us. It's out there somewhere. Stanley knew its whereabouts.'

'Unfortunately, he's dead.'

'I told you, that was an accident.'

'Well,' Haldine said. 'Our best hopes—'

'If he found it, so can we. Let the Erimus Detective Agency do our dirty work for us. We'll keep a close watch, and be there when they do. Only we'll have the upper hand. A gun.'

Haldine rang off and dialled again. 'I've been to the agency. They're a lot cleverer than we thought. I've muddied the water a little with them over George Knight.'

'What are you thinking?'

Haldine rubbed his chin. 'I've told them about his prison sentence. I don't trust him. I think we should do this on our own. The bodies are mounting up.'

'They are.'

'We're not killers,' Haldine said. 'I can't believe the murders aren't linked.'

'George Knight has an alibi for Randy's killing.'

Haldine scoffed. 'Yeah. That's easy to arrange. We keep our cards close to our chest from now on.'

Sam leant back on his chair and put his feet on his desk. 'That was interesting.'

Phillip viewed him. 'Why?'

Sam pulled a face. 'Didn't like that bloke.'

Albert straightened the pens on his desk. 'I thought he was very nice.'

'Albert,' Sam said. 'You see good in everyone. Sometimes in life, you have to employ a little cynicism.'

Albert looked across at Phillip. 'What did you think, Phillip?'

'He seemed ok to me.'

Sam stared out of the window and into the street. 'Definitely something …' He narrowed his eyes. 'odd, about him.'

The door opened and Baggage raced in, closely followed by Kim. 'How did that go?' she said.

Phillip glanced at Sam. 'Ok. Didn't tell us anything we didn't already know. Although Sam thinks he's a bit odd.'

Baggage stared at Sam, cocking his head to one side. 'What's the matter, boy?' Sam said.

Kim smiled. 'Luggage is tormenting him.'

Phillip huffed. 'Well he should have behaved himself, shouldn't he?'

Sam ruffled his ears. 'Pay no attention, boy. That poodle was gagging for it.'

'Is Zeus ok?' Albert said.

Kim smiled. 'Zeus is great. He's so well behaved. He goes on his puppy pad in the same place at the same time, every day. However, those doggy biscuits you got him.' She laughed. 'He'll only eat the round ones. He doesn't touch the square ones.'

'How peculiar,' Albert said. 'I hadn't noticed that.'

Sam rolled his eyes, looked upwards and blew out hard. 'It's obviously the females that are the problem. Southgate's a little sod.'

'It was your decision to have a bitch,' Phillip said. 'You could have had Cobra. You did have the choice before Tommo and Deb.'

'Yeah,' Sam said. 'Living in a house with three females is a nightmare.'

Kim glanced at Phillip and raised her eyebrows.

Sam stood. 'How do you fancy a walk, boy?'

Baggage wagged his tail furiously and ran to fetch his lead. He returned seconds later and dropped it at Sam's feet.

'Where are you off to?' Phillip said.

'A walk on the beach to stretch my legs.' He clipped the lead on Baggage and headed off.

Kim moved closer to Phillip. 'Has Sam mentioned anything about, you know who?' she whispered.

'No,' Phillip said. 'He's never said a word.'

Sam unclipped Baggage, threw the stick for him, and watched as the dog bounded off along the sand. Sam's phone rang as Baggage returned. He viewed the name.

'Hi,' he said.

'How are you?' Lisa said.

'I'm good.'

'How was Alnwick?'

Sam picked up the stick and threw it again. 'Ok.'

'When are we going to meet and have that drink?'

'I'm not sure—'

'No agenda, Sam. Just two mates meeting innocently.'

Sam threw the stick again. 'We'll see. Later in the week, maybe?'

'That'll be good. You'll text?'

Sam glanced around. 'Yeah.' He hung up, dropped to his haunches, and took hold of the dog's face between his hands. 'What do I do, boy? What do I do?'

The dog barked and wagged his tail, looking at the stick. 'Yeah,' Sam said. 'I wish I was a dog.'

CHAPTER FIFTEEN

FIVE MONTHS EARLIER - Stanley Knight read through his emails. One jumped out at him.

'Dear Mr Knight. I was interested in reading your message on social media regarding Stainton. I no longer live in the area, but my family lived there for over a hundred years. I have a great deal of letters and other documents, along with photographs. I would be happy to show them to you. Kindest regards, Timothy Blackburn.

Knight picked up his mobile and telephoned.

'Hello,' a female voice said.

'Oh, hello there. I'm trying to get in touch with Timothy Blackburn.'

'Tim? I'll give him a shout. Can I ask who's calling?'

'Stanley Knight.'

'I won't be a minute,' she said.

'Hello, Timothy Blackburn.'

'Hi, there. It's Stanley Knight. You emailed me regarding Stainton.'

'Yes, of course,' Blackburn said. 'I'd forgotten about it.'

'In your email, you said you had past family members who lived in Stainton?'

'I did. My great-grandfather was the vicar at the church. His family lived there until the 1950s. I lived in Acklam. I used to visit the church regularly until my wife and I moved to Ruswarp.'

'Near Whitby?'

'Yes,' Blackburn said.

'I wonder, Timothy—?'

'Tim, please.'

'I wonder, Tim, if it would be possible to meet with you and have a look at what you have?'

'Yes, of course.'

'I'm free tomorrow,' Knight said. 'Would that be convenient?'

'Yes, I don't see a problem with that. I'll sort out what I have in readiness.'

'Superb. Shall we say one? Email me your address.'

'One is fine. I'll send it now.'

Knight rang off, opened his diary, and made a note.

Albert paused his reading of the diary and rubbed at his eyes. He yawned and stretched.

Phillip watched him. 'Anything?'

'Not really. I've read this several times, but there's not much of any help. There are a few names and times.'

'No entries saying, *the cross is hidden …*?' Sam said.

'I'm afraid not,' Albert said.

Sam stood. 'Let me have a look. A fresh pair of eyes.'

Albert handed him the diary and stood. 'I'm making a cup of tea. Any takers.'

'Yes, please,' Phillip said. Sam put his thumb up and returned to his desk. Adopting his usual position with his feet up and propped unsteadily on the back legs of his seat, he began flicking through the pages as Albert left, and Phillip resumed his paperwork.

Albert returned with three steaming cups and placed them down. 'Anything?' he said to Sam.

'Nah. Most of its just boring stuff.'

'We need a eureka moment,' Phillip said.

Sam picked up his mug and took a sip. 'Yeah.' Sam paused at one of the final entries. 'Ruswarp,' he said.

Phillip and Albert looked at him. 'Ruswarp?' Phillip said.

Sam smiled. 'Ruswarp Ruth.'

Phillip rolled his eyes. 'Not another Samuel Davison conquest story?'

'I'm surprised you remember them all,' Albert said. 'There have been so many.'

'Well,' Sam said, and stood, placing his hands behind his back. 'Some are more memorable than others. Ruswarp Ruth.' Sam grinned. 'Had a piercing.' He laughed. 'A brave lass, Ruth.'

Phillip briefly raised his head upwards and groaned loudly. 'I know I'm going to regret asking this, but where did this *Ruswarp Ruth* have the piercing?'

Sam grinned again. 'There,' he said, and glanced down.

Albert shook his head. 'Where?'

Phillip pointed to his groin. 'Her lady-bits, Albert.'

Albert's mouth dropped open. 'Why on earth would anyone allow someone to do that to you? It's, it's … mutilation.'

'Apparently,' Sam said. 'it heightens the pleasure.'

Albert gasped and brought his hand to his mouth. 'It can't be hygienic. It would be a breeding ground for germs.'

Sam scoffed. 'It's no wonder you're single.'

Albert folded his arms together. 'Well if I did have a girlfriend, I wouldn't want one with ...'

'Anyway,' Sam said. 'You wouldn't know that when you first meet them, would you?'

'I would imagine,' Phillip said. 'It isn't mentioned in the first conversation.'

'She also had nipple-rings,' Sam said.

'Good God,' Albert said. 'Wouldn't that cause problems at airport security?'

'Maybe she didn't travel abroad,' Phillip said.

Sam stood and took a large gulp of tea. 'She had numerous other piercings as well. It was touch and go whether I bedded her or weighed her in for scrap.'

Phillip snorted. 'Good one, Sam.'

Albert shook his head. 'I don't like the sound of this Ruth one bit.'

'Don't worry, Albert,' Sam said. 'I can't imagine you being her type.'

'So,' Phillip said. 'This Ruth, was she a one-night stand or something a little more lasting?'

'I saw her for a couple of weeks,' Sam said. 'She worked at The Railway Arms in Ruswarp. She did the best Shepherd's pie I've ever tasted.' He licked his lips as the memory arrived.

'Is that a euphemism?' Phillip said.

Sam winked. 'Maybe we should have a run out there.'

Phillip sneered. 'What? To meet one of your old conquests? I think we have more important things to do.'

'No.' Sam picked up the diary. 'To speak to Timothy Blackburn.'

'Who?' Albert said.

'Stanley Knight visited him. It's in Knight's diary.'

Phillip made his way over to Sam's desk and took the book from him. 'Timothy Blackburn, 13.00,' he said aloud. 'It could be anyone?'

Sam sat. 'This is what detectives do. They follow leads.'

'Is this an excuse to go to a pub and have Shepherd's pie?' Phillip said. 'Because if it is, I won't be happy.'

'We haven't much else to go on, have we?' Sam said. 'It's probably a waste of time, but what happens if it isn't? If we don't go, we'll never know. There could be a clue waiting for us.'

'And Ruswarp Ruth?' Albert said.

'It's over ten years,' Sam said. 'She probably left ages ago.'

'Yeah.' Phillip folded his arms. 'Why not.'

'Albert?' Sam said. 'Do you fancy a run-out?'

'Along the moors road?'

'That's the usual way you get to Ruswarp,' Sam said.

'I'm not sure. There was a crash last week on that road. Do you know how many deaths a year there are on the Whitby road?'

Sam rolled his eyes. 'Funnily enough, I don't have that information. You look after the shop, and Phillip and I will do the legwork.'

FIVE MONTHS EARLIER - Stanley Knight made his way along the path of the pretty cottage and stopped at the door. He briefly surveyed the beautiful garden before knocking.

The door swung open, and an elderly man stood there. 'Tim?' Knight said.

'You must be Stanley,' Blackburn said. 'Come in.'

Knight followed Blackburn through into the dining room and over to a large table covered in photos and papers. 'Have a seat, I'll fix us some drinks. Tea ok?'

'Tea's fine,' Knight said. 'Milk, no sugar.'

Blackburn nodded towards the table. 'I've got everything I can find there.'

Blackburn returned with the beverages and took a seat at the table opposite Knight. 'As you can see,' he said. 'There is quite a bit of stuff.'

'Yes. I hope you don't mind, but I've had a quick look.'

'Not at all,' Blackburn said. 'That's what you're here for.'

'You said your great-grandad was a vicar in Stainton?'

'Yes,' Blackburn said. He picked a snap from the pile. 'This is Rufus Blackburn.'

Knight took the photo from him and studied the old man in the picture.

'That's him in his later years,' Blackburn said. 'After he'd retired. I think he's about eighty in that photo. He was ninety-five when he died.'

'That's a great age for someone back then,' Knight said. 'Ninety-five. I hope I live to that age.'

'What is it you are doing? If you don't mind me asking?'

'I'm planning a history of Stainton. It's a bit of a diversion, really. I was a history teacher, and I was very interested in a Celtic cross which was held on Lindisfarne. There's a possibility … well, evidence really, that it somehow got across to the mainland and may have ended up in Stainton.'

'How wonderful. It must be ancient?' Blackburn said.

'Over a thousand years.'

'So, your interest in Stainton around the turn of the twentieth century concerns the cross?'

'Yes and no,' Knight said. 'In searching for clues, I fell in love with the village. It dates back a very long time. There's been a church in Stainton for many years.'

Blackburn smiled. 'It's been a long time since I visited. I must go back some time.'

'There's an ancient route through the village called the Monk's Trod. It stretched from Durham to Whitby.'

'My word. Is that how the cross got there?'

'We think so,' Knight said. 'A couple of friends of mine are assisting me. I would love to locate it before I shuffle off.'

'What would you do with it? I suspect it's worth a great deal of money?'

'The money's not important to me. At my age, I'm quite comfortable. I would give it to The British Museum.'

Blackburn smiled. 'That sounds wonderful.'

'Well,' Knight said, gazing across the paperwork. 'Let's see if there's anything we can glean from this lot.'

PRESENT TIME - Sam and Phillip exited the car, and Sam made his way across the road towards the pub.

Phillip hurried after him. 'I thought we were looking for this bloke?'

Sam stopped. 'We are. Pubs are the best place to find stuff out.'

'And get Shepherd's pie?'

'Exactly,' Sam said.

The pair made their way inside and to the bar. A woman popped her head up from below the counter. Her ears full of piercings. Her arms covered in tattoos. 'Now then, guys,' she said, in a thick Yorkshire accent.

Sam smiled. 'Ruth.'

She studied him for a moment and then smiled herself. 'Fresh-cream-Sammy.'

Phillip gazed at Sam. 'What?'

Sam waved a dismissive hand. 'Don't ask.'

Ruth leant across the bar and grabbed the sides of Sam's face, planting a kiss on his lips.

'I didn't think you'd still be working here,' Sam said.

'I'm the landlady, now,' she said. 'All this ...' She waved her arms around. 'Is mine.'

'Tell me,' Sam said, and leant across the bar. 'Do you still make that gorgeous Shepherd's pie?'

She winked. 'Fresh today. Do you and your pal, here.' She smiled at Phillip. 'Want to give it a try.'

'I've heard a lot about it,' Phillip said. 'So I better had.'

'Have a seat, you two. I'll rustle some up.' She stood straight and pinched Sam's cheeks. 'You're still as gorgeous as ever.'

Sam looked her up and down. 'You've added a few more piercings, I see. And some tats.'

'There are lots more hidden.' She laughed. 'Sammy hasn't been telling all our little secrets, has he?'

Phillip fixed Sam with a stare and grinned. 'No. *Sammy* hasn't. He's been very discreet.'

'Two pints?' she said.

'Yeah,' Sam said. 'Phillip?'

'I'll have what *Sammy's* having.'

Phillip and Sam picked up a knife and fork each as Ruth placed two plates in front of them. 'Tell me what you think, boys?' she said.

Phillip surveyed the mountain of food. 'We will,' he said.

'No husband?' Sam said.

Ruth winked. 'Why? Were you fancying a wander down memory lane?'

'Afraid not, Ruth. I've got a girlfriend and a toddler at home.'

'Lovely. Have you any pictures?'

Sam showed a picture on his mobile to Ruth. She smiled. 'She's bloody gorgeous. My Stacy's twenty-eight next week. She's a solicitor.'

'That's great,' Sam said.

'As for men,' she grinned. 'You very nearly ruined me for other men. After you, Sammy, it took me years to get over it. I finally did, though. I met a lovely man called Gary. We've been married for eight years.'

'Where is he, then?'

'He drives forty-footers. At this time ...' She glanced at the clock. 'He'll be nearing Barcelona. Anyway, you two crack-on with your meal, and we'll have another chat before you leave.'

'Yeah,' Sam said. 'There's something we need to ask you.'

'Oh,' she said. 'Sounds very intriguing.'

Sam watched as she made her way behind the bar. He picked up the little gravy boat and poured some of the thick liquid over his pie. 'Now then, Phillip,' he said. 'Prepare to be blown away.'

Phillip placed the knife onto his empty plate and patted his stomach. 'You were right,' Phillip said. 'That was amazing.'

'Told you,' Sam said.

Ruth came over to their tables and smiled. 'Did you enjoy it, lads?'

'We certainly did,' Phillip said.

She collected the empty plates. 'What about a nice sweet?'

Phillip shook his head. 'I couldn't eat another thing.'

'I'll pass too, Ruth. I'm stuffed.'

'What was that thing you wanted to ask me?' she said.

'Do you know a Timothy Blackburn?' Sam said.

'Tim, yeah.' She nodded at a grey-haired man in the corner, reading a paper. 'That's him there. One of my best customers.'

The cousins headed across to the man. He looked up as they reached him.

'Timothy Blackburn?' Phillip said.

'Yes.'

'Sorry to interrupt you, Mr Blackburn. My name's Phillip Davison, and this is my cousin, Sam Davison.' Phillip pulled a card from his pocket and handed it to Blackburn. 'We run a detective agency on Teesside.'

Blackburn studied the card and smiled. 'The Romanov Eagle.'

'That's right,' Sam said.

'I remember it from the news. Did you ever discover its whereabouts?'

'I'm afraid not,' Phillip said.

Blackburn folded his paper and placed it aside. 'How can I help you, gentlemen?'

Sam and Phillip sat. 'We're investigating the death of someone we think you knew,' Phillip said. 'Stanley Knight.'

Blackburn's mouth dropped open. 'Yes. I didn't know he'd died though. How awful.'

'He fell to his death,' Sam said. 'His brother thinks it's suspicious. The police think it was an accident.'

'Right,' he said. 'Suspicious you say?'

'We're open-minded,' Phillip said.

'I'm not sure how I can help, though.'

'He had an entry in his diary that he spoke with you,' Phillip said.

'Yes. He came here to visit me. That was the only time I ever met him.'

'So you didn't know him well?' Sam said.

'No. Stanley put a notice on social media, asking for information about Stainton. Specifically, before the turn of the twentieth century.'

Sam glanced at Phillip. 'Can we ask—?' Sam said.

'I had some family who lived there dating back nearly a hundred years. Stanley was particularly interested in my great-grandfather, Rufus Blackburn. Rufus was the vicar at the church for quite a number of years.'

'Did he tell you why he was interested in Stainton?' Phillip said.

'Yes. He was quite candid about it. He was searching for a Celtic cross which may have made its way over to the mainland from Lindisfarne. He had evidence, he said, that it was sighted in Stainton around the time Rufus lived there.'

Sam glanced at Phillip again. 'Did he find anything?' Sam said.

'I don't know. Rufus kept diaries, and I loaned them to Stanley. He posted them back to me a few days later.'

'You still have them?' Phillip said.

'I do.'

'I don't suppose ...?' Sam said.

Blackburn smiled. 'I'd be delighted to lend them to you.'

'That's very kind, Mr Blackburn,' Phillip said.

'Did Stanley Knight talk with you about the diaries?' Sam said. 'I mean ... What he found?'

'Not really in-depth. We had a brief conversation about them. He said he found them interesting, and there were some avenues he could explore. He said he'd let me know how he got on. I think he was going to Alnwick.'

'That's where he died,' Phillip said.

Blackburn slowly shook his head. 'Very sad. We'll finish these drinks and then pop over the road.'

Phillip slammed the boot shut and climbed into the driver's seat next to Sam. The pair gave a brief wave to Blackburn, who stood on the doorstep of his house, as they headed off.

'I didn't realise there would be so many,' Sam said.

'Me neither,' Phillip said. 'The thing is, Knight only had the diaries for a few days before he returned them to Blackburn.'

'Yeah,' Sam said. 'He must have known what he was looking for.'

'The problem is ...' Phillip glanced across at Sam. 'We don't.'

'We'll enlist Albert. The three of us should be able to discover what Knight found.'

The car following Phillip and Sam pulled into a layby allowing the cousins to disappear into the distance. George Knight pulled out his mobile and dialled.

'George?' Haldine said.

'I followed them to Ruswarp near Whitby.'

'And?'

'They went into the pub and stayed there for about an hour. They came out with another man and went into a house across the road, opposite the pub. They were in there for about thirty minutes.'

Haldine grunted. 'It must be a lead. I remember Stanley telling me he was travelling to somewhere near Whitby. I wonder what was said?'

'I don't know, but they left with a box.'

'A box?'

'Yeah,' Knight said. 'I'm going to drop into the detective agency and see what they say. I'll probably tell them to end the investigation into Stanley's death.'

'Right. Why?'

'We've piqued their interest. There's no point in shelling out good money when we don't have to.'

'True enough. Keep me informed,' Haldine said.

Haldine hung up and dialled.

'Hi, Bob,' a voice said.

'Knight followed the cousins to Ruswarp. They met with a man there. Have a run up there and see what you can find out. Be discreet.'

'What about George Knight?'

Haldine rubbed his chin. 'Like I said, I'm not sure we can trust him anymore. I still think he killed Stanley.'

'What about Randy? Have you managed to find anything on that?'

'I'm sure Knight has someone helping him,' Haldine said. 'This person may have killed Randy.' Haldine rubbed his chin again. 'The police think his murder was a jealous husband or boyfriend of a lover.'

'Plausible, I suppose.'

'Follow Knight,' Haldine said. 'See if he contacts anyone. We need to know what we're up against.'

'The detective agency?'

'I think they must be getting close,' Haldine said. 'We have to be ready to pounce. I have a buyer for the cross. The money he's offering is enormous.'

'We could do with an extra pair of hands. Someone with fewer scruples than us.'

'Rudy?' Haldine said.

'Yeah, that's what I was thinking.'

'I'm reluctant to involve anyone else,' Haldine said. 'But I think you're right. Just give him the bare bones of the case. Imply that Knight killed his brother. That way he'll be more loyal.'

CHAPTER SIXTEEN

Albert put down the phone. 'That was George Knight,' he said. 'He doesn't want us to continue with the case.'

'Right,' Phillip said. 'That's a turn-up.'

Sam leant back in his chair. 'We still think his brother was murdered.'

'But without Mr Knight funding the investigation …' Albert said.

'I think,' Sam said. 'The search for the cross is more important. We'll just have to fund it ourselves.'

'It could become expensive,' Phillip said.

Sam leant back on his chair. 'But if we find it …'

The door opened, and Kim entered with Baggage and Luggage. 'Will you look after Baggage?' she said to Phillip. 'I'm going out with Luggage. She's just annoying him all the time.'

Phillip smiled. 'It's his own fault. Where you off?'

'I'm meeting Emily. We're taking Luggage and Southgate to a dog café.' She looked at Albert. 'Would you like me to take Zeus too?'

'Yes please,' he said.

'Deb's meeting us there with Cobra, and another woman I used to work with. She's got a Cockapoo.'

Albert tilted his head. 'A Cockapoo?'

'It's a cross between a Cocker Spaniel and a Poodle,' Kim said.

'Baggage's puppies have a Poodle mother, don't they?' Albert said.

'Yeah,' Kim said. 'But Baggage is a mixed breed.'

'What breed would you call the puppies then?' Albert said.

'A Bagapoo?' Phillip said.

Sam laughod. 'Good ono Phillip.'

'Phillip,' Kim said, bending lower to ruffle Baggage's ears. 'You can't call him that.'

'Well,' Phillip said. 'When I've taken him for a walk, that's what I normally come back with.'

'Anyway,' Kim said. 'I'll leave you boys, to it. You're obviously run off your feet.' She closed the door behind her.

Sam placed his feet on the desk and rocked back on two legs. 'Maybe we should phone Comby, and see if he has any information on Aaron's murder.'

'Not a bad idea,' Phillip said. 'But maybe I should ring. You always wind him up.'

The door opened again, and Tommo came in. 'Greetings and salutations,' he said. Baggage padded over and sat next to him, wagging his tail rapidly.

Tommo ruffled his ears. 'How are you, fella?'

'What are you doing here?' Sam said.

'Cheers, Sam. I've come around to see my buddies, and I get slagged off. I've just seen Kim leaving.'

'Yeah,' Phillip said. 'She's meeting the girls.'

'Anyway.' Tommo smiled. 'How are my favourite chums?'

Sam groaned. 'What do you need doing?'

'Don't I get a cuppa?' Tommo said.

Albert stood. 'I'll make one for you.'

'Lovely,' he said. 'Plenty of biscuits too.'

'Who's looking after the pub?' Phillip said.

'Gene and Marie. But it's always quiet on a Wednesday. What case are you working on?'

'The Lindisfarne Liturgy,' Phillip said.

Tommo nodded. 'The Celtic cross. Any developments?'

'We've got a load of diaries to look through,' Phillip said. 'It's all a bit tedious.'

'That's detective work,' Tommo said. 'Sam?'

Sam threw his hands up. 'Here it comes.'

'Can you spare an hour or two?'

Albert returned with a mug of tea and a plate of biscuits.

'Cheers, Albert,' Tommo said.

'I am rather busy,' Sam said.

'I'm sure Phillip and Albert can spare you?'

Phillip nodded. 'Yeah. Fine by me.'

'What are you doing?' Albert said.

'My aunt needs a couple of things shifted from her café. I said I'd do it for her.'

'Will we get lunch?' Sam said.

'You know Annie. She has a soft spot for you. I'm sure she'll you'll get fed.'

Sam stood. 'What are we waiting for?'

Tommo held up his mug. 'Let me finish this first, and then we'll get going. She didn't specify a time.'

Phillip placed his pen on his desk as the door opened and Comby and Hardman strode in.

'Good morning, gentlemen,' Comby said.

Albert put down the diary he was reading, allowing his gaze to follow the officers.

'No Sam?' Comby said.

'He had to go somewhere,' Phillip said.

'Shame ...' Comby said, as he picked up one of the vicar's diaries and flicked through it's pages. 'I do love that sparkling wit of his.'

'Is there anything, in particular, we can help you with?' Phillip said.

'Just a social visit,' Comby said. He wandered over to Albert. 'I was hoping Albert, here, would make me one of his delicious brews.'

'Of course,' Albert said. He stood and made his way towards the door.

'And some biscuits,' Hardman said.

Comby rolled his eyes and tossed the diary back onto the desk. 'My colleague in Alnwick. You remember him?'

'I do,' Phillip said, folding his hands behind his head. 'Lovely chap.'

'Mmm,' Comby said.

Baggage got up from his beanbag and stretched. The three men watched as he yawned, performed a pirouette and lay back down.

'I spoke with him today. Apparently, having done a thorough search of Aaron Morgan's flat, they discovered some class A drugs along with a quantity of cash. It appears he was a dealer.'

'Right. And?' Phillip said.

'Inspector Steadman believes that his death is drug-related.'

Albert returned with a tray. He handed a mug to Hardman and one to Comby.

'What do you think, Inspector?' Phillip said.

'I have to agree with him. He went through the investigation concerning Stanley Knight's death, and it appears it was an accident.'

'And yet?' Phillip said.

Comby sipped at the steaming liquid. 'Have you gentlemen come by any other information?'

'Stanley Knight's brother has asked us to end the investigation,' Albert said.

Comby placed his mug down. 'Did he say why?'

'The expense and ...' Albert said.

'And?' Comby said.

'He doesn't think it's worth pursuing?'

'Well, there you go,' Comby said. 'It appears everyone is in agreement.'

'Have you any more of these chocolate Hobnobs?' Hardman said.

'No,' Albert said. 'They were the last.'

'Shame. They're really nice.'

Comby shook his head at his junior. 'Have you two any thoughts? Any further information you want to share?'

Phillip smiled. 'No.'

Comby pushed one of the diaries a little. 'What's with all the books?'

Albert coughed 'Another case, Inspector.'

'How's your love life going?' Phillip said.

'He's going to an opera,' Hardman said, through his biscuit-filled mouth.

'An opera?' Phillip said.

Comby glared at him. 'Yes. In the West End.'

'I didn't know you were a man of culture.'

Comby took a large swig of his tea. 'This really is delicious. Lapsang?'

'Darjeeling,' Albert said. 'What are you seeing?'

'Les Miserables.'

'Oh, I'd love to see that.'

Comby looked towards Phillip. 'So that will be the end of the Stanley Knight case?'

Phillip shrugged. 'Looks that way. We're not going to carry on investigating if no one's paying us.'

'And the cross?'

Phillip smiled. 'Probably just a wild goose chase. A one thousand-year-old cross in Middlesbrough? It's a bit far-fetched.'

'I suppose so.' Comby drained his cup. 'Well, gentlemen. Our business is concluded.'

'Looks that way,' Phillip said.

'Come on Hardman,' Comby said. 'We have work to do.'

Phillip waited for them to leave, then pointed at Albert. 'Quick thinking, Albert.'

He grinned. 'I'm getting the hang of this lying.'

Hardman slumped into the car next to Comby, put his hand inside his coat pocket, and pulled out a Penguin. Comby rolled his eyes. 'Don't you ever stop eating?'

'I'm hungry.'

'Hungry. You're like a one man, eating machine.' Comby stared upwards at the office window.

'What are you thinking, guv?'

'I'm thinking those two weren't being totally honest. Nice tea, though.'

Hardman pulled another biscuit from his pocket. 'Yeah.'

Sam nudged Tommo as they drove along Guisborough High Street. 'Pull over at the betting shop,' he said.

'What for?'

'I want to put a bet on.' He smiled at Tommo. 'I've got a tip.'

'Not from Timmy the Tipster?'

'Yeah. He said it's a cert.'

Tommo sneered. 'A cert. They always lose.'

'Not always. I've had a few winners.'

'One, Sam. You've had one in ten years.'

Sam sighed. 'I know. But I know about the horse now. If I don't back it, and it wins ...'

'A fool and his money.'

'It's 12-1 in the paper.'

Tommo shook his head. ' How much are you putting on?'

'Twenty quid.'

Tommo blew out hard. 'Twenty quid!'

Sam opened the door. 'Nothing ventured, nothing gained.'

As Sam put a foot outside, Tommo took hold of his arm. 'Are you backing it each-way?'

Sam scoffed. 'Each-way! Straight on the nose, mate. Each-way is for wimps.'

Tommo pushed his hand into his pocket and pulled out a £20. 'Put this on it.'

Sam grinned. 'I thought—'

'I know, I know, but if it wins I couldn't put up with all your gloating.'

Sam plucked the note from his hand and headed into the shop. He returned moments later and got into the car next to Tommo. 'Forty quid on Slippery Sid,' he said.

'That's what it's called?' Tommo said.

'Yeah. I thought you'd like that name. With your passion for snakes.'

Tommo nodded. 'I suppose it does have a ring to it.'

'I got 14-1 as well.'

'Well,' Tommo said, starting the engine. 'Let's hope it wins.' He put the car into gear, and Sam grabbed hold of his arm. Tommo spun around and gawped at him. 'What's the matter with you?'

'I've just seen a ghost,' Sam said.

Tommo followed Sam's stare. 'Isn't that Randolph Edwards' shop?' Tommo said. 'It looks as if it's under new management.' Sam continued to stare across the road, and Tommo nudged him. 'Sam,' Tommo said. 'Are you listening to me?'

Sam rubbed his eyes. 'I've just seen Randy going inside.'

Tommo scoffed. 'Randy's dead. You and Phillip found him.'

'I know. But I swear I've just seen him.'

Tommo laughed. 'He'd been hit over the head with a shoehorn and strangled.'

'I know,' Sam said. 'I was bloody there.'

'So how can you have seen Randy?' Tommo waved his arms about. 'Maybe he's come back from the dead. Maybe it was Zombie Randy you saw?'

Sam opened the passenger door. 'I'm going over.'

Tommo laughed again. 'Have you got your pump-action in case he tries to bite you?' Sam got out and walked across the road as Tommo huffed, clambered out of the vehicle, and followed him. Sam reached the top of the stairs and peeped around the corner into the shop. A large black man stood with his back to Sam.

'Randy?' Sam said. 'Is that you?'

The man turned around and peered over the top of his spectacles. 'Can I help you?'

'You're not Randy?' Sam said, as a panting Tommo joined him.

The man guffawed. 'Well, it's not unheard of, even this early in the day.' His voice a deep, treacle-coated baritone.

Sam and Tommo stepped inside the shop. 'I thought …' Sam said.

The man nodded. 'I'm Rudolph, Randolph's brother. Come inside, gentlemen. You can tell me what you think of these.' He moved over to a rack of suits. 'From my Italian contacts.'

'Have you taken over?' Tommo said.

'Yes. Randy owed me quite a bit of money, and when he died, I got the shop. Randy wasn't very good with money.'

'Sorry about Randy, Rudolph,' Sam said. 'I really liked him.'

'Call me Rudy,' he said. He pondered for a moment. 'It was a dangerous game he was playing. I counted over two-hundred women in his little … well not so little, black book.'

Sam sucked in air. 'Two-hundred! Jesus. That's like a full-time job.' Sam stroked the arm of one of the suits. 'I like this.'

Rudy guffawed. 'They're top quality. Randy …' He clasped his hands together. 'One shouldn't speak ill of the dead, but he had let the shop slide a little. There were also rumours.'

'Rumours?' Tommo said.

'That he was dealing in stolen goods. The police confiscated some of his merchandise. Everything in here is legit, though.'

'Are you going to be running the shop now?' Sam said.

'I already have two. One in Richmond, and the other in Harrogate. This shop will become the next to join the ranks of *Rudy's Dudes*.'

Sam took out a card. 'Sorry, I haven't introduced us. I'm Sam Davison, and this is my friend, Howard Thomson. Tommo to his mates.'

Rudy studied the card. 'Erimus Detective Agency? How did you get to know Randy?'

'We're working on a case,' Sam said. 'And we wanted to ask some questions.'

'Oh, yes?'

'A friend of Randy's, Stanley Knight, died. His brother asked us to investigate his death.'

Rudy regarded Tommo. 'And you two are part of this detective—?'

'No,' Tommo said. 'I'm a publican. I own The Sidewinder and Black Mamba, in Middlesbrough. I'm Sam's mate.' He pulled out a card and handed it to Rudy.

'I see. Well, gentlemen,' Rudy said. 'If ever you need suiting and booting, I'm your man.'

'We'll bear that in mind,' Tommo said.

'I bought a suit for my daughter's christening,' Sam said. 'It's unlikely I'll need another. It's the first I've ever owned.'

'Well, if you change your mind. One can't have too many suits.'

The pair shook hands with Rudy and moved towards the door. Sam paused. 'Do you think I would suit a cravat?' he said.

Phillip stretched and yawned. 'This is tedious. The vicar's diaries are full of boring, day to day stuff. Sermons, christenings, funerals etc.'

'I suppose that was a vicar's life back then,' Albert said.

'Bloody Sam's getting off lightly.' Albert stared at the diary. 'I said Sam's getting—' Phillip said.

'I may have found something.' Albert stood and moved across to Phillip's desk. 'Look.'

Phillip read the entry. *"Had to administer the last rites to Walter. The poor man was in distress. Asking for Gods forgiveness and rambling about some past misdemeanour involving a cross."* The next line had been crossed out. *"I will have to arrange his funeral for next week. He had been a great servant to our church. He deserves a fitting send-off."*

Phillip looked up. 'A cross?'

Albert smiled. 'Do you think...?'

'This line,' Phillip said. 'It's been crossed out.'

Albert flicked the pages over. 'There are several crossings out throughout the diaries.'

'I know,' Phillip said. 'But look.' He held it for Albert to view and then continued. 'This pencil looks new.'

Albert scrutinised it. 'Yes, I think you're right.'

Phillip grinned as Baggage padded over to the pair and sniffed at the book. 'What do you think, boy?' Phillip said.

Baggage cocked his head to one side as if deep in thought, and then barked.

Tommo and Sam entered the café and made their way over to the counter. A young woman looked at the pair of them and smiled. 'Can I help you guys?'

'Is Annie in?' Tommo said.

'Yes, she out the back. Can I get her for you?'

'Thanks,' Tommo said. 'Tell Annie, her favourite nephew is here.'

The woman disappeared and returned moments later. 'She won't be long, she's dealing with a delivery.'

'The smell is making me hungry,' Sam said.

'Yeah,' Tommo said. 'I could go a sandwich or something.'

Annie entered from out the back. 'Boys.' She raced around the counter and planted a kiss on Tommo's cheek. She pushed Tommo towards the young woman. 'Look at this handsome brute, Kerry. Isn't he gorgeous?'

Kerry pulled her gaze away from Sam. 'Yeah.'

'And, Sam,' Annie said. 'Look at you. That Emily's a lucky girl.' She moved forward and hugged him tightly, kissing his cheek. 'Have you two eaten?'

'I'm famished, Annie,' Sam said. 'I only grabbed a slice of toast this morning.'

Annie tutted. 'We can't have a handsome chap like you wasting away. Kerry, plate up some steak pie dinners for these two. And don't skimp on the portions.' She caught sight of the bag in Sam's hand. 'I thought Randy Ted's was closed?'

'His brother has taken over. Rud—' Sam said.

She beamed. 'Rudolph.'

'You know him?' Tommo said.

'Oh, yes,' Annie said, her words heavily coated with intrigue.

'Tell me more,' Sam said.

'He was in our choir until he moved away.' She gazed into the past. 'What a baritone. Like Paul Robeson.'

'Who?' Sam said.

'A black actor and singer,' Tommo said. 'He sang Old Man River.' Tommo lowered his voice in an effort to impersonate.

'Ah,' Sam said.

Annie clasped her hands together and smiled. 'What a voice. What a man.'

Sam glanced at Tommo. 'You didn't …?' Sam said.

'Two hours of Rudy belting out his stuff, and any female chorister worth her salt would succumb.'

'He's just like his brother, then?' Sam said.

'Randy couldn't hold a candle to him.' She gazed, longingly again.

'Why did he move away?' Sam said.

'I'm not sure. There were all sorts of rumours flying about.' She waved them closer. 'I heard he went to prison.'

'What for?' Sam said.

'I've no idea. Rudy always was a bit of a ducker and diver. Anyway, lads. You two come this way. Kerry, we'll be fifteen minutes.'

Sam and Tommo followed Annie. 'What did you buy?' she said, glancing at the bag in Sam's hand.

Tommo rolled his eyes as Sam pulled the item from the carrier and held it up. 'A cravat,' he said.

'Oh, how rakish,' she said.

CHAPTER SEVENTEEN

FIVE MONTHS EARLIER - Stanley Knight pulled on his jacket and snatched up his mobile as it rang.

'Hi, Randy.'

'You left a message?'

'Yeah. I may have found something.'

'Regarding the cross?' Randy said.

'Yes. I've photocopied a page from a diary. I'll explain about it later. Can you keep it safe?'

'Yeah. Are you still in Alnwick?'

'I am. Bob Haldine is supposed to be meeting me here later.'

'Why don't you give Bob the page?'

Knight rubbed his chin. 'Bob and I had a bit of a heated row. If we find The Liturgy, he doesn't want it to go to a museum.'

'But we agreed.'

'I know. He implied we could sell it on … Well, let's just say, under the radar of the academic world.'

Randy grunted. 'Stanley,' he said. 'My business could do with an injection of cash, I won't lie to you. But this find, if we do find it, is of such importance it needs to be in a museum. Not some millionaire collector's mansion.'

'That's what I said. We'll still do ok out of this, won't we?. We'll get money when it's valued under treasure trove. It's not as if we'll be left with nothing.'

'Stanley,' Randy said. 'You're talking as if you've found the cross.'

'I'm not certain. I may be totally wrong here. But I'm optimistic.'

'And Bob?'

'I'm just going to keep him in the dark for the moment.'

'This piece of paper,' Randy said. 'When are you going to send it?'

'I'll post it tonight.'

Sam and Tommo entered the office. Phillip jumped to his feet and beamed at the pair. 'We have a clue,' he said.

Sam pulled off his jacket and tossed it onto the coat rack. 'Clue?'

Phillip opened the diary and showed it to Sam. Sam slowly read the words and smiled. 'The Liturgy.'

Tommo slumped onto a chair. 'Is anyone going to enlighten me?' Baggage padded across and nudged his leg. 'Hello, boy,' he said, and ruffled the dog's ears.

'You know we're looking for a cross?' Albert said.

'The Lindisfarne thingy?' Tommo said.

'Liturgy,' Sam said.

'Well,' Phillip said. 'We may have found a clue to its whereabouts.'

Tommo balled his fists. 'A caper?'

'Here we go,' Sam said. 'You don't even work for this agency.'

Tommo stood, walked over to Sam and placed a large hand on his shoulder. 'I'm your protection. We went through this with The Eagle. No offence boys, but if this turns nasty ...'

'I think Tommo should be in on this,' Albert said.

'But this is different.' Sam said. 'No one knows about The Liturgy.'

Tommo guffawed. 'You fool. Someone will be looking for it. Something as precious as this …' He narrowed his eyes. 'There always is.'

Phillip looked at Sam. 'It wouldn't harm.'

Sam threw his hands upwards and blew out. 'Ok. But I don't want you taking over like you did last time.'

Tommo grabbed Sam in a bear-hug. 'Would I?'

Sam wrestled out of his grip. 'Get off me you big galute.'

Baggage barked and wagged his tail. 'The famous five ride again,' Tommo said. 'Now.' He clasped his hands together. 'Where do we start?' Sam rolled his eyes.

Sam rubbed his eyes. 'We still don't know what it says under the crossed out section.'

'Yeah,' Phillip said. 'It was obviously important otherwise Stanley Knight wouldn't have crossed it out.'

'How do you know it was Stanley Knight who crossed it out?' Tommo said.

'It must have been,' Albert said. 'Who else could it be?'

Sam's phone beeped indicating he'd received a message. He read it and stood. 'Trouble is …' He stared out of the window. 'Knight has taken it to his grave,'

'That's it,' Tommo said, jumping to his feet. 'Grave.'

The three cousins looked at him. 'The guy Walter. It says he served the church well. The vicar said he would organise his funeral.'

Phillip grinned. 'He must be buried in Stainton churchyard.'

'Stands to reason,' Tommo said.

'Wait a minute,' Sam said. 'You're not suggesting it's buried in his grave, are you?'

'It could be,' Tommo said.

Sam flopped back down. 'Well, that's that then. We can't go digging up graves.'

Tommo smiled. 'Why not?'

Sam's jaw dropped open. 'Why not? Let me think.' He narrowed his eyes as if deep in thought, and threw out his arms. 'Because it's illegal. Against the law. Frowned upon.'

'Sam's right,' Phillip said.

'I don't think it's in his grave,' Albert said.

The other three focused on him. 'He was dying. How could he have got the cross into his grave? The vicar obviously didn't know any more about the cross. Look ...' He took hold of the diary and flicked through the pages. 'Walter's funeral went well. A huge turnout for a well-liked man and a great servant to our church.'

'Why don't we go to Stainton and find his grave?' Phillip said. 'There might be a clue there.' He looked to Tommo, who nodded and then to Sam, who shrugged. 'You three go,' Sam said. 'I have an errand to do.'

'I have a session with my therapist,' Albert said.

'Cancel it,' Phillip said.

'I can't.' Albert lowered his eyes. 'Charles doesn't like it when I cancel.'

'Well.' Tommo patted Phillip on the back. 'Just you and me blue-eyes,' he said, in his best Humphrey Bogart voice.

Sam made his way along the road and into the bar. He glanced about and spotting Lisa in a booth, headed over to her. She smiled as he slipped into the opposite seat.

'I got you a drink,' she said. 'Beer. I take it you still drink beer?'

Sam nodded. 'Cheers.' He picked up the pint and downed a third.

'Thirsty?'

He smiled. 'Bit of a hectic day.'

'So.' She leant forward. 'You've had big changes since I moved away?'

'Yeah. I'm a dad. Can you believe that?'

Lisa smiled at him. 'Yeah. I think you're probably a great dad.'

'I'm getting there. What about you? No kiddies to talk of?'

'No children,' she said. 'I've just come out of a long relationship. I thought he was the one, turns out he wasn't. He was seeing someone behind my back.'

'Sorry about that.'

She studied her perfectly manicured hands. 'It was my best friend.' She stared into his eyes. 'It made me think about what I did to you with Ewen all those years ago. What goes around, comes around.'

Sam lowered his eyes. 'A lot of water has passed under the bridge since then. We were just kids.'

'I suppose. We were ... just daft kids then.'

Sam glanced around the room. Lisa placed a hand on his. 'I picked this booth especially. Discretion and all that. I understand.'

Sam puffed out his cheeks. 'It is a bit close to home.'

Lisa grinned 'I'm thinking of moving back to Middlesbrough. My smoggy blood runs deep.'

'Yeah? You've cut the ties completely in ...?'

'Cardiff. I think so. Mam's ailing a bit as well. I can't leave it all to our Billie.'

Sam glanced about again. 'Look, Lisa. You know how I felt about you all those years ago. It ...' He pondered, looking for the right words. 'I took it hard. But Emily and me are ...'

'You and Emily are good?'

'Yeah. And there's Daisy of course.' Sam smiled as he thought of his daughter.

Lisa reclined in her seat and grinned. 'I'm not trying to break you up, Sam. That's not my intention at all. Just two mates having a friendly drink.'

'Sorry ... I didn't mean to imply—'

'Sam,' Lisa said, gently touching his hands. 'Don't worry.'

'It's just ...' Sam glanced to his left as the door swung open, and a couple came in. 'It's just, I feel that I'm cheating on Emily just by being here.'

Lisa pushed her hands through her hair. 'You're being silly. It's not like we're in bed together having sex.' She licked her lips and smiled. 'Is it?'

'No one knows I'm here. That in itself is wrong. I'm sure you understand. With what happened to you in Cardiff.'

'Yeah. You didn't have to come, Sam. I would have understood.'

'No, I didn't.'

Lisa locked eyes with him. 'Yet you came.'

Sam dropped his head. 'I did. I felt I owed you that much.'

'I never forgot about you. You were always here.' She placed a hand on her chest. 'Maybe if I hadn't been so stupid all those years ago, you and I would have had a baby or two.'

Sam forced an unconvincing smile. 'I should go.'

'Will I see you again?' she said, as Sam stood.

'I don't know.'

'You've still got some beer left.'

Sam swirled the beer in the half-empty glass. 'You finish it for me. I'm not really in the mood for drinking.'

Lisa stood. 'See you later.' She put her arms around him and hugged tightly. Sam resisted the urge to pull away and hugged her back. His face pushed into her auburn tresses, which smelled wonderful, briefly transporting him back to their youth. He slowly pulled away and headed for the door. Sam stopped at the threshold and looked back at Lisa. She smiled and waved, and then he was gone.

Lisa picked up Sam's glass and took a swig. She smirked, leant back in her seat and pushed a hand through her hair.

Ewen, who was sat in the corner behind a large column, watched the unaware Lisa rise from her chair and leave. He picked up his drink and slowly shook his head.

Albert waited quietly in his therapist's room. He pondered the cross and where it could be. He would have another look through the diaries when he got back to the office. His thoughts interrupted abruptly as the door opened and Charles strode in.

'Morning, Albert,' Charles said, as he entered. 'You were miles away.'

'I was just thinking about a case we're working on.'

'Oh, yes? Anything interesting?' Charles said, dropping into the seat opposite Albert.

Albert was about to speak but stopped himself. He mustn't discuss the agency's cases with anyone from outside the agency. Sam had been explicit on this.

'A cross,' he said.

'Cross. Sounds interesting. Anyway,' Charle said. 'We have lots to discuss this morning.' He leant back in the chair and smiled.

Albert stared out of the window into the distance. 'The vicar said Walter had been a great servant to the church.'

Charles frowned. 'Who's Walter?'

'Someone who died over a hundred years ago.'

Charles laughed. 'It's the living we must worry about. Not the dead.' He scoffed. 'A century ago?'

Albert clenched his jaw. 'The vicar said he had been a great servant to the church.'

'Who?'

'Walter. He read him his last rites.'

Charles looked skywards. 'Is this Walter important? Is he going to help you with your biscuit issues? Because I'm pretty sure he isn't.'

'Well no,' Albert said. He lowered his head and picked at his thumbnail. 'But …'

Charles scowled. 'Maybe he was a curate or something.'

'Yes,' Albert said. 'A curate. But how—?'

Charles rolled his eyes. 'You have his name?'

'The curate?'

'No, this Walter.'

Albert's brow furrowed. 'Only his Christian name. Why?'

'If you can find out his last name, and where he's buried ... Bob's your uncle.'

Albert's eyes narrowed. 'I can. But ...?'

'The census, man. The census.'

'Of course.' Albert beamed. 'It would have his occupation on the census.'

'Eureka!' Charles said, and gazed wistfully into the distance. 'Kevin and I once trawled through the census. When he was looking into his family tree.'

'Really?'

'Oh, yes. We spent weeks looking through documents. One of Kevin's antecedents was hanged for murder. Can you believe that? He hit a man with a shovel. Some argument over a sow.'

'I'm not sure you should call a woman—'

'Not a woman, you fool. The animal. Female pig. Porcine.'

'Ah,' Albert said.

'It made the local newspaper. He became quite the cause celeb. *Butcher kills a local man with a shovel.* The headlines said.'

'So he was a butcher then?' Albert said.

'Yes. Kevin and I laughed.' Charles stared stern-faced at Albert. 'Not about the murder. About the sow.'

'How did you come by all this information?'

'Middlesbrough archive is a great place to start. It has copies of local papers. You can get a census online. And then there are those sites.' He stroked his chin. 'Ancestry something. It's quite enjoyable once you start.'

Albert nodded. 'Yes, we could—'

'Anyway, Albert. More pressing matters.' He pulled a card from his pocket. 'Look what I have?'

Albert's eyes widened, and he leant forward. 'What is it?'

Charles beamed. 'It's a postcard from Kevin. All the way from the Seychelles.' Albert rolled his eyes, sagged back in his chair and inwardly screamed.

'Do you mind if we have something to eat first?' Phillip said to Tommo. 'I'm starving.'

'I've eaten,' he said. 'But I'll have a pint.'

Phillip parked outside the pub. 'The church is over there.' He nodded out of the window. 'I'll have some grub, and then we'll have a look.'

The pair got out and headed inside the restaurant. 'A tall blonde haired woman moved across to them. 'Hi,' she said. 'Table for two?'

'Yes please,' Phillip said. 'Although I'm the only one eating.'

She looked at Tommo. 'Not hungry? Our parmos are lovely.'

'Just a pint of beer,' he said. 'Maybe another day.'

The pair moved across to a table. 'I'll have a pint of beer too.'

'Hobgoblin?' she said. 'We have ruby and gold.'

Tommo smiled. 'The ruby.'

'The same,' Phillip said.

Phillip pushed aside his empty plate. 'That hotshot was fantastic.'

'I could see that by the way you devoured it,' Tommo said, and drained his beer. 'Not a bad pint that.'

'I'll pay the bill,' Phillip said

Tommo stood and waited at the door as Phillip settled up and then made his way over to him.

'What's the plan?' Phillip said.

'We separate, and each check one half of the graveyard.'

'We're looking for the Christian name, Walter,' Phillip said. 'Let's hope it wasn't the most popular man's name back then.'

They made there way over to the churchyard and inside. 'Shall we have a wager?' Tommo said.

'A wager?'

'Yeah. I had a bet with Sam, and it's got me in the mood.' He rubbed his hands together.

'What were you thinking?'

Tommo smiled. 'The first one to find a Walter wins a tenner.'

'You're on.' Phillip handed Tommo a small pad and a pen. 'Good luck.'

Tommo whooped. 'I've got one.'

Phillip let out a loud groan and wandered over to him. Tommo grinned and nodded towards the gravestone. The name on it read, *Walter Farrow.*

'1930,' Phillip said. 'It's too late. We're looking for a Walter from the nineteenth century.'

'You didn't say that when we had a bet,' Tommo said.

'I thought it was understood.'

'No,' Tommo said. 'It wasn't.'

Phillip pushed his hand into his pocket and pulled out a note. 'Here.'

Tommo beamed. 'Quite a productive day. Don't worry,' he said. 'I'll buy you a couple of pints back at The Sidewinder.'

'You beat me to it,' Phillip said.

'What?'

Phillip moved towards a gravestone nearby. 'I was just about to shout.'

Tommo glanced at the headstone. He pushed the note back inside Phillip's pocket. 'Call it a draw,' he said. He dropped onto his knees and read. 'Walter Littleby, died 1886.'

'What do you think?' Phillip said.

'Fits with your date.'

'Have you many more to check?'

Tommo took stock of the graveyard. 'No, not many.'

'Finish off yours, and I've only got a handful to check myself. Just in case there's another Walter.'

CHAPTER EIGHTEEN

Albert stared into the box. 'What do you think?' Charles said.

'Fishing flies?' Albert said.

Charles clasped his hands together. 'Not just any fishing flies. Kevin made these.'

'They're very delicate.'

'They are, Albert. Had you seen Kevin, you would have been very impressed indeed.' Charles glanced into the distance. 'How those strong, manly hands could have produced a thing of beauty like this.' He plucked one of the flies from the box and held it aloft. 'This is a dry fly. It's used for trout fishing. I can still see Kevin labouring over it. Those delicate fingers.' He let out a huge sigh.

'Did you only go fishing for trout?' Albert said.

'No. We fished for salmon, bream, carp and more. You name it, we fished for it.'

'Did you fish from a bridge?'

Charles laughed. 'No. You have to get into the water, Albert. A pair of waders. The water lapping around your nether regions. There really is nothing in life more liberating.'

'I'm not sure I'd like that. Couldn't the water be contaminated.'

Charles laughed again. 'This is Britain, Albert. Not Chernobyl.' He narrowed his eyes. 'This is your problem. You worry about things you shouldn't. Worry is your enemy. It chips away at your self-confidence.'

'I can't help it.'

Charles patted him on the arm. 'Don't worry, we'll get to the bottom of it. Cognitive behavioural therapy.'

'I've heard of that,' Albert said.

'That's what we'll use, Albert. The cutting edge of psychological science.'

Albert smiled. 'Will it help?'

'It will. The success rate is high.'

'When can we start?'

'Soon, Albert. Soon. First, I want you to have a look at this.' He picked up a magazine and opened its pages.

'What is it?' Albert said.

'It's a new keep-net I'm thinking of buying. What do you think?'

Albert rolled his eyes and inwardly screamed again.

Tommo and Phillip, holding their steaming mugs, looked across as Albert trudged into the office. He took off his coat, tossed it over the coat stand, and slumped onto his seat. He placed his head on the desk and groaned.

Tommo glanced at Phillip before standing and making his way over to Albert. 'What's up, buddy?'

Albert sighed. 'I don't think I'm ever going to get better.'

Tommo placed a hand on his shoulder. 'Of course you are. We all have bad days.'

'Didn't your therapy go well?' Phillip said.

'Not really.'

'Can't you try another therapist?' Tommo said.

'I've built a relationship with Charles. It would be so hard to begin anew with someone else.'

'What does this *Charles* think?' Tommo said. 'About your condition?'

'He said we're going to try cognitive behavioural therapy.'

'There you go,' Phillip said. 'I've heard good things about that.'

Albert straightened. 'Have either of you two ever fished?'

Phillip shook his head, and Tommo grinned. 'I have. Me and the old fella would go most weekends.' Tommo crossed his arms. 'When he died, I stopped. I couldn't bring myself to go alone.'

'It's all so depressing,' Albert said. 'The Boro are struggling as well.'

'Would you like to go fishing?' Tommo said.

Albert smiled. 'With you?'

'Yes, with me.'

'But I thought you said ...'

'That was years ago,' Tommo said. 'I'm over that now. I kept a lot of my old gear. You can have Dad's. It's packed away somewhere.'

'When?'

Tommo rubbed his beard. 'This weekend. We'll put together a packed lunch. We'll take the dogs. How does that sound?'

'Brilliant.'

Sam strode in and threw his coat onto the hat stand. 'Morning,' he said. He pulled a wad of notes from his back pocket and handed it to Tommo.

Tommo grinned. 'It won?'

'Yep. You won £180 plus your stake. That's £200.'

'Brilliant,' Tommo said. 'The pints are on me.'

Sam dropped onto his seat and put his feet on the desk. 'How are we getting on with the case?'

'We have a name,' Phillip said. 'Walter Littleby.'

Sam smiled. 'What do we know about him?'

'Not a lot,' Tommo said. 'Except, he died in 1895 and is buried in Stainton graveyard.'

'We could check the census,' Albert said. 'See if we can find any more information about him.'

'Good idea,' Phillip said.

'The cross,' Sam said. 'We're not saying it's buried in his grave, are we?'

Phillip threw open his arms. 'I don't know.'

'Because if it is, we can't go digging it up.' Sam said. 'I'm sure I read somewhere that you need a court order to disinter a corpse.'

'It can't be in the grave,' Albert said. He opened the diary. 'Like I said, the vicar said Walter mentioned something about the cross being buried earlier.'

Phillip stood. 'That's right. He did.'

'So, we're back to square one?' Sam said.

'Looks that way,' Tommo said.

'The vicar said he had served the church well,' Phillip said. 'Maybe he was a curate or something. The census might help with that.'

'It still doesn't help with its location,' Sam said.

Tommo stood. 'I have to go. Pubs don't run themselves. Pop in later, boys. And I'll buy you a couple of pints.' He looked at Albert. 'I'll have a look for that fishing gear.' Albert beamed.

'What we need to find out,' Phillip said. 'Is, what Stanley Knight crossed out of the vicar's diary. He must have kept a note of it.'

'Not necessarily,' Sam said. 'He may have committed it to memory.'

'Maybe we should ask George Knight?' Albert said. 'There's nothing in the paperwork he gave us. Maybe he has some other bits and pieces.'

Phillip bit his bottom lip. 'It's worth a try.'

George Knight sipped on his brandy as he looked out of the window of his house, and into the garden.

His mobile sounded. 'Hello, George Knight,' he said.

'Mr Knight,' Albert said. 'It's Albert Jackson from The Erimus Detective Agency.'

'Albert,' he said. 'What can I do for you?'

'I know you asked us to end the investigation into your brother's death, but ...'

'But ...?' Knight said.

'We've come by some information.'

'Albert.' Knight sighed. 'The police are certain it was an accident. I can't go on funding what appears to be a fruitless exercise.'

'It doesn't really concern his death. It's more to do with the Lindisfarne Liturgy.'

Knight sat. 'Oh, yes?'

'We've come by some information.'

'Regarding its whereabouts?' Knight said.

'Possibly. We've tracked it down to Stainton. We were wondering if you have any more of Stanley's papers?'

Knight sipped his drink. 'Such as?'

'An entry from a diary.'

'Diary? Stanley's, you mean?'

Albert coughed. 'No. A nineteenth-century vicar.'

Knight laughed. 'A what?'

'Stanley borrowed some diaries from a man in Ruswarp. This gentleman was related to the vicar, and in one of his diaries, he mentioned a man called Walter.'

'Oh, yes. And this Walter?'

'We're not sure who he was, but the vicar wrote that Walter mentioned a cross in his diary.'

'Albert,' Knight said. 'It could be any cross.'

'We realise that. The cross would be priceless. If we found it, there would be enough money for all of us.'

'I've given you all the paperwork I have,' Knight said. 'What is it exactly you're searching for?'

'There is a sentence in one of the diaries which is crossed out. We think Stanley may have crossed it out so no one else would know what it said.'

'I see. I'm sorry Albert, I don't think I have anything resembling that. I will have a good look, though.'

'Thank you, Mr Knight.'

Knight rang off and stared at the phone. He quickly dialled and waited.

'It's George. The people at the detective agency have come up with something. We need to meet to discuss our next move. We'll keep Haldine in the dark. If the cross is out there, it's ours.'

Sam held his hands out as Albert rang off. 'Well?' Sam said. 'What did he say?'

'He's going to look.'

Phillip looked at Sam. 'What do you think?' Phillip said.

Sam parked himself on the edge of his desk. 'I don't trust him.'

'You don't trust anyone,' Phillip said.

Sam furrowed his brow. 'There's something about George Knight that doesn't ring true.'

'He seems perfectly trustworthy to me,' Albert said.

Sam rolled his eyes. 'Everyone seems trustworthy to you, Albert. That's one of your biggest weaknesses. You trust everyone. Whereas me.' He pointed to his chest. 'Trusts no one.' He glanced between Albert and Phillip and laughed. 'I'm not a 100% sure about you two either.'

'Yeah, yeah, very funny,' Phillip said.

'Isn't there any way we can decipher what it says under the pencil?' Albert said.

Sam walked back to his desk and slumped onto the seat. 'This is not CSI, Albert. We haven't got some special gadget to do it for us.'

Phillip scratched his head. 'We need to find a bit more about Walter Littleby. See if that gives us any help.'

'I can check the censuses online,' Albert said.

'Yeah,' Phillip said. 'You do that. We may have reached a dead-end, though.'

Sam put his feet on his desk. 'To think, the cross could be buried in that graveyard. A few feet from where you and Tommo stood.'

'Yeah.' Phillip returned to his desk. 'So near …'

FIVE MONTHS EARLIER - Stanley Knight headed downstairs and into the reception of the hotel. He waved across at Aaron behind the reception desk.

'Mr Knight,' Aaron said.

Knight stopped and made his way over to the desk. 'Yes, Aaron.'

'There's a message for you.'

'From whom?'

Aaron pulled a piece of paper out of the pigeon-hole behind him. 'From Randolph Edwards.'

Knight took the paper from him and read the message. *'Meet me at the castle. Urgent we talk. 20.30.'*

Knight looked at Aaron. 'Who took the message?'

'One of the others,' he said. 'Not sure who. I think they've gone off shift.'

'Thanks.' Knight made his way into the restaurant as Aaron watched him. Aaron took out his mobile and moved into the office behind the reception desk.

'It's Aaron. I gave him the message.'

'Good,' the voice on the other end said.

Knight headed off in his car and away from the hotel. Within minutes he reached the castle and made his way around to the meeting place. The wind, accompanied by increasingly heavy rain, swirled around him.

Pulling the collar of his overcoat tight around his neck, he pushed his hat firmly on his head and moved towards a sheltered area. He waited as a figure loomed into view and made his way towards him. Knight strained to decipher who it was, the shape and form unlike Randolph Edwards. The man reached Stanley Knight and unzipped his parka hood. Stanley Knight's brother, George, stood there.

'Hello, Stan,' George Knight said.

'What are you doing here?'

'We need a chat.'

Stanley Knight turned and moved off, his brother quickly closed the gap and took hold of him by the arm. 'Just wait.'

'I have nothing to say,' Stanley Knight said. 'I told you what will happen to the cross.'

'You've found it?'

'Let's just say I have a good idea where it is.'

'I have a buyer,' George Knight said. 'He's willing to go as high as ten-million.'

Stanley Knight scoffed. 'You're mad if you think I would sell such a historically important relic to the highest bidder.'

'Bob Haldine wants to sell it too. And Randy could be persuaded.'

Stanley Knight sneered. 'You've never changed. You were always a wrong-un. The cross goes to the museum.'

George Knight grabbed his brother by the lapels. 'Listen, old-man. If you think we'll allow you—'

Stanley Knight shrugged him off. 'I'm phoning the police.'

George Knight pushed a hand into his pocket and pulled out a cosh. Quickly catching Stanley, he struck him across the head. Stanley fell forward onto his knees and then onto his side. He let out a groan as George squatted and rifled through his pockets. The older man regained his senses and struck out, catching George on the side of the head. George fell backwards, allowing Stanley enough time to scramble to his feet. He set off along the track as George, who was upright by now, reached him. Stanley turned and flailed at George but the younger man, anticipating what he would do, barrelled into Stanley who stumbled and slipped on the wet grass. Unable to keep his feet as they gave way beneath him, he let out a scream and tumbled down the steep embankment coming to a rest at the bottom with a loud thud. George bolted for cover. Panting, he watched as a woman walking a dog came into view. She moved towards the edge of the bank and gasped. George continued to watch as the woman took out her phone. He slipped further into the darkness and disappeared quickly into the stormy night.

CHAPTER NINETEEN

Sam woke early and went for a walk with Southgate. He headed into some open ground and stood, as the dog played, watching the sun rise in the sky. He pulled out his phone and read the message from Lisa.

'Loved seeing you. Great to have a catch-up. We need to do it again, Lisa x.'

Sam closed his phone and pushed it back into his pocket as Southgate bounded over to him and dropped her ball at his feet. Sam picked it up and tossed it across the field, the dog raced off to retrieve it.

Sam hung the dog lead over the back of a kitchen chair. Emily, who had her back to him making a cup of tea, turned to face him. 'You were awake early. Couldn't you sleep?'

Sam grunted. 'No. Crap night's sleep.'

Emily wandered closer and handed him a mug. 'Do you want some breakfast?'

He perched on his elbow at the table, cradling the drink. 'Not yet. I'm not really hungry.'

Emily sat opposite and took hold of his hand. 'Is everything ok, Sam? You seem a bit ...'

Sam forced a smile, resisting the urge to pull his hand away. 'Yeah, fine. Like I said, crap night's sleep.'

Emily lowered her head. 'What are you up to today?'

Sam sipped at his tea. 'Still working on the case.'

'I thought your client had halted it? I thought—?'

'We've got a lead on the cross.'

Emily smiled. 'The one from Lindisfarne?'

'Yeah. What are you ...?'

'I'm meeting Deb for a coffee. Kim's meeting us later.'

Sam nodded and gazed out of the window. Emily followed his gaze outside. 'Could you pick up a few things for Daisy while you're out?' she said. Sam continued to stare blankly. 'Penny for them?' she said, and lightly tapped his hand.

Sam faced her. 'Sorry, what did you say? I was miles away.'

'I've made a list of things for you to get.' She picked up a pad and tore off a piece of paper.

Sam plucked the paper from her hand, folded it, and thrust it into his pocket. 'Do you want me to feed Daisy?' he said.

'She's still asleep. I wouldn't wake her. You know how crabby she can be when you do.'

Sam stood. 'I'm going for a shower.'

Emily grasped his arm. 'Are you sure everything's ok? You would tell me?'

Sam forced a smile. 'Of course. Everything's good. You know what I'm like when I haven't had my sleep. Daisy must take after me.'

Emily nodded. 'Ok. If you're sure.'

Sam's eyes narrowed as he glanced at the pad. He picked it up from the table and stared at the blank piece of paper.

'What's up?' Emily said.

Sam kissed her on the cheek. 'I've got an idea.'

Sam bounded into the kitchen of the detective agency. Phillip and Kim extricated themselves from their embrace and sheepishly looked at Sam.

'Get a room, you two,' Sam said, as a huge grin filled his face.

'You're in a good mood,' Phillip said.

'I may have cracked this case.'

'Really?' Phillip said. 'Pray tell.'

Sam tapped the kettle. 'A cuppa first. Where's the OCD kid?'

'In the office,' Kim said.

'Good,' Sam said. 'Milk no sugar.' With that, he spun on his heels and marched into the office. 'Morning Albert,' he said.

'Morning, Sam. You're in—'

'I know. A good mood. Anyone would think I'm a grumpy get.'

'You can be ... Occasionally.'

'Well, Albert, my old friend. This morning finds me in fine fettle. I may have an answer to our problem.'

'What problem?'

Sam sat at his desk and adopted his usual position with his feet up. 'Wait for Phillip, and then we'll begin.'

Phillip entered with Kim. He placed a mug on Albert's desk and one on Sam's before sitting at his own. Kim perched on the edge of his desk, her eyes on Sam.

Sam held up the pad he had brought with him from home. 'Exhibit one.'

'A notepad?' Phillip said.

'Emily wrote a shopping list for me on this notepad this morning.'

'I'm meeting Emily later,' Kim said.

'I'm sure that's very interesting,' Sam said. 'But this is more important.'

Phillip drew in a breath. 'This is going to get very tedious, very quickly.'

Sam ignored him. 'When I ripped off the list, guess what I found underneath?'

'Another list?' Albert said.

'Good guess, Albi, but wrong.'

'A blank sheet of paper,' Phillip said. 'That's the normal thing you find in a notebook. You write on one sheet, tear it off and voila ... a blank sheet.' Kim giggled.

Sam stood. 'Putting aside your sarcasm, Phillip. You are right. However, on that blank sheet of paper was an indentation of the list Emily had written for me.'

'Ah, I see,' Phillip said. 'So now you have two lists.'

'The diary,' Albert said.

'Exactly,' Sam said, and pointed a finger at his cousin. 'The diary.'

'So,' Phillip said. 'What you are saying in a long and convoluted way, is, whatever was scrubbed out by Stanley Knight may be visible on the page underneath?'

'What was scrubbed out?' Kim said.

Phillip tapped her hand. 'I'll explain later.'

'It's better than that,' Sam said. 'I've been on the internet this morning.'

'Oh, aye,' Phillip said. 'On one of those dodgy sites.' Kim and Albert giggled.

'Good one, Phillip. This site explained how to decipher writing that had been scribbled out.'

Albert picked up the diary, found the appropriate page, and carried it over to Sam's desk. 'What do we do?'

Sam pulled a small torch from his pocket and switched it on. 'Here is exhibit two. I purchased it this morning on my way in to work. Who knew you could still buy torches so readily? Batteries included.'

'What's wrong with using your mobile, like normal people in the twenty-first century?'

'Watch and learn, Phillip,' Sam held up a hand. 'We shine the light at an oblique angle.' He waved Albert closer. 'Hold the torch here.' Albert did as he was asked. 'Now ...' Sam pulled out his phone and took a picture.

Phillip and Kim joined them. 'Can you see how the writing underneath is visible?' Sam said.

Phillip strained his eyes. 'It's still not decipherable.'

Sam held his mobile aloft. 'We put the photo on a computer and enlarge it. Hopefully, if we're lucky, we will be able to see what it says.' Sam quickly loaded the image onto his laptop.

Phillip glanced to his left at Sam. 'Sam, you're a genius.'

'What does it say?' Albert said, straining to read the writing.

'He said he buried it in an unused grave on the Jesmond's plot,' Sam said. 'Or that's what it looks like to me.'

Phillip nodded. 'I agree.'

'So, it could still be there?' Albert said.

'It could,' Sam said.

'It still doesn't alter the fact that it's a graveyard,' Phillip said.

'No,' Sam said. 'No, it doesn't.'

The three cousins returned to their desks.

Sam leant back on his chair. 'Do we know any more about Walter Littleby?'

Albert opened his emails. 'Hold on,' he said. 'I might have something here. I've got the census.'

Phillip made his way over as Albert opened the file. The pair scanned the list of names and stopped halfway down. 'Walter Littleby,' Phillip said, and showed the list to Sam. 'Gravedigger and gardener.'

Sam grinned. 'That seals it, then. Walter was a gravedigger. He would have had ample opportunity to bury the cross.'

'But if it's buried in a grave,' Albert said. 'How can we retrieve it?'

'The cross belongs in a museum,' Phillip said. 'Maybe we should let the authorities deal with it.'

'And miss out on our reward,' Sam said. 'No way.'

Albert frowned. 'How could we explain how we found it?'

Sam pondered. 'We could concoct a story later. Does it give an address for where Walter lived?'

'Yes,' Albert said. 'On Hemlington Road.'

'If the property is still standing,' Sam said. 'We could lie and say we found it there.'

Phillip scoffed. 'The current owners aren't going to be happy with us doing that.'

'And,' Albert said. 'We can't go digging in cemeteries.'

'Read me what it says in the diary again,' Sam said.

Albert looked at the words. 'It says that he buried it in an unused grave ...' Albert squinted. 'On the Jesmond's plot.'

'It sounds,' Sam said. 'Like he didn't complete the digging. I'm sure Walter wouldn't have put it inside the grave of some poor deceased parishioner.'

'Wait,' Phillip said. 'First, we need to revisit the graveyard. Albert, find out what you can on this Jesmond family. If they were notable, there might be stuff on Wikipedia.'

'Good idea,' Sam said.

Kim popped her head inside the door. 'I'm off out. I'll be about an hour. Do you boys want anything bringing back?'

'I'm good,' Sam said.

'I fancy some fish and chips,' Phillip said.

'Oh,' Kim said. 'I haven't had those for ages. Albert? Do you want anything?'

'No, thanks. I've brought a packed lunch.'

'Can you three look after Baggage? I'll take Luggage and Zeus with me. We're going to the puppy café.' Baggage's head appeared around the door. He trotted inside and over to the beanbag in the corner. He performed a quick pirouette, flopped onto the bed, yawned and closed his eyes.

'What a life,' Sam said.

'Don't be too long,' Phillip said. 'We have an errand to run this afternoon.'

'Ok, bye,' Kim said, as she left.

Albert paused his typing. 'The Jesmonds were a well-to-do family from Teesside. They had a large house on the edge of Marton village. They were well-known philanthropists who gave many charitable gifts to schools and churches. They also held a fair every year for the villagers in Stainton. Joseph Jesmond, who was born in the village, was married to his wife in the parish church in 1745. The family continued the tradition of marriages and funerals at the church until the end of the nineteenth century. The family ceased burials at the church after the tragic death of William Jesmond's only son, Daniel. He fell from a horse at the village fete and was subsequently interred near to the family home in Marton. The now childless couple moved further north soon after.'

Sam smiled. 'The boy wasn't buried at Stainton, then?'

'It doesn't look like he was,' Albert said.

Emily planted herself next to Kim in the café with the four puppies at their feet as Deb got served.

'Everything all right, Emily?' Kim said.

'Yeah, why?'

'You seem a little quiet.'

She smiled. 'I'm fine.'

Deb arrived and placed the tray on the table. 'I got us a cake each. I thought a little sugar was in order. Right, Emily Simpson. What's up?'

Emily stiffened. 'Like I've just told Kim, there's nothing up.'

Deb sneered. 'Of course there is. I've known you for years. I can tell when you've got something on your mind.'

Emily sipped her tea. 'The puppies enjoy it here.'

'Don't try and change the subject,' Deb said.

'Maybe she doesn't want to talk about it,' Kim said.

'Well, she's bloody going to. I'm sick of looking at her miserable clock.'

'Deb!' Kim said. 'That's a bit harsh.'

'Cruel to be kind,' Deb said, and took a large bite of cake.

Emily put her hands up. 'Hello. I am here you know,'

Deb threw out her arms. 'Then bloody tell us. Kim and we can dissect your problem and then give you some of our priceless advice.'

'Who are you?' Emily said. 'The local agony aunt?'

'I'll be honest about it,' Deb said. 'You've always said you like my honesty.'

'Brutal honesty,' Kim said.

Deb groaned. 'Emily likes me because I'm like a bloke. Some women are awful. All they do is snipe behind your back. I tell it as it is. Straight from the lip.' Deb blew on two imaginary guns.

Emily lowered her head. 'Sam and I haven't … you know … had much action in the bedroom of late.'

'At last,' Deb said. She rolled her eyes. 'How long?'

'Two weeks.'

'Two weeks!' Deb spluttered through her cake-filled mouth. 'That's hardly a drought.'

'Two weeks is not a long time,' Kim said.

'I'm new to this heterosexual game. What's normal?' Emily said to Kim.

'Erm, well,' Kim said. 'I suppose about two or three times a week. Sometimes more, sometimes less.' Kim made a face at Deb. 'That's about right, isn't it, Deb?'

Deb took another bite of cake. 'Every night if I can.'

'Every night!' Kim said. Her jaw dropped open. 'I don't think I could find the time?' The last sentence whispered.

Deb let out a roar of laughter. 'You have to make time. Sex is a good barometer for how the relationship's going. The truth is.' She winked. 'If I'm not having sex with the big guy, I'm thinking about it. By the time Tommo gets in, I'm good to go.' Emily stopped with her éclair just short of her mouth and placed it back on the plate.

Kim raised her eyebrows. 'Doesn't Tommo ever get tired of it?'

Deb laughed again. 'In my experience, Kim, men rarely turn down sex. Admittedly, he is sometimes tired. So, if he's had a hard day at the pub, I just sing him a lullaby.'

Kim frowned. 'Sing him a lullaby?'

Emily rolled her eyes. 'She helps him out.' Emily huffed. 'I thought you were supposed to be helping me?'

'Really?' Kim said. 'But what do you get out of that?'

'I'm doing something nice for someone I love. It's an unselfish act.'

'Love?' Emily said.

Deb slurped her tea. 'Yes. You heard me right. I love that big fella, and I love his big fella.'

'Too much information, Deb,' Kim said. 'Don't put that image in my head.'

'Besides,' Deb continued. 'If you do that for your man, it releases feel-good hormones into his bloodstream. He has a good night's sleep, and in the morning he's ready to rock and roll again. I read it somewhere.'

'Your sex life sounds almost clinical,' Kim said.

Deb drained her cup. 'I'll be honest, Kim ...'

'Again,' Emily said. 'Let's not.'

Deb ignored her. 'I love sex. I like lots of sex.' Emily waved for Deb to lower her voice as people in the café looked in her direction. 'Sex is good for you. It makes you look younger. It keeps you fit. Sex is fantastic.' She threw wide her arms with the last words.

'Thanks for that party-political broadcast on behalf of the shagging party, Deb,' Emily said. 'Can we please concentrate on Sam and me.'

'Well, I'm just saying.' Deb leant back in her chair and folded her arms.

'I think we got the message,' Kim said.

'My gran once told me,' Deb said. 'That she and Granddad were still doing it in their late-seventies.' Deb pondered. 'Hardly a wrinkle on her face. She could pass for at least ten years younger.'

'Ok,' Kim said. 'I get your point.'

'Listen ...' Deb said, as Emily rolled her eyes again. 'Sex is your not-so-secret weapon. If you want a shelf putting up, offer him sex. If you want the bin putting out ...'

'Offer him sex,' Kim intoned.

'Sex is the biggest weapon in your arsenal,' Deb said.

Emily stood. 'I'm going to get another coffee. I feel sick.'

Deb pulled her back down. 'Wait a minute. We're sorting out your love-life here.'

'No, you're not. You are giving us the sex world according to Deb.'

Deb tapped her arm. 'Ok. Here goes. Two weeks for most people isn't a long time. You could try seducing him? Cook his favourite meal. Get your mam to look after Daisy. Spend some time together.'

'I'm not much good at that ... Seduction stuff,' Emily said. 'I'd feel proper daft.'

Deb scoffed. 'What about all the women you bedded?'

'That was different. I felt I was on an equal footing with them. It was much easier. And ...' She paused, searching for the right words. 'I was usually drunk.'

'So, get pissed and seduce him,' Kim said.

'Put on some sexy gear,' Deb said. 'Basque, stockings, sussies etc.'

'Isn't that a bit tacky?' Emily said.

'Of course it is. But men love all that crap. Personally, I hate wearing that rubbish, but if it gets him going ...'

Emily blew out. 'He mentioned a name in his sleep.'

Kim threw a glance at Deb. 'A name?' Kim said.

'Lisa.'

Deb rolled her eyes and rubbed her face. 'In his sleep? So what?'

'It might not have been—' Kim said.

'Don't be daft, Kim,' Emily said. 'It was Lisa. He's dreaming about her.'

'It's a dream,' Deb said. 'We can't help what we dream.'

Kim knitted her brow. 'A friend of mine divorced her husband because she dreamt he was having an affair.'

Deb glared at Kim. 'Kim, you're not helping.'

'Oh, sorry,' Kim spluttered. 'I'm not saying Sam is ...'

Emily stood again. 'I'll go and get us another coffee.'

The other two watched as she walked off. 'What did you say that for?' Deb said.

'Sorry, it just came out.'

Deb scoffed. 'Divorcing your husband because you dreamt he was having an affair. How stupid is that?'

'The thing was,' Kim said. 'He was. He'd been shagging a woman he worked with for months.'

Deb's eyes widened. 'Don't tell Emily that for God's sake.'

'No. Mum's the word.'

Deb glanced over to Emily still at the counter. 'We may need to have a word with Lisa.'

Kim moved in closer. 'You mean, frighten her off?'

'That's exactly what I mean.'

CHAPTER TWENTY

Comby and Hardman loitered in their car and watched from a distance as Sam, Phillip, Albert and Baggage entered the graveyard.

'What do you think they're up to, guv?' Hardman said.

'I don't know. It must have something to do with that case they're working on.'

'They could be visiting the church?'

'Give over, Mick. A group of less likely religious people would be hard to find.'

'It was a bit of luck we were outside the detective agency.'

'Yeah. Sometimes serendipity shines on us coppers.'

'Seranne who?' Hardman said.

'Good fortune, Mick.'

'What are we going to do?'

'Nothing. I don't want them to know that we know what they're up to.'

Hardman frowned. 'But we don't know.'

'Yeah, all right, Hardman. But we will know what they know, but they won't know that we know. Understand?'

Hardman scratched his head. 'I suppose.'

'Leave the thinking to me, Mick. Obviously, I'm the brains in this partnership.'

Hardman gazed across at the pub. 'They do a good parmo in there.'

'Do they?'

'Home-cooked chips too.'

'Hardman,' Comby said. 'Is there ever a time when you're not thinking about your stomach?'

'I missed my breakfast this morning.'

'No, you didn't. You had a bacon and egg sandwich. The remnants of which are still adorning your chin. You don't have to be a detective to deduce that.'

Hardman began rubbing his chin. 'That was only a snack. I missed my breakfast at home. Me and the missus were cementing our affection for each other, and I was nearly late.'

Comby held up a hand. 'Please don't give me the details. I'm feeling bilious just thinking about it.'

'What about you and your lady friend?'

Comby blew out. 'I'm not discussing my relationship. I have said this before.'

'I know. I'm just curious.'

'Well, you know what curiosity did? Let's see if you can sit in silence for the next ten minutes. If you do, I'll buy you lunch. Ok?' Hardman grinned like a little schoolboy who had just been promised the very latest computer game.

Phillip, Baggage and Sam made their way to the back of the churchyard towards Albert.

'Here it is,' Albert said. Phillip and Sam joined him. 'The Jesmond family plot.'

Sam squatted next to the graves and then looked at his cousins. 'It could be buried around here.' He stood again and swept a hand in front of him.

'It could,' Phillip said. 'But look.' He waved an arm around. 'It's so open. Anyone could see us.'

'We can't go digging in a graveyard,' Albert said. 'Even if there is a priceless cross buried in it. We'd go to prison. Who'd look after my Zeus?' Baggage edged forward and sniffed at the ground.

'Yeah,' Sam said. 'We need to know for sure that there is something buried.'

Albert gaped at Phillip. 'You're not considering ...?' Albert said.

Phillip's eyes widened. 'He's right, Sam. We'd end up inside. I thought you said you wouldn't consider digging in a graveyard?'

Sam squatted again. 'I know I did, but that was before I knew for sure that the cross existed. But somewhere here.' He picked up a small branch and tapped the ground. 'Is a priceless artefact. Besides, It doesn't look as if it's buried in a grave.' He stood and studied the other two. 'I can't leave something as precious as this undiscovered.'

'I know but ...' Phillip held out his hands.

George Knight watched Sam, Phillip and Albert from his vantage point. 'It's got to be in the graveyard,' he said into his mobile. 'The cousin's are in there now ... I'll pop around to their office. I have my final bill to pay. I'll call you later.'

He continued to watch as the three of them, with the dog, exited and climbed into their car.

'Couldn't we pay someone else to dig it up for us?' Sam said.

'Who?' Phillip said. 'Who would be discreet enough?'

Albert leant forward from the back. 'What would stop them from keeping the cross for themselves?'

'Obviously,' Sam said. 'It would have to be someone we can trust.'

Phillip glanced across at him. 'You have someone in mind?'

'Ewen.' he said.

'Ewen,' Albert repeated. 'He was discreet about ... you know what.'

Phillip nodded. 'He was. But would he?'

'For a share in the reward money,' Sam said.

'What reward money?' Phillip said.

Sam grinned. 'I have a plan.'

Phillip groaned. 'I'm not sure.'

'Phillip,' Sam said. 'Take us to Tommo's. We'll ask him. Tommo can have the deciding vote. Agreed?'

Phillip stopped at a red light. 'Agreed.'

'Albert?' Sam said.

'Yes,' Albert said. 'Tommo will do the right thing.'

Tommo pulled the pint and placed it in front of Ewen. 'There you go.'

Ewen pushed a note across the counter. 'Bit quiet in here, Tommo.'

'You missed the rush,' Tommo said. 'It was rammed earlier.'

'Where're the Erimus boys?'

'Not sure. Sam said he might pop in later.'

Ewen glanced about. 'Can I trust you with a secret.'

Tommo pulled himself a half. 'Absolutely.'

'Sam.'

'What about him?'

'I saw him in The Pirate Bar the other day.'

Tommo adopted a mock-shock face. 'Oh, no. The scoundrel. Spending money in someone else's pub. He is allowed to.'

'If you're not going to be serious,' Ewen said. 'I won't tell you.'

Tommo held up his hands. 'Sorry. Go on.'

'I was in the Pirate Bar and guess who was in there?'

Tommo shrugged. 'Captain Hook?'

Ewen ignored Tommo's sarcasm. 'Lisa.'

'Lisa Sandsfield?'

Ewen took a sip of his drink. 'Yeah.'

'Ewen,' Tommo said. 'It's a free world.'

'I know it is, but aren't you a little worried? Sam's your best mate.'

Tommo covered his face with his hands. 'Bloody Sam. He's an idiot if he has anything to do with her.'

'Yeah. Neither of them saw me, I was hiding behind a pillar. I do that because my bother-in-law has a habit of following me around.'

'Sexton?'

Ewen blew out and covered his eyes with his hands. 'Yeah. The most boring man in the world. An hour with him is like an eternity.'

Tommo nodded. 'He came in here once when we were really quiet. Bored me for two hours talking about the best way to cook a poached egg.'

Ewen laughed. 'Surely you drop a raw egg into boiling water?'

'Not when Sexton's explaining it. What kind of name is Sexton, anyway?

'His mam liked a detective called Sexton Blake.'

'Good job she wasn't a fan of Conan Doyle. He'd have been walking about with a pipe and a deerstalker.'

'Exactly,' Ewen said. 'Anyway. About Sam?'

Tommo drained his glass. 'What do you want me to do?'

'Well, I thought with you being his best mate, you might be able to talk a bit of sense into him.'

'Ewen,' he said. 'What makes you think Sam will listen to me?'

'It's worth a try.'

Tommo smiled. 'Why the concern over Sam? You and he hated each other for years.'

Ewen waved his hand. 'That's in the past. I like Emily. And what about little Daisy?'

'That's up to Sam.'

'Come on, Tommo, Lisa's poison. She caused the rift between Sam and me in the first place. She just likes to cause trouble.'

Tommo picked up a bar towel, scrunched it in his hands and tossed it to the floor. 'Ok, ok. I'll have a word.'

Ewen drained his pint. 'Good lad.'

Sam, Phillip, Albert and Baggage entered The Sidewinder. 'Here comes the Erimus Detective Agency,' Tommo said, as Ewen swivelled on his stool.

The three cousins and the dog made their way to the bar. 'Have you got ten minutes to spare, big fella?' Sam said.

Tommo consulted his watch. 'Gene will be in shortly. Why?'

Sam tapped the side of his nose. 'Erimus business.' He put a hand on Ewen's shoulder. 'We want you in on it as well.'

Ewen's eyes widened. 'Me?'

'Yeah. We need a favour.'

He raised his eyebrows at Tommo. 'No problem.'

'In the meantime,' Phillip said. 'We'll have some beers.'

Tommo began pulling them. 'I found the fishing gear, Albert. Are we still on for Saturday?'

'Definitely. I'm looking forward to it.'

Sam nudged Albert. 'What's this about?'

'Tommo's taking me fishing.'

'Really?' Sam said. 'It's been years since you went fishing, Tommo.'

'Not since Dad was around.'

'Yeah. He's been dead some years.'

Tommo nodded. 'Twelve, next week. Anyway.' Tommo smiled. 'Let's not get maudlin. Grab yourselves a table, and I'll bring the beers over.'

Phillip slipped onto a chair opposite Sam and Albert. Baggage did his usual pirouette before laying under the table.

'What's the plan?' Phillip said to Sam.

'Right,' Sam said. 'We find the cross.'

'If it's there,' Albert said.

'Yes, if it's there,' Sam continued. 'We locate a place on farmland nearby and re-bury the cross.'

Phillip glanced at Albert then back to Sam. 'Why?' he said.

Sam put his hands out, palms upwards. 'We can't tell people we found it in a graveyard.'

'We know that,' Phillip said.

'I have an acquaintance,' Sam said. 'Well, actually, he's a friend of a friend. Monty Lowry.'

Phillip shrugged. 'And he's ...?'

'He's a detectorist. He searches all over the North-East for precious artefacts. I'm going to ask him to loan us his metal detector.'

'To find the cross?' Albert said.

'Exactly. Monty will have the top of the range model, I'm sure. Once we're certain there's something in the graveyard, we dig it up.'

'Then re-bury it,' Phillip said.

'And then find it,' Albert said.

Sam held his arms wide, triumphantly. 'Yeah. Great idea, isn't it?'

Phillip shook his head. 'It will seem a bit suspicious. I mean, asking to borrow the detector and then finding a priceless cross soon after.'

'I agree,' Albert said. 'Why don't we just buy one?'

'Have you seen the price of them?' Sam said. 'We tell everyone that we had information leading us to the place we found it.'

'What if they ask us about this information?' Phillip said. 'Then what do we say?'

'We'll be vague.'

'What happens when, and if, we find the cross?' Albert said. 'We can't just auction it.'

'The cross will be classed as treasure trove,' Sam said. 'The crown puts a value on it, and we share that money.'

'What about the farm we find it on?' Phillip said.

'We'll have to split it fifty-fifty,' Sam said.

'But that means,' Phillip said. 'They'll get more than us.'

Sam adopted a serious face. 'This could be the biggest historical find of this or any other decade. We can sell our story like last time. Maybe even get an agent. The money we'll get will be significant, I'm sure.'

'I've never seen you so passionate about anything,' Phillip said.

'Phillip,' Sam said. 'This cross is over a thousand years old. It deserves to be in The History Museum, not in some collectors mansion.'

Phillip looked at Albert. Albert tapped his chin with a finger and then nodded. 'Ok,' Phillip said. 'Sounds good. There's just one small problem. How do we dig up a graveyard without anyone in Stainton village seeing us?'

Sam put his hands onto his head. 'I haven't quite figured it out yet. But I will.'

Tommo carried three pints across to their table and placed them down. 'I'll be five-minutes, boys. Gene's just arrived.'

Tommo put his hand into his pocket and pulled out a pie. He bent down, broke it into pieces, and watched as Baggage wolfed it down. 'Good boy,' he said, rubbing the dogs head. 'I'll go and get you a drink, Bagsy.'

Sam narrowed his eyes at Ewen. 'Maybe Ewen might have an idea.'

'About the graveyard?' Albert said.

'Yeah.' Sam smiled. 'He's quite adept at problem-solving. Cunning as a fox is Ewen.'

'Will he go along with your scheme, though?' Phillip said.

'With the money he'll get from finding it, I'm pretty sure he will.'

'And Tommo?' Albert said. 'Will he? You know how religious he is. Do you remember the statue?'

'Oh, yeah. I'm pretty sure he will.' Tommo peered across, and Sam raised his glass to him. 'Tommo will be a pushover.'

Tommo waved over to Albert, Phillip and Sam who, accompanied by Baggage, made their way into the Black Mamba. The three cousins sat, as Tommo and Ewen slid onto seats opposite. Baggage briefly popped his head onto the table and, satisfied there was nothing of note happening, curled up on the floor.

'I thought it would be more private in here,' Tommo said. 'He took a large gulp of his pint and smiled at the assembled group. 'Ok. What's going on?'

Sam leant forward. 'We may have found the location of the cross.' He patted Ewen on the arm. 'I'll explain fully later. But briefly. There's a priceless Celtic cross buried somewhere. We think we know where it is.'

Tommo eyed Sam. 'So, what's the problem? Get a spade and just dig it up.'

'Mm,' Phillip said. 'That is the problem. It's buried in a graveyard.'

Tommo chuckled. 'You're not scared, are you?'

'No,' Sam said. 'We think it's buried in a graveyard in the middle of Stainton.'

Tommo tugged on his beard. 'The one I went to with Phillip?' Sam nodded.

'Sam,' Phillip said. 'Tell them the full story.'

Sam took a deep breath and began. He explained about the evidence they had pointing to the location of the cross. And also the plan he had conceived about re-burying the cross and concocting the story that they found it at a later date. Sam finished, eased back in his chair, and swigged greedily on his pint.

Tommo sucked in air through his teeth. 'I'm going to state the obvious here. If you, we, got caught digging up a grave we would all be sent to prison.'

'That's what I think,' Albert said. 'Like I said, who would look after Zeus?'

Sam took in a lungful of air and glared at Albert. 'Never mind a bloody dog. This is a priceless artefact.'

'It probably isn't a grave, to be fair,' Phillip said. 'We don't think there's a body in it.'

'But what if there is?' Albert said.

'Jesus, Albert,' Sam said. 'It's 125 years old. There wouldn't be anything left of anyone.'

'Even so,' Tommo said. 'I'm not overly happy desecrating—'

'It's not Catholic,' Sam said.

Tommo threw his hands out. 'What does that matter? I still have nightmares over the statue of the Virgin Mary.'

Sam rolled his eyes. 'You didn't smash it.'

'I know. But ...'

Sam focused on Ewen. 'What do you think?'

Ewen took a gulp of his drink. 'Yeah, I'm up for it. I don't mind digging in a graveyard.'

'That's because you're a bloody Heathen,' Tommo said.

Ewen laughed. 'Just say a few extra Hail Mary's.'

Tommo ignored him. 'What happens if it's not where you think it is? Do you dig another hole, and then another?' Tommo stood for effect. 'Morning, Vicar.' He waved to the imaginary clergyman. 'Dammed sorry about all the holes, old man. We're looking for a priceless relic. We'll fill them in once we locate it, old bean.' Tommo slumped back into his seat.

'Stop being sarcastic,' Sam said. 'I'm going to borrow a metal detector from a friend of a friend. That way we can be sure that it's there before we dig.'

Tommo slowly shook his head. 'I'm still not certain. I've been to the graveyard. You couldn't dig there without being seen.'

'Why don't I go and have a look,' Ewen said. 'I'll see if it's possible.'

All eyes zoned in on Tommo. ‘I don’t know what you’re looking at me for.’

‘You’re important to this,’ Sam said. ‘We won’t do it if you don’t agree.’

Tommo rubbed his face with his hands. ‘Let Ewen have a look. Then we decide. But I’m not saying I agree.’

Sam patted him on the arm. ‘Good lad.’

CHAPTER TWENTY-ONE

Sam, Ewen, Tommo, Albert and Phillip waited in the car, parked along the road from the church.

'You three stay here,' Sam said. 'Me and Ewen will go and have a look. It'll look a bit suspicious if all five of us pitch up.'

'Ok,' Tommo said.

Ewen and Sam climbed out and headed towards the graveyard. 'It's a bit open,' Ewen said.

'I know. We'd have to do it at night.'

They marched through the gates and around to the back, making their way down a slight slope to a plot with six or seven headstones.

Sam looked at Ewen. 'What do you think?'

Ewen glanced around. 'It's a bit more secluded here. Where do you think it's buried?'

Sam walked forward and stopped near a grave. 'This is the last Jesmond to be buried here. The others that way are older. We think …' he lowered his voice further. '… that the cross could be buried here.'

Ewen dropped to a squat. 'Ok.' He remained like that for a few seconds and then stood. 'We'd need some cover.'

'What like?'

Ewen raised his eyebrows. 'A tent or something.'

Sam sneered. 'We can't put a tent up. It'd be spotted.'

Ewen nodded behind him. 'What about those.'

Sam spun on his heels and viewed the large pile of branches. 'To cover the tent?' he said.

'Exactly.'

'But someone will see you putting it up.'

'I've got one of those pop-up ones. I bought it for my nephew. It takes seconds.'

Sam smiled. 'We would need to be sure that the cross is there.'

'Your friend, the detectorist?'

Sam nodded. 'He's a friend of a friend, really.'

'Hello there.' a man's voice said.

Sam and Ewen spun around. 'Oh ... hello,' Sam said.

'Are you looking for anyone in particular?' He nodded at the graves. 'I'm the vicar.'

Sam held out a hand. 'Sam. This is a friend of mine, Ewen.'

'If you are looking for anyone in particular,' the vicar said. 'I know this graveyard like the back of my hand.'

'Well,' Sam said. 'As a matter of fact, I'm interested in the history of Stainton.' He turned back to the graves. 'The Jesmonds?'

'Ah, yes,' The vicar said. 'The Jesmonds.'

'What can you tell me about them?'

'They were quite a wealthy family from Stainton. They owned a manor house. They were close friends of the Pennymans.'

'Of Ormesby Hall fame?' Sam said.

The vicar smiled. 'Yes. The Pennymans lived here too.' He pointed away from the churchyard. 'Up there. They had a hall. It's a bit of a mystery what happened to it. There are still remnants of the wall of the property.'

'Didn't the Pennymans flee to France?' Sam said.

'They did. They backed the wrong side in the civil war. When the monarchy was reinstated, they returned. The King gifted them some land for their support, and they built Ormesby Hall.'

'What about the Jesmonds?' Ewen said.

'Ah, the Jesmonds. They weren't as wealthy. They lived, married and were buried here for a long time. Until the death of Daniel Jesmond.'

Sam raised his eyebrows. 'Daniel Jesmond?'

'Yes,' the vicar said. 'He was killed when he fell from his horse while riding through the village. His family decided that they did not want him buried here. A lot of this information is contained inside. There's a comprehensive record of all the births, deaths, marriages and christenings.'

'I don't suppose I could have a look?' Sam said.

'Certainly.'

'I'll stay here and have a look around the graveyard,' Ewen said.

Sam followed the vicar inside the church and through into a side room.

Ewen leant against the wall of the graveyard as the vicar and Sam emerged. 'Thanks for that,' Sam said. 'It was fascinating.'

'If you need any further information ...'

'Thank you. I have your card.'

Ewen stood upright. 'Gorgeous churchyard,' he said to the vicar.

'Yes, it is.'

'You even have a commonwealth grave, I noticed?'

'Yes we do. Some of the graves are ancient.'

Ewen shoved his hands into his pockets. 'I don't want to alarm you, or anything.' He moved towards the far corner, closely followed by the other two. 'But your wall is in danger of collapse.'

The vicar's eyes widened as Sam frowned. 'See here?' Ewen said, tapping the stone. 'You have a crack. That crack will almost certainly run right through the wall.'

The vicar stepped forward. 'Oh, dear. Is it serious?'

'Very much so. One bad winter and ...' Ewen threw up his hands. 'Crash. The whole lot will come tumbling down.'

'Oh no,' the vicar said. 'That's terrible. Would it be expensive to fix? Only we're struggling with our roof, you see. We've had quite a large amount of lead stolen.'

'It's not a huge job,' Ewen said. 'A day, maybe two.'

The vicar lowered his eyes. 'I don't know what the Bishop will say. It seems all I do these days is go cap in hand to him.'

'Look,' Ewen said. 'You've been very helpful to Sam. I'll do it for free.'

The vicar stared wide-eyed. 'Really?'

'Yeah, I've got some free time next week.' Ewen glanced at Sam, who nodded. 'I've got the materials left over from other jobs. Maybe Sam here could help as my labourer.'

The vicar turned his attention to Sam. 'Yes,' Sam said. 'As a thank you for your assistance.'

The vicar clasped his hands together. 'Well, I must take you to the vicarage and introduce you to my wife. She's been baking today, so there may be a cake or two to be had. Come this way, gentlemen.'

Ewen winked at Sam who smiled back, as the pair followed after the clergyman.

'Bloody hell,' Tommo said. 'You've been a long time.'

Sam and Ewen climbed inside the car. 'We had a lot to discuss,' Sam said. 'It's definitely the place the Jesmond family intended to bury their son. The vicar kindly showed me the burial records. No one else was buried there.'

'So,' Phillip said. 'If the cross is there, there isn't a body?'

'That's the size of it,' Sam said.

Tommo huffed. 'Why did you involve the vicar?'

'We didn't,' Ewen said. 'He just turned up.'

'Well, that's great,' Tommo said. 'You can't go digging there now. He'll remember you were there and put two and two together.'

'We'll be fine,' Ewen said. 'I've offered to do a bit of restoration on the wall of the graveyard. The wall is close to the site. He's going to open the gate on the far side. I can back my van up, which will cover us from the road—'

'But what about the grave,' Albert said. 'Anyone passing the graveyard by the front of the church, will—'

'It slopes down, Albert,' Sam said. 'And, Ewen's got one of those pop-up tents. We'll cover it with branches, there are loads of those near the grave, and dig from inside there.'

Tommo tugged on his beard. 'I'm still not sure.'

Sam huffed. 'We've thought of everything.'

'What about after we fill the grave in?' Phillip said. 'Won't they know someones been digging.'

'We'll have to make a good job of it,' Ewen said. 'And I'll back over it as well. The vicar won't know. He won't be expecting anyone to be digging holes in his graveyard.'

'If all this works,' Tommo said. 'And by some stroke of fortune we don't get arrested, won't he be suspicious when you're in the news having discovered a priceless cross?'

Sam grinned. 'I've thought of that. I'm loaning a metal detector from a friend of a friend.' The others nodded. 'I'm going to go metal detecting away from the graveyard. We've already been around to the vicarage and met the vicar's wife.'

'For scones and tea,' Ewen said.

'I'll make sure he sees the metal detector,' Sam said. 'Then it won't come as a surprise when I announce my discovery.'

'We've pencilled it in for next Friday,' Ewen said. 'Put a note in your diaries.'

All eyes centred on Tommo. He glanced at the others in turn. 'What are you all looking at me for.'

Sam rolled his eyes. 'For some reason, this lot need your approval before they agree.'

Tommo closed his eyes and slowly shook his head. 'I must be mad. Ok. We'll do it.'

Sam patted his arm. 'I knew you would, big fella.'

'We'll need tools,' Tommo said. 'Well, spades.'

'Sorted,' Ewen said.

'One more thing,' Sam said. 'We don't mention this to anyone. Not even the girls. They'll only try to talk us out of it.' Sam waved his finger at Albert. 'No telling your therapist, either.'

Albert looked down. 'I wouldn't.'

The sleeping Baggage woke, stretched and yawned. 'Baggage we can trust,' Sam said, ruffling the dog's ears.

'Can we get something to eat?' Phillip said. 'I'm ravenous.'

'I don't want anything,' Sam said.

'Me either,' Ewen said.

'That's because of all those scones you've been eating,' Tommo said. 'We'll go to the pub. You two can have a pint. Or a cup of Earl Grey.'

George Knight watched the three cousins, along with Ewen, Tommo and Baggage get out of the car and head inside the pub. He narrowed his eyes at the bald, thick-set man next to him. 'What are they up to, Crusher?'

'No idea, George. Do you want me to go and knock it out of them?'

Knight patted his arm. 'There will be plenty of opportunities to inflict a bit of GBH on them later.'

'That big guy with the beard reminds me of a bloke I fought in my amateur days.'

Knight smiled. 'Oh, yeah. How did that turn out?'

Crusher boomed. 'I put him in the hospital for three weeks.'

CHAPTER TWENTY-TWO

Comby walked along the corridor and, knocking at the door, entered the office. 'You wanted to see me, sir?'

'Sit down, Comby.' Comby complied as his superior flicked through some paperwork. 'Samuel Davison?' he said.

'From the Erimus Detect—'

'I know where he's from. Is there any reason you're investigating him?'

'He's up to something, sir.'

The senior officer leant back in his chair. 'Up to something?'

'I'm not sure what, but—'

'Listen to me, Comby. I'm getting grief from the top brass about our clear-up rate. I can't have my best coppers running around on wild goose chases.' Comby smiled as his superior continued. 'I can't even afford to have you and your dim-witted sergeant not pulling their weight.'

The smile fell from Comby's face. 'But, guv—'

'I hope this isn't becoming some sort of vendetta.'

'Vendetta?' Comby said.

'Yes. Because of the article Mr Davison wrote in the Gazette. Because what I read of it, summed you up pretty well.' Comby started to speak, but the DCI held up his hand. 'Mr Davison has not done anything wrong. He hasn't even got a parking ticket to his name.'

'I know that—'

The DCI stood. 'Comby!' He slid a file across the desk towards his junior. 'DI Stamp is on sick leave. He was working on a missing person's case. I want you to take over.' The DCI sat again and stared at Comby. 'Off you trot.'

Comby stood, paused about to speak, but then thought better of it and left. He made his way downstairs, stormed outside and jumped into the car.

Hardman, breakfast bun in hand, stared at him. 'All right, guv?'

'No, I'm bloody not all right. Why did you tell the DCI that we were watching Samuel Davison and his cohorts?'

Hardman pulled a sausage from the bun and bit half of it off. 'I didn't know it was a secret.'

'Sometimes, Hardman, words fail me. He's just given me a dressing down and assigned me to a missing person's case because of your big mouth.'

Hardman frowned. 'Sorry, guv. I got you a bacon and egg butty.' He pulled a paper bag from the driver's side door.

'I don't want a butty.' Comby huffed. 'Bloody food, that's all you ever think of. If you put half as much effort into your police work as you do in shovelling food down your throat, you'd be twice the copper you are now. And that's not saying much.'

Hardman pondered. His brow deeply knitted. 'Sorry, guv, I didn't think it would get you into bother.'

'That's your problem,' Comby said. 'You never think. Except to decide where your next pit stop is going to be. Well, from now on, it's going to change. Have you got it?'

'Yes, guv.'

'Before you speak to the chief or anyone else, run it past me first.'

'Is it because your lady friend stood you up?'

'No!' Comby said.

'So, you don't want the bun then?' Nodding at the paper bag on the dash.

Comby grabbed the bun, and also the one Hardman held, lowered the window, and launched them outside. Hardman's jaw dropped open, his fingers still holding onto the half-eaten sausage.

'From now on, fatty,' Comby said, poking his junior in the chest. 'No food in this car. I want you to clean all this crap out as well.' He pointed into the back at the array of empty packets and cartons. Comby opened the door and stepped outside, then lowered his head back inside. 'For your information, she didn't stand me up. Her mother was ill.' With that, he marched back inside. Hardman stared at the forlorn sandwich on the tarmac outside, pouted, then popped the remainder of the sausage into his mouth.

Albert sat opposite Charles, waiting for his therapist to end his phone conversation.

Charles hung up and smiled at Albert. 'Sorry about that. Apparently, the police are coming to see me.'

'The police?' Albert said.

'Yes, some trivial matter. Anyway.' He clasped his hands together. 'How has your week been?'

'Good.' Albert smiled. 'I went fishing this weekend.'

Charles furrowed his brow. 'Fishing?'

'Yes. With a friend.'

Charles drummed his fingers on the table. 'I see.'

'With my friend, Tommo.'

Charles huffed. 'Is this … Tommo, a proper fisherman? Or is he one of those annoying novices?'

'He seemed to know what he was doing,' Albert said.

'What rod was he using?'

'Oh, I'm not sure. I remember it was black.'

Charles huffed again. 'Black! And bait. What bait?'

'I'm not sure of that, either.'

'Come, come, Albert,' Charles said. 'Is this Tommo real, or are you making him up? You're not having some sort of illusory episode, are you?'

Albert winced. 'No. He runs a pub in town. He's a very good friend of one of my associates.'

'Had you told me you wished to go fishing.' Charles reached for a tissue and blew his nose. 'I would have been happy to take you. You only had to ask.'

'I'm sorry. I didn't think. You're a busy man, and—'

Charles stood with his back to Albert. 'Et Tu, Albert.'

Albert stood as well. 'I didn't mean to offend you, Charles.'

'Just go, Albert. I feel betrayed.'

Albert moved towards him, paused, lowered his head and hurried off. Charles picked up the photo of himself and Kevin. 'Oh, Kevin. How I miss you.'

Albert tramped into the office, tossed his coat over the hat stand, and slumped into his chair.

'You all right?' Phillip said.

Albert lay his head on the desk. 'It's Charles.'

'You therapist?' Phillip said.

'Yeah.'

Sam slumped back in his chair and put his feet on the desk. 'Didn't the session go to plan, then?'

'He was upset because I went fishing with Tommo.'

Sam and Phillip shot a glance at each other and pulled a face. 'Upset?' Phillip said.

Albert lifted his head. 'I think I offended him. He said he would have taken me if only I'd asked.'

Sam scoffed. 'I don't know why you just don't find another therapist. This Charles sounds like a proper loon.'

'But,' Albert said. 'We've built a rapport.'

Sam jumped to his feet. 'I'll leave you to sort this drama, Phillip. I'm off out.'

'Where are you going?' Phillip said.

Sam pulled on his coat. 'I told you. I'm meeting a mate of mine. He has a friend who is a detectorist. I'm hoping to borrow a metal detector from him. For you know what.' Sam tapped the side of his nose with his index finger.

'Will he loan you one?' Albert said.

'Ways and means,' Sam said. 'I'll see you two later.'

Albert stood, and Phillip regarded him. 'Where are you off to?' Phillip said.

'I'm going to see Mary Hough.'

'Why?'

'She told me my chakras were all to pot. She offered to assist in realigning them. I'm hoping she can help me.'

Phillip shook his head as Albert left and scoffed. 'Chakras.'

Sam strode along the path and knocked on the door of the house. The door opened, and a portly man smiled at him. 'Sam. Come in,' he said. Sam followed the man along the hall and into the lounge. A woman reading in a chair, looked up as they entered. 'Cathy. Look who's here.'

'Sam. How are you?' She stood, moved across, and kissed him affectionately.

'Put him down,' the man said. 'You don't know where he's been.'

'Hi, Cathy,' Sam said. 'Nice to see you.'

Cathy moved aside. 'Sit down, I'll get you a drink. Tea ok?'

'Tea's fine.' Sam glanced around. 'I see you've done quite a bit to the house.'

'We only finished it the other week.' She glanced at the man. 'You know how long it takes Gary to do anything.'

Gary put his hands behind his head. 'Work and football get in the way.'

'And pubs,' she said, as she left.

'Are you still running the team?' Sam said.

'Yeah. Our Ryan's at the Boro academy now.'

'Really?'

'Yeah,' Gary said. 'He's doing well. Hopefully, if he gets his head down, he may make it.'

'Great. They could do with some new blood now.'

Gary pointed to a chair, and Sam sat as Gary eased himself onto the settee opposite. 'Are you still going?'

Sam shook his head. 'No. I gave it up this year. With Daisy coming along, and that ...'

'Sorry we couldn't make the christening.'

'It was a good day. How were the hols?'

Gary smiled. 'Excellent. Spent a fortune though.'

Cathy returned with tea and biscuits. 'Here you are, lads. You'll have to excuse me, Sam. I'm just baking. Pop in before you go.'

Gary picked up his mug and leant forward on the seat. 'So, what brings you here?'

'I'm after a favour.'

Gary bit into a biscuit. 'Yeah. Fire away.'

'I remember you told me a mate of yours was a detectorist.'

Gary nodded. 'Monty Lowry. What about him?'

'I'm after borrowing a metal detector, and a quick lesson on how to use one.'

'Oh, yeah. Treasure hunting?'

'It's a case we're working on. I can't say too much at the moment.'

Gary tapped the side of his nose. 'I understand.' He rubbed his chin. 'Monty's a bit … a bit eccentric.'

'In what way?'

'You'll have to meet him. We need something, though.'

Sam frowned. 'What do you mean?'

'Something to entice him.'

'Money, you mean?'

'No. Monty keeps everything he finds, and I mean everything. We'll need something to entice him to loan you a detector.'

'If not money …?'

Gary stood and opened a drawer, pulled something out and tossed it across to Sam, who caught the coin and studied it.

He gawped at Gary. 'An Edward the first silver penny.'

'Yeah.' Gary sat back down. 'It hasn't got a great value, but it'll be enough to entice Monty.'

'How much is it worth?'

Gary shrugged. '£20-£30.'

Sam pulled out his wallet. 'I'll pay you for it.'

Gary waved his hand. 'I got it from Monty. He was cataloguing his coins one day, and I found it on the floor. He'd pissed me off. Monty's a bit tight, and he never pays for a round of drinks if he can help it. So, while he wasn't looking, I nicked it. Served the greedy bugger right.'

Sam grinned. 'I must give you something for it.'

'Wouldn't hear of it.' Gary stood and closed the lounge door. 'I do need a favour from you. It's a bit fortuitous you coming here.' He sat again. 'Cathy's been acting a little strange. She goes out a couple of times a week. She says she's visiting her sister.'

'And isn't she?' Sam said.

'No. But I don't know where she goes. I want you to follow her.'

'Are you sure you—?'

'Sam,' Gary said. 'It's eating away at me. I think she might be having an affair.'

'Cathy? No,' Sam said. 'I think—'

'Please, Sam.'

Sam rubbed the coin between his fingers and pushed it into his pocket. 'Ok.'

'Great. I'll give Monty a ring. See if we can visit today.'

Albert tapped on the door of Mary's flat and nervously waited. He prepared to knock again as it swung open. A smiling Mary stood there, her clothing a mass of rainbow-coloured taffeta and satin. Her Doc Martin boots, bright red. Her multicoloured hair flowed majestically behind her. 'Albert,' she said. 'Come in. Come in.' She moved aside and hurried him along the passageway. 'I was just about to have a herbal tea. Come with me.' Albert followed the ebullient Mary as she bounced into the lounge.

'I hope I'm not too ...' Albert stopped mid-sentence and stared around the room. He had never seen so many different colours outside of B&Q's paint department in one place. The curtains, the cushions – of which there were dozens – shone with every shade imaginable.

'Do you like what I've done to the place?' she said.

'Yes ... It's amazing. I've never seen—'

'Anything like it?'

Albert shook his head. 'No.'

'I must have colour,' she said. 'Can't abide drabness. Right.' She clasped her hands together. 'I'll make us that drink. I have a special herbal infusion for you, Albert. You'll love it. Have a seat, my boy,' she said, then Tigger like, she bounced from the room.

Albert sat, and almost disappeared into the softness of the chair. He stared around the room again, as his eyes picked out new colours and hues in every corner. He almost wished he had brought some sunglasses.

Mary re-entered carrying two steaming cups. 'Get that down you,' she said, offering him one of the drinks. She draped herself onto the chaise opposite, narrowed her eyes, took a sip of the liquid and purred, like some giant feline dressed in a coat borrowed from Joseph. 'Your chakras.'

Albert nervously sipped at his drink. 'Yes.'

'Emotional and compulsive behaviours. That's what you have.'

'Yes. That's it exactly.'

She smiled, and her eyes widened as if a giant, probably multicoloured, lightbulb had just lit up. 'Orange.'

Albert beamed. 'Orange?'

'Orange is your colour. You should wear more orange.'

'Yes, yes, I will.'

Mary wagged a finger. 'Your element is water.'

Albert nodded enthusiastically. 'Orange and water.'

'Yes. You have a blocked Sacral Chakra.'

'Is that serious?'

Mary guffawed. 'Not with me to help you. With a blocked Sacral Chakra, you're likely to feel bored, listless and uninspired.'

'Yes,' Albert said. 'I do.'

Mary moved forward onto the edge of her seat. 'You may have a low sex drive.' Albert blushed as Mary lowered her brow. 'Have you a low sex drive?'

'Well ... I ... I wouldn't like to say.'

'Have you had many sexual partners?'

Albert blushed again. His colour rivalling Mary's boots. 'No. I haven't. Well ... you see.'

'No need to explain, Albert. You're a virgin.' She clasped her hands together. 'I understand. By the time I've finished with you, Albert, you won't be a virgin anymore.'

Albert's mouth dropped open, and Mary laughed. 'Not me, Albert.' She belly-laughed again. 'My days of popping someone's cherry has long gone. I meant ...' She leant closer still and tapped his knee. 'The girls will be throwing themselves at you. It's all about confidence. Women love a confident, assertive male.'

Albert forced a smile. 'I wouldn't know what to say to a woman.'

'Having a blocked Sacral Chakra also makes you resistant to change.' Albert nodded. 'Urinary discomfort,' she continued. Albert shook his head. 'Increased allergies, and ...' She put a finger in the air. 'An attraction to addictive behaviours. Not drugs or alcohol, more shopping, gambling—'

'And OCD,' Albert said.

'And OCD.'

Albert grinned. 'Can you really help?'

'Of course. It doesn't end there, either. A misaligned or blocked Sacral Chakra also affects your sexuality and capacity to change. You, Albert Jackson, are going to be a changed man. The rest of your life begins today.'

'I am?'

She stood. 'You are. Follow me. We will begin with some meditation.' Albert eagerly trailed in her wake as she made her way into the dining room. 'I have cleared some space.' She pointed to the middle of the room and gently led him to the centre. Mary appraised him, frowned and clasped her hands together. 'You can't really meditate in those clothes. In the bathroom, you will find some jogging bottoms and a t-shirt. They should fit you.'

Albert hurried away. 'Chop, chop, Albert,' Mary called after him. 'The new you starts here.'

Sam followed Gary inside the house. 'Monty,' Gary shouted.

'I'm in here,' a voice said.

Sam and Gary made their way along the passage and into the kitchen. Monty sat at a table. Its surface strewn with coins of every shape.

'Monty,' Gary said. 'This is a friend of mine, Sam.'

Monty peered up, the monocle in his left eye held precariously. 'I haven't time to make tea,' he said. 'If you want one—'

'We haven't come here to drink tea,' Gary said.

Monty sighed. 'What have you come here for? I'm extremely busy.'

'I like your monocle,' Sam said.

Monty pulled it from his eye. 'You do?'

'Yeah. Makes you look rakish.'

Monty grinned. 'Sit,' he said to the pair. He smiled at Sam. 'Monocles have been given a bad press,' he continued. 'Everyone imagines upper-class British officers or SS thugs as the only people that wear them.'

'I've recently purchased a cravat,' Sam said.

Gary stared across at him. 'Really?' Monty said. 'I have several myself. Silk, of course.'

'Of course,' Sam said.

'What are you doing?' Gary said.

'Cataloguing some of my coins.'

'Didn't you do that last week?'

'Well, I'm doing it again. I wasn't satisfied with last week's outcome. It was slapdash at best.'

'You'd get on well with a friend of mine,' Sam said. 'He's punctilious like you.'

'Yes, I am punctilious. I'm going to write that word down, so I don't forget it.' Monty took out a small pad and pencil from his shirt breast pocket and jotted down the word. He fixed Sam with a steely stare. 'Sam?'

'Yes,' Sam said.

'I'm going to call you Samuel. I can't abide abbreviated names. If your parents were good enough to give you such a wonderful name, you should have the grace to use it.'

Gary sneered. 'But your name is abbreviated?'

'That's different.'

'How?' Gary said.

Monty put his monocle back in. 'It just is.'

'I've brought you something,' Sam said. 'Gary told me you were a prodigious collector.'

Monty removed his monocle again, took out his pen and pad, and jotted the word down. 'Prodigious,' he said, allowing the word to reverberate around the room. 'I suppose I am. Some people view it as a weakness, Samuel.'

Sam scoffed. 'How can being meticulous be a bad thing?'

'Gary,' Monty said. 'Make yourself and Samuel here a brew. We have much to talk about.' He preceded to jot down the word meticulous.

Gary rolled his eyes and moved over to the kettle as Sam pulled out the coin. 'This is for you, Monty.'

Monty plucked the coin from his hand and examined it. 'An Edward the first silver penny. The Mint that stamped it is pretty common. Not of great value.' He looked at Sam and smiled. 'But a lovely coin nonetheless.'

Sam perused the array of coins on the table and whistled. 'Talking of lovely coins, Monty. You have some exquisite examples here.'

Monty wrote down the word. 'Exquisite,' he repeated. 'Yes I do.'

'Is this your full collection?'

Monty's eyes widened, and he beamed. 'No.' He stood. 'Follow me, Samuel.'

'What about your tea?' Gary shouted after them as the pair exited the room.

They reached the top of the stairs and Monty stopped outside a bedroom. 'Have a look at this.' Pushing the door open, he moved aside, allowing Sam to enter. Sam's eyes slowly scanned the shelves and glass cases that filled the room. He ventured forward and examined them. Coins, neatly laid out in glass-fronted cabinets. On the shelving, artefacts of every size, shape and colour.

'Everything I've ever found is in this room,' Monty said.

'Wow,' Sam said. 'Look at these Roman coins. He leant over one of the cabinets and viewed the dozens of coins.'

'The coins are cased in eras. Roman, Anglo-Saxon, right up to the Victorian era. I lose interest in history after that time.'

Sam gestured towards the shelves. 'And these?'

'Every artefact I've ever found.'

Sam bent and allowed his eyes to examine the pieces. Each one with a small label describing the article, its date and the time and place it was found.

Gary entered carrying two mugs. 'Tea,' he said, holding up the cups.

Sam moved to another set of shelves. 'Those are partefacts,' Monty said.

'What's a partefact?' Gary said.

'Part artefact,' Sam said. 'When a find is incomplete.' Gary shrugged.

Sam faced the pair and raised his eyebrows. 'It's a portmanteau word.'

Gary frowned. 'A what?'

'A word constructed from other words. Like brunch. A portmanteau of breakfast and lunch.'

Monty took out his notepad and began scribbling.

'This is all very interesting,' Gary said. 'But, do you want this tea?'

Monty took the cups from him. 'Can't you see Samuel and I are discussing more important things than tea.'

Gary folded his arms. 'What do you want me to do? I find all this stuff boring.'

Monty sneered and swivelled around in his seat. 'You can have a read of those.' He pointed to a small pile of magazines in the corner.

'What are they?' Gary said, and moved over to them.

'Nudie mags,' Monty said. 'I was having a clear-out. I bought them in my youthful days, and I don't want them now.'

Gary glanced at them. 'Nudie mags?'

'Yes. There's one called buxom babes. I thought that might appeal to you. I know you love cleavage.' Monty sniggered. 'It verges on obsession.'

'I don't know, Monty,' Sam said. 'I like an impressive décolletage myself.'

Monty smiled and took out his pad. 'Yes. Decolle …'

'Tage,' Sam said.

Gary hoisted the magazines into his arms and opened the top one 'Bloody hell, she's sat on a space hopper. How old are these mags? Monty waved a dismissive hand. 'They're probably collector's items you know.

'Well,' Gary said. 'I'll go and have a gander while you two … Get on with this.'

Monty turned to Sam. 'You like my collection?'

Sam nodded enthusiastically. 'I do. It would rival most museums. Some of these items must be worth a penny or two.'

Monty waved a dismissive hand again. 'I have no interest in money. It's the piece I admire. The thought that someone who lived such a long time ago held it in their hands.'

Sam smiled. 'I know exactly what you mean.'

Sam climbed into the car next to Gary. Gary glanced at the metal detector in Sam's hand and started the engine. 'You got it then?' Gary said.

'Yeah. He was only too willing in the end. You're right about him being eccentric, mind. His back bedroom was full of metal detectors. They were mounted on the walls as if they were guns or swords. He's kept every one he's ever bought.'

Gary slowly moved off. 'He's a strange one all right.'

'In the box-room, he had hundreds of metal detecting magazines. It's a wonder that the ceiling hasn't come down. All in all, a satisfactory day.'

Gary nodded behind him. 'It was a good day for me too. A load of nudie-mags and …' He pushed his finger into his top pocket. 'This.' He handed Sam a coin.

'Your coin back?'

Gary grinned. 'My coin back. Don't forget our deal.'

Sam examined the detector. 'I won't.'

CHAPTER TWENTY-THREE

Sam entered the office with a steaming cup of tea and a bacon sandwich in his hand. He hung up his coat and slid onto his seat. Phillip popped his head inside the door. 'I hope you have one of those for me?'

Sam took a massive bite of his bun and held it up. 'Sorry, mate,' he said, through his full mouth. 'Never gave it a thought.'

'Charming. Did you do that thing for your mate?' Phillip said.

Sam nodded. 'I followed Gary's wife last night to a dance studio in Darlington.'

'Dance studio? Let me guess, she's having an affair with her dance instructor?' He pulled off his coat and hung it up.

'How cynical,' Sam said. 'Actually, she was doing a really nice thing for Gary.'

Phillip sat. 'Yeah?'

'Gary can salsa, but Cathy can't. Apparently, it's Gary's birthday coming up, and she decided to learn how to salsa as a surprise. No clandestine meetings, no illicit affair.'

Phillip smiled. 'Sometimes, in our job, it's nice to get a surprise like that.'

Sam took another bite of the bun. 'It is. I told Gary, who was understandably relieved and very happy. He's going to act surprised when his birthday comes.'

'So no divorce?'

'No divorce,' Sam said.

Phillip nodded at Albert's desk. 'And no Albert? I wonder where he is?'

Sam shrugged. 'No idea.' He checked his watch. 'We were late as well, and he's normally in before us.'

'Maybe he got held up at Mary's yesterday.'

Sam rolled his eyes. 'Yeah. What on earth has Miriam Margoyles been telling him? Medium! She's a 3XL if I've ever seen one.'

Phillip sat. 'Yeah. How did you get on with ...?'

'Monty,' Sam said.

'Yeah, Monty. Did he loan you a metal detector?'

Sam grinned. 'I can convince anyone to do anything. It's just this gift I have.' He cocked his head to one side. 'The detector's in the car.'

'So the plan is?'

Sam took a bite of his sandwich and pondered, chewing slowly. 'I need to find a farm near to Stainton village that will let me detect on it. And then ...'

'The real thing,' Phillip said.

'Here he is,' Sam said, as Albert entered. 'Jonny-come-lately.'

Albert smiled at the pair. 'Morning Phillip, morning Sam.' He pulled off his coat and hung it up.

Sam and Phillip stared at the shirt Albert was wearing. 'Nice shirt,' Sam said.

Albert gracefully lowered himself onto the chair behind his desk. 'Thank you.' He straightened his collar and adjusted the buttons on his cuffs.

'I think Sam was being sarcastic,' Phillip said.

'I don't think I've ever seen a shirt as orange as that,' Sam said. 'Where on earth did you get it.'

'I'm not rising to your bait, Samuel. I'm rising above it.'

Sam stood and wandered over to him with his hands inside his trouser pockets. 'Not rising, rising. Make your mind up.'

'You haven't gone all Hari Krishna on us, have you?' Phillip said.

'Mary told me I would face negativity. Orange is my colour.'

Sam rolled his eyes. 'What rubbish has she been telling you?'

'It's not rubbish. I found it enlightening. My Chakra's were misaligned.'

'Misaligned?' Sam said. 'Who'd have thought.'

Albert fixed Sam with a stare. 'Mary isn't keen on you. She says you have a spiky aura.'

Sam sneered. 'A spiky aura.'

Albert stood. 'I feel invigorated. I feel like a new man.'

Phillip narrowed his eyes. 'So what did she do?'

'I haven't time to go through what we did, but Albert Jackson was reborn yesterday.'

Sam ambled back to his desk. 'You do realise, Albert, that all that eastern mystical stuff is a load of baloney.'

'Well, you would say that. I'm going to meditate for a few minutes, and then make myself a herbal tea.' He smiled. 'Body and mind in perfect synergy.'

Sam sat and leant back in his seat. 'Yeah, you do that, mate.'

Phillip stared across at Sam as Albert left and closed the door behind him. 'He does seem different,' Phillip said.

Sam rolled his eyes. 'It's all rubbish. That Mary, I don't know why we let her have that flat … Filling Albert's head with mumbo-jumbo.'

'It won't harm him,' Phillip said.

Kim came into the office and closed the door behind her. 'What's up with Albert? He's inside the broom closet.'

Sam sneered. 'Well, it won't be news to anyone when he finally comes out of the closet.'

'Rubbish,' Kim said. 'Albert's straight.'

'He's meditating,' Phillip said. 'He needs peace and quiet.'

'What?' Kim said.

Sam glanced at his phone as he received a text. 'I'll let Phillip explain.'

'Mary's realigned his Chakras,' Phillip said.

Kim perched on the edge of Phillip's desk. 'Oh, I've heard that's good.'

Sam scoffed. 'Not you as well? You're all so gullible.'

'Well, I don't know,' she said. 'I think Mary has something about her. She's …'

Sam stood. 'She has something about her, all right. She a bloody fraud. A charlatan. A bloody con-woman.' He moved across to the coat stand and snatched his coat. 'Mark my words. She's a quack.'

'Emily still away?' Kim said, as Sam reached for the door handle.

'Yeah. She's gone with her mam and Daisy to see her aunty. She should be back today, though.'

'Where are you off?' Phillip said.

'Out,' Sam said, as he exited.

Kim cocked her head to one side. 'Phillip, can I ask you about Sam?' she said.

'What about him?'

'Come on, Phillip. He's not himself either.'

Phillip shrugged. 'We all have our off days,'

'It's that Lisa.'

Phillip scoffed. 'You don't know that.'

'She has her hooks into him.' She moved around to Phillip's side of the desk. 'Phillip?' she said. 'Can you have a word with him?'

'About Lisa?'

'Yeah. Deb's going to ask Tommo to have a chat. See if we can stop Sam from doing something stupid.'

'How do you know he already hasn't?'

Kim widened her eyes. 'What's he told you?'

'Nothing. Sam doesn't tell me much these days.'

'Well,' Kim looked away deep in thought. 'We have to assume nothing has happened yet.' She turned back to face her boyfriend. 'I want you and Tommo to make sure nothing does.'

Phillip rolled his eyes. 'Sam's an adult. I can't, we can't, tell him what to do.'

'Phillip,' Kim said. 'Please. Think of Emily and little Daisy.' She tapped the desk with her hand. 'Our goddaughter.'

Phillip rubbed his face. 'I'll try. But I can't—'

Kim hugged and kissed him. 'Thanks, gorgeous. I won't be ungrateful.' With that, she sexily sashayed out of the room.

Sam wandered along the seafront and took out his mobile.

'Hi, sexy,' Lisa said.

'Hi. I got your text.'

'Obviously. That's why you phoned.'

'I have something to do this morning,' Sam said. 'An errand to run. I can be at your mam's early afternoon.'

'Shall we say, one?' Lisa purred.

'Yeah, one o'clock is good. I'll have to be discreet.'

Lisa giggled. 'Of course. I can do discretion.'

'One it is.' Sam hung up. He blew out hard and then headed back to pick up his car.

Phillip entered the Sidewinder and made his way to the bar. Tommo folded his newspaper and pushed it aside. 'Hi, Phillip. What are you doing here?'

'Can we talk?'

Tommo folded the paper and pushed it under the bar. 'Yeah. I can't leave the pub, though. I'm on my own and …' He gestured around the room.

Phillip glanced about. 'You've got a lot in for a Monday.'

'I know. Normally it's dead, but today … You just can't gauge it. So, what is it you wanted to talk about?'

'Sam,' Phillip said.

Tommo held up a hand. 'Don't tell me, Kim's been bending your ear.'

'Yeah. I take it Deb's …'

'The same.'

Phillip pulled out a note and handed it to Tommo. 'Get us a pint each.'

Tommo began pulling the drinks. 'I told Deb,' he said. 'Sam's an adult. I can't tell him what to do.'

'Did she mention Emily and Daisy?'

Tommo sighed. 'Yeah. And reminded me that I'm her godfather. I wouldn't have agreed to that if I knew I had to be Sam's conscience.'

'Same here. What do we do?'

'I'm just going to remind him of what he'll lose if he goes ahead with this ...'

'Yeah,' Phillip said. 'That's what I was going to do.'

'We can't allow Sam to know we're plotting against him. Trust me, if he finds out, he'll go ballistic.'

Phillip picked up his pint and took a large swig. 'No. This conversation never happened.'

Albert, bolt upright at his desk, recited his mantra as someone tapped on the door. Mary pushed her nose inside. 'Morning, Albert,' she said.

Albert stood. 'Oh, hi. I wasn't expecting you.'

Mary bounced inside closely followed by a trail of rainbow covered material. 'I thought we could move your training to a new level.'

'Really?'

Mary clasped her hands together. 'Absolutely. You're one of the best students I've ever had.'

Albert moved around to the other side of the desk. 'I'm about finished here.'

'Good,' Mary said. 'Follow me.'

Mary watched as Albert locked the outer door to the office and pushed the key into his jacket pocket. She smiled to herself, as the pair headed towards her flat.

'How do you feel?' Mary said.

'Incredible,' Albert said. 'I feel as if I can take on the world.'

Mary walked into the kitchen and returned with a plate of biscuits. 'What is your biscuit of the day?'

'Blue Ribband,' he said.

'I don't have any of those. Would you like another kind?'

Albert smiled. 'Yes, I would.' He picked up the Kit-Kat, opened the wrapper, and took a bite.

'I think,' Mary said. 'Our work is almost done. I have a few more mantra's for you to try. These will reinforce what you already do. Come this way, young man. Thirty minutes and we'll be done.'

Albert thanked Mary, pulled on his coat, and almost skipped from her flat.

Mary grinned and slipped her hand into the side pocket of her burgundy, linen trousers. She pulled out the set of keys and tossed them into the air, caught them again, and placed them on the dining table.

Sam made his way along the path to the farmyard. In a field adjoining the track, a man on a tractor carried out his work. Sam paused at the gate and shouted to him. The farmer manoeuvred his vehicle over to him and switched off the engine.

'Mr Sproggs?' Sam said.

'Aye,' he said.

'My names Sam Davison. I was wondering if you had any objection to me doing a spot of metal detecting on your farm?'

Sproggs jumped from his vehicle and ambled across. 'Metal detecting?'

'Yeah. I'm new to the metal detecting malarky, but fields are often good places to find things.'

'I'm not sure—'

'I asked your neighbour ...' Sam pointed across the road. 'But he wasn't keen.'

The man sneered. 'Dolby.'

'Yes, that's him.'

'Gerald Dolby is one of the most miserable men you're ever likely to encounter.'

'Yeah,' Sam said. 'He was a little surly.'

'Turned you down, you say?'

Sam nodded. 'Flatly. He said he'd always fancied doing it himself.'

Sproggs laughed. 'He'd never get off his fat arse and do that.' The farmer moved closer. 'Now young man ...'

'Sam.'

'What's in it for me?' Sproggs said.

'A fifty-fifty split.' Sam put a hand inside his jacket pocket and pulled out a piece of paper. 'I have an agreement here. We both sign it and have it witnessed. If I find anything, we split the money between us.'

'Well,' Sproggs said. 'I think we have an agreement. I'd love to get one over on Dolby.'

Kim and Deb lingered in the car. 'She might not come back out,' Kim said.

'Maybe we should knock?' Deb said.

'Should we?'

Deb nodded. 'Yeah. Come on.' The pair climbed out of the car and headed up the path. Deb glanced at Kim before knocking on the door.

Lisa opened it, the smile on her face quickly evaporating. 'Yeah.'

'Do you know who we are?' Deb said.

Lisa sternly folded her arms. 'I know who you are. But I'm not familiar with your friend.'

'We're both mates of Emily Simpson,' Deb said. 'We've come around here to give you a bit of friendly advice. Stay away from Sam.'

Lisa sneered. 'Who the hell—?'

Kim moved closer to Lisa, pushed her in the chest and glared. 'Listen you slapper. If you want to hang on to those porcelain veneers, you'll do what we say.'

Lisa stared wide-eyed as Kim was joined by Deb. 'It would be best for all concerned if you left town,' Deb said. 'Sam's happy.'

Lisa stepped further back. 'You can't just go around threatening people. In any case, I don't want anything to do with Sam.'

Deb and Kim glanced at each other. 'Good,' Kim said. 'Make sure it stays that way.' The pair of them headed off as Lisa slammed the door, took out her phone, and called Sam.

Lisa checked her appearance in the mirror as she waited for Sam's arrival. She dabbed at her red and puffy right eye, smiling at her own handiwork. Lisa spun around as the doorbell chimed, wiped the smile from her face, and headed to answer it. Sam stood outside, he frowned as she beckoned him inside, glanced in both directions, and then shut the door.

'What happened?' he said.

Lisa slowly turned to face him. Sam sucked in air as he spotted the developing shiner on her right eye, and winced. Sam stepped forward and placed a hand on her cheek. 'Did they do this?' Lisa tearfully nodded. 'Wait until I see them—' He growled.

Lisa shook her head. 'It's ok. I was just a little shaken, that's all.'

'I'll make us some tea,' Sam said.

'I was hoping for something more than tea.'

Sam smiled. 'All in good time. Come on, let's have a sit-down.'

The pair headed into the lounge and sat on the settee. 'I haven't pulled you away from something important, have I?' she said.

'No. I'd finished what I was doing.' Sam glanced around the room. 'I'll tell you what, forget about the tea. You haven't got something a little stronger, have you?'

'Wine ok?'

'Yeah. Wine is great.'

Lisa stood and entered the kitchen. Sam pulled out his mobile as he felt it vibrate. He viewed the three missed calls from Emily and one text. Sam pushed the phone back inside his pocket, paused, took it back out and read the message.

Lisa came back carrying two glasses. 'Here you are?' she said, offering Sam one.

'I have to go,' he said.

'Go, why?'

'Daisy's not well, she's at the hospital. Sorry, Lisa. I have to go.'

Lisa put a hand on his arm. 'Of course.' Sam kissed her and left.

Lisa fumed, downing both glasses of wine in succession.

Sam raced through the corridors of the hospital and into A&E. Emily sat with her mother as Daisy happily played with a toy.

'Is everything ok?'

Emily stood and threw her arms around Sam. 'Oh, Sam. I thought you'd never come.'

'Is Daisy ok?' he said.

Emily's mother smiled. 'She's fine. She had a temperature, that's all. Emily panicked when she couldn't get hold of you.'

Sam lifted his daughter into his arms and kissed her. His eyes glistened as he hugged her close. 'I thought …'

'It was awful, Sam,' Emily said. 'She was so hot, and I didn't know what to do.' Emily started to sob, and Sam took hold of her hand, pulling her close. 'Don't worry. I'm here now.'

'We're just waiting for the doctor to say we can go,' Emily said.

Sam kissed Emily, and then his daughter. 'How about we go for a meal, my treat.'

CHAPTER TWENTY-FOUR

Sam stared out of the office window to the street below. 'Sam,' Phillip repeated. 'Do you want a tea?'

Sam turned. 'Yes, please. Sorry I was miles away.'

Phillip edged closer. 'Can I have a word before Albert comes in?'

Sam slumped onto his chair. 'Yeah. Fire away.'

'Is everything ok with you and Emily?'

Sam rubbed his face. 'I was a bit shook up yesterday.'

'But Daisy's fine?'

'Yeah. She was full of beans this morning.'

Phillip glanced over his shoulder towards the door, then fixed his gaze back on Sam. He coughed. 'You and Emily?' he said quietly.

Sam lowered his eyes. 'Phillip,' Sam said. 'This isn't going to be a lecture, is it? Because I would never tell you how to run your life.'

'I know. It's just ... This Lisa ...?'

'I would quit now, Phillip. Before we fall out.'

Phillip nodded and moved over to the door. 'I'll make the tea.' He stopped at the threshold. 'I wouldn't like to see you do something you may regret later, that's all.' Sam spun in his chair and looked out of the window. 'Once the die is cast ...' Phillip said. Sam said nothing as his cousin left, but then swivelled his chair around and viewed the space Phillip had occupied.

Phillip glanced at the clock. 'Where the hell is Albert?' he said.

Sam drained his cup. 'God knows. He's getting tardy of late.'

'What's your plan for today?'

Sam leant back in the seat. 'I'm going over to Stainton to do a bit of detecting.'

'So, the farmer is letting you go on his land?'

'He is. I'll do it for a few days as cover. And then ...'

'And then …?' Phillip said.

'Ewen's doing the work in the churchyard on Thursday and Friday. I spoke to him yesterday. He's going to leave his van there on Friday night.'

Phillip frowned. 'Won't the vicar be suspicious?'

Sam smiled. 'Ewen's thought of that. He's going to tell the vicar that there's something wrong with it. That way, it will cover us from the road. The only way anyone could see us is if they venture inside the churchyard.'

'And we're going to have the tent covering the dig?'

'Yeah. Hopefully,' Sam said. 'We can do it quietly.'

'You're sure it's there?' Phillip said.

'I ran the detector over it yesterday. There's definitely something there. Something made of gold.'

Phillip smiled and rubbed his hands together. 'I'm excited and nervous.'

'We'll be fine. Don't …'

Albert entered took off his coat and wandered across to his desk. He smiled at the other two and slid onto his seat.

'I don't think I've ever seen orange trousers,' Sam said.

'I bet you got some funny looks on the way in,' Phillip said.

Albert leant back in his seat and placed his feet on the desk. 'You're right, Sam. This position is really comfortable.'

Phillip stood and stared at Albert's footwear. 'Are those flipflops?'

'Yes,' Albert said. 'Very comfortable.'

Sam narrowed his eyes. 'Are they monogrammed?'

Albert grinned. 'I thought they would add a bit of style to them. What do you think?'

Sam stood and walked across to Albert. 'Lovely,' he said, as he examined them. He bent down and viewed Albert. 'You haven't shaved.'

Albert waved a dismissive hand. 'Shaving's a chore. I've been a hostage to the razor blade far too long.'

'You're growing a beard?' Phillip said.

'Yeah. It's all part of the new Albert Jackson.'

Phillip tutted. 'It'll look a bit scruffy while it's growing.'

'I've purchased a beard trimmer. When it's long enough, I'll style it.'

'Well,' Sam said. 'I'm impressed by Mary Hough. She's managed to transform you from a smartly dressed individual to a tramp within a couple of days.'

'Your negativity doesn't affect me, Sam. I am inured to it.'

'What about your counselling sessions?' Phillip said.

Albert scoffed. 'I don't need them anymore. I have one scheduled today, actually. I'm going along to tell Charles that I won't require his services from now on.'

'What if you have a relapse?' Sam said. 'And your biscuit obsession returns?'

'I won't. I am at one with myself.' Albert placed his hands behind his head.

'What's that on your wrist?' Phillip said.

Albert grinned. 'It's my bracelet. It has all the colours of the Chakras.'

'Why don't you get a tattoo?' Sam said. 'Go the whole hog.'

'And a piercing,' Phillip said.

Albert stood. 'I may well. But for now, I will sate my appetite with herbal tea. Laters,' he said, as he wandered out.

Sam blew out hard. 'Just when you think someone can't get any weirder, he jumps on the bus to Lunatic-Ville and books himself into the Mad as a Hatter Hotel.' Phillip chuckled.

Albert strode into Charles' office and slumped onto the seat. Charles concentrated on his paperwork as he flicked through it. 'I'll be with you in a minute,' he said.

Albert shuffled in his seat. 'Charles,' he said. 'I have something important to tell you.'

Charles noisily rustled his papers. 'Can't you see I'm …' He looked up and stared at Albert. 'What on earth are you wearing?'

'What I'm wearing isn't important at this moment.'

Charles tossed aside the papers. 'You haven't been drinking, have you? Or worse, dabbling with illicit substances?'

'I'm stone-cold sober.'

'But – but – but, your attire. It's …'

Albert glanced down at his shirt. 'Orange.'

'Yes. Orange. Your condition is worse than I thought.' He stood and moved across to the shelf. 'There's a similar case in here. I was reading it last week.'

'Charles,' Albert said. 'I've had my Chakras realigned.'

'Chakras? Not eastern mystic medicine rubbish? You do know it's a load of—'

'Yes, yes. The upshot is …' Albert stood. 'I won't be needing any more sessions. I'm completely cured of my OCD. I only came here to thank you for your help and say goodbye.' Albert inched towards the door. Charles dropped the book and put himself between Albert and the exit.

'Now, Albert. Let's not be hasty.'

'But I'm cured.'

'Perhaps you are, but what about me?'

Albert's jaw dropped open. 'You?'

'I thought we had built a rapport? A glorious meeting of intellects.'

'Well …'

'What about our fishing exploits? I know you went fishing with your friend ...'

'Tommo,' Albert said.

'But does he really know the ins and outs of angling? The nuances? The passion and rapture of holding that fish in your hands. Does he, Albert? Does he?' Charles thrust a fist upward.

'He seems quite—'

Charles scoffed. 'Seems. There you go. He's just a novice. I have loads to show you. Lots to teach you. I haven't even mentioned my collection of keepnets. I have nearly ten. Some dating back years.'

Albert mumbled. 'I've sort of enjoyed the sessions, but I can't keep paying—'

'I'll give you a discount. 20%. There you go. You can't say fairer than that.'

'Charles—'

'40%,' Charles said. 'That's more than I gave Morley, and he was skitzo.'

'Skitzo? Is that even an appropriate term?'

Charles dropped to his knees and pawed at Albert's trouser leg. 'Please, Albert. I implore you. I'm begging you. Bugger it. I'll do it for nothing.' He stood. 'There, I've said it now. For free, Albert. Free,' he screeched.

Albert took off his orange-tinted sunglasses and blew on them. 'Free, you say?'

'Yes,' Charles said, grasping hold of his lapels. 'Free. Gratis. Buckshee.'

Albert put his glasses back on. 'I'm not sure—'

'I'll pay you. I have the money.' He pulled out his wallet. 'Look,' he said, holding it open. 'What good is money to me if I haven't got you.'

'I can't take money from my therapist. That would be unethical.'

'Of course you can. You can help me with some therapy.' Tears formed in Charles' eyes. 'I'll tell you about my childhood, and my brute of a father.'

'Your father?'

'He'd beat me, Albert. With a copy of Who's who.'

'Good God,' Albert said.

'And he would lock me in the under-stairs cupboard. Harry Potter's life was nothing compared to what I had to endure. Oh, the torture I went through, and I didn't get the chance to become a wizard.'

Albert lifted his eyes and pointed to the chairs. 'Shall we sit?'

'Yes,' Charles said. 'I'll make us some tea.'

Someone knocked on the door, and Charles groaned loudly. 'Who the hell is this?' He held up his hand to Albert. 'I'll be two minutes. Don't go anywhere.'

Sam entered the Sidewinder and made his way across to the bar. 'What's the emergency?' he said.

Tommo handed a customer his change. 'No emergency, mate.'

'You said on the phone you wanted a word.'

'I did.' He motioned for Sam to follow him into the cellar room. 'How's the plan going?'

'I was on my way over to see Ewen until you called.'

Tommo forced a smile. 'Sorry about that.'

Sam shrugged. 'He's working on the wall. He'll probably finish it tomorrow.'

'Good.' Tommo stroked his beard.

'He's concocted a plan. He's going to tell the vicar that his van has something wrong with it. That way, he can leave it there tomorrow night. It will screen us from the road.'

'And the tent and tools? He's got those?'

Sam frowned. 'You know all this, Tommo.'

'What about when we find the cross?'

Sam groaned. 'I told you. I'm going to re-bury it in a field. I've got the location. While Ewen is getting everything ready, I'll dig a hole in readiness.'

'This will be great,' Tommo said. 'We'll be rich.'

'You do realise that the cross will be classed as treasure trove.'

'Yeah, you explained.'

'We should still do ok out of it, but we won't be millionaires.'

'I know.' Tommo opened the door and peeked out into the bar. 'We'll meet here tomorrow at 5pm.'

'Sounds good to me,' Sam said. 'Now, if that's everything? I have places to be.'

Tommo grabbed his arm. 'There is one more thing.'

Sam raised his eyebrows. 'Go on.'

'Lisa.'

Sam fixed Tommo with an icy stare. 'What about her?'

'You haven't ... Have you?'

'What business is it of yours?'

Tommo rubbed his face. 'I'm thinking of Emily and Daisy.'

'Have I ever interfered in your life?'

'Well, no.'

'Right,' Sam said. 'So, what's makes you think you can interfere in mine?'

Tommo held his hands up. 'Fair point.'

Sam reached for the handle. 'All I'm saying,' Tommo said. 'Once the die is cast.'

Sam spun around to face him. 'What did you say?'

'Eh, I said—'

'The die is cast.'

'Yeah.'

'Funny thing to say. Phillip said exactly the same thing the other day to me.'

'Ah,' Tommo said. 'I can explain.'

'Have you and him been talking about me behind my back?'

'Sam,' Tommo said, and placed a hand on his arm. 'It was the girls that—'

Sam pushed his arm away. 'Fuck you,' he said. 'And Phillip, and the girls. Stay out of my business, all of you.' He pulled the door open and stormed out. Tommo slammed his fist on the bar, huffed loudly and poured himself a very large whisky.

Sam screeched to a halt in Stainton, still seething. He put his head on the steering wheel and groaned as his phone rang.

'Hi,' he said.

'Everything ok?' Lisa said. 'With Daisy?'

'Yeah, she's fine. False alarm.'

'Are you busy today?'

'I've got a couple of things to do. But I could …'

'I've got the house to myself. Bring a bottle of wine, we'll have a reminisce.'

Sam peered out of the window as Ewen approached. 'Shall we say two?'

'Two it is,' she said.

Sam opened the car door and got out. 'How's it going?' he said to Ewen as he reached him.

'Good,' Ewen said. 'I've just about finished the wall. I'm just padding it out for tomorrow. The vicar's wife's been over with tea and sarnies all day. She's a bit flighty. She even felt my muscles.'

Sam moved around to the boot and pulled it open. 'She seemed so prim the other day.'

Ewen raised his eyebrows. 'She is when her husband's about, but when he's not …'

Sam lifted the detector from the boot and slammed it shut. 'You're not thinking of …'

'Christ, no. Even if I did find her attractive, I wouldn't. I couldn't do the dirty on Steph. I'd never forgive myself.'

Sam gazed into the distance. 'I'm going to the field again. Just keeping up the pretence. I've found a nice spot to bury the cross.'

'If it's in the graveyard?' Ewen said.

'Well, there's definitely something made of gold buried in there. I'll come and see you before I leave.'

Ewen nodded. 'You ok? You look a bit preoccupied.'

Sam groaned. 'Just other people. Tommo and Phillip, sticking their noses into my life.'

'Do you want to have a cup of tea before you crack on? The vicar's wife has just brought some over.'

'Maybe I should get on.'

Ewen pulled a spliff from his pocket. 'I've got one of these we can share.'

'I thought you were laying off the wacky baccy?'

Ewen smiled. 'I am. This is only lightweight stuff. I have one occasionally. When I'm a little wound up. This whole cross thing has got me on edge. In a good way.'

Sam nodded. 'Yeah, ok.'

The pair made their way over to the churchyard and reclined against a wall. Ewen lit the cigarette, took a long drag and gave it to Sam.

Sam drew deeply on it and passed it back. 'It's tranquil here.'

'Yeah,' Ewen said. 'We couldn't have asked for a better place to dig. With the van covering us from the roadside, no one can see us. And if anyone comes into the graveyard, or even the church, with the tent they can't see a thing.'

'I can't wait to hold it,' Sam said.

'You love all that stuff, don't you?'

Sam smiled. 'When I was at University, I did a lot of research into Lindisfarne. To think I could be holding something that the monks on the island had made over a thousand years ago.'

Ewen held the spliff out to Sam, who shook his head 'I suppose when you put it like that,' Ewen said. He held out the cigarette again. 'Sure?'

Sam shook his head again. 'It's not really for me. I prefer a drink.' Sam glanced away. 'Lisa,' Sam said.

Ewen said nothing. He took another draw on the cigarette and tossed the butt into the grass. 'You're right about this. It's doing nothing for me either.'

'What you were saying earlier ...' Sam said. 'About not doing the dirty on Steph.' Ewen nodded. 'I'm about to do the dirty on Emily.' Ewen stared across the graveyard.

'Any thoughts?' Sam said.

'You've already said that you're sick of people interfering.'

'You're different. You know Lisa.'

Ewen laughed feebly. 'I think the old Sam would have already done the dirty.'

Sam shrugged. 'Maybe.'

'Do you remember Nathan from school?' Ewen said.

'Nathan Skully, yeah.'

'I still keep in touch with him on Facebook and that.'

'Oh, yeah. How's he doing?'

Ewen plucked a piece of grass from the ground and started playing with it. 'He lives near Hull.'

'Hull, eh?'

'Lisa lived there for a while. I remembered him telling me he ran into her.' Sam remained silent. 'I rang him up,' Ewen continued. 'She apparently caused a lot of bother while she was there. Managed to break up three relationships, he told me …' Ewen glanced at Sam. 'She was virtually run out of town. One of the blokes she messed about with was a traveller. His wife's family weren't happy.'

'That's why she's here?' Sam said. 'She told me she lived in Cardiff.'

'Maybe she did.' Ewen lowered his eyes. 'There were other men, apparently. She's a bit of a dab hand at causing mischief by all accounts.'

'What are you saying, Ewen?'

Ewen shrugged. 'I try not to dispense advice. It's usually not that great.'

Sam smiled to himself. 'I sense a but?'

Ewen lowered his eyes and ran a hand through his hair. 'We've been trying for a baby, Steph and me.'

'I didn't know.'

'We've kept it quiet. We've had tests done, and … Well, let's just say, the chances are slim. Not impossible, but slim.'

'What about IVF?'

'Done it. From this point on we'll have to pay.' Ewen picked up a small stone and lobbed it across the churchyard.

Sam nodded past Ewen. 'If the cross is there …'

'Steph wants a baby more than anything. What you and Emily have with Daisy is …' He turned his head away. 'We'd give anything for that.'

'I'm sorry, mate.'

'Steph loves me, but things like this drive a wedge between couples. It eats away and erodes their relationship.' Ewen rubbed his face.

'Emily loves me. I know that.'

Ewen turned to face Sam again. 'She adores you, mate. If you're going to play poker with your life … well,' he said. 'You get the picture.'

'And Lisa?'

Ewen stood. 'Lisa's poison. I know how you felt about her. I understand how you feel about her, but …' He bent and took hold of his trowel. 'Is she worth losing what you've got?'

Sam watched as Ewen walked away. He stood, picked up the detector, and left.

CHAPTER TWENTY-FIVE

Albert sat in his therapist's office, trying to decipher what was being said. He stood, wandered over to the door and opened it.

'Charles,' he said. 'I have to ...'

Inspector Comby and DS Hardman stood near to Charles. Comby glanced in Albert's direction. 'I'm sorry, sir. We will have to curtail your session. Mr Hurworth, here, has to accompany us down to the station.' Comby turned away to face Charles again. 'If you could get your coat, Mr ...' Comby spun around. 'Albert Jackson?'

'Hello, Inspector.'

'What are you doing ...? And what the hell are you wearing?'

'Charles is my therapist.'

'I see. Unfortunately, Mr Jackson, you may have to find yourself a new one.'

'What's happened, Charles?' Albert said.

Charles put his hands over his face. 'I didn't mean to do it. It was a moment of madness. An aberration.'

Phillip entered the Sidewinder and strode across to the bar. Gene smiled at him. 'Hi, handsome,' he said.

'Hi, Gene. Where's Tommo?'

'He's next door. On his third whisky.'

'Really?' Phillip said. He pulled a note from his pocket and popped it on the counter. 'I'll have a pint of the American IPA, and get one for yourself.'

'Cheers,' Gene said. 'I'll bring it through to you.'

Phillip walked through into the cocktail bar and slumped onto a seat next to Tommo, who was doing the accounts.

'On the whisky?' Phillip said.

Tommo shut the book. 'Yeah. Want one? I've got a spare glass.'

'Gene's bringing me a beer.'

Gene came into the bar and placed Phillip's drink and change onto the table. 'I think the stouts going off,' Gene said to Tommo.

'Give me five minutes, and I'll change it,' he said. Gene nodded and left.

'Did you talk to Sam?' Phillip said.

Tommo picked up the bottle. 'Why do you think I'm on this?'

'Didn't he take it well?'

Tommo held the half-empty bottle aloft. 'Not really. He told me to eff off.'

'Yeah,' Phillip said. 'I didn't have much luck, either.'

'I told Deb when she asked me to speak to him what would happen,' Tommo said. 'I knew Sam wouldn't be happy.'

'I got off lightly,' Phillip said. 'He didn't swear at me.'

'He twigged when I said that thing about the die being cast.'

'I said that.'

Tommo sighed. 'I know. He stormed out of here in a right huff.'

'What do we do now?'

'Nothing,' Tommo said. 'We have tomorrow to think about. I don't want Sam walking around with his pet lip on.'

Phillip picked up the whisky. 'I think I will join you.'

'Tommo,' Gene shouted.

Tommo groaned. 'I said I'd be five minutes.' He hauled himself to his feet and wandered into the Sidewinder closely followed by Phillip.

'Jesus, Gene,' he said. 'You're an impatient—' Gene nodded over Tommo's shoulder.

Phillip and Tommo turned and honed in on Albert, who sat staring vacantly into space.

The pair walked over. 'You ok, Albert?' Tommo said.

Albert didn't answer. Tommo clicked his fingers. 'Gene, get Albert a drink. He looks in shock.'

'What should I get him?' Gene said.

'Orange juice,' Phillip said. 'It'll match his outfit.'

Tommo frowned at Phillip. 'Brandy.'

Gene poured a large brandy and carried it across to his boss. Tommo and Phillip parked themselves opposite Albert. 'What's up, Albert?' Tommo repeated, placing the drink in front of him.

'Charles,' Albert said.

Phillip pushed the drink towards Albert. 'Your therapist?'

Albert nodded. 'The police arrested him.'

Tommo rolled his eyes. 'Don't say he's a fake—'

Albert shook his head. 'Inspector Comby and Hardman came to his office.' Albert stared wide-eyed at the others. 'They say he murdered his wife and friend.'

'Kevin?' Phillip said.

'Yeah. He'd buried them under the patio.'

'How cliché,' Phillip said.

Tommo glared at Phillip. 'Just because Sam's not here, Phillip, it doesn't mean you have to stand in for him.'

'Sorry,' Phillip said.

'Buried under the patio?' Tommo said.

'Yeah. Apparently, Kevin was still wearing his waders.'

'What?' Tommo said.

'That's what pushed Charles over the edge, you see.' Albert slowly shook his head. 'He said that he couldn't stand the thought of losing Kevin. He came home early and found his wife and Kevin leaving with half his fishing gear.'

'And he murdered them?' Phillip said.

'He hit Kevin over the head with a fishing stool and choked his wife to death with a fishing line.'

'Bloody hell,' Tommo said.

Albert downed his drink in one. 'That could've been me. He wanted to take me fishing.'

'But it isn't, Albert,' Tommo said.

Albert stared directly at Tommo. 'Do you mind if we don't go fishing again, Tommo. I couldn't face it.'

Tommo patted his arm. 'No. To be honest, standing in cold water up to my gonads didn't seem as exciting as it once was. I was only going fishing for you.'

'My Chakras are all over the place now,' Albert said.

'You'll get them back,' Tommo said. 'I'm sure.'

The door opened, and Lisa stood there. 'I thought you were never coming,' she said to Sam.

Sam followed her through into the lounge. He held out the bottle of wine to her. 'I had some thinking to do.'

Lisa took the bottle and pouted at him. 'Oh, yeah?'

'I can't do this, Lisa. I love Emily and Daisy too much.'

Lisa forced a smile. 'Come on. I said I'd be discreet.' She stepped closer and placed a hand on his cheek. 'You and I had something special once.'

'Once,' Sam said, and removed her hand. 'That was the past.'

'Emily won't keep you happy. You know that?'

Sam shook his head. 'She will.'

'You're just feeling guilty because of Daisy. Emily's gay for god's sake.'

'I should go.'

'What did you bring the wine for then?'

'Old-time's sake.'

'You're going to lose what we have for a born-again dyke? She's probably in bed with some woman as we speak.'

'If you're coming back to Teesside because of me, you're wasting your time. I heard about what happened in Hull.'

'Sam,' she said. 'Who's been filling your head with rubbish?'

'It wouldn't matter, anyway,' he said. 'I love Emily.'

Lisa sneered. 'Love! Don't make me laugh. This is why I cheated on you. You try to make out you're edgy, but deep down you're still the spineless Sam from all those years ago.'

Sam looked her up and down. 'Goodbye, Lisa,' he said. 'Maybe you did deserve that blackeye.'

Lisa scoffed. 'They didn't do it. They never laid a finger on me. Neither of them has the guts.'

Sam shook his head. 'I should have known you were lying. Ewen was right about you.'

'Ewen wasn't the only one, you know. I had all your mates.' Sam walked outside and closed the door behind him. He took in a deep breath and smiled to himself.

Lisa scrutinised the wine in her hand, turned to face the fireplace, and smashed the bottle on the marble hearth.

Tommo pulled his coat off and tossed it over the bannister. Deb's head appeared around the corner. 'Good day?'

Tommo groaned and followed her into the kitchen. 'Not really.'

'Aw,' Deb said, kissing him on the cheek. 'What's up?'

'Sam's not speaking to Phillip or me.'

'Why?'

Tommo scoffed. 'Why do you think?'

'Oh, you mentioned Lisa?'

He sighed. 'Yeah. He told me to eff off.'

'God. Sorry about that.' She put her arms around him. 'I'll make it up to you after tea.'

'Albert's looking for a new therapist.'

Deb snuggled into him. 'What's wrong with the one he's got?'

Tommo slumped onto a chair. 'He murdered his wife and best friend, then buried them under the patio.'

'Really?' Deb said, donning her oven gloves. 'Will cottage pie do?'

Baggage jumped onto the sofa next to Phillip. 'You know, Bagsy,' Phillip slurred. 'It's been an eventful day.'

Baggage cocked his head to one side as if listening intently. 'Albert's therapist is a murderer. Sam's fuming, and we're digging up a grave tomorrow.' He held a finger to his lips. 'Shh. Don't tell Kim.'

Kim popped her head around the corner. 'Who are you talking to?'

'Baggage.'

Luggage came bounding in and jumped at the settee, trying to get next to Baggage and Phillip. Baggage looked at the pup and then at Phillip before placing his head between his paws.

'Anything interesting happen today?' Kim said.

'Funny you should ask,' Phillip said. He stood, and unsteadily followed Kim as Luggage finally succeeded in getting onto the sofa. She playfully jumped on top of Baggage who gave a doggy sigh.

Albert lounged cross-legged in the middle of his sitting-room as incense burned steadily in the corner. He closed his eyes and repeated the mantra Mary had given him. His orange-clad form mumbling to himself as the day's stresses slowly evaporated. Zeus, nearby, watched on as if in some kind of trance himself.

Sam entered the sitting room and made his way over to Emily and Daisy. He bent down and kissed the pair of them. 'I thought I might cook tea,' Sam said.

'Oh,' Emily said. 'That would be nice.' Southgate stirred and moved towards Sam wagging her tail. He ruffled her ears.

'I've got a bottle of wine, too. I thought once Daisy goes off, we may put on a movie and have a glass or two.'

'That would be lovely.'

'Right,' he said. 'I'll get started.' He stopped at the threshold of the door.

'Good day?' she said.

'Yeah.' Sam smiled. 'Monumental.'

'Good. Are you and the boys still doing that thing tomorrow?'

'Yeah. Can't tell you too much yet.'

'Kim and Deb are meeting me in the Black Mamba tomorrow. Girlie afternoon. Mam said she'll babysit.'

'Em?' Sam said.

'Yeah?'

'I do love you.'

Emily smiled. 'I know.'

'I don't tell you often enough.' Emily nodded. Sam smiled. 'I'll get the tea on.'

CHAPTER TWENTY-SIX

Emily and Deb sat in the corner of the Sidewinder, while Phillip got served by Tommo.

'Where's Sam?' Tommo said, placing a pint on the bar top.

'I don't know. He didn't come into work today. Neither did Albert.'

'Mm,' Tommo said. He placed the second pint on the counter. 'He's probably still mad at us.'

'I spoke to Emily. She said he's coming in. He had an errand to run.'

Tommo raised his eyebrows. 'I hope he's not with you know who?'

Deb stood and walked across to them. 'Is this mine, big fella?' she said, and picked up one of the pints.

'Yeah. The gin's Emily's.'

'How's Emily and Sam?' Phillip said.

Deb glanced back at Emily, who was fiddling with her phone. 'I think they're good. They had sex last night.'

'She told you that?' Tommo said.

'No, but I can just tell. She's in a much better mood.'

'You don't tell them about us, do you?' Tommo said, as Phillip smirked.

'No one needs to hear about that, Tommo,'

'You're not wrong there,' Phillip said.

Tommo blushed a little. 'Good.'

The door opened, and Sam strode in. 'I have an announcement,' he exclaimed. The customers in the pub looked towards him as a hush descended. Sam dropped onto one knee, pulled a box from his pocket and grinned. 'Emily Jane Simpson. I bloody love you. Will you marry me?'

Emily smiled and took the box from him. She opened the lid, removed the ring, and stared at it. 'Oh, Sam,' she said. 'It's beautiful.'

'Well?' a woman on a nearby table said. 'Is that a yes?'

Emily beamed and slid the ring on her finger. 'Yes.' Sam moved near to Emily and hugged and kissed her as the place erupted into clapping and cheering.

Deb glanced at Tommo. 'If you ever do that to me,' she said. 'I'll bloody chin you.'

Tommo's eyes widened. 'Wouldn't you marry me?'

'I'd marry you all right. I just wouldn't want to be embarrassed like that.'

Tommo picked up his glass. 'I'll bear that in mind.' He raised his glass high. 'Cheers, Sam.'

'Yeah, cheers,' Phillip said.

Deb made her way over to Emily and kissed Sam en route. 'Congratulations,' she said.

'Thanks, Deb.'

Sam stopped at the bar. 'Get a drink for everyone,' he said. 'On me.'

'Sam,' Tommo said. 'About yesterday. I want to apologise.'

Sam waved a hand dismissively. 'Forget it. That's all sorted.' He looked back towards Emily, who was proudly showing her ring to Deb. 'Emily's the girl for me.'

'Right,' Tommo said, raising his voice above the hubbub of noise. 'Sam's buying everybody a drink.'

Albert walked into the office carrying a bag. 'Hi, Kim. You haven't seen Mary, have you?'

Kim nodded behind Albert, who turned to find a seated Mary pointing a gun at him. 'Take a seat, Albert,' she said.

Albert stared at Mary, who was dressed in black jeans, and a black turtle-neck jumper. 'What the—?' he said.

'Sit,' she bellowed. 'Like I told Kim here. This gun is real, loaded, and I do know how to use it.'

Albert slumped onto a chair. 'I was hoping that you would realign my Chakras.'

Mary sneered. 'You didn't believe all that mumbo jumbo, did you?'

'Well,' he glanced at Kim. 'It seemed to work.'

'Placebo effect, Albert. That's all it was.'

'I'm not convinced,' he said. 'You were very good at it.'

'Albert,' Kim said. 'Aren't you puzzled as to why Mary is holding us at gunpoint?'

Albert glanced between the two of them then focused on Mary. 'Why *are* you holding us at gunpoint, Mary?'

'The cross,' Mary said.

'The cross?'

'Yes. The Liturgy. We know you've found it. We know you're going to retrieve it later tonight.'

'Ah,' Albert said.

Mary stood. 'Ah, indeed.'

'And Stanley Knight? Did you kill him?'

Mary shook her head. 'His brother George did that. Although he claims it was an accident. But we don't believe him.'

'I suppose you're going to sell the cross?' Albert said.

'That's the plan. Poor Stanley wanted it to go to a museum.'

'We were hoping it would end up in a museum too.'

Mary smiled. 'How noble. Sadly, it will end up in the private collection of someone from China. However, he is paying us handsomely for it.'

Albert glanced at Kim again. 'And what about us?'

'Do as we say and you won't come to any harm. First things first, though. Give me your mobile.' Mary held out her hand, and Albert passed her his phone. 'My colleague is going to follow your friends. Once they have the cross, we'll get them to come here.' Mary leant back in her seat. 'Why don't you make the three of us a nice cuppa?'

Albert beamed. 'I've got some new herbal ones we can try.' Kim rolled her eyes as Albert pulled out a box from his carrier.

'I can't abide them, Albert. I'm afraid that was all for show. Yorkshire will do nicely.'

A crestfallen Albert dropped the box back into his bag and went to make the tea.

Tommo hung up. 'He's still not answering.'

Sam huffed. 'Typical. The most important night of our lives and he's at home contemplating his navel.'

'We can go without him,' Phillip said.

'But we're the ones taking all the risks,' Sam said.

'To be honest,' Tommo said. 'There are already plenty of us. Albert's been a little preoccupied since his therapist got arrested.'

Sam gaped. 'His therapist got arrested?'

'Yeah,' Phillip said. 'He murdered his wife and best mate.'

'Bloody hell,' Sam said. 'Albert can't half pick them.'

Emily walked over to the boys. 'Kim hasn't phoned, has she?' Emily said to Phillip.

'No. Why?'

'She's not answering her phone.'

Phillip took out his mobile and rang. '... It's gone straight to answerphone.' He pondered. 'It's not like her. She always has her phone with her.'

'I've only had one drink,' Emily said. 'I'll have a run over to your house.'

'Yeah,' Phillip said. 'Good idea. I'll come with you.'

Deb joined them. 'What's happening?'

'Kim's not answering her phone,' Emily said.
'She'll have run out of power or something.'
'Kim's rarely late,' Emily said. 'And when she is, she always rings.'
'We're going over to my house,' Phillip said.
'You two aren't going anywhere, are you?' Deb said to Tommo and Sam.
'Yeah,' Tommo said. 'I told you.'
Deb huffed. 'Well, I'm not staying here on my own. I'll come with you Em.'

'No answer, guv,' Hardman said to Comby. 'Jackson must be out.'
'What a great piece of detective work, Mick,' Comby said under his breath, as he reached the car. 'Your powers of deduction never cease to amaze me.'
Hardman made his way back to the car and squeezed into the driver's seat. 'What do we do now?'
'We'll go around to that pub he frequents. I need to ask Albert Jackson about his therapist.'
'The Sidewinder?'
'Yeah.'
Hardman glanced at his watch. 'It's after five, guv.'
'And?'
'Well,' Hardman said. 'I haven't had any tea.'
Comby rolled his eyes. 'Is that all you think of?'
'Natalie was doing pork chops.'
'Bung it in the microwave when you get in.'
'Pork,' Hardman said. 'Oh, it's dodgy warming pork up.'
'Phone your lass and tell her you're going to be late. You can have the chops another day.'
'Ok. But what about tonight?'
Comby blew out hard. 'Stop somewhere on the way and grab a sarnie, but I don't want you taking all night over it.'
Hardman grinned. 'I know just the place.'

Phillip came out of his house and jumped inside the car. 'She's not there.'
'I've tried ringing again,' Emily said. 'Still no answer.'
Phillip gripped the steering wheel. 'I think we should go to the office. She might be there.'
Deb pushed her head forward from the back of the car. 'She can't still be at work, surely.'
'It's as good a place as any to begin,' Phillip said. 'It won't take us long to check.'
'Yeah,' Deb said. 'I suppose so.'

Hardman stopped the car across the road from the Sidewinder. He pulled out his massive kebab wrap and took a bite.

'You stay here,' Comby said. 'I'll pop inside.'

'Isn't that Davison?' Hardman said.

Comby looked across the road. 'Yeah. And his pub-owning friend.'

Hardman took another bite of his sandwich. 'Aren't you going in?'

'No. We're going to follow those two.'

'The guv won't be happy. He said you have to stop harassing Davison.'

Comby growled at Hardman. 'I wasn't harassing him. Samuel Davison is a dodgy character, sooner or later he'll slip up, and I'll be there when he does.'

'If the chief finds out—'

'He won't if you keep your trap shut.' Comby got out of the car as Tommo's disappeared around the corner. 'Budge over. I'll drive.'

Emily parked on Redcar High Street. 'The light's still on,' she said.

'Yeah. Maybe she just lost track of time,' Deb said.

'We'll go and see,' Phillip said.

The three of them climbed from the car and headed inside.

'Looks like they're heading for Stainton,' Hardman said.

'I have got eyes.'

'They do a nice parmo in there,' Hardman said.

Comby glanced at him. 'You're not having a parmo, so you can put that idea to bed.'

Tommo pulled into the pub carpark and switched off the engine. 'Ready?' he said to Sam.

'Absolutely.'

'Should we wait for Phillip?'

'No. Let's crack on. Phillip will join us later.

'They've probably come for some grub,' Hardman said. 'Or maybe the Karaoke.'

'Yeah,' Comby said. 'Looks like my hour of retribution will have to ... Wait, there they are.'

The two officers watched as Sam and Tommo made their way over to the graveyard and inside.

'Got them,' Comby said.

'They haven't done anything wrong, guv.'

Comby stared at him. 'They're in a graveyard at night. What do you think they're doing, putting flowers on a loved one's grave?'

Hardman frowned. 'I didn't see any flowers.'

'That's because they haven't got any, you numbskull.'

'Harsh,' Hardman said.

'They're probably nicking the lead,' Comby said. 'It's the sort of thing those two would do.'

Hardman opened the car door, and Comby grabbed his arm. 'What are you doing?' Comby said.

'I thought we were going to nab them.'

'No, no,' Comby said. 'I don't want them wriggling out of a charge by making up some lame excuse. We wait until they come back out.'

Phillip finished tying Deb and Emily to the chair and looked towards Mary. 'What now?' he said.

Mary glanced towards the door as someone climbed the stairs. 'Sit, and be very quiet.'

The door opened, and Rudolph Edwards walked in. 'Ah, Rudy,' Mary said. 'Just in time. I could do with an extra hand with all these.'

Rudolph chuckled. His voice a deep baritone. 'You have been busy.'

'Can you fasten Mr Davison to his chair, please?' she said.

'Yes of course.'

'Bob's in Stainton,' Mary said. 'Keeping an eye on the others.'

'Baggage,' Kim said. 'He's locked in the other room.'

'He'll be fine,' Mary said.

'He gets a bit upset if he's left on his own,' Phillip said.

Mary tutted and motioned to Rudy. 'Go and get the dog. He's well behaved.'

Rudy went into the kitchen and returned with Baggage. 'He's a handsome chap,' he said, ruffling the dog's ears.

Baggage yawned and stretched. Viewed the occupants of the room in turn, and then lay on the floor.

CHAPTER TWENTY-SEVEN

Ewen popped his head out of the tent. 'Evening boys,' he said.
'How's it going?' Sam said.
Ewen held back the flap. 'I'm about two feet down. But it's easy digging.'
'I'll take over,' Sam said. 'We'll have to be careful from now on. I don't want to damage what's down there.'
'Ok,' Tommo said. 'I'll keep watch.'
'I'm going to nip over to the pub,' Ewen said. 'For something to eat.'
'Don't be too long,' Tommo said.
'I won't. I'm only after some nuts or crisps.'

Comby nudged Hardman. 'Who's he?' Comby said, as Ewen emerged from the churchyard.
Hardman shrugged. 'No idea, but he's going into the pub.'
Comby rubbed his hands together. 'The more arrests, the better.'
'What do you think they're doing in there?'
'No idea,' Comby said.
Hardman's eyes widened. 'You don't think it's an occult thing?'
'Occult thing?'
'Yeah. Devil worshippers.'
Comby sneered. 'Don't be stupid, Mick. This is Stainton, not bloody Salem.'
'I don't know,' Hardman said. 'I was watching a programme on Sky the other week. This group of people down south were creeping into graveyards and sacrificing chickens.'
'I don't think they're doing that.'
'How do you know?'
Comby rubbed the back of his neck. 'Because they haven't brought any chickens.'

'Oh, yeah,' Hardman said. 'I forgot about that.'

Comby rubbed his chin. 'Go inside, but be discreet. See what he's up to.'

'Ok, guv.'

Hardman disappeared inside as Comby stared over to the graveyard. 'Banged to rights, Davison,' he said.

Hardman walked through the crowded pub and past Ewen who was stood at the bar. He made his way towards the far side but paused as a familiar looking face came from out of the toilets. Hardman turned his face away from the man as he sat with his back to the officer. Retracing his way back through the bar, Hardman headed outside and climbed into the car next to Comby.

'That was quick,' Comby said.

'I've just seen a familiar face in there.'

'Oh, yeah. Who?'

'Crusher Grainger.'

'Crusher Grainger?' Comby rubbed his temple. 'No, you're mistaken. He's still inside.'

'No, he isn't. I swear it's him, guv.'

'He didn't see you, did he?'

'No. That's why I was so quick.'

'What about the other guy?' Comby said.

'He was at the bar getting served.'

'I suppose Crusher could just be on a night out?' Comby said.

'He was at a table.'

Comby nudged Hardman. 'Look.'

Hardman followed Comby's gaze as Crusher Grainger came out of the pub, crossed the road, and climbed into a car.

'What's he doing?' Hardman said.

'There's someone else in the car with him. It looks as though ...'

'They're watching the church?' Hardman said.

'Yeah.'

George Knight looked at Crusher as he lumbered into the car. 'That Ewen bloke is in the pub,' Crusher said.

'Yeah? I wondered where he was going. Sam Davison, and his mate who runs the pub, have arrived. This could get ugly.'

Crusher pushed his right fist into his left hand with a smack. 'I'll handle any rough stuff.'

Hardman stared through the windscreen then back to Comby. 'What are we going to do, guv? It took four uniforms to get Crusher into the van last time.'

'Phone for some backup. Tell them to wait on the edge of the village out of sight. We'll call them when we need their assistance.'

Hardman took out his phone. 'Ok.'

'Better ask for armed police too. He's been known to carry a shooter.'

'Right, guv.'

Ewen made his way from the pub and back into the graveyard. 'I got some crisps and nuts if anyone's interested,' Ewen said.

'I'm fine,' Tommo said.

Ewen nodded towards the tent. 'How's he doing?'

Tommo pushed his head inside. 'Any luck?'

Sam, who was on his knees, stood. In his hand, the cross gleamed where he'd rubbed off the dirt. 'I've got it.' He came out of the tent and held it out for Tommo and Ewen to see.

'Can I hold it?' Tommo said.

Sam passed the cross to his friend. 'Wow,' Tommo said. 'It weighs a ton.'

'That's gold for you,' Sam said.

Tommo passed it to Ewen. 'God, it does.'

Sam searched on the floor and located a small sack. Ewen passed the Cross back to Sam as if it was the most delicate object, he or anyone else, had ever held.

'What now?' Tommo said.

Sam placed the cross inside the bag and wrapped it up. 'I'll go and bury it if you two can start filling the hole back in?'

'Yeah, I'll start now,' Ewen said. 'You keep watch, Tommo.'

'Is the side gate still open?' Sam said to Ewen.

'It's closed but not locked.'

'I'll be as quick as I can,' Sam said.

Professor Haldine took out his mobile and answered. 'Hi, Mary,' he said.

'Any news?' she said.

'Not yet.'

'We've got quite a number here,' Mary said.

'Who?'

'Albert Jackson, Phillip Davison and three women.'

'Right, is Rudy there?'

'Yeah. Don't worry, they're all secured.'

'Good. When they come out of the graveyard, I'll ring you.'

'Ok.'

Sam surveyed the surrounding area, but nothing stirred. He entered the field and quickly located the hole in the corner that he had previously excavated. Dropping to his knees, he placed the cross inside. Immediately replacing the earth, he pressed the soft soil down, until it was almost level. He searched around and, finding some bits of detritus, covered over the former hole. Making his way back over to the field entrance, he scanned the area. Satisfied, Sam headed back.

Ewen threw the tools and tent inside the back of his van. 'Get some of those leaves and twigs,' he said to Tommo. Tommo gathered together some of the cuttings from a pile close by, and the pair of them covered over the previous excavation. 'I'll back my van over it,' Ewen said. 'It will help disguise that there's ever been a dig.'

'Good idea,' Tommo said.

Sam appeared at the side entrance and slipped in through the gate. 'All done?'

'Yeah,' Tommo said. 'You?'

'All done too.'

'Ewen's going to back his van over the dig,' Tommo said.

'Good thinking.'

Ewen performed a few backward and forward movements before driving his van to the now open gates. He lowered the window. 'Lock the gates when I'm gone, will you?' he said to Tommo, who held one of the gates open.

'I'll see you two tomorrow,' Ewen said, and quietly made his way out, heading away from the village and towards Thornton. Sam and Tommo quickly closed the gates, and Tommo clicked the padlock back in place.

'Job's a good un,' Sam said.

Tommo put an arm around his friend and man-hugged him. 'It certainly is.'

Hardman hung up. 'The guys are all in place, guv.'

'Good,' Comby said.

'Here they come,' Hardman said.

'Where's the other one?' Comby said.

'He might be still in there.'

Comby rubbed his chin. 'Yeah. But what do we do with those two?'

Hardman nudged Comby. 'Look.' Crusher exited the car and walked over to Sam and Tommo. 'Excuse me, mate. You couldn't tell me the way to Hemlington, could you?'

'Yeah,' Sam said. 'It's over …'

Crusher pulled out a gun. 'Get in the car.'

Tommo stared at the weapon. 'We'd better do as the man says, Sam.'

The three men made their way across the road but stopped as the noise of sirens, and the flashing of blue lights caught their attention.

'The filth,' Crusher said. He reached for the door handle of the car, but could only watch on helplessly as it screeched away.

Comby and Hardman emerged from their vehicle, and Crusher levelled his gun at Comby.

'You'll never take me alive, copper.'

Sam laughed, and glanced at Tommo. 'It's a James Cagney movie,' Sam said.

Comby stopped in his tracks and held his hands up in a futile defence and dropped to his knees. Crusher squinted and took aim, but Sam moved quickly and knocked the weapon from the big man's hand. Crusher roared and turned on him, grabbing hold of Sam by his jacket. Tommo waded in, hitting Crusher square on the jaw. He stumbled backwards, but regaining his equilibrium, launched himself at Tommo. The two giants fell in a heap on the floor. Sam kicked out, hitting Crusher between the legs as he and Tommo grappled. He let out a loud groan, and the now upright Tommo caught him with a perfect uppercut. Crusher fell backwards, hitting the ground with a loud bang. Comby and Hardman, accompanied by armed officers, joined Sam and Tommo.

'Right, you two,' Comby said. 'Now I've got you.'

Sam glanced at Tommo. 'What's he on about?' Sam said. 'We saved his life. You were crouched on the floor crying like a little girl, Inspector.'

An armed officer glanced at Comby. 'He's right about that, sir.'

'Crusher would have shot you, guv,' Hardman said.

'I was making myself as small a target as possible. That's all. It's what we're trained to do.'

Sam threw his head backwards and laughed. 'Is that what you were doing?'

'Are the tears part of the training too?' Tommo said.

'I wasn't crying ... Never mind all that,' Comby said. 'I want to know what you lot were doing in the graveyard?'

Sam smiled. 'Helping a mate get his van started.'

Comby scoffed. 'Helping a mate? Do I look stupid? Follow me,' he said, heading across to the graveyard. 'Show me this van.'

Tommo and Sam walked across to where the van had been. 'It was here,' Sam said.

'Ewen has gone,' Tommo said.

'Why would his van be parked in a graveyard?'

Sam pointed to the wall. 'He was doing some work on the wall for the vicar. His van wouldn't start, so he phoned Tommo.'

'I'm his cousin,' Tommo said.

'And a dab hand at getting vans going,' Sam said.

'I don't believe you,' Comby said. 'What was the altercation with Crusher?'

'Who?' Sam said.

'The big goon outside who you had a fight with.'

Sam grinned. 'Mistaken identity.'

'Hah!' Comby said. 'You must think I was born yesterday.'

Sam nudged Tommo. 'Not with those wrinkles,' he said.

Comby raised a finger about to speak. 'Guv,' Hardman said. 'The Chief's here.'

Comby rolled his eyes. 'Hardman,' he said. 'Go to the vicarage and ask the vicar what these jokers were doing in his graveyard.'

'Ok, guv.'

'You two come with me.'

Sam and Tommo followed Comby as he stomped out of the churchyard. He marched over to the Chief Inspector. 'I can explain everything, sir,' Comby said.

'No need, Comby,' the Chief said. 'Hardman has explained it all. A brilliant stroke of luck spotting Crusher Grainger. He's been on the run for weeks.'

Comby's jaw dropped open. 'Eh, yes.'

'Ah,' he said, moving towards Sam and Tommo. 'These must be the two gentlemen who assisted you in his capture.'

'Who?' Comby said. 'These two?'

'I was in the area when I got the news. I heard they saved your life, Comby.' He shook Sam and Tommo's hands. 'Well done, gentlemen. It was an incredibly brave thing to do. If I have my way, I'll see you two get rewarded.'

Comby glowered at Sam, who winked at him. 'Oh, it was nothing,' Sam said. 'Anyone would have done the same.'

'Right, thanks again,' the Chief said. 'I'll see you two later.' He waved a hand at Comby. 'Carry on,' he said, and marched back to his car.

'I don't believe this,' Comby said.

Hardman returned. 'The vicar confirmed the story, sir. Apparently, a man called Ewen, I haven't got his surname, has been repairing the wall. He knows Sam, too. He said Ewen told him his van wouldn't work.'

Comby threw his hands up and faced Sam and Tommo. 'You two were up to no good. I will get to the bottom of it, mark my words.'

'But Tommo and I are getting a bravery award,' Sam said, waving at the Chief as he drove by.

Comby turned. 'You haven't heard the last of this,' he mumbled, as he walked off.

Sam nudged Tommo. 'Call Ewen and tell him the score. We all need to be singing from the same hymn sheet.'

'Appropriate that,' Tommo said, and nodded towards the church.

'Hey,' Sam said, as Tommo rang Ewen. 'What the hell happened to Phillip and Albert?' Tommo shrugged, and carried on making the call.

CHAPTER TWENTY-EIGHT

Mary answered her phone. 'Yeah,' she said, and wandered into the corridor.

'All hell's broke loose here,' Haldine said. 'Knight and that thug he uses tried to abduct Davison and his mate.'

'What happened?'

'The police arrived. Knight drove off, and the coppers have arrested Crusher.'

Mary glanced back into the office. 'What do we do? Rudy and I can't keep this lot prisoner forever.'

'Don't do anything yet until I know what's happening.'

'What about the cross?' Mary said.

'I don't know,' Haldine said. 'They weren't holding anything.'

'Ok, keep me informed.'

Tommo talked to Ewen on the phone as Sam tried to ring the others.

'Don't worry, Tommo,' Ewen said. 'I'll handle the police.'

'Good, lad.' Tommo said. 'Ewen's got the full picture,' he said to Sam.

Sam stared at his phone and frowned.

'What's up?' Tommo said.

'I can't raise the others,' Sam said. 'Any of them.'

'Phillip and Albert?'

Sam shook his head. 'Or Emily and Kim.'

Tommo waved him closer. 'That big guy.'

Sam nodded. 'He must have known about the cross.'

'But how?'

Sam shrugged. 'I don't know. But every time we have a big case, every man and his dog seem to find out about it.'

'The driver,' Tommo said. 'The one who drove off when the police came.'

'I didn't get a good look.'

Tommo rubbed his beard. 'Neither did I.' He held up a hand. 'Hold on, I'll phone Deb.' Tommo searched his contacts and rang. He muttered something under his breath and then dialled a second number.

'Hi, Gene. Is Deb there ...? Any of the others ...? No. Don't worry. She's probably gone home.'

Sam locked eyes with Tommo, who was already dialling another number. 'Any luck?' Sam said. Tommo shook his head and then blew out.

'Nothing,' Tommo said. 'Deb's not answering her mobile or our home number. They haven't been back to the pub.'

Sam glanced over at Comby and Hardman who were making their way over. 'Something's up, mate, but don't tell Comby.' Tommo nodded.

Comby and Hardman reached the pair. 'The driver of the vehicle that sped off?' Comby said.

'We didn't see him,' Tommo said.

'Didn't you two diligent officers get a licence plate?' Sam said.

Comby glanced at his junior. 'Unfortunately, not.'

'Can we go, inspector?' Tommo said. 'It is getting late.'

'We need statements,' Hardman said.

'Can we pop into the station tomorrow?' Sam said. 'It's been a long night, and us heroes need our sleep.'

Comby narrowed his eyes and muttered something under his breath. 'I suppose so. First thing in the morning.'

Sam gave a salute. 'Yes, sir.'

'We'll bid you good night,' Tommo said. He and Sam headed towards the car park. 'I wish you wouldn't wind him up,' Tommo said.

'I love it,' Sam said. 'It's my raison d'etre.'

'What do we do now, guv?' Hardman said.

'I don't suppose Crusher said anything?'

Hardman shook his head, took out a bag of crisps, and began eating them. He offered the packet to Comby. 'You know Crusher. He never says anything.'

'When did you get those?' Comby said.

Hardman glanced at the crisps. 'I popped into the pub while you were speaking with the chief.'

Comby pushed Hardman in the chest. 'What did you tell the Chief that Davison saved me for?'

Hardman stuck out his bottom lip. 'Well, he did, guv. In any case, one of the armed lot told him as well.'

'I still think they were up to something.'

'Maybe it was a case of mistaken identity?'

Comby scoffed. 'Yeah, right. Come with me.'

Hardman followed his superior as they made their way back to the car. 'Where are we going?' Hardman said.

'We're going to follow those two.'

'Oh, guv. Have you seen the time?'

Comby stared at him. 'You know, Hardman,' he said. 'There are times when I don't think your heart is in the job.'

Hardman pouted. 'They're probably going home for some supper.'

'Well,' Comby said. 'If they are, we'll go home ourselves.'

Tommo made his way out of the car park and headed away from the pub. 'Anything?' he said.

Sam shook his head and put the mobile away. 'No.'

'Where to?'

'The office,' Sam said.

'You think they're there?'

'That's where Emily, Phillip and Deb were heading. They were looking for Albert and Kim if you remember?'

'Yeah. Good call.'

Tommo headed for Redcar, closely followed by Haldine.

Mary answered her phone. 'Yeah, Bob?'

'The police have let them go. They're on their way somewhere else.'

'Where?'

'I don't know, but we're just coming on to the Parkway.'

'Could they be heading here?' Mary said.

'Maybe. I'll let you know when we're closer.

'Ok.'

'It looks as if they're on their way to Redcar,' Hardman said, eating his second bag of crisps.

'I told you they were up to something,' Comby said. 'Hah! Bravery award indeed. That Davison and his big mate will be doing a five-year stretch if I get my way.'

'He did save your life, though.'

Comby groaned. 'Will you stop saying that.' He knocked the bag of crisps from Hardman's hand onto the floor. 'And stop bloody eating!' Hardman folded his arms, stuck out a pet lip, and nearly shed a tear.

Tommo parked the car some distance from the office and gripped the steering wheel. 'The light's still on.'

Sam pushed his face closer to the windscreen. 'Yeah. What do you think?'

Tommo tapped the steering wheel. 'I don't know. But I hope there isn't any more like that big bloke. My knuckles are still hurting me.'

'We'll have to tread carefully,' Sam said. 'Have you got anything big and heavy in the boot.'

Tommo raised his eyebrows. 'Like what?'

'I don't know. A crowbar or a baseball bat.'

'Yeah, because I expected to have to knock the hell out of some thugs.'

'Hey,' Sam said. 'Don't be getting all arsey with me. Save it for them upstairs.'

'Sorry,' Tommo said. 'But they've got our family and friends in there.'

'What if I draw them out and you batter them?'

Tommo shrugged. 'Not the best plan you've ever come up with, but in the absence of anything else ... Although ...' Tommo pondered. 'I may have another plan.'

Comby nudged Hardman who was looking at the scattered crisps beneath his feet. 'That car,' Comby said.

Hardman lifted his head. 'What car?'

'It's parked across the road from Davison and his mate.'

'So?'

'Are you going to be like this the rest of the night? Because catching criminals is going to be a lot harder with you in a mood.'

'Well, there was no reason to do that with my crisps.'

Comby brought his hands to his face and groaned. 'Give me strength. I'll buy you another bag when we've sorted these miscreants out. Jesus, it was a bag of crisps, not a five-course dinner.'

Hardman pushed out his bottom lip. 'They were Walkers.'

'Yeah, all right, Mick. I'll buy you a bag of Walkers. I'll buy you a bloody family pack. It's like having a petulant kid.'

Hardman smiled. 'That car,' he said. 'Could it be the one from Stainton?'

Comby patted him on the arm. 'My thoughts exactly. I'm sure it's been following them from the village.'

'They're getting out,' Hardman said.

Comby and Hardman watched as Sam and Tommo exited the car. 'They definitely up to something,' Comby said. 'I mean, why park so far away from the office when there are parking spaces outside?'

'Someone is getting out of the other car.'

'We'll wait and see what he does,' Comby said. 'With a bit of luck, he'll shoot the pair of them.'

'Guv!' Hardman said.

'I'm only joking.' Comby pulled out his phone as it beeped. He read the message. He looked across at Hardman. 'Get on the blower to the firearm boys, and get them to come here. Pronto,' he said.

'Will do.'

'Do you know any Paul Robeson?' Albert said.

Rudy chuckled. 'Would you like a rendition of Ol' Man River?'

Albert and Phillip shot a glance at each other. 'Yeah.' Emily, Deb and Kim stared on in astonishment.

Rudy began singing. 'Ol' Man River, that Ol' Man River ... His voice a rich bass-baritone.

'Shh,' Mary said. 'I thought I heard something.'

Rudy jumped to his feet and pulled out a gun. 'Turn the lights off,' he said.

Mary hit the switch, and the room was plunged into darkness. 'Not a sound, you lot. I've got enough bullets for everyone.'

Sam switched on the hall light and whistled the theme tune from *the great escape*, as he climbed the stairs.

Rudy stepped out of the darkness and into the light. 'Hold it there, Mr Davison.'

'Rudy,' Sam said, feigning surprise.

'Where's your friend?'

Tommo moved from around the corner and knocked the gun from Rudy's hand and down the stairs. Rudy lunged for him, but Tommo quickly sidestepped the big man and stuck out a foot sending him sprawling.

'Get the gun, Sam,' Tommo said.

Sam raced down the stairs, but as he bent to pick up the gun, Haldine levelled his own. 'Don't move a muscle,' Haldine said, and placed the tip of the weapon on Sam's temple.

'Or you,' Mary said, as she placed her pistol on the side of Tommo's head.

Tommo closed his eyes and held his hands up as Haldine encouraged Sam upstairs. Mary flicked on the light and Sam and Tommo were bundled inside.

'Nice try, boys,' Haldine said. 'Lock the door, Rudy, we don't want to be disturbed.' Rudy moved across to the door and pretended to lock it.

Sam glared at Mary. 'Mary Hough. I knew you were a fake.'

Mary smirked. 'Maybe so, but I fooled all your friends.'

'Have a seat,' Rudy said, pushing a couple of chairs towards them. 'We saved them for you.'

Sam sneered at Rudy. 'It was you who killed Randy, wasn't it?'

Rudy laughed. 'Randy was a fool, and utterly useless with money. He didn't quite understand the gravity of the situation when I got some suits for him. The people I deal with don't supply them sale or return. He wanted nothing to do with them when he found out they were knock-off. We got into a heated argument, and well ... You know the rest.'

'And you killed him because of that?' Tommo said.

'He threatened to go to the police,' Rudy said. 'I couldn't have that.'

Haldine perched on a desk. 'In any case,' he said. 'Randy would never have gone along with our plan to sell the cross on the open market.'

'The cross is a priceless artefact,' Sam said. 'It belongs in a museum.'

Haldine scoffed. 'You're just like Stanley with your romantic vision of our past. This is the twenty-first century, Mr Davison. Everything has a price.'

Sam edged towards Mary. 'And you?'

Mary smirked. 'We've been selling artefacts for years. Under the radar of the establishment, of course. But the cross …' Mary smiled. 'Will be the most valuable object we've ever shifted.'

'And George Knight?' Tommo said.

'We recruited George,' Haldine said. 'But he became a little unpredictable killing Stanley before he'd found the cross. We've managed to keep him at arm's length. Once we have The Liturgy, we won't need dear George's help anymore.'

'You won't get away with it,' Phillip said.

Haldine laughed. 'Of course we will. Anyway ...' He fake-smiled. 'Enough of this chatter. We have work to do.' He waved his hand at Rudy. 'Fasten Mr Thomson up. Mr Davison and I will be going for a little drive.'

'Where?' Sam said. 'We haven't a clue—'

Haldine walked over to the sleeping Baggage. 'Would you like me to put your dog to sleep permanently?'

'You can't,' Kim said.

'Mr Davison?' Haldine said. 'The choice is yours. The dog first, and then we'll start with your friends.'

'You sent that thug tonight, didn't you?' Sam said.

Haldine smiled. 'No. That was George Knight. As I said, he can't be trusted.' He motioned toward Rudy and Mary. 'George got greedy and thought he could double-cross us. Hopefully, the police will arrest him when I make an anonymous tip-off.'

'What do you want?' Sam said.

'Where is the Cross?' Haldine said.

Sam puffed out his cheeks. 'We haven't got it.'

'Mr Davison,' Haldine said. 'Do you expect us to believe that?'

'Ask Tommo.' Haldine wandered towards the now tethered Tommo.

'He's telling the truth,' Tommo said. 'We thought we had a location for it in the cemetery, but when we dug …'

'Nothing?' Haldine said.

Tommo put his hands together. 'Yeah, nothing.'

The door burst open, and George Knight stormed in. He pointed his gun at Haldine. Rudy levelled his weapon at Mary.

'Rudy?' she said. 'I thought you were on our side?'

'Sorry, Mary. George has promised me a bigger cut.'

Haldine placed his pistol on a desk. 'Let's not do anything stupid, George.'

'Fasten them up, Rudy,' Knight said. 'Then Mr Davison and I can have a word.'

Sam folded his arms. 'There's no honour among thieves,' he whispered to Tommo.

'Yeah,' Tommo said. 'A proper pack of back-stabbers.'

'George,' Haldine said. 'There's enough for all of us. We could still share the money.'

'It was my brother who found the cross.' Knight said. 'My brother who never stopped looking for it.'

'The brother you killed?' Mary said.

'Stanley would have given the cross to a museum,' Knight said. 'Stuck in some glass case for people to gawp at for £5 a go.'

'And what about you, Rudy?' Haldine said. 'We had a deal.'

'I lied earlier.' Rudy said. 'Randy was buying knock-off suits himself. He was the same as Stanley, though. He had this pathetic belief that the cross belongs in a museum. He only told me about the cross when he got into money difficulty. Bragged, when he was drunk, that he had money coming his way from the reward for finding it.' Rudy smiled. 'Never could handle his booze.'

'Why kill your own brother?' Tommo said.

'I told Randy, George and I had an overseas buyer. He was livid. I told him if he didn't go along with our plan, I'd tell the police about the suits. He lost his head and came at me with a shoehorn.'

'The shoehorn you hit him with?' Sam said.

'Yeah,' Rudy said. 'Poor Randy wasn't much good at anything, apart from bedding women. It was my idea for George to get in touch with Stanley. George and I go back a long way. Isn't that right, George?'

'We do,' Knight said. 'The pair of us spent a couple of years together at Her Majesty's pleasure.'

'And Aaron?' Phillip said. 'Who killed him?'

Rudy put a hand up. 'That was me as well. Aaron was unreliable. When you visited him, he panicked. So …' Rudy shrugged. 'He became a loose end we had to tie up.'

'I don't know why you're all arguing over the cross,' Sam said. 'We didn't find it.'

Knight sneered. 'You expect me to believe that? You had a metal detector. You must have located something for you to dig.'

'Just a ring pull,' Sam said.

Knight moved closer to Sam. 'Now you listen carefully. I'm not like these two jokers.' He pointed at Haldine and Mary. 'I'll have no trouble inflicting pain on you and your friends. I know you found it. You were detecting at a farm in Thornton, as well. I watched you enter a field. You know exactly where it is.' He put the muzzle of the gun to Sam's head. 'And you will tell me.'

'Tell him, Sam,' Tommo said. 'And maybe we can all go home.'

Sam scowled at his friend. 'Tommo?'

Tommo shrugged. 'It's not worth anyone dying over.'

Sam held his hands up. 'Ok. I'll take you to it, as long as you let the others go.'

'Once we have the cross and we are far enough away,' Knight said. 'Then we'll phone the police and tell them where your friends are.'

'And me?' Sam said.

'We'll drop you off somewhere, safe and sound.' Knight said. 'As long as you do what we say.'

Haldine looked at Knight. 'I have a buyer, George. He has promised us twenty million. He will transfer the money into an account of our choice. Five million is still a lot of money.' He glanced at Mary. 'Mary?'

Mary nodded. 'Yeah.'

Knight moved across to Haldine and hit him across the side of the face with his gun. 'You're just like my brother. You academic types are all the same, high and mighty.' Haldine groaned, as blood ran down the side of his head.

'Ok,' Mary said. 'Let's not do anything stupid.'

Knight sneered. 'One more word from you two and you'll go the same way as Stanley and Randy. For your information, Bob ....' He squatted and put his face near to Haldine. 'We have a buyer. You can do anything on the internet.'

Sam locked eyes with Tommo and mouthed. 'He's mental.' Tommo nodded.

'Mr Davison,' Knight said, turning to face Sam again. 'You can drive.' He put the gun on Sam's forehead. 'No funny business. And to make sure you comply ...' He signalled towards Rudy. 'Grab the bag from the hall.'

Rudy moved into the corridor and returned with a holdall. He opened it and pulled out a small explosive device.

'Fasten it to Mr Davison's girlfriend's chair,' Knight said.

Rudy squatted, taped it to the leg, and stood. 'All done, George.'

Knight pulled out his phone. 'All I have to do is make the call, and ... Boom!'

'Ok,' Sam said. 'I get the picture.' He glanced across at Tommo, who blew out hard. 'I'll take you to the cross.'

'Do you copy, Inspector?' A voice said on the radio.

'Yeah, I copy.'

'Everyone's in position, sir.'

'Wait for my command,' Comby said. 'We don't want a blood bath.'

'There's movement from the premises,' the radio voice said. 'I think someone's coming out.'

'Let them reach the car, and then take them.'

'Yes, sir.'

Sam exited the building closely followed by Knight and Rudy.

'One of them could be armed,' a voice on the radio said.

'Hold your fire,' Comby said. 'If he doesn't drop his weapon when we order him to, you have my permission to shoot.'

The trio slowly walked along the High Street towards Knight's car. 'I don't like this, Rudy,' he said. 'It's too quiet.'

Rudy glanced up and down the road. 'Yeah. Where is everyone?'

Knight pushed Sam forward. 'Quicker. It's the black Merc.' The three arrived at the vehicle and Sam reached for the door.

'Drop your weapon.' An officer, clad in black and holding a gun, ordered.

Knight tossed the gun down. 'On the floor,' another commanded.

The three men dropped to the floor, and several armed police emerged and swarmed over them. Sam lay still as someone loomed over him.

'Well, well, well. If it isn't Mr Davison.'

Sam sat. 'There's a bomb in the office. He can detonate it with his mobile.'

Comby stared wide-eyed. 'Get the bomb disposal,' he said to Hardman, who appeared at his side. 'And someone search them for their phones.'

'Yes, sir.'

'You got the text, then?' Sam said, and climbed to his feet.

Comby narrowed his eyes. 'You and Mr Thomson have a bit of explaining to do.'

CHAPTER TWENTY-NINE

Sam and Tommo waited in the interview room as Comby and Hardman entered and sat opposite the pair.

'Mr Davison, Mr Thomson. How are you two today?' Comby said.

Sam glanced at Tommo. 'Fine, Inspector,' Sam said.

'It appears that you two are blue-eyed boys. The Chief is singing your praises in a press conference as we speak.'

'Heroes, I think you'll find,' Sam said.

'We did save your life,' Tommo said. 'And we sent you that text.'

'Only because your loved ones were being held captive.'

'The bomb was a dummy,' Hardman said. 'Just plasticine and a clock.'

'We didn't know that,' Sam said.

'Anyway,' Comby said. 'More pressing matters. I'd normally interview you two separately, but no doubt the pair of you have concocted some wonderful tale.'

'Not really,' Tommo said.

Comby leant back and held out his hands. 'Come on then. Let's hear it.'

Tommo motioned for Sam to begin. 'We were employed, as you know, by George Knight, to investigate the death of his brother. And in doing this, certain clues about the whereabouts of a valuable Celtic cross—'

'The Lindisfarne Liturgy,' Tommo said.

Sam nodded. 'Were discovered. The people you arrested last night, and don't ask me why …' Sam laughed. 'Thought we knew where it was. Utterly preposterous.'

'Utterly,' Tommo said.

'And, of course …' Comby leant forward. 'You don't?'

Tommo and Sam shook their heads. 'Nope,' Sam said.

'My sergeant and I had a run over to the graveyard this morning.' Comby folded his arms. 'Where your friend ...?'

'Ewen,' Tommo said.

'Ewen,' Comby continued. 'Had his van parked. The ground around there looks as though it has been disturbed. Dug up even.'

Sam scoffed. 'Don't be daft. Who would dig up a graveyard?'

'You two would,' Comby said. 'Along with your mate. Do you know it is an offence to desecrate a grave?'

'Is it?' Sam said. He raised his eyebrows at Tommo. 'Did you know that?'

Tommo shook his head. 'Well, I had an inkling.'

Comby stood. 'I want full statements from you two.'

Sam saluted. 'Yes, sir.'

Comby glanced between the two. 'The pair of you have bested me twice. It will not happen a third time.' He huffed and marched off.

Sam leant forward. 'He's in a right mood, Mick.'

Hardman rolled his eyes. 'Tell me about it. I haven't had any breakfast yet.'

Tommo and Sam exited Middlesbrough police station and headed for The Sidewinder.

'What do we do about the cross?' Tommo said.

'We'll have to leave it a week or two,' Sam said. 'It'll look a bit suspicious if we unearth it now. I was thinking ...'

'Yeah?' Tommo said.

'Do you think the others will mind if we give the church in Stainton a little of the reward money for their roof?'

'I don't think so. You're getting generous these days.'

Sam held out his hands. 'Easy come, easy go.'

Phillip, Albert, Kim, Emily and Deb, along with Baggage and the puppies waited in the Sidewinder.

'I've never been so scared,' Emily said. 'My life passed before my eyes.'

'Phew,' Deb said. 'I bet that was some sight.'

Phillip laughed. 'Sam and Tommo, heroes. I can't believe it. I bet you Comby is hopping mad.'

'He'll always be a hero to me,' Emily said.

'Aw,' Kim and Phillip said in unison, as Deb leant forward and feigned being sick.

Baggage padded across to them, closely followed by the puppies. He turned to face them and barked. The puppies stopped in their tracks, and all but Zeus cocked their head to one side. Baggage put his paws on the table and stared at Kim and Phillip.

'I know they're a pain, Bagsy,' Phillip said. 'But it's your own fault. If you'd behaved yourself and not snook into next door's garden …'

Kim rubbed his head and kissed him. 'I'll put them out back in a minute, Baggage.' Baggage, seemingly satisfied, lay on the floor as the puppies mobbed him.

Sam and Tommo entered. The whole pub rose to their feet and applauded them.

Sam held up his hands. 'It was nothing, people.'

Albert walked across and shook hands, first with Tommo, and then with Sam. 'It was incredibly brave. I'm so proud of you both.'

Tommo patted him on the arm. 'Cheers for that, Albert.'

'Yeah, thanks,' Sam said. Albert headed off.

'I wish you would have a pep talk with Albert,' Tommo said.

'Me? Why me?'

'Because he looks up to you.'

Sam scoffed. 'Don't be daft. It's you he's having a bromance with.'

Tommo patted his friend on the shoulder. 'Sam,' he said. 'I know that behind all that jokey banter of yours, you do care about people.'

'Why me though? I don't want to be his agony aunt. Can't he find another therapist?'

Tommo sighed and glanced across at Albert stood at the bar on his own. 'He took it badly about Mary. He feels that he always makes the wrong choice. He's depressed.'

Sam groaned. 'Oh, all right. What do you want me to say?'

Tommo patted his arm. 'You'll think of something.'

Sam took a deep breath and headed across to Albert. He put an arm around his shoulder. 'How are you, Albi?'

'Ok, I suppose.'

'Ok?' Sam said. 'This is a celebration.'

'I don't really feel like celebrating if I'm honest.'

'You know your problem?' Sam said. Albert shook his head, and Sam continued. 'You're very trusting, and sometimes people take advantage of that.'

'I can't help it.'

Sam hugged him with one arm. 'Seeing the best in people is not the worst attribute to have. In fact, it's admirable.'

Albert frowned. 'I know you have Emily now, but you were very successful with the opposite sex.'

'Bloody right I was.' Sam glanced towards Emily and smiled. 'I'm happy now, though. I wouldn't change a thing.'

'Weren't you happy before?'

'I thought I was, but …' Sam smiled meekly. 'I don't think I was.'

'I wish I could find someone nice like Emily.'

'You will,' Sam said. 'It's only a matter of time. Let me get you a pint.'

Sam precariously carried two large cocktails across to the table and placed one in front of Emily before sitting into the seat beside her. 'I haven't a clue what's in these,' he slurred, raising his glass. 'But it tastes all right.'

Emily nudged Sam. 'You see that woman at the bar?'

Sam followed her gaze. 'What about her?'

'She's been looking at Albert all night.'

Sam chuckled. 'Well, he does act strangely at times.'

'Sam,' Emily said. 'Stop being awful. I think she fancies him.'

Sam looked her up and down. 'Surely not.' He focused on Emily again. 'Do you really think so?'

'Yeah. Why don't you go and have a word with him about her?'

'I think he's a little old for the birds and the bees.' Sam took a swig of his drink and chuckled.

'He'll miss his opportunity. Go on, Sam. You know what to say to get a woman interested.'

'Oh, God,' Sam said. 'Why does everybody think it's my job to look after Albert? I only gave him a pep talk a few hours ago.'

Emily kissed him on the cheek. 'Please, for me.'

Kim and Phillip slid into the seats opposite Emily and Sam. 'What the hell are you drinking?' Phillip said.

Sam shrugged. 'Haven't a clue. Tastes all right though.'

Emily nudged Sam. 'Go on.'

Sam blew out hard. 'I should be charging for this,' he said, and unsteadily got to his feet. 'Watch the expert.' He straightened his shirt and tottered off.

'What's he doing?' Kim said.

'Trying to get Albert fixed up,' Emily said.

Phillip folded his arms and watched Sam wander across to Albert. 'This should be interesting.'

Sam put an arm around Albert, as much to aid his own balance as affection. 'How are you, mate?' Sam said.

'I'm ok.'

'Right,' Sam said, winking across at Emily, Phillip and Kim. 'Don't look, but that woman at the bar has been clocking you all night.'

'Which woman?' Albert said, glancing past Sam.

'Albert,' Sam said. 'I told you not to look.'

'Sorry, I got excited.'

Sam attempted to put his elbow on the table, succeeding at the third attempt. 'You have to play it cool,' Sam said. 'Don't be so eager. It's all in the chase.'

'What do I do?' Albert said.

Sam grinned. 'Go and strike up a conversation with her.'

Albert shook his head. 'I don't think I could—'

Sam put a finger to his own lips. 'Shh. I don't want to hear that defeatist talk.' He waved Albert closer. 'You have to talk to her. Reel her in, like a fish.'

'Like a fish?'

'Yeah. You reel her in with some sparkling conversation. Then ...' Sam said.

'Then?'

Sam burped. 'Sorry about that. Then,' he continued. 'If you're lucky, you scoop her up with the net thingy.'

'The keepnet?'

'Yeah,' Sam said. 'The conversation is the rod and reel. The keepnet is your house, where you woo her.'

'I woo her?' Albert said, and Sam nodded. 'Right.'

'Then comes the bedroom.'

'What's the bedroom?' Albert said.

Sam's elbow slipped off the table. 'Oops,' he said. Then waved Albert closer. 'The bedroom is the frying pan.'

'I don't know,' Albert said. 'Maybe she'll come over and talk to me.'

Sam grabbed hold of Albert's lapels. 'That's not how it works, mate. You have to go over there. Grasp the bloody nettle.'

Albert surreptitiously glanced again. 'What happens if she tells me to go away?'

'Well,' Sam said. 'She obviously wouldn't be a very nice person, and you wouldn't be interested in her anyway.'

'Is that what I should say if she—?'

'Knocks you back,' Sam said.

'Knocks me back.'

'If you like.'

Albert sighed. 'Did you always have to go and talk to a woman?'

Sam laughed. 'No. But I was a babe magnet.'

'What would I say to her?'

Sam fixed him with a stare. 'You strike up a conversation.'

'About what?'

Sam rolled his eyes. 'Small talk. You're a bright lad. Talk about something interesting. Not bloody court cases about biscuits, though. You don't want to put her to sleep.' Sam patted his arm and slumped forward. 'I have the utmost faith in you.'

Albert peeped across at the woman, steeled himself, and set off. But as he approached her, the woman moved across to the door that led to The Sidewinder. She stopped to talk to Tommo and Deb, who had just entered. Albert glanced at Sam, who threw up his hands. The woman kissed Deb and Tommo then headed for the exit. Albert's shoulders drooped, but then spotting a scarf on the stool the woman had been sat on, he scooped it up and headed after her.

'Excuse me,' he said, as he neared her.

The woman turned around and smiled. 'Hi,' she said.

Albert held out the scarf. 'Is this yours?'

'Oh, god, yeah,' she said. The woman blushed a little. 'I'm always forgetting things.'

The pair locked eyes. 'Erm,' Albert said. 'I don't suppose … well, I'm sure you don't want one … What I mean is—'

'I'd love a drink,' she said.

Albert beamed. 'I thought you were leaving?'

'I was. I only came to see Deb. She's my cousin. And I liked it here, so I stayed a little longer. I don't get out much.'

Albert ushered her towards the bar. 'Why's that?'

She lowered her eyes. 'I'm not very good with crowds. It can all be a little overwhelming.'

Albert scanned the room. 'Are you ok here?'

'Yeah, it's not too crowded. My … Well, let's just say, people, think I need to get out a bit more.'

'How rude of me,' Albert said, holding out a hand. 'I'm Albert.'

'Alice,' she said.

Albert smiled. 'Alice was my mother's name. What can I get you … Alice?'

'I was drinking a cocktail.' She squinted at the menu board and blushed. 'That one.'

'Porn star martini it is. I think I'll join you.' Albert caught the attention of the bar staff and ordered the drinks. He watched as Alice straightened the beer mats on the bar. She then squared the drink-stirrers and placed the straw holder, which was lying on its side, upright.

She pursed her lips and blushed again. 'Sorry, it's a habit of mine.'

Albert grinned. 'Me too. I can't abide a mess.'

'Really?'

'Really,' he said.

Tommo and Deb joined the others. 'Who's the woman with Albert?' Phillip said.

'My cousin,' Deb said, and rolled her eyes. 'Alice.'

'Your cousin?' Emily said. 'I've never seen her before.'

'She lives in Darlington. She doesn't get out that much. She's a little weird … In a nice way.'

Sam joined the group. 'Success,' he slurred. 'One lesson from me and Albert's pulled. I am.' He slumped onto a chair. 'The master.'

'Christ,' Tommo said. 'How much have you had?' Sam put his head on the table and chuckled. 'Lots.'

'It's those cocktails,' Emily said. 'He's been drinking those all night.'

'Why didn't you say you had a cousin who's …?' Kim said to Deb.

'Weird,' Deb said.

'Yeah,' Emily said. 'We could have introduced her and Albert sooner.'

Deb scoffed. 'Who am I, Cilla Black?'

Sam, with his head still on the table, groaned. 'Can someone take me home to bed, please?'

CHAPTER THIRTY

'Hi,' Comby said.

'Sorry I haven't been in touch, Clive. What with my mother being ill.'

'I understand, Barbara. How is your mum?'

'Much better, thanks. She's back home and coping well.'

'Good, good.'

'How have you been?' Barbara said.

'Busy. A couple of complex cases.'

'I saw the piece in the paper about the men from the detective agency—'

'Sam and Howard.' Comby rolled his eyes.

'I didn't realise how dangerous your job was. You must be very brave.'

Comby pumped out his chest. 'All in the line of duty. Someone has to do it.'

'Even so. Listen,' she said. 'Now that my mum's better and you've managed to clear up some of your cases, would you still like to go for that meal?'

'I'd love to.'

'Splendid. Shall we arrange a date?'

Comby glanced at the memo on his desk. 'The two chaps who saved me ...'

'Yes?' Barbara said.

'They're having a reception at the town hall. The Chief Inspector is giving them a bravery award. There's a dinner afterwards. How would you like to come?'

'I'd love to.'

'Fantastic.' Comby beamed.

'Why don't you pop around to my house tonight, when you're finished catching all those ne'er-do-wells of course. I can rustle up a little something. We could have a wine or two, and perhaps you could stay over.'

Comby gulped. 'I'd love to. I'll bring a bottle, shall I?'

'Oh, yes. Eight ok?'

Comby loosened the collar on his shirt. 'Eight's fine. See you tonight.'

There was a knock at the door and Hardman walked in carrying an iPad. 'Have you seen the local news?' he said.

Comby leant back in his chair, deep in thought.

'Guv?' Hardman said.

'Sorry, Mick,' Comby said. 'I was miles away.'

'The local news?'

Comby shrugged. 'No, why?'

'You're not going to like it.'

'Mick,' Comby said. 'You find me in a wonderful mood today. Nothing is going to dampen it.'

Hardman passed the iPad to Comby who studied the news item. 'I knew it,' he said. 'I knew those buggers were hiding something.'

'It's all over the national news, as well.'

'*Hero detective finds a priceless artefact,*' Comby said. 'I'm going to have a word with Mr Davison.'

'Now, guv?'

'I'll be five minutes,' Comby said. 'I'll meet you in the car park.'

Hardman nodded and moved towards the door. 'Mick,' Comby said.

Hardman moved closer. 'Yeah, guv?'

'Those little blue pills ...'

Hardman smiled. 'Yeah.'

'Do you still have any?'

'Lots, guv.'

'I don't suppose?'

'I've got them downstairs in the car.'

Comby widened his eyes. 'They are safe?'

'Yeah. Don't worry.'

'And, Mick ...' Comby said. 'This is between us two.'

Hardman drew an imaginary zip across his mouth. 'Mum's the word, guv.'

Sam and Phillip sat in the office drinking tea. Kim popped her head inside the door. 'Comby's on his way up,' she said.

Sam leant back in his chair and propped his feet onto his desk. 'This should be good.'

Kim moved aside as Comby and Hardman entered.

'Inspector,' Sam said. 'And to what do we owe this pleasure?'

Comby looked across at Albert's empty desk. 'Where is your colleague, Mr Jackson?'

'He's off today,' Phillip said. 'Taking his young lady out.'

'So,' Comby said, moving nearer to Sam. 'You found the cross?'

'Yeah.' Sam grinned. 'Bloody stroke of luck, really.'

'Of course it was,' Comby said. 'You just happened to be detecting in the neighbourhood of Stainton—'

'Technically it was Thornton,' Sam said.

'Thornton? Yeah. Which is several hundred yards from the churchyard.'

'What churchyard is that, Inspector?' Sam said.

'I won't beat about the bush,' Comby said. 'You knew all along where it was, that's why the others came after you and your mates.'

'Interesting hypothesis,' Sam said. 'But that's just conjecture.'

'Mmm,' Comby said. He reached into his inside pocket and pulled out an envelope. 'The Chief Inspector asked me to give you this.'

'What is it?' Phillip said.

'Believe it or not, Mr Davison, it's an invitation to attend an award ceremony at the Town Hall.'

Sam took the envelope from him. 'Cheers, Clive.' He read the letter. 'It's an invitation for us all,' Sam said. 'Tommo and I are getting a bravery award. No money though.'

'The award is prestigious,' Comby said. 'And I wouldn't have thought you needed any money after your stroke of good fortune.'

Sam nodded. 'True enough. The cross is treasure trove, though. It has to be valued. The farmer who owns the field I found it on will get half, and we all thought it would be nice to gift the church some money for the roof. Apparently, they've had a lot of problems with lead theft and the police have been next to useless.'

Comby smiled. 'Uniform stuff. Outside of my jurisdiction.'

'Well,' Sam stood. 'Thanks for this.' He held out the letter and waved it at Phillip. 'I'll be able to wear my suit again.'

Comby eyed Sam. 'For the record …' He stepped forward and held out a hand. 'Thanks.'

'Your welcome,' Sam said, and shook it firmly. 'Oh, before I forget,' he said. 'We're having a little get together at Tommo's pub next week. The Sidewinder … You and your sergeant are welcome to come along.'

'It's to celebrate our good fortune,' Phillip said. 'You can bring your other halves as well.'

Sam winked at Hardman. 'They'll be a nice buffet on, Mick.'

Hardman grinned. 'I'll be there.'

'You, Inspector?' Sam said.

'Yes,' Comby said. 'I'm sure I'll make it too.'

The Sidewinder thumped to the sound of music as Tommo cracked open the bottle of Champagne. He filled some of the glasses lined on the bar top before repeating the process. Albert and Alice huddled in the corner as Zeus slept next to his owner's feet. Ewen stood with his arm around his wife talking with Emily and Kim.

Sam joined Tommo at the bar. 'Do you want a hand with those?' Sam said.

'Yeah. I'm having to do the bar work. Gene's missed his bus. I told him to get a taxi in so I can enjoy the evening.'

Phillip joined Sam and Tommo. 'I never thought I would say this,' Phillip said. 'But that cravat suits you.'

Sam winked. 'You'll all be wearing them shortly. Give us a hand dishing these out, will you?'

Tommo patted Sam on the arm. 'Who's the guy with a monocle?'

'Monty. He's the one who leant me the metal detector.'

'Ah. He's a little odd.'

Sam smiled. 'He certainly is.'

Sam, Tommo and Phillip handed around the glasses. 'There's no show without Punch,' Sam said, and nudged Tommo.

Tommo cast a glance towards the door as Hardman and Comby entered with two women.

'Clive,' Sam said, holding out a glass. 'Nice of you to come.'

Comby coughed. 'Thanks for the invite ... Sam. Tommo.' He put his hand on the arm of the woman at his side. 'This is a friend of mine, Barbara.' He smiled at her. 'Barbara, this is Sam and Tommo.'

Sam took hold of her hand and kissed the back of it. 'Delighted to meet you. Clive's told me so much about you, but he didn't tell me how attractive you are.'

Barbara blushed a little. 'Oh, thank you.'

Sam handed her a glass. 'Help yourselves to food. Tommo's aunty did the catering, and it's fabulous.'

Hardman waved away the champagne. 'Me and Natalie aren't big on the fizzy stuff,' he said. 'We like our lager.'

Tommo patted Hardman on the arm. 'Well, get yourself to the bar. The drinks are on the house.'

Sam and Tommo watched as Hardman and his wife attacked the buffet.

Comby put his ear near to Tommo. 'I'm not sure you'll have enough grub. Mick and his missus can eat their body weight in food at one sitting.'

Tommo laughed. 'If we get short, I'll send out for pizzas.'

Comby put his arm around Sam's shoulder. 'I know we've had our differences, Sam, but I like you,' he slurred. 'I like you a lot.'

'I like you, Clive. And I'm glad you didn't get shot.'

Comby squeezed him. 'Thanks.'

'Barbara seems very nice.'

Comby grinned and studied Barbara deep in conversation with Emily. 'She is.'

Sam pushed a large whisky across the bar to Comby. 'Try this,' Sam said. 'Twenty-year-old single malt.'

'I'm not sure I should. I'm feeling a little merry as it is.'

'A toast,' Sam said. 'To us.'

Comby steadied himself on the bar and picked up the glass. 'To us,' he said. Sam nodded behind the bar at the picture of Comby in the middle of Sam and Tommo, handing them their bravery award.

Emily joined Sam at the bar as the guests made their way off. 'What's Comby been drinking. He can hardly walk.'

Sam smiled. 'I've been loading his drinks all night. He'll have a right head on him in the morning.'

Emily tutted. 'Sam.'

'Barbara was quite tipsy as well.'

Emily giggled. 'We had her drinking cocktails.'

Hardman waved at the pair as they made for the door. 'Great night, Sam. The food was fantastic.'

Sam and Emily waved back. Tommo locked the door to the cocktail bar and joined them. 'Great night,' he said.

'Yeah,' Sam said, as Baggage padded across to them. He barked and wagged his tail.

'I think Bagsy's had enough,' Tommo said. 'Where's Phillip and Kim?'

'Here they are now?' Sam said, as Phillip and Kim came into the pub.

'Your dog wants to go home,' Sam said.

Deb joined Tommo and put her arm around him. 'He's not the only one,' she said. 'I'm knackered, and Cobra will need a walk when we get home.'

'Where's Albert?' Phillip said.

Sam raised his eyebrows. 'He left with Alice ages ago.' Sam consulted his watch. 'She should have popped his cherry by now.'

'Sam,' Emily said. 'You don't know he's a virgin.'

'He told me,' Sam said. 'I gave him a packet of condoms too.'

'You didn't?' Kim said.

'I did. I had to give him a brief explanation of how you put them on. I'm like a dad to that bloke.'

The door opened, and a man pushed his head through the door. 'Sorry, mate, we're closed,' Tommo said.

'I don't want a drink. I'm looking for Sam and Phillip Davison.'

Sam and Phillip stepped forward. 'That's us,' Sam said.

The man stepped closer and handed Sam a card. 'I was told you might be here. My names Paul Maddock.'

Sam studied the card and handed it to Phillip. 'What can we do for you, Mr Maddock?'

'Have you heard of Captain Henry Morgan?'

'The privateer?' Sam said.

'Yes. He was also the governor of Jamaica.'

'I know a little about him,' Sam said, as the others all moved closer.

'An ancestor of mine, James Maddock, was on Morgan's ship. There was a cutlass … A ceremonial one.'

'Cutlass?' Sam said

'It was silver,' Maddock said. 'With a golden handle. The King had it made and presented it to Captain Morgan.'

'A gift?' Sam said.

'Yes. As a reward for his great work against the Spanish.'

'This silver Cutlass?' Phillip said.

'Gentlemen,' Maddock said. 'I want you to find it.' Baggage padded forward, sank to the floor in front of Maddock and yawned, cocking his head to one side.

Sam gaped at Phillip. 'Morgan's Cutlass,' Sam said.

Phillip grinned and looked back at Maddock. 'It sounds right up our alley.'

NOTES ABOUT THE AUTHOR

John Regan was born in Middlesbrough in 1965. He currently lives with his partner in Stainton Village near Middlesbrough.

This is the author's sixth book and a follow-up to his third – **The Romanov Relic** – A comedy thriller, set in and around the Teesside and North Yorkshire area.

At present his full-time job is as an underground telephone Engineer at Openreach and he has worked for both BT and Openreach for the past twenty years.

He is about to embark on his seventh novel and hopes to have it completed sometime next year.

August 2020.

The author would be happy to hear feedback about this book and will be pleased to answer emails from any readers.

Email: johnregan1965@yahoo.co.uk.

OTHER BOOKS BY THIS AUTHOR

THE HANGING TREE – Even the darkest of secrets deserve an audience.

Sandra Stewart and her daughter are brutally murdered in 2006. Her husband disappeared on the night of Sandra's murder and is wanted in connection with their deaths.
Why has he returned eight years later? And why is he systematically slaughtering apparently unconnected people? Could it be that the original investigation was flawed?
Detective Inspector Peter Graveney is catapulted headlong into an almost unfathomable case. Thwarted at every turn by faceless individuals, intent on keeping the truth buried.
Are there people close to the investigation, possibly within the force, determined to prevent him from finding out what really happened?
As he becomes ever more embroiled, he battles with his past as skeletons in his own closet rattle loudly. Tempted into an increasingly dangerous affair with his new Detective Sergeant, Stephanie Marne, Graveney finds that people he can trust are rapidly diminishing.
But who's manipulating who? As he moves ever closer to the truth, he finds the person that he holds most dear threatened.
Graphically covering adult themes, 'The Hanging Tree' is a relentless edge of the seat ride.
Exploring the darkest of secrets, and the depths people will plunge to keep those secrets hidden. Culminating in a horrific and visceral finale, as Graveney relentlessly pursues it to the final conclusion.

'Even the darkest of secrets deserve an audience.'

PERSISTENCE OF VISION – Seeing is most definitely not believing!

Amorphous: Lindsey and Beth, separated by thirty years. Or so it seems. Their lives about to collide, changing them both forever. Will a higher power intervene and re-write their past and future?

Legerdemain (Sleight of hand): Ten winners of a competition held by the handsome and charismatic billionaire, Christian Gainford, are invited to his remote house in the Scottish Highlands. But is he all he seems, and what does he have in store for them? There really is no such thing as a free lunch, as the ten are about to discover.

Broken: Sandi and Steve are thrown together. By accident or design? Steve is forced to fight not only for Sandi but for his own sanity. Can he trust his senses when everything he ever relied on appears suspect?

Insidious: Killers are copying the crimes of the dead psychopath, Devon Wicken. Will Jack be able to save his wife, Charlotte, from them? Or are they always one step ahead of Jack?

A series of short stories cleverly linked together in an original narrative with one common theme—Reality. But what's real and what isn't?

Exciting action mixed with humour and mystery will keep you guessing throughout. It will alter your perceptions forever.

Reality just got a little weirder! Fact or fiction...You decide!
Seeing is most definitely not believing!

THE ROMANOV RELIC – The Erimus Mysteries

Hilarious comedy thriller!

Private Detective, Bill Hockney, is murdered while searching for the fabled *Romanov Eagle*, cast for The Tsar. His three nephews inherit his business and find themselves not only attempting to discover its whereabouts but also who killed their uncle.

A side-splitting story, full of northern humour, nefarious baddies, madcap characters, plot twists, real ale, multiple showers, out of control libido, bone-shaped chews and a dog called Baggage.

Can Sam, Phillip and Albert, assisted by Sam's best friend Tommo, outwit the long list of people intent on owning the statue, while simultaneously trying to keep a grip on their love lives?
Or will they be thwarted by the menagerie of increasingly desperate villains?

Solving crime has never been this funny!

THE SPACE BETWEEN OUR TEARS

If tears are the manifestation of our grief, what lies within the space between them?

After experiencing massive upheavals in her personal life, Emily Kirkby decides to write a novel. But as she continues her writing, the border between her real life and fiction begin to blur.

Sometimes even the smallest of actions can have far-reaching and profound consequences. When a pebble is cast into the pool of life, there is no telling just how far the ripples will travel.

A rich and compelling story about love in all its many guises. A story about loss and bereavement. A story about guilt and redemption, regret and remorse. But mainly, chiefly, it's about love.

THE FALLING LEAVES – One of the most perplexing cases Inspector Peter Graveney has worked on. A car is dredged from the bottom of a deep pond after twenty years. The grisly remains of two bodies locked inside. Why is Graveney certain that this discovery is linked to a dubious businessman and the murders of the men working for him? And why does a young woman's name keep surfacing within the investigation after her release from prison for murder?

As Graveney digs deeper, he finds more missing pieces to the puzzle and is faced with his biggest struggle yet – his own mind. As the body count escalates, Graveney battles with his own demons and in his desperation to solve the case, he allows himself to be guided by an unlikely source from his past.

A gruesome and provocative sequel to the author's first novel, 'The Hanging Tree'. The Fallen Leaves takes the reader on a breath-taking journey, from the graphic opening chapter to the emotionally charged denouement.

If you bury the past, bury it deep.

Printed in Great Britain
by Amazon

81461040R00140